LOVE REBRANDED

SEEKING PROVIDENCE
BOOK ONE

JILL BURRELL

CHERRY CREEK PRESS

To my Writing Sisters.
You ladies are the best at keeping me on track, giving me reality checks, and
providing the words of encouragement I need to hear.

Trigger Warning: Love Rebranded is a clean and wholesome romance, however, it deals with sexual assault and alcohol addiction. Though not graphic, the discussion of some events may trigger some readers.

CHAPTER 1

*R*iley stifled a yawn before putting a cheerful smile on her face and opening the door to exam room four. "Good news, Jayden. Your arm isn't broken. Again."

"Yay! No cast!"

"Not so fast, young man." Riley sat on the swivel stool and parked herself in front of Jayden. "If you don't give the sprain the time it needs to heal, you could cause more damage to your wrist." She motioned for him to hold out his arm then strapped on the brace she'd carried in with her. "You need to wear this for four to six weeks."

"Ah man." Jayden scowled at Riley.

"I'll be lucky to get him to wear it for two." His mom rolled her eyes.

Eight-year-old Jayden was the oldest of three active kids who kept the single mom on her toes. Jayden was by far the most rambunctious, always jumping off things, popping wheelies on his bike, or trying new stunts on his skateboard.

Normally, Riley would suspect a parent of child abuse when their child had this many injuries, but Jayden always had a story to tell about how he injured himself. The logic behind his antics were way

1

too entertaining, not to mention detailed and age-appropriate, to be mistaken as abuse.

A few minutes later, Riley ruffled Jayen's hair as she followed mother and son out of the exam room. "No more trying to jump your skateboard off the front porch steps."

He was her last patient of the day. They had been squeezed in at the last minute as it was. She stifled another yawn as she made her final notes in Jayden's chart. Exhaustion weighed heavily on every muscle of her body. Sleep had been nearly impossible since her date with Collin last Friday night, and she was exhausted.

She contemplated asking Dr. Nelson to prescribe her something to help her sleep. But he'd want to know why she wasn't sleeping well, and she didn't want to talk about it. Telling the police how she was sexually assaulted by the pharmaceutical rep, who frequently came into Dr. Nelson's office, had been hard enough. She didn't want to relive the whole ordeal again. And she certainly didn't want to be viewed as a victim. Besides, she feared her coworkers wouldn't believe her.

Collin Ainsworth was so charming and charismatic that he was every nurse's favorite rep. He always brought baked goods and chocolates for everyone in the office, but he always managed to make Riley feel singled out, which she hated.

After calling in sick for the last two days, it was easier to cover the bruise on her temple with makeup than to try to convince her friends what a dirtbag he was.

Zoe, her medical assistant, pitched forward in her seat and gave Riley a mischievous grin from behind her desk. "Hey, you have one last patient in room two. A walk-in."

Riley sighed. "Why didn't the front desk send them to the walk-in clinic?"

Zoe shrugged but her grin only grew. It was way too big for five-thirty in the afternoon. "He insisted on being seen by his favorite medical professional."

Favorite?

Riley treated many young patients who preferred to be seen by a female nurse practitioner over Dr. Nelson, who was a large, barrel-chested man with a deep voice, but she'd never been called anyone's favorite.

She loved working with Dr. Nelson, who was nothing but a big teddy bear, but she'd struggled to breathe earlier this afternoon when she conferred with him behind closed doors about a patient. What little lunch she'd managed to choke down had nearly come back up.

She cursed Collin in her head for the hundredth time since Friday night. It was his fault she feared being alone in a room with a man. Thanks to her cousin Paige's timely arrival, Collin hadn't achieved his goal, but he'd taken something from her. Something Riley feared she'd never get back. She doubted she'd ever be able to trust and feel safe again?

Riley chided herself for even accepting that first date with Collin, let alone the second. She should have listened to the voices in her head, telling her to steer clear of him.

Heaving a sigh, she approached exam room two and pulled the chart from the pocket on the wall.

Jon Johnson. Twenty-nine.

Great, a man. Just my luck.

A cold sweat pricked her brow, and a band tightened around her chest. The paper chart shook in her clammy hand so badly she struggled to read the rest of Jon Johnson's stats.

Six foot, one hundred eighty-five pounds. Temp and blood pressure, both normal. Complaint: chest pains.

Not likely a heart attack. He's too young. Maybe a panic attack, but probably indigestion.

She looked at the patient's name again. She didn't know Jon Johnson, so how could she be his favorite medical professional?

Because Zoe still grinned at her from behind her desk, Riley rolled her neck to loosen the tension that threatened to give her a headache, then she sucked in a deep breath, and pushed open the door.

I can do this.

Her brow furrowed as she took in the empty room. A movement

3

behind her caught her attention at the same moment the doorknob jerked from her hand, and the door slammed shut.

"Hello, Riley Darling."

The seductive tone in the tenor voice filled her veins with ice, and her heart pumped so fast she feared she might have a heart attack. Praying the familiar voice belonged to someone other than the man who was supposed to be in jail, she spun around.

Her stomach plummeted, hardening like concrete before hitting bottom.

It's not possible.

She'd filed a restraining order. He wasn't supposed to come within 100 hundred yards of her.

Yet, there stood Collin Ainsworth, looking as cocky as ever, smiling at her and blocking the only exit.

"You made a big mistake, Cowgirl." He advanced on her.

"You're not s-supposed to be here." She backed away from him until she hit the exam table. With nowhere to retreat, fear consumed her, freezing her limbs—like it had Friday night.

Scream. Help is just beyond the door.

She couldn't seem to make her lungs work, though. Her chest was so tight, she could hardly breathe. Besides, screaming and fighting had only aroused Collin more last week. A wave of dizziness hit her as she recalled how weak and powerless she'd felt when he'd pinned her to the sofa and groped her body.

If I'd only had the courage to tell everyone, Zoe never would have let Collin in.

Her medical assistant probably thought she was doing Riley a favor by creating a bogus chart and sneaking Collin into an exam room for a lover's tryst, but she couldn't be more wrong.

"You should have known better than to go to the police." Collin laughed as he took another step toward her. "Did you really think they'd charge me after I explained how you'd been coming onto me all night and showed them the pictures of us together? I mean you could hardly keep your hands off me."

The pictures Collin took during their date should have clued her in that he had an agenda. Pictures that made her increasingly more uncomfortable as the night progressed. The way Collin repeatedly invaded her space, putting his arm around her and pressing his cheek to hers made her uneasy. He even took her hand and placed it on his chest for one of the photos.

Relief filled her when he finally brought her home. Except he didn't leave like she'd expected. Instead, he took the keys from her hand, opened her apartment door, and sauntered inside.

"You attacked m-me." The words were barely more than a whisper because Riley couldn't draw in a full breath. Dark shadows danced at the edges of her vision.

"Oh, come now." His voice took on that sultry quality all the nurses loved. "We were only making out."

"Do you always hit the women you make out with?" She squared her shoulders, but her voice was still weak. She hated that he had such a debilitating effect on her.

People often said, "You need to face your fears to overcome them," but no matter how many times she looked at Collin Ainsworth's pretty-boy face, she'd never feel anything but fear and disgust.

He tapped a finger to his lips. "Now, see, I explained to the police that when things got passionate, we fell off the couch and you hit your head on the coffee table."

She eyed the door, willing herself to make a run for it, but her knees shook so badly she had to put her hands on the exam table behind her to steady herself. Despite knowing there was help on the other side of the door, she felt as trapped and hopeless as she did Friday night.

"You ripped my blouse." He'd done a lot more than that, but Riley couldn't vocalize the ways he'd violated her.

"It was only a few buttons, darling. I'll buy you a new shirt." He kept himself positioned between her and the door as he closed the distance between them. "I can buy you all kinds of nice things."

"I don't want anything from you." Her voice was a little stronger now, but her breaths came so fast she risked hyperventilating. "You stay away from me."

"I can't do that, sweetheart. You stir something inside me." He stood toe-to-toe with her now. His hot breath brushed her face, reminding her of the stench of alcohol on his breath a few days ago. He ran a finger down her cheek. "You belong to me."

A shudder of disgust laced with fear ricocheted through her, both from his words and his touch. She slapped his hand away. "Don't touch me."

His eyes darkened, and she recalled the pain of the punch he landed to the side of her face last Friday and the throbbing headache she'd nursed all weekend. Despite wanting to be brave, she felt like curling up in a ball and crying, like she had for two days straight after his assault.

"You want me. I can see it in your eyes." He leaned closer. "Just think of how amazing it could be between us if you'd only let go of your puritan values and give in to the attraction."

Attraction? More like repulsion.

Riley shoved against his chest and forced all the vehemence she could muster into her words. "I'll never give in to you!"

Again, something dark and dangerous flashed in his eyes, and he let out a sinister chuckle. He leaned closer still until he pinned her against the exam table, his thighs pressed against hers. She opened her mouth to scream, but he clapped one hand over her mouth while the other cupped the back of her head.

"Mark my words, Riley, you *will* be mine."

She tried to fight and shove him away again, but he barely budged.

His grip on her face and neck tightened. "Don't get any heroic ideas about going to the police again. If you try to press any more charges against me, my dad's team of lawyers will chew you up and spit you out so fast you won't know what hit you."

When Collin told her his father was Senator Ainsworth, it had given him near-celebrity status in her eyes, but now, the knowledge that the senator used his money and position to cover his son's sins sickened her.

Riley swallowed down the bile that rose in her throat. Her brain screamed at her to run, but every muscle in her body trembled so badly she couldn't move.

Then Collin's mouth was on hers, crushing and bruising. His arms wrapped around her, pinning hers to her sides.

Her stomach roiled, and a bitter taste filled her mouth. She tried to pull away, but he held her so tightly she couldn't move. She couldn't even knee him in the groin, because his thighs pressed too firmly against hers.

Desperate to free herself, she clamped her teeth down on his lip.

He jerked away and let loose a string of vulgar swear words. He raised his hand as though intending to backhand her, then he froze at the sound of laughter out in the hall.

She glared at him as she swiped the back of her hand across her mouth. If only she could wipe away his vile attack so easily. Countless showers hadn't helped rid her mind of the memory of his last assault.

She pulled her phone from her pocket and dialed 911. "Go ahead, I dare you."

Why did it have to take her so long to find the courage to stand up to him? She showed him the screen as her thumb hovered over the call button. "Touch me again, and I'll scream so loud security at the other end of the hospital will hear me."

He grabbed a tissue off the counter and dabbed at his bloody lip. He swore again, then pointed at her as he backed toward the door. "This isn't over." He walked out, slamming the door behind him.

Riley's knees gave out, and she sank to the floor. Burying her face in her hands, she sucked in deep breaths as hot tears stung her cheeks.

She grew up on a ranch, working her butt off to keep up with the strongest of ranch hands, but Collin Ainsworth made her feel weak and helpless.

He's never going to leave me alone.

The victim's advocate the police referred her to had warned her Collin would likely be out on bail soon, but from the way Collin described it, he wasn't even formally charged and arrested. Her advocate had also warned her that a restraining order would only protect her if Collin obeyed it. Which he clearly hadn't.

He'd violated her a second time, making her feel vulnerable and powerless. Next time, she might not be so lucky to have help just beyond the door, or Paige might not show up.

She swiped away her tears and pushed to her feet as the fear turned to anger.

I won't sit around and wait for there to be a next time.

RILEY WAS CURLED up in the armchair with her arms wrapped around her knees when her cousin Paige walked through the door later that evening loaded with groceries.

Paige took one look at her and dropped the bags on the floor before hurrying over to sit on the end of the couch nearest to Riley. "Looks like you had a rough day. I knew you should have given yourself more time before returning to work."

Riley stared at the cheap charcoal gray sofa. She hadn't been able to bring herself to sit there since Collin pinned her down on it Friday night. She could barely stand to be in this room as it was. That's why she'd gone back to work today. Trying to forget how close Collin had come to raping her while spending all day, every day, in the apartment where it happened was impossible.

"He showed up again." The words Riley forced through her dry throat were little more than a whisper.

Paige's brows drew together. "Who showed up?" Then her expression quickly morphed into one of shock, her eyes practically bulging from her head. "Do you mean Collin?"

Riley shuddered at the mention of that man's name. She gave a curt nod.

"Collin Ainsworth showed up at the clinic and confronted you in front of everyone?" Paige asked.

"No, he was hiding in an exam room, waiting for me."

"That snake!" Paige pounded her fist on the arm of the couch. "Is he out on bail already?"

"He was never arrested." Heat surged through Riley's body at the statement.

"What? Why?" Paige's jaw dropped.

A pit opened in Riley's stomach as she told her best friend how Collin convinced the police they'd only been making out. Then tears filled her eyes as she told her how helpless she'd felt all over again when Collin assaulted her a second time in the exam room.

"Oh, Ri, I'm so sorry." Paige squeezed into the armchair with Riley and wrapped her in a hug. "What about the restraining order? Did you call the police?"

The pit in Riley's stomach widened as she related Collin's threat about using his dad's lawyers to discredit and defame her. Then she reminded Paige of the victim advocate's warning that the restraining order would only protect her if Collin obeyed it.

"Which he clearly isn't." Paige's nostrils flared now, and her face turned red. She made a growling sound. "I should never have gone to that movie with Jen and Shaylee last Friday. If I'd been here, he wouldn't have—"

"It's not your fault, Paige."

"It's not yours either. You remember that." Paige pointed a finger at Riley. "You did not bring it on yourself. That slimeball had no right to do what he did to you."

"I know, but I can't help but second guess everything I said and did." Riley pulled her knees tighter to her chest in a defensive gesture.

"Stop it! That man is a scumbag and should be in jail."

"We both know that's not going to happen." The pit in Riley's stomach had become a gaping hole now.

"Gah, it sickens me that his father uses his power that way." She pounded the armrest again.

"Me too." Riley's voice was quiet, resigned. "That's why I've decided to leave for a while."

"Leave?" Paige's brows drew together as she studied Riley's face. "To go where?"

"Home." The word lit a tiny spark of hope in Riley's chest. "To the Double Diamond."

Thinking about the beautiful ranch she grew up on in south-eastern Washington provided a balm to Riley's tormented soul. "Dr. Nelson promised to talk to the pharmaceutical company about Collin, but he suggested I take a leave of absence for a while."

"Yes!" Paige's excited outburst startled Riley. "You need to leave Seattle for a while. The ranch is the perfect place for you to heal."

"But I don't want to leave you alone here. What if Collin comes back? I don't want you to be his next victim."

Paige pinched her lip, deep in thought. Then she snapped her fingers. "I'll talk to Jen and Shaylee next door and see if I can stay in their extra room for a while."

"Are you sure?" Riley felt bad leaving her cousin and best friend. "I don't know how long I'll be away, but I'll keep paying my share of the rent."

"Yes, I'm sure. You should go home to the Double Diamond."

Now Riley studied Paige. Should she take offense at Paige's eagerness to get rid of her?

It doesn't matter.

Going home was the right move.

Will putting two hundred miles between me and Collin help erase the memory of what he did to me?

DANIEL'S WORLD tilted a little as he straightened from returning the wheelbarrow to where it belonged. He put a hand against the wall to steady himself. His jaw stretched in a wide yawn.

His dad stepped into the doorway of the tool room. "Thanks for cleaning the stables." He pointed a finger at Daniel. "Now get some lunch, then get some sleep."

Zane Hamilton was a man of few words, but when he spoke people listened, especially around here because he was the ranch foreman. Even Jake Winters, the owner of the Double Diamond, deferred to Zane's expertise. After all, Daniel's parents had been working and living on the ranch since before Jake was born.

Daniel hoped to be half the man Jake was by the time he reached his early thirties. He could never aspire to be as good as his own father because his dad had been smart enough to shun alcohol like the plague. Something Daniel hadn't been strong enough to do.

"Yes sir." Daniel nodded at his dad. He would have given a mock salute if he'd had the energy to lift his arm that high.

He made his way to the big house where his mom, housekeeper for the Winters family, prepared all the meals. After washing up, he dropped into a chair at the kitchen table. He yawned again, so big his jaw popped. He was tempted to lay his head on the table and take a nap but knew his mother wouldn't approve.

Who needs food? All I want is sleep.

Mom slid a bowl of beef stew and a grilled cheese sandwich in front of him. "Here, eat something before you fall flat on your face." She made tsking noises as she returned to the stove. "I don't understand why you insist on burning the candle at both ends. When you pull an all-nighter at the calving sheds, you're entitled to sleep the next day. But no, you insist on mucking out the stalls and doing anything else your dad or Jake ask."

The way he saw it, he owed Jake a huge debt. He and his older brother Robert, who happened to be the sheriff, went to court with him when he faced jail time. They managed to convince the judge to let him fulfill his community service hours here on the ranch.

He'd paid off that debt a long time ago, but when his dad and Jake had to drag his butt out of jail again last fall and bring him home to dry out, Daniel promised himself he wouldn't let them down again. However, what little sleep he'd snatched here and there after covering so many nights at the calving shed wasn't enough anymore.

Maybe I'll skip tonight's AA meeting to catch up on sleep.

His sponsor would be on his case, but Daniel was too tired to care at the moment.

He was halfway through his lunch when Jake's wife, Emily, walked in with three-month-old Adam in her arms.

"Smells delicious as usual, Lottie," Emily said as she settled the baby into a bouncy infant recliner contraption.

His mom waved away the praise. "Just something I threw together."

Jake's mother had insisted it was ridiculous to expect Lottie to cook for them then turn around and cook for her own family. So, the Hamiltons always ate their meals at the big house with the Winters. When Jake married Emily, she'd insisted on keeping the tradition. Emily worked part-time as a psychologist at the hospital and part-time at the high school, so she was grateful to keep Daniel's mom on as cook and housekeeper.

"You look tired." Emily studied Daniel's face. "How are you doing?"

"I'm fine." He lied. "Just tired."

"Let me know if you need to talk, okay?" Emily waited for him to nod before she broke eye contact. She got herself some food, then sat across from Daniel at the table. "Jake got a phone call from Riley, so it might be a bit before he joins us."

Daniel didn't know if she was talking to him or his mom, but his heart stumbled at the mention of Jake's younger sister.

Riley hadn't been home to visit since Christmas. Even then, she'd spent most of her time in town with her mom and her Aunt Charity.

Riley used to be his best friend, and at one point, he was certain she was the woman he would marry. That is until she dumped him and returned to college, leaving him feeling like he'd been nothing more than a summer fling.

The last three years since she broke up with him had been strained and awkward between them when she came home. It was just as well because he didn't want her to know the things he'd done and the depths to which he'd sunk.

Jake joined them a few minutes later, sliding into his seat beside Emily. He put his arm on the back of his wife's chair. "Riley wants to come home. I told her she's always welcome here. I hope that's okay with you."

Daniel's heart tripped up again, and he held his breath waiting for Emily's response.

"Of course, it is. How long does she plan to stay?"

"I'm not sure." Jake scratched the back of his neck. "She asked if she could work on the ranch for the summer." He lifted one shoulder in a shrug. "That's one less ranch hand we'd have to hire."

For the summer? Riley's coming home? For months?

"For the summer?" Emily echoed Daniel's thoughts. "What about her job?"

"I asked her about that, and she said she's taking a leave of absence."

"But why?" Emily's brow furrowed. "It's not like her to leave her job."

"I know." Jake shrugged. "But the more I pressed to try to figure out what was going on, the more upset she sounded."

"Upset?" Daniel's mom spoke up now. "Upset how?"

"Her voice got shaky. Like she was on the verge of tears."

Daniel's chest tightened. Riley was one of the most level-headed and even-tempered people he knew. It must be something big to upset her enough to make her come home for months.

Emily's brow furrowed. "I wonder what's going on with her?"

Jake squeezed her shoulders before pulling his arm away and picking up the sandwich Daniel's mom placed in front of him. "I don't know, but if we can't help her figure it out, I know an excellent psychologist who can."

Daniel could attest to that. Emily had helped him work through a lot of things. But after falling off the wagon twice, the underlying fear lingered in the back of his mind that he'd never be able to stay sober if he left the ranch for good.

He looked up to see three sets of eyes on him, a mixture of compassion and concern in each. He clenched his jaw so tight it ached. Were they worried about how having Riley around would affect his sobriety? Or were they concerned, like he was, about what Riley would think of him when she discovered the reason he was back home, living on the ranch at the age of twenty-seven?

Ignoring everyone's stares, he put a spoonful of stew in his mouth. It didn't taste nearly as good as it had a few minutes ago. He dropped his spoon into the bowl.

"Why don't you go get some sleep?" Jake said.

Daniel couldn't find the energy to argue as he had on other days. He doubted he'd sleep, though, because from the moment Emily first mentioned Riley's name, he'd been reliving their history together—their carefree childhood here on the ranch and that blissful summer three years ago when they dated. His heart bolted like a racehorse when Jake said Riley was coming home, and it had yet to stop racing.

He excused himself and walked out the back door of the ranch house.

"Daniel." Emily stopped him as he stepped off the deck.

He turned to face her and waited for her words of wisdom. She always said what he needed to hear.

"Riley is a piece of your past that you need to face and come to terms with. But don't worry, you're strong enough now."

"I'm not so sure about that." He didn't feel very strong most days. He'd only been sober for eight months.

"You don't need to stay hidden behind the walls you've built around yourself. If you let people in, they can help you when you're struggling."

But letting people in meant admitting the things he'd done, and he didn't want them to see the monster he'd become.

The trek down the lane to his parents' cottage-style home was only a hundred yards, but it felt like a mile as he contemplated how he would keep his secrets hidden while working with Riley this summer. Even more important, how did he guard his heart from the woman he'd loved his whole life?

As he trudged up the steps to the house, he decided he needed to attend the AA meeting tonight after all. Because right now, the desire for a stiff drink was even stronger than the pull of his bed.

CHAPTER 2

The knot in Riley's stomach slowly eased as she drove down Providence's Main Street. Memories of being a teenager dragging Main with her cousin Paige and milkshakes at Aunt Charity's diner filled her mind as she noted how nothing had changed since she left this small town seven years ago.

As an ambitious eighteen-year-old, she couldn't wait to get out and experience the world. She hadn't exactly *experienced* the world over the last seven years, but she'd never regretted leaving. Until last week.

Riley often came home for the holidays, but going to the ranch wasn't the same anymore. Not since her dad died five years ago. Then a year later, her mom moved into town to live with her sister Charity after Riley's Uncle Rich passed away.

That's when the family agreed to let her second oldest brother, Jake, buy the ranch. He'd been depositing money into a trust fund for her ever since. She'd been grateful for the money that paid for her schooling, but she'd wished many times that things didn't need to change.

She hadn't thought much about the trust fund for some time. There was probably a nice little nest egg there now.

Riley turned onto the road that led to the Double Diamond and picked up speed as she headed out of town. The sight of animals grazing in green pastures brought a smile to her face, and she relaxed a little more. She rolled down her window and breathed in the fresh air.

Coming home might be just what I need.

Her smile soon faded when she spotted a herd of cattle and a lone man on horseback in the middle of the highway. The horse and cows were too far away to see a brand, but she knew by the white rail fence that ran along the highway they belonged to the Double Diamond.

She looked more closely at the cowboy in the saddle who wore a baseball cap instead of a cowboy hat. His tall, lean figure had filled out over the past two years, becoming broader and more muscular, but she'd recognize that physique anywhere.

Daniel Hamilton.

Her breath hitched. She'd forgotten Daniel moved back home to the ranch last fall. She'd have to work with him all summer. The thought both excited and terrified her.

Daniel used to be her favorite person in the whole world—next to her cousin Paige. The two of them often vied for the title of "Riley's Best Friend." But she and Daniel had a history that won him the title for an entire summer, until she put an abrupt end to their relationship almost three years ago, costing her one of her best friends.

She wasn't ready for marriage back then, and she'd panicked at the prospect of putting her schooling on hold to follow him to Portland. It was all too much at the time. So she'd ended it between them.

She forced a smile as she pulled her Jeep up beside the rugged yet handsome cowboy.

His eyes widened in surprise, then a grin filled his face. "Boy, am I glad to see you!"

Riley felt her own eyes widen. That was not the reaction she'd expected from the man she'd dumped. "You are?"

"Yes. I need your help." He motioned to the herd of cows blocking the road.

Her brow furrowed. "Why are you herding cows down the highway?"

"I'm trying to get them back into the Dry Creek pasture, but they're being stubborn."

The small creek that ran through the southeastern most part of the land wasn't dry, but it was considerably smaller than any of the other water sources on the ranch, hence the name Dry Creek. The forty-thousand-acre ranch was so large they named the tracts of land to help them keep track of the locations of various herds.

Riley hooked a thumb over her shoulder. "Dry Creek is back there." Beyond where the rail fence ended, of course.

"I know, and I had them headed in the right direction, but then Madam Houdini decided she didn't want to go back yet. She bolted the other way and the rest followed. I need someone to head them off."

They rarely named cows on the ranch, instead they put a numbered tag in their ear after they were born that linked them to their pedigree. D-258's behavior, however, had earned her a name. She was an escape artist, always finding a weak spot and figuring out how to exploit it. It never failed, she always took her herd with her.

During the summer Riley and Daniel had dated, they'd had to herd Madam Houdini and her crew back to where they belonged half a dozen times.

"Where are Jake and your dad?"

"At the auction."

"Give me five minutes. I'll get Misty saddled and come help you."

"Hurry before Madam Houdini decides to take her posse down the lane and onto the front lawn of the ranch house. Mom and Emily will kill me if I let that happen."

Riley wove her way through the herd of cattle doing her best not to drive them further down the highway. Parking beside the house, she jumped out of her Jeep and whistled for Misty as she jogged toward the corral where they kept the stock horses.

The beautiful, dappled gray Arabian, sporting a black mane and tail, lifted her head and trotted over to the gate. She nickered as she put her head over the gate to nuzzle Riley.

"I've missed you too, girl." She rubbed Misty's neck, grateful the horse was so forgiving considering Riley hadn't been home for over four months. She opened the gate. "Come on, we've got work to do."

An hour later, Riley and Daniel reined in their horses beside the stables after repairing a ten-foot patch of fence Madam Houdini and her girls had trampled.

Riley slid down and patted Misty's neck. "We'll go for a long ride later, girl." Then she set to work unsaddling her horse.

Daniel did the same. "Thanks for your help. Houdini and her herd would be halfway to Seattle by now if you hadn't shown up when you did."

The joking comment surprised Riley. They'd talked while they repaired the fence, but only about the job at hand. And although she'd talked to Daniel several times over the past few years, their conversations had always been stilted and awkward.

"She was in a mood today, wasn't she?" Riley didn't doubt that Daniel could have gotten the cows back in by himself if she hadn't come along. He was good with animals and a skilled horseman.

"She gets that way every few months." He set to work removing Rebel's saddle. "I was...surprised to hear you were coming home for the summer."

And there it is.

Everyone would want to know why she'd come home.

She didn't want to tell them. Never mind that they were her family —even Daniel's parents, who weren't related by blood, were like a second set of parents to her. Telling them would mean reliving the whole ordeal.

She shuddered with fear and revulsion at the memory of Collin's hard mouth bruising hers with greed and possessiveness. Bile filled her mouth as she recalled the predatory way his hands groped her body. Her left temple still sported a greenish-yellow bruise from the punch he'd landed to the side of her face.

"Hey, you okay?" Daniel's concerned face peered at her over Misty's back.

Riley didn't realize she'd abandoned the task of unsaddling Misty and wrapped her trembling arms around her body. She shook off the apprehension that still plagued her even though she was two hundred miles away from Collin.

"I'm fine." She forced a smile. "I just needed a break this summer."

Daniel stared at her through narrowed eyes for a long moment as though he didn't believe her.

Eager to put some distance between her and the one person who knew and understood her almost as well as Paige did, she pulled the saddle from Misty's back and retreated to the tack room.

Less than a minute later, he followed her, carrying his saddle. He'd shed his flannel shirt while they fixed the fence, and now, his biceps bulged beneath the sleeves of his t-shirt. The sight, attractive as it was, caused her heart to race with apprehension.

Daniel was so much stronger than he used to be, and he was even taller than Collin.

Riley grabbed a horse brush and darted out of the tack room.

"Why the whole summer?" Daniel said from behind her.

She jumped and spun around. He wasn't that close, but she couldn't help the spike in adrenaline that warmed her veins, making the unseasonably warm early-April day even warmer.

"What?"

"I understand needing a break, but why take the whole summer off?" He tossed his horse brush in the air then caught it again. "Couldn't you have cut back on your hours at the clinic for a while?"

She could have, but that wouldn't change the fact that Collin knew where she lived and worked.

"I... I needed a change of add—I mean a change of scenery." She switched her choice of words mid-sentence, hoping to avoid raising even more questions.

Once again, Daniel's gaze fell on her face, a small furrow creasing his brow.

He doesn't believe me.

Or maybe he did, but he knew there was more to the story.

His eyes narrowed, and he tilted his head as though trying to get a better look at her left temple.

She turned away from him. She should have covered the bruise with makeup this morning but getting out of town had been her only goal. Needing to deflect, she went on the defensive. "Why are *you* back here again this summer? I thought the architect firm agreed to let you finish your internship after you recovered from your broken leg."

His lips set in a firm line and a muscle in his jaw jumped. The concerned look he'd given her turned hard. He pivoted and walked to Rebel's side where he brushed the chestnut stallion with short, rapid strokes.

Daniel's internship with a prestigious architectural firm in Portland was interrupted two years ago when he wrecked his motorcycle and broke his femur. He'd come home to the ranch to recuperate, but a few months later, he'd returned to Portland to finish his internship.

Riley never understood why he chose to come back to the ranch again last fall. But she'd overheard her mother and aunts talking about how quiet and withdrawn Daniel was. And when she came home for Thanksgiving, she'd seen firsthand how much he'd changed.

The Daniel she saw then was not the same carefree, adventure-loving boy she grew up with. He seemed more himself now, but there was still something different about him.

Riley grimaced. She'd hit a sensitive spot. Apparently, Daniel hadn't gotten the position he'd hoped for with the firm after finishing the internship.

But why come back here? Why not apply to other firms?

They finished brushing down their horses in silence and turned them back into the corral.

After latching the gate, Riley brushed her hands on her jeans then slid her hands into her back pockets. She rocked up on her toes, trying to think of something to say to the man who used to be her best friend but now felt like a stranger.

Apparently, he couldn't think of anything to say either, because he just stared at the horses in the corral.

She pointed over her shoulder. "I guess I'd better get unpacked."

"I'll help you carry in your luggage." Daniel followed her to her Jeep.

Riley wanted to argue that she could do it herself because

accepting his help made her feel weak. And she'd had enough of feeling weak and helpless to last her a lifetime.

When he grabbed her largest suitcase, she bit her tongue to keep from snapping at him. She couldn't explain the sudden irritability that hit her, but she wanted to be left alone. He was halfway to the house before she'd composed herself enough to grab the smaller suitcase and duffel bag.

She paused after stepping into the house to study the great room that consisted of the living and dining spaces. It wasn't the first time she'd seen the changes Emily had made over the past two years, but she still hadn't gotten used to seeing the dusty rose curtains frame the floor-to-ceiling windows in the family room instead of the navy-blue drapes that had hung there her whole life. A new gray rug with rose-colored accents covered the hardwood floor near the setting of leather sofas that Jake and Emily had replaced last year.

Riley let her gaze continue to roam, taking in the changes, most of them subtle, yet jarring, nonetheless. Tears filled her eyes when her gaze landed on the new gray and dusty rose tablecloth covering the large dining table on the far side of the room instead of the checkered one that had been there for so many years.

It was such a little thing that Emily had every right to change, but it felt like a betrayal to Riley, who sought the comforts of home. She blinked away the tears and followed Daniel down the hall.

He stood at the end of the hall, looking at her expectantly. "Which room do you want?"

Riley stopped in the doorway of her childhood bedroom. Her stomach dropped when she spotted pastel walls with colorful farm animals painted on them, a crib, and rocking chair. She'd forgotten that Jake had asked her at Christmastime if she would mind them turning her old room into a nursery, since it was the closest to the master bedroom. At the time, she hadn't minded, because she didn't think she'd ever come home to stay for more than a weekend.

But now, she minded.

Again, she blinked back the tears. "I'll sleep in Robert's old room." She deposited her things in the next bedroom.

Emily had changed the decor in this room too, replacing the Americana theme with tans and blues that reminded her of the beach. It looked nice, but it felt all wrong. It simply wasn't home anymore.

Daniel set down her suitcase and rotated in a circle, taking in the room. Then he shuffled his feet and swiped his hands down the front of his jeans.

"I uh..." He stepped toward her, hesitated, then closing the distance between them, he wrapped his arms around her in a hug that was like so many of the hugs they'd shared in the past. "I'm glad you're home."

But it all felt different.

Daniel was bigger and stronger than he used to be. The muscles in his arms were corded and firmer, his chest rock hard. The boy she'd grown up with was a man now. A strong man who could hurt her if he wanted to.

Her mind jumped to the brute strength Collin used on her when he pinned her to the sofa.

She flinched and gasped, then stood immobile in Daniel's arms. Every muscle in her body trembled. She couldn't move, couldn't hug him back. She couldn't even breathe.

Her heart pounded so hard against her ribcage she felt the reverberation in her ears, and her stomach spasmed so tight she thought she might be sick. She opened her mouth to scream but couldn't seem to find the air to do so.

Just when she thought she might pass out from the rush of blood to her head, Daniel released her and stepped back.

A frown and a look of disappointment filled his face. "I guess I'll let you unpack." Then he turned and left the room. Judging by the slamming of the back door, he didn't stop until he'd left the house.

Riley collapsed on the bed and gave into the tears that had been threatening to fall ever since she walked through the door.

Why did I think coming home would make everything better?

Things had changed. Not only around the house but between her and Daniel.

She hated that what Collin did to her made her fear everyone, including the one person she used to trust more than anyone else. The one who picked her up and dusted her off the first time she got bucked off a horse. The one she cried with after her dad died.

The pounding in her heart settled into a dull ache.

She'd burned a bridge three years ago with Daniel that she wasn't sure she could rebuild. She wasn't even sure if she wanted to. Because even though she found him incredibly attractive still, he'd changed somehow. He was more serious and pensive now and seemed less sure of himself.

And she'd changed.

She was broken. Damaged.

Things could have turned out so much worse with Collin. She knew that, and she was so grateful they hadn't, but it didn't change the fact that she viewed the world differently now. She didn't trust anyone anymore. Especially not men.

I can come home, but I can't go back to the way things were.

Daniel was the last to arrive at the dinner table that evening. He wasn't eager to face Riley again after the way she reacted when he hugged her this afternoon.

He hadn't meant anything by it. He'd only been trying to make Riley feel welcome. When he asked her why she'd chosen to come home for the summer, something dark and troubled filled her eyes, and he could have sworn he saw a faint bruise near her left eye.

He also saw the tears in her eyes when she remembered her old room was no longer hers. Working with her this summer would be difficult enough, so he figured he may as well smooth the waters as much as possible early on. He hadn't expected her to freeze up and be repulsed by his touch.

Now, here she sat, directly across the table from him. She was as beautiful as ever with her long dark hair and expressive blue eyes, but there was something about the way she avoided eye contact and kept her head downcast that affirmed what Daniel already suspected.

Something serious drove Riley home.

After the blessing on the food, Emily immediately turned her attention to Riley. "It's good to have you home, Riley. Working with Dr. Nelson must have grown pretty difficult for you to decide you'd rather work on the ranch this summer."

A flash of something—alarm maybe—filled Riley's face before she schooled her features. "No, Dr. Nelson is great. I love working with him."

"Then why did you take a leave of absence this summer?" Jake asked.

Riley's gaze dropped to her plate where she repeatedly stabbed her fork into her meatloaf. "I just...needed a change of scenery."

That was the same answer she'd given Daniel earlier, although he could have sworn she'd almost said she needed a change of address before she corrected herself.

Did she and Paige have a falling out?

They'd been best friends since they were babies. Sure, they'd had their share of disagreements, but they always worked things out. They were too close to stay mad at each other. For Riley to choose to leave a job she loved, something big must have happened. If not with Paige, then with someone else.

A boyfriend, perhaps.

A knot formed in Daniel's stomach. He hadn't heard any of her family mention Riley being in a relationship, but he'd mostly kept to himself since coming home seven months ago.

She was such an amazing woman. It wouldn't surprise him if she had dozens of men after her. Sure, she was opinionated and as stubborn as a mule at times, but he loved that about her. She was also driven and motivated, spunky, and fun to be around. And she was pretty. Her laughing blue eyes and cheerful smile used to brighten his days and dance through his dreams at night.

There was no laughter in her eyes today, though. And nowadays when he saw her face at night, it was in his nightmares. The lifeless face of the little boy who haunted his dreams often morphed into Riley's, and he experienced the pain of losing her all over again.

He shook off the images that drove him to drink and focused on the conversation.

"You realize it's irresponsible to up and quit a job when the going gets rough, don't you?" Jake's expression was grim.

A spark of anger flashed in Riley's eyes and her lips pressed into a thin line for a moment before she spoke. "I didn't quit my job."

"You left Dr. Nelson without a nurse practitioner."

"Dr. Nelson understands that I needed a break. He's the one who suggested I take a leave of absence for a while." Her fork continued to pulverize her meatloaf.

"Well, *I* don't understand. If you love working for Dr. Nelson so much, why do you need a break?" Jake was usually patient and soft spoken, but his words were forceful enough that Emily put a hand on his arm to calm him.

Riley's older brothers had always been protective of her, so even though Jake's words sounded critical, Daniel knew he spoke them out of concern for his little sister. He recognized, like Daniel did, how out of character this was for Riley.

"There's a lot of things men don't understand about women." Riley's words were defensive and sharp. "They think they can do whatever they want. Take anything they want. They don't care what we think or what we want." She was on her feet now, shoving her chair under the table. "Excuse me. I've lost my appetite." She was halfway down the hall before she slowed her steps and in a much softer voice said, "Thanks for dinner, Lottie."

At least Riley recognized his mom's effort of making her favorite dinner even if she'd hardly touched it.

Jake set down his fork and ran a hand over his face. He looked at Emily. "I blew it, didn't I?"

She gave him a soft smile. "Just a little."

"I'd better apologize." He started to stand, but Emily stopped him.

"I think she needs a few minutes to calm down." She took a drink of water. "I hate to say it, but I think whatever is bothering her goes much deeper than her job."

The meatloaf in Daniel's stomach turned to lead.

So, there are man problems.

Had Riley been in a serious relationship? Did he dump her? Had she come home to nurse a broken heart?

I know how that feels.

~

RILEY WISHED she'd stormed out the back door instead of to her room. No, this wasn't her room. But it was no longer Robert's old room either.

Even though the new decor was pleasant enough, it felt all wrong. Everything had changed, and she hated change. Even Jake, who was only six years older than her, thought he had the right to act like her father.

She plopped on the bed and punched a pillow.

No one understood what she was going through, and she couldn't bring herself to tell them. She didn't want to see their pity or judgmental stares. Would they question whether she'd brought it on herself by the way she'd dressed or acted? Would they insist that she led Collin on?

She sprang to her feet and paced her room, hating the anger and defensiveness coursing through her. Collin had stolen her agency, and now she felt the need to reclaim it by being aggressive and contentious.

Her phone rang, and she sighed in relief when she saw Paige's picture on the screen.

"Hi, Paige." She tried to force enthusiasm into her voice.

"You were supposed to call me when you got home."

Riley grimaced as she dropped onto the bed again. "I know. I'm sorry. There was a bit of a crisis when I arrived, and I totally forgot."

"What kind of crisis?" Alarm filled Paige's voice.

"A bunch of cows got loose on the highway and Daniel needed help to herd them back to where they belonged."

"So, you've seen Daniel already? How is he?"

He wore his hair a little longer now than he used to, but he was more attractive than ever and as strong as an ox. She recalled the way he stretched the fence wire with gloved hands while she twisted the broken pieces together.

"Is he still withdrawn and broody?"

Oh. Paige wanted to know how he acted, not how he looked.

"Sort of, I guess. We haven't talked much yet." Riley poked at a pillow. "I forgot Daniel was here at the ranch when I decided to come home."

"I didn't. That's why I encouraged you to go back to the Double Diamond. It's time for you two to make up and figure out how to build a future together."

A little surge of electricity sparked in Riley's heart. "It's not that easy, Paige."

"I know, but with the way you two looked at each other at Jake and Emily's wedding last year, it was obvious you're still in love."

Riley let her mind drift back to the wedding. All her old feelings for Daniel had resurfaced while she danced a slow dance with him, encircled in his arms. She could have sworn he'd been about to kiss her when the song ended, but then her mom announced that it was time for the couple to cut the cake, and they were jostled off the dance floor.

She focused again on Paige's voice. "He no longer has a job keeping him in Portland and you've finished your Nurse Practitioner degree. Marriage and family are the next step."

"After last Friday, that's the last thing on my mind." Riley's voice was heavy and flat.

"I know. You need time to heal." Compassion filled Paige's voice. "But you were miserable after you broke up with Daniel. I think you should give things with him another chance this summer."

Riley recalled her reaction to Daniel this afternoon and how it sparked the memory of Collin's assault.

"I can't." The words were little more than a whisper.

"Give yourself some time, Ri, but in the meantime, don't push him away."

"I kind of already did," Riley said quietly.

"What do you mean? What did you do?"

Riley stood and paced her room again. "He...he hugged me."

"Really? What kind of hug?" Paige's voice rose in volume. "Was it like 'I'm so excited to see you!'? Like he wants to pick up where you guys left off three years ago? Or was it like 'Oh hey, hi. It's good to see you again.'?"

"I think he just meant it as a welcome home hug but..." Riley squeezed her eyes shut and drew in a steadying breath.

"But what?"

"I totally freaked out." Her breathing came a little faster as she told Paige how she'd frozen when Daniel touched her and how she'd wanted to scream but couldn't.

"Oh Ri, I'm so sorry." Paige's voice was gentle again. "I'd hoped getting away from Seattle and that scumbag would help you be able to distance yourself from what happened. But I guess it's not that easy."

"No, it's not that easy."

A part of her feared if she got too close to Daniel, he would hurt her in some way. The other part feared he would find out what she didn't want anyone to know and judge her for it. Nor did she want him to think less of her or pity her.

Daniel would think her rude, but it was probably best she avoided getting close to him.

"Hopefully, some time on the ranch will help you heal a little and decide what your next step will be."

Heal? Next step?

Riley hadn't suffered near the anguish most rape victims did thanks to Paige's timely arrival, but she'd been traumatized in a way that she didn't know how to handle. And would she ever be able to go back to Seattle?

"It might be good to talk to Emily while you're there." Paige's voice was soft and encouraging now. "Maybe she can help you."

Even though Emily was a nice person, having a psychologist for a sister-in-law was weird. Riley always felt like Emily analyzed everything she said and did. In fact, she probably thought Riley was really messed up for her outburst at dinner tonight, and she'd be right.

So many emotions flowed through her that she didn't know how to suppress or express. Anger and fear, desperation, and anxiety.

"I don't think I can...yet."

"That's understandable, but remember they are your family, and they love you."

Poor Jake. She shouldn't have lashed out at him like that.

"I'm worried about you." Riley changed the subject as she sat on the bed again. "I'm afraid my leaving might make you a target."

"Don't worry about me. I moved everything I need into Jen and Shaylee's apartment this afternoon. Besides, I spend most of my time with Phillip nowadays anyway."

Phillip seemed smitten with Paige, but there was something about him that bothered Riley. She couldn't put her finger on what it was though, so she'd kept her mouth shut.

A soft knock sounded on Riley's bedroom door.

"Can I come in, Ri?" Jake called.

"Hey, I need to go, Paige. I'll call you tomorrow."

"Okay, bye. Love you."

"Come in," Riley said as she ended the call.

She couldn't bring herself to meet Jake's eyes, so she stared at the floor. She owed him an apology, but not only was she as prideful as her brothers, she didn't want to have to explain why she blew up at him.

Jake shuffled his feet then cleared his throat. "Lottie wanted to make sure you got some of the apple crisp she made to welcome you home."

Riley looked at him. He held a plate of not only a generous serving of apple crisp but also a heaping scoop of vanilla ice cream. A smile lifted her lips. "Let me guess, you're the one who served the ice cream."

Finally, she'd found something that would never change.

All the Winters enjoyed ice cream, but Jake loved it more than the rest of them combined.

"Can you tell?" He smiled then cleared his throat again. "I thought it might help you forgive me. I'm sorry I got all critical of you and your life choices. You're welcome here anytime and for as long as you want. I hope you know that."

"Thanks." Riley accepted the plate but lowered her gaze again. "I'm sorry I got huffy with you too. I just have some...things I need to...work through right now, and I get...defensive sometimes, I guess."

"Well, you take your time." He stepped toward the door. "Remember we're here if you want to talk about whatever it is that's bothering you."

Talking was the last thing Riley wanted to do. She wanted to go for a run—although she'd fallen out of that habit years ago—or hit something. She wanted to scream and yell and throw things. But she didn't want to talk.

"Thanks," she said before Jake closed the door.

She needed to get out of this house and go for a ride on Misty. A fast one. But no way would she let Lottie's apple crisp and Jake's peace offering go to waste.

CHAPTER 3

*T*he house was dark when Riley returned from her ride. Exhausted, she took a quick shower and fell into bed.

Sleep came quickly, but so did the nightmares. Vivid dreams of Collin's face sneering at her. The evil intent in his eyes. His crude words. His hot breath on her face. And then always came his mouth followed by his rough hands fondling her and ripping her shirt. His body pinning her down as he continued to assault her.

Riley shot upright in bed, gasping for air. Her unfamiliar surroundings only accelerated her heart rate even more, and a sharp pain filled her chest. Her whole body shook uncontrollably as she broke out in a cold sweat.

It's fine. I'm fine.

She gradually recognized her surroundings as she tried to convince herself she wasn't in danger, but a total recall of everything that happened with Collin continued to flood her mind. Her chest grew so tight she struggled to breathe. Hot bile filled her mouth, and she threw back the covers and raced to the bathroom.

Tears streamed down her face as she emptied the contents of her stomach into the toilet. When the retching finally subsided, she turned on the shower as hot as it would go and stripped off her clothes again with shaky hands.

All the scalding-hot showers she'd taken over the past week, where she'd scrubbed her body until she was chafed and raw, hadn't been able to erase the feel of Collin's hands on her body. She should have known this shower wouldn't help either.

Still feeling desperate and agitated, she dressed and walked out of the bathroom. She stopped short when Emily walked out of little Adam's room at the same moment.

Emily's brows furrowed and concern filled her face. "Are you okay?"

"I'm fine." Riley wrapped her arms around herself and pushed past her sister-in-law to get to her room. Once inside, she couldn't bring herself to go back to bed. The nightmares would only return, setting off her PTSD.

Or is it my PTSD causing the nightmares?

After pacing for a few minutes, she changed into jeans and a sweatshirt, picked up her boots, and tiptoed out the back door. She sat on the top step of the deck and pulled her boots on, wishing she'd changed into running clothes and brought her sneakers out instead.

It's too dark. I can't run alone.

With nowhere to go and nothing to do, she walked to the stables. She contemplated taking a different horse out for another ride, but it was too dark tonight. She'd only put the horse and herself in danger. Besides, she was saddle-sore from her earlier ride.

She let herself into the stables through the small side door and flipped on the single light. No point in disturbing the horses just because she couldn't sleep. She wandered deeper into the massive stables to the storage room at the far end where she flipped on another light.

She'd heard music playing and caught a glimpse of Daniel in here earlier when she took Misty out for a ride. She'd contemplated inviting him to join her, but decided she wasn't in the mood to make conversation. The last thing she wanted was him questioning her again about why she chose to come home for the summer.

The small room that used to be filled with miscellaneous tools and odd junk while she was growing up had been cleaned out and turned into a weight room by Jake and Daniel a couple years ago. Riley had never understood why the two of them felt driven to revert to their teenage fascination with body building, but now she understood why Daniel was so ripped.

The small room was well stocked with a bench press, a rack of weights plus a wide assortment of dumbbells of varying sizes and weights. A punching bag hung from the rafters near the corner.

Just what I need.

She searched the room until she found boxing gloves on a shelf. Pulling the door closed, so she wouldn't disturb the horses too much, she pulled on the gloves. Their bulkiness felt strange on her hands, but she didn't care. She had no idea what she was doing, but she turned to the punching bag and pictured Collin Ainsworth's face.

DANIEL SHOT UP IN BED, gasping for air. Groaning, he pressed the heels of his hands to his eyes, trying to rid his mind of the images that invaded his dreams.

Vivid images of a young blond-haired boy on his bike, darting into the road in front of Daniel's truck. His inability to stop in time.

The boy's still body.

Screaming sirens.

Flashing lights.

The boy's face often morphed into Riley's, and no matter how hard he tried to wake her up, she never responded.

Thankfully, he hadn't had this particular nightmare for some time. The lack of nightmares made it easier to remain sober. But having Riley home must have triggered something.

Daniel stared at the extra dark spot on the wall that was a picture of him wrestling a steer back in his high school rodeo days. He focused on his breathing, slowly counting backward from one hundred. By the time he reached seventy, his breathing had calmed and so had his thoughts.

Then the urge for a stiff drink hit him like a freight train. He threw back the covers and darted to the bathroom to splash cold water on his face.

Once again, he focused on his breathing as he stared at his reflection in the mirror.

You don't need that stuff.

You're stronger than that.

It'll pass in a few minutes.

The urge to grab his truck keys and drive to the liquor store didn't subside as fast as it usually did, so he grabbed his guitar, slid his feet into slippers, and headed outside. It was late, and he didn't want to wake his parents, so he sat on the front porch, far away from their bedroom at the back of the house. Settling into a wicker chair, he strummed a few notes.

Working out, whittling, and playing the guitar. Those had become his coping mechanisms when the cravings hit. But he'd already worked out tonight before heading to his AA meeting, and whittling in the dark was a bad idea. He often called his sponsor or talked to Emily when things were bad. But he'd already talked to Tom tonight at the meeting, and Emily was asleep. She often woke up at night with little Adam who was only two and a half months old, so Daniel refused to bother her when he had a rough time in the middle of the night.

Despite plucking out his favorite church hymn that usually calmed him, he couldn't help but replay the scene at dinner in his head. Sure, Jake had been out of line, but Riley had reacted much stronger than was typical for her.

In fact, she wasn't acting like herself at all.

A scream split the air, and Daniel bolted to his feet. He stood frozen, listening for more screams as he tried to figure out where it had come from. The whinny of a horse floated on the evening breeze, then a faint but steady thudding reached him.

He left his guitar on the wicker chair and walked toward the lane that led to the big house. Dim light shone through the window at the front of the stables and more light filtered through the window at the back.

That's odd. I'm sure I turned the lights off after my workout.

The sound of dull thuds continued to sound at frequent intervals. Curious, he jogged down the lane.

The small door to the right of the big double doors was slightly ajar, so Daniel slipped inside. His slippers made no sound on the wooden floor as he walked to the other end of the stables. The frequency of the thuds grew more rapid and louder as he approached the door to the storage room that he'd turned into his weight room.

Another yell sounded as he reached for the doorknob. This one was decidedly feminine.

He jerked his hand back.

It came from Riley; he was sure of it, even though it was deep and guttural and full of pain. Knowing he shouldn't intrude, but feeling the need to protect Riley from whatever tormented her, he quietly opened the door.

Her back was to him, but perspiration soaked through her shirt and curled the tendrils of hair at the nape of her neck. He was about to say her name when a tortured sob tore from her.

She threw another forceful punch. "I hate you!"

And another sharp jab. "I hate what you did to me!"

Then she stopped and hugged the bag, leaning her head against it. Anguished sobs shook her shoulders.

Whatever demons Riley was trying to outrun, they were every bit as formidable as his own.

Daniel ached to pull her into his arms and take away her pain. But he feared he might be the source of her misery. Some of it anyway. He recalled the way she tensed up when he hugged her that afternoon. She'd never reacted that way before, so he couldn't help assuming his touch repulsed her.

Was she tormented by the fact that she'd have to work with him every day? Or was this a carryover of her annoyance with Jake?

No. Something—or rather someone—drove her home.

He had to believe he and Riley would find a way to work together peacefully this summer. Otherwise, he'd never be able to stay sober.

Recalling how angry he'd been at his parents and Jake when they dragged him home last fall and forced him to dry out, he decided he needed to give Riley some grace and space to work through whatever tormented her.

So, even though it was the last thing he wanted to do because he'd loved this woman all his life, he backed out of the room and softly closed the door between them.

CHAPTER 4

*D*espite the amazing smells of bacon and waffles that assaulted Daniel when he stumbled through the back door of the big house for breakfast on Saturday morning, he wished he'd decided to forgo food in favor of more sleep. It had been close to two by the time he finally fell into a deep sleep, so his six-a.m. alarm went off way too early.

Jake stood from the table and carried his plate to the sink before Daniel could even sit down with his food. "Zane, keep an eye on 168 today. She's in labor, but I recall she had trouble delivering her last one, so she might need help with this one too."

Ah, Jake must have spent the night at the calving sheds.

Daniel should have volunteered to work the calving sheds for all the sleep he'd gotten last night. Choosing to walk away from a distraught Riley had been hard. Blocking out the memory of her tortured cries even after he'd returned to his bed had been even harder.

Daniel's dad nodded. "I'll be glad when we finally get all these calves here."

"Me too. Only a couple dozen to go." Jake gave a half-hearted wave before pushing open the swinging door that led to the great room.

"Let me catch a few hours of sleep, then we can discuss bringing on some ranch hands. Hopefully as early as next week."

"Sure thing." Daniel's dad turned to him after the door swung closed behind Jake. "You look like you could use a few more hours of sleep yourself."

His mom slid into a chair across the table from Daniel. "Did you have a bad night?"

Daniel scrubbed a hand over his face and let out a sigh. "Yeah."

"Was it the same nightmare?" Her voice was gentle. At his nod, she asked, "Did Riley coming home cause it?"

Daniel cut a bite of waffle but didn't bring it to his mouth. "I don't know. Maybe."

"I imagine her being home stirs up all kinds of emotions in you, but stay strong and focus on your goals." She put a hand on his arm. "If it's meant to work out between you two, it will. Stressing over it won't change anything."

Daniel only had one goal: stay sober.

After six months of almost constant inebriation, the seven months he'd remained sober weren't enough to dull the frequent desire for a drink. As for things working out between him and Riley... He couldn't go there. He needed to prove to himself he could stay sober long-term before getting into a relationship. The last thing he wanted was to let down a woman he cared for. Especially the one woman who meant more to him than even his family.

Considering the way Riley took out her rage on the punching bag the last night, a relationship was the last thing on her mind right now too. Which was probably for the best.

Daniel gave his mom a tight smile and a nod before shoving the bite of waffle in his mouth. He thought about the things Emily had taught him. The only things he had control over were his words, behavior, and mindset. So that's what he'd do. It didn't matter that Riley was back at the ranch, acting strange, he would focus on the things he could control.

His dad rose from the table. "I'm going to start feeding the cattle. You hit the stables when you're done eating."

With thousands of heads of cattle in the surrounding corrals and pastures, getting feed to them every day was a monumental task even with the help of a tractor. It would be a lot less work after they moved most of the herds to summer grazing pastures.

"We also need to move more straw to the stables today."

Daniel acknowledged his dad's words with a nod.

His dad paused by the door to the mud room before walking out. "Hopefully, Riley will come help you when she surfaces, but I'm not sure what to expect from her yet."

Riley was a hard worker, but she was not a morning person. Considering what he witnessed last night, Daniel doubted he'd see her before noon.

Fifteen minutes later, he pushed open the big double doors and walked into the stables. After ensuring there was enough straw for today, he turned the horses out into the corrals and set to work cleaning the stalls. He'd finished the third one by the time Riley walked into the stables.

Despite his thoughts at breakfast about avoiding a relationship right now, his breath hitched, and his heart rate kicked up a notch. She'd always had that effect on him. When he was young, it was because she was fun to be around. Then just before he left for college, she blossomed into a young woman, and he'd started to see her in a different light. He'd been attracted to her ever since.

Shadows ringed her eyes that had a decidedly pink tint to them, and exhaustion lined her face, but she was still pretty in her faded jeans, pale pink t-shirt, and layered pink and gray flannel shirt with her hair pulled back into a ponytail.

"Sorry, I'm late." She barely glanced at him before looking at the blank job board. "I assume I'm supposed to help you?"

"Yeah, Dad will probably start listing the jobs on the board next week. But for now, we need to clean out the stalls then haul more straw over from the hay sheds."

"Oh yay." Sarcasm filled her voice. "At least straw is lighter than hay." She walked over to the cabinet where they kept a store of gloves and other supplies.

39

"Good luck finding gloves small enough to fit you. I don't think we've had a ranch hand with hands as small as yours since..." his voice died off as he recalled that summer three years ago.

She raised an eyebrow. "Since I left?"

"Probably." He forced his lips into a grin, trying to keep a positive mindset.

She didn't return his smile.

After pulling on the smallest pair of gloves in the cupboard, Riley grabbed a wheelbarrow, pitchfork, and shovel from the tool room and stood at the head of the long line of stalls. Her shoulders slumped. "Usually when you grow up and go back to visit places from your childhood, you think, 'I recall it being much bigger than this.'" She shook her head. "Not this place. It's still as big as ever."

Daniel's gaze followed hers. "Yeah, it still has *sixteen* roomy stalls. At least now I have help and don't have to do it all myself." He gave her another broad grin.

One corner of her mouth lifted a little this time.

He leaned on his pitchfork. "Just like old times, huh?"

The hint of her smile faded, and Riley pushed her wheelbarrow to the far end of the stables.

Okay then. I guess it's not going to be like old times.

They used to always work next to each other, leap frogging around one another, so they could talk while they worked. Was the cold shoulder her way of saying she had no intention of getting involved with him again, even as a friend? Or was it something else entirely?

He hated to admit it because it would probably be the worst thing for his sobriety, but if Riley was interested in the two of them trying to make a go of it again, he had a feeling he would cave rather quickly. Like he did three years ago. Because even though he didn't want to be, he was still attracted to her and cared for her deeply.

After last night, the desire to protect and comfort her was stronger than it had ever been in his life, which was saying something, because it had always been his job to look out for Riley.

Twenty minutes later, he spotted her standing in the aisle at the other end of the stables. She repeatedly stretched her arms over her head, behind her back, and across her body, doing anything and everything to loosen up her shoulders.

He recalled his first workout after hanging the punching bag. He'd been determined to work up a sweat, and he did, but he could hardly lift his arms the next day. Considering how aggressively Riley attacked the bag last night, she no doubt had sore muscles today.

They finished cleaning the stables in record time. Daniel appreciated Riley's help, but with the way she barely acknowledged him, he may as well have been working alone.

This is going to be a long summer.

CHAPTER 5

The knot that formed in Riley's stomach when Jake and Emily insisted she ride to church with them expanded as she walked up the front steps of the modest ivory sandstone church. She hesitated on the threshold.

I don't belong here. I'm not worthy to step foot in this building.

What happened to her wasn't her fault, she knew that, but it still made her feel filthy and tainted.

"Riley, honey." Riley spun around at the sound of her mom's voice behind her. "Jake told me you were home for a while. I planned to come out to the ranch to visit you yesterday, but I got tied up helping a sick friend."

Her mom pulled her into a tight hug, and Riley had to squeeze her eyes closed at the rush of emotion that filled her. A part of her wished she was still an innocent little girl who could run to her mom for every little bruise and scrape. But the other part of her didn't want to burden her mother's compassionate heart with her problems. A mother's kiss couldn't heal the kind of pain Riley suffered now.

Her mom pulled her through the doors of the church after releasing her. "We're blocking traffic."

Before Riley knew it, she sat beside her mom in the fourth row, with Jake, Emily, and little Adam on one side and Robert, Jessie, and baby Blake on the other. She loved being surrounded by family, but Robert's whispered, "What are you doing at home?" as he gave her a one-armed hug made her dread the interrogation she'd get later, during family dinner.

Daniel and his parents slipped in just before the services started to sit in their usual spot at the end of the third row. Riley's breath caught at the sight of Daniel in a suit. He sure filled out a pair of Wranglers well, but there was something compelling about this rugged cowboy in a suit.

Riley's gaze repeatedly drifted to him as she listened to the sermon about Unity in Christ. Sitting behind Daniel made it easy to watch him without getting caught. He bowed his head as soon as he sat down, and now, he leaned forward, elbows propped on his knees, head in his hands.

She thought maybe he was sleeping, like he used to do when they were teenagers, but he scrubbed his hands over his face or tugged at the collar of his shirt every so often. Not once, however, did he look up at the pulpit.

Riley leaned close to her mom and whispered, "What's wrong with Daniel?"

Mom's gaze followed hers. "I don't know. He's been like that ever since he came home last fall. Always broody. Always closed off."

Closed off. That's exactly what he is. But why?

Over the past three years Riley had only visited the ranch for an occasional weekend a dozen times or so. Except for during Jake and Emily's wedding early last year, her encounters with Daniel had been brief and uncomfortable, but she'd noticed a change in him. Ever since he broke his leg a couple years ago, he'd been withdrawn and guarded.

She thought it was because she'd broken up with him, but there seemed to be something more bothering him. She did her best to listen to the pastor, but she wasn't very successful in keeping her gaze from repeatedly drifting to Daniel.

Later that afternoon, Riley found herself surrounded by her family again. Sunday was the only day Lottie took off. So Riley's mom, Faith

Winters, came to the ranch and cooked for her family. Everyone gathered in the kitchen to help. It was one of Riley's favorite traditions.

There was always so much work to do on the ranch that it was rare for the family to be together for longer than the time it took to eat a meal. Riley enjoyed watching her brothers peel potatoes and toss a salad. It reminded her of how her dad used to help and steal kisses from their mom while they worked together in the kitchen on Sundays.

She missed her father terribly, but it was fun to have two adorable nephews to distract her. In fact, she spent most of the meal prep time in the living room playing with the babies, so it shouldn't have surprised her when her oldest brother Robert decided to grill her the moment they all gathered around the dinner table.

"Jake says you plan on working all summer on the ranch, Ri. What's up with that?"

Riley's defenses immediately rose, and she itched to go for a ride so she could avoid this conversation yet again. She chewed on the inside of her cheek for a moment before giving the response she'd given everyone else. "I needed a change of scenery for a while. So, I took a leave of absence."

"But you have a full-time job with a doctor and patients who rely on you. You can't just walk away from that."

"I didn't walk away from it."

Except she had. She wasn't sure when or if she'd ever be able to go back. Certainly not as long as Collin was around. Would his obsession with her be gone by the time summer ended? As much as she no longer wished to be the target of his attention, she couldn't wish that on any other woman.

"Didn't you?" Robert's raised eyebrow lowered until he studied her through narrowed eyes. "Did something happen with Dr. Nelson, like misconduct?"

As the county sheriff, Robert was suspicious by nature, so naturally, he would jump to those conclusions.

"No. Nothing happened. Dr. Nelson is great to work with!"

"Then why did you come home?" Robert's voice rose in volume.

Their mom held up a hand at the same moment Robert's wife, Jessie, put a hand on his arm.

Jessie spoke first. "Sometimes life throws you a curve ball and you need to take a breather."

Riley shot Jessie a look of gratitude. If anyone understood what Riley was going through it was Jessie, whose first husband had physically and mentally abused her. Not that Jessie knew exactly what Riley was going through, but judging by the sympathetic look her sister-in-law gave her, she understood a lot.

Riley's gaze jumped to Emily's next. Once again, the look on her psychologist sister-in-law's face was a combination of I-know-something-is-wrong and please-let-me-help. But Riley wasn't ready to talk yet. She wasn't sure she ever would be.

Her gaze continued to travel around the table to find everyone's eyes on her, including her mom's, whose brows creased in a deep furrow.

Riley ducked her head and studied her mashed potatoes.

"Robert," Jessie said, "why don't you tell your family about your experience with Mrs. Silverstone this week?"

Riley shot Jessie another appreciative glance when Robert launched into his story about how he'd pulled over the ninety-year-old woman for driving on the wrong side of the road and the public dressing down she'd given him.

Having lost her appetite, Riley itched to go for a ride or even a long walk, but she dug into her meal instead. Her mother wouldn't approve of her excusing herself without even touching her food.

Gratefully, conversation continued around the table with little input from Riley. Once dinner wrapped up, Riley took her plate to the kitchen and quickly helped clean up, intending to break away as soon as she could to go for a ride. But her mom had other ideas.

She followed Riley to her room and stood in the open doorway, arms folded. "Are you okay, honey?"

Riley gave her mom a stiff smile. "I'm fine." When the doubt on her mother's face grew, she went on. "Really, I'm fine. I just needed a break and a change of scenery."

"But for the whole summer?" Mom stepped into the room. "This is so out of character for you. We all recognize that, so we know something's wrong."

Riley turned away from her mother's penetrating gaze and wrapped her arms around herself. A part of her wanted to cry on her mom's shoulder and tell her what happened even though she didn't want to have to relive it. The other part didn't want her family to know, because she was so ashamed that she'd ever gotten into that position with Collin in the first place and that she hadn't been able to stop him sooner.

"It's not something you can fix, Mom." Her quiet voice broke on the last word.

"Oh, sweetheart." A gentle hand landed on her back. "Is it a problem with a boyfriend? I didn't know you were dating anyone seriously." Mom stroked her back from shoulder to shoulder. "I know a broken heart can feel like the end of the world, but time heals all wounds."

Does it?

Would time take away the feelings of irritation, anger, and anxiety? Would it dull the memories of Collin's hands and mouth violating her? Would it take away the shame that she knew she shouldn't feel but did anyway?

Maybe time would *help with those things.*

But Riley wasn't a patient person. She wanted to feel better now. Since that wasn't possible, she took the next best thing: a lengthy hug from her mom.

CHAPTER 6

*M*onday morning Daniel walked into the stables to find his dad writing on the job board.

Of course, Riley's name sat next to his own. So far, they were the only two ranch hands listed, but Jake hoped to hire more men by the end of the week. That meant Hank would be returning too. The ornery old man, who cooked for the ranch hands and kept the bunkhouse clean, was almost as good of a cook as Daniel's mom. Not that he'd ever admit that to her.

The first item on the list of chores for Daniel and Riley was cleaning the stalls and feeding the horses, of course. The animals always took precedence.

"Spring cleanup?" Daniel read the second task on the job board.

His dad slapped a paper against his chest.

Daniel quickly scanned the list. "Wait, you want me and Riley to prune the trees in the orchard? I don't know how to do that."

His dad turned back. "Of course, you do. You've helped me do it many times."

"Helped. I never had to do it on my own. I don't know which branches to cut."

"Keep all the small branches on the five main branches unless they

47

cross or interfere with each other." His dad held up his hand with his fingers splayed in a wide curved position as though he meant to catch a baseball. "Use the saws-all on the branches that are too large for the pruning shears."

Daniel looked at the list again. "Trim the raspberries?"

"Same thing, son. Just cut back last year's growth."

Like I know what that is. I wasn't here last summer.

"I'll switch you jobs, if you want." His dad grinned. "You can drive the honey wagon instead."

"Nope. I'm good. I'll figure out how to prune everything."

Even if I have to look it up on YouTube.

Daniel would rather prune any day over hauling the manure from the corrals to spread over the alfalfa fields. That was the dirtiest and smelliest job on the ranch. His dad always called the manure spreader the Honey Wagon, even though it was the farthest thing from it.

"I'll be back and forth between here and the hay fields, so let me know if you have any problems." His dad stepped out the door of the stables then turned back. "Don't bother Jake before noon. He pulled another all-nighter at the calving sheds."

"I could have taken another turn at the sheds."

"Don't worry, you'll get another chance or two." His dad waved a hand. "We still have a couple dozen babies coming."

Daniel had cleaned two stalls by the time Riley walked into the stables.

Shadows once again ringed her eyes, and he wondered if she'd spent half the night taking her frustrations out on his punching bag again.

"Sorry, I'm late." She barely glanced at him before studying the job board. "Spring cleanup?"

Daniel pointed to the list sitting on a nearby shelf. "Dad wrote us a whole list of things to do in the orchard and gardens."

She grimaced. "I'd rather fix fences."

"Me too."

Cleaning the stables went about the same as it did the last two days. Riley worked from the other end, and even when they met in the middle, they hardly talked.

Before long, they gathered a different set of tools and headed to the small orchard behind his parents' house. His mom always insisted on keeping a garden and growing as much of their own food as possible. They grew almost every fruit and vegetable possible, making for a massive garden. The ranch hands often had to help with the weeding, but when they were rewarded with corn on the cob, new potatoes, and fresh watermelon, they stopped complaining.

"Do you remember how to prune the fruit trees?" Daniel asked as they entered the small orchard.

Riley shook her head. "I haven't helped with the pruning for years, so I have no idea."

He pulled his phone from his pocket. "Okay, give me a minute to make sure we don't screw this up."

He quickly searched for YouTube videos, fast-forwarding through them until they got to the part where it explained exactly what branches to trim off and where to make the cuts. Then he did another search to see if all fruit trees were supposed to be pruned the same.

Daniel struggled to keep his attention on his phone screen, however, because Riley stood ten feet away from him, doing all the arm stretches he'd seen her do in the stables on Saturday.

She'd likely spent another late-night session in his little gym, which only raised more questions in his mind. Did Riley struggle to fall asleep? Or was she waking from nightmares, like he often did? And what happened to cause all this unrest in her?

Once he was sure about what they were supposed to do, they got to work. The job required them to work closer together than they had in the stables.

Any time he stepped close to Riley, she sucked in a sharp breath and tensed. He wanted to believe it was the attraction between them. It was certainly still there on his part. But he recalled the way she tensed up and practically recoiled when he hugged her the other day.

No, Riley was fighting something, but it wasn't attraction.

Hating the uncomfortable silence between them, Daniel searched for something to talk about that wouldn't add to the awkwardness or set her off like Jake did at dinner the other night.

"Do you remember how we used to play Hide-and-Seek with Damon and Paige here in the orchard?"

Damon and Paige were Riley's cousins, who visited the ranch often when they were young. Damon was Daniel's age, so the two of them were good friends. They always got stuck playing with the girls, even though they were two years older, because their older brothers decided they were too young to hang out with the big boys.

A genuine smile filled Riley's face, and she snorted. "Paige was afraid of heights, yet she loved climbing the trees."

"She went too high every time and freaked out. Then she demanded I get the ladder so she could climb down."

Riley chuckled. "I remember the time Damon snagged his pants as he jumped out of the cherry tree, ripping a gaping hole across the backside."

"I remember the time you got hung up, literally, in the apricot tree." Daniel couldn't help laughing at the memory of a seven-year-old Riley hanging by the back of her shorts from the remnants of a trimmed branch.

Whoever did the pruning that year, didn't cut off the branch as close as they should have.

"I can't believe you just left me hanging there while you went to get our moms and insisted they take a picture before they helped me down." Riley dropped the branch she'd been holding and shoved his shoulder.

"Even your parents agreed it was a priceless picture."

"So was the memory of the wedgie it gave me. I swear it took a month for that sensation to go away."

For the next two hours they continued to reminisce as they worked, and it felt like old times. Riley finally relaxed around him, and Daniel realized how much he'd missed working with her. He loved the way he and Riley could talk about anything and everything.

Even after they finished pruning the orchard, they continued to chat while they ate sandwiches for lunch, and Daniel recognized that he hadn't only missed working with Riley, he'd missed his best friend.

"What's left on our list?" Riley asked as they walked out of the house after lunch. Again, she stretched her arms, trying to loosen up her muscles.

Daniel pulled the paper from his back pocket. "We need to till the garden, and mow and weed whack all the grounds."

"Mowing and weed whacking takes all afternoon," Riley said with a sigh that sounded like it came more from exhaustion than frustration or disappointment.

He looked around at the unkempt backyard of the big house. It definitely needed a mow. It would be the first mowing of spring and they'd had enough late-fall growth that the yard was a mess.

"I don't think my dad and Jake expect us to get all of this done in one day. So, I say let's do whatever makes it look like we put forth our best effort."

"Mowing and weed whacking it is." Riley headed toward the stables again, for yet another set of tools and equipment. She rotated her arms in big windmill-like circles as she walked.

Daniel wanted to ask her what made her so upset that she needed such an aggressive outlet, but she'd be embarrassed if she knew he saw her crying on Saturday night. Despite all the conversation they engaged in while they worked and ate lunch, none of it was even remotely personal. Daniel preferred it that way, and he assumed Riley did too.

"I know you hate carrying the weed whacker around for hours, so I'll do that."

Weed whacking killed his back because it was six inches too short for his tall frame, but he'd deal with it to save Riley's arms.

She stepped in front of him and grabbed the handle of the weed whacker before he could. "I'm not some weak female. I can run a weed whacker."

"I never said you were weak. I just know you don't like—"

"I don't need to be coddled. I'm as competent as anyone else around here." Her words were sharp and forceful.

Daniel wasn't sure what triggered this sudden change in her mood, but he raised his hands in surrender and stepped away. "Okay, you can weed whack."

He stood by as Riley checked the gas and the string, then when she walked toward the entrance, he picked up a pair of safety glasses. "You should probably wear—"

"I don't need you to tell me how to do my job."

Daniel let out a low whistle. He sure would like to know who ticked Riley off, because he was getting whiplash.

IT TOOK ONLY a minute of weed whacking for the wind to whip the cut grass and weeds back into Riley's face, and she realized what Daniel had been about to say as she walked out on him. She should have known to grab safety glasses, but her pride wouldn't let her get them now. Especially after snapping at Daniel.

Five more minutes of running the cumbersome weed whacker, and her shoulders burned. It didn't help that every muscle from her wrists to her neck ached from punching the bag so aggressively the last two nights. Last night's nightmare wasn't as bad as her first night home, but she'd been unable to go back to sleep without working off her frustrations.

There was something cathartic about expressing the emotions raging inside her through physical exertion. But cleaning out stalls and constantly reaching overhead to prune the fruit trees had left her arms feeling like jelly.

Daniel was only trying to do her a favor by offering to weed whack because he knew she hated this chore. But all she heard was him calling her weak. She couldn't be viewed as weak and vulnerable. It would make people think they could take advantage of her again.

So she pressed on, even though her arms ached and the muscles in her shoulders burned.

She was half done with the backyard of the main house when the wind blew debris into her right eye. With a shriek, she shut off the weed whacker and pulled off her gloves. She turned her back to the wind and doubled over, hoping gravity would help pull out whatever it was that made it feel like needles stabbed her eye.

The mower shut off across the yard and Daniel yelled. "Are you okay, Ri?"

She didn't bother answering, because she was too busy trying to rid her eye of the irritation.

Rapid footsteps drew nearer, and from the corner of her good eye she saw Daniel running in her direction. Warning bells sounded in her head, growing louder with each step he took.

"What's going on?"

"I got something in my eye." A growl of frustration punctuated her words.

"I'm not surprised." He put a hand on her shoulder and pushed her upright.

Her whole body tensed at his touch. She turned away from him, but he sidestepped, keeping his body squarely in front of her. "Let me see."

Even though she'd straightened to her full height, he loomed over her, tall and broad, his breathing labored. Her breath hitched, and a band tightened around her chest.

Her right leg bounced, tapping the heel of her boot against the ground, as she struggled to draw air into her lungs. Instinctively, she balled her hands into fists.

It's Daniel. He won't hurt me.

He used to be her best friend. The one who carried her on his back for a whole mile when she sliced open her knee in the creek.

Large hands cupped her face with thumbs pressed to her cheek bone. His long fingers pushed against the erratic pulse racing under her jaw.

But he could hurt me if he wanted to.

Daniel leaned closer, and his warm breath hit her cheek.

Her heart raced faster as she recalled the smell of garlic and whiskey on Collin's breath the night he attacked her. A cold chill snaked down her spine, and a flood of adrenaline made her whole body tremble.

The pain in her eye forgotten, she jerked back. She needed to get away from him.

His hands held firm. "Hold still!"

Daniel's lips moved, but she heard the demanding tone of Collin's voice when he pressed his hand to her neck and sternum, pinning her down. She'd struggled so hard for air that shadows filled her vision.

Just like now.

Not again!

A surge of adrenaline fueled by fear and self-preservation set her body in motion.

She put both hands on his shoulders and brought her knee up as hard as she could. "Get your hands off me! Don't you ever touch me again!"

Collin doubled over.

No, wait.

It was Daniel's dark head that doubled over, a loud groan emanating from him.

Mortified by what she'd done and still fighting the panic surging through her, she turned and raced into the house.

CHAPTER 7

*D*aniel paused to brush the grass and weeds off his pant legs before hurrying through the back door of the ranch house. He'd just finished mowing and weed whacking around the big house, up the lane to the highway, and down the lane to his parents' house by himself.

He should be awarded a medal for getting any work done at all after Riley kneed him in the groin that afternoon. Although, he had laid on the ground for a full five minutes after she ran off.

"Ah, there you are." His mom pulled a casserole dish from the oven and straightened. "Perfect timing. Dinner's ready."

Daniel washed his hands then slipped into the dining room as his mom laid the lasagna on the table. He would've liked to shower before eating, but his mom was a stickler for schedules, and everyone was already seated. Everyone except for Riley.

He didn't know what her deal was, but he hoped she got over it soon. Otherwise, his sobriety wasn't likely to survive the summer. Alcohol dulled all kinds of pain.

"Where's Riley?" His mom asked as she took her seat.

Jake got to his feet. "I knocked on her door a bit ago and told her it was dinner time, but apparently she needs an extra invite today."

I should have taken time to shower.

When Riley slid into her seat across from him less than a minute later, he caught a glimpse of red-rimmed eyes again. The resentment he'd harbored toward her all afternoon dissipated.

He could count on one hand the number of times he'd seen her cry since she turned twelve. She'd rarely had emotional outbursts like she'd been prone to lately.

Someone—probably a man—has wrecked Riley.

His heart twisted in his chest at the thought of someone hurting her, and he ached to punch something. In truth, he longed for a stiff drink, but he couldn't give in. Not once. Not even a little one. Or he would spiral out of control again. He'd have to settle for punching something after dinner.

Riley was distant a few nights ago, but that was nothing compared to the way she refused to look at him tonight. Her eyes never left her plate, yet she picked at her food and hardly ate a bite. She didn't look at anyone else either, except for a quick glance and a mumbled response when someone asked her a question.

Daniel wasn't the only one who watched Riley with concern. His parents and Jake and Emily all had eyes on her as well. He must have been too quiet because they watched him too.

At one point, Emily caught his eye. When he tried to look away, she tilted her head and held his gaze. Her right eyebrow raised ever so slightly, asking him a question.

How are you doing?

It had become a silent way for him to communicate with his therapist.

If he smiled or gave a brief thumbs up, Emily knew he was okay. But if he shrugged or shook his head the slightest bit, she usually fabricated a task that she needed his help with so they could talk.

He'd never been good about seeking her out when he struggled. And he didn't know how to respond now. Having Riley home was bad enough, but every interaction with her seemed to end in disaster, and that only amplified his cravings. His non-response would probably have Emily seeking him out after dinner.

Daniel tuned into his dad's voice. "I'll take a turn at the calving sheds tonight. Daniel, can you cover tomorrow night? We have half a dozen cows and about ten heifers that have yet to deliver."

"I can take a turn at the calving sheds," Riley said, surprising everybody.

Jake and his dad looked at each other with raised eyebrows, then finally Jake gave a small shrug.

His dad cleared his throat. "Daniel, will you and Riley work the calving sheds tomorrow night?"

Riley's eyes darted to Daniel's face, but she looked away again so fast he thought he'd imagined it.

"I can work the calving sheds by myself," Daniel said.

He was exhausted, so he shouldn't volunteer for more solo night shifts. The last thing he wanted was to spend all night with Riley while waves of animosity continued to roll off her like an avalanche barreling down the mountainside toward him. It was only a matter of time before he found himself buried, and his sobriety a casualty.

"I can too. I don't need Daniel's help." Riley's voice was defensive.

Jake and his dad locked gazes again, then Jake shook his head. "I don't know, Ri, it's been a long time since you've had to watch for the signs of a cow in distress or deliver a calf. I'd feel better if you worked with Daniel this time."

"I don't need a babysitter." Riley's words were sharp.

"I know you don't, but you've been away for a long time, and it takes a lot of strength to pull a calf."

"Are you saying I'm weak?"

There was that word again. *Weak.* Riley had gotten mad at him this afternoon, thinking he had called her weak.

Who called or made Riley feel weak?

"No, I don't think you're weak." The slowness with which Jake spoke showed he was trying not to lose his patience. "You just don't have any recent experience."

"So I'm incompetent?"

Jake's brow furrowed. "What? No—"

"I'm sorry you feel saddled with me when you don't think I'm up to

57

the task of working on the ranch." Riley bolted to her feet. This time she didn't take the time to push her chair in or thank his mom for dinner, she simply stomped out the back door, slamming it behind her.

Silence fell around the table.

Jake hung his head and rubbed the back of his neck as though fighting a headache.

Emily stared at Riley's back through the glass door, a frown marring her face and a deep V creasing her brow.

His parents stared at each other, confusion written on their faces.

Daniel kept telling himself not to take Riley's outbursts personally. But she'd looked right at him this afternoon before she rammed her knee into him and shouted at him to never touch her again. He couldn't help thinking that maybe she'd learned the things about him that he tried to keep hidden. Things that repulsed her.

"Did...one of you..." He fiddled with his fork as he struggled to find the words to voice his thoughts. "Did one of you tell Riley about me? I mean...about the little boy and my drinking?" He looked at the faces surrounding the table, finding only puzzled looks.

"It's not our story to tell," Jake said with a shrug.

"It's in the past, Daniel." Emily leaned forward in her seat. "Riley doesn't need to know, unless you want her to."

Daniel's dad rested a hand on his shoulder, and his mom studied his face a moment before speaking. "Did something happen between you two? Is that why she wouldn't look at you?" Her eyebrows inched up as she waited for an answer.

It wasn't his place to tell them what was going on with Riley—not that he knew exactly what was going on with her—but maybe if they could make sense of her behavior, they could figure out how to help her.

He stared at his plate for several long moments before speaking.

"This afternoon...she got something in her eye while she was weed whacking. I stopped the mower and hurried over to see if I could help her." His grip on his fork tightened until the metal dug into his hand. "She...she got really defensive when I touched her. Then she..." He didn't want to admit how Riley had laid him out. "She shoved me away and shouted at me to never touch her again."

"Oh dear." Emily's quiet words only added to the puzzlement on everyone's faces. Her gaze shifted to the glass door again, and Daniel's followed.

Riley had Misty tied to the hitching post and was working on saddling her.

Daniel looked back at Emily. Her frown had deepened along with the worry lines across her forehead.

She knew what Riley's problem was, Daniel was sure of it. But he also knew she'd never tell them unless Riley wanted her to. Emily was good at keeping confidences. He liked that about her.

Daniel looked out at the backyard again. He had no desire to ride with Riley, but a fast ride on Rebel sounded tempting.

His time would be better spent attending an AA meeting, though. Never mind that he went to one three days ago. Besides, after the way Riley assaulted him this afternoon, sitting in a saddle would be mighty uncomfortable.

FEELING OVERHEATED despite the cool spring evening, Riley walked straight to the corral and whistled for Misty. She felt like an idiot for blowing up and storming out on dinner again, but she couldn't help the agitation and defensiveness that consumed her. At least this time she'd had the foresight to go outside.

Her emotions were like a roller coaster repeatedly plummeting to new depths that left her head spinning every time she turned around. This was not her. She didn't get angry and act irrationally. But she couldn't seem to stop feeling like she was under attack. Couldn't stop feeling like a victim. Couldn't stop remembering the things Collin did to her.

She was halfway through saddling Misty when she stopped and considered how her actions affected everyone around her. She practically snapped at Jake every time he talked to her. Her stomach hardened, and she cringed as she recalled her panic attack this afternoon and the way she took out her fear on Daniel. She'd still been so embarrassed at dinner that she couldn't meet his eyes.

The poor man probably thinks I'm psychotic.

She felt like she was losing her mind, so if Daniel thought she was crazy, he wouldn't be far off. She needed to figure out how to stop taking her uncontrollable emotions out on her family though. It wasn't fair to them, especially when she wasn't ready to tell them why she was so upset.

A measure of peace settled over her much quicker than she expected as she rode, and she didn't feel the need to ride as long as she did on her first night home. She turned Misty around after only half an hour. Despite taking a nap this afternoon—for which she felt guilty because it left Daniel to finish all the work by himself—she was still exhausted.

She hadn't had a full night's sleep since Collin's attack, and it was taking a toll on her. Taking her frustration out on Daniel's punching bag helped, but she was beginning to think she might not ever be able to put the attack behind her.

A surge of guilt settled like a ten-pound weight in the pit of her stomach after she turned Misty back into the corral with the other stock horses. She owed Daniel an apology. But how did she give him a sincere one without explaining why she freaked out this afternoon?

Trying to formulate the words she needed to say in her head, she headed toward the tree-lined lane that led to the Hamilton's house. She'd walked this path almost daily when she was a child. Sometimes multiple times a day. Once she and Daniel were old enough that their moms didn't feel the need to keep a constant eye on them, they often went to Daniel's house to hang out because his mom spent the bulk of her day at the main house.

Feeling nostalgic, she stepped off the road and into the trees. She chuckled as she remembered how Daniel at eleven years old climbed up three different trees and tied a long rope high up in each. He planned to swing from tree to tree like Tarzan. However, with his first swing, he couldn't find his footing on the second tree and ended up falling and severely spraining his ankle.

Halfway to Daniel's house, she looked up at the remnants of the tree house that their older brothers had built. Girls hadn't been allowed inside until their older brothers were old enough to lose interest. Then Daniel and her cousin Damon had to share it with Paige and Riley.

She laughed out loud as she recalled the many arguments she and Paige had with the boys over calling the tree house their princess palace. The boys had stopped talking to them for a whole week after Riley convinced her mom to make pink curtains for their palace. Damon and Daniel's fortress and hideout had been sullied.

Riley was still smiling by the time she reached the Hamiltons' house. She had no idea what she would say to Daniel, but she decided to ask him to join her for a walk. Maybe that would give her time to find the right words.

She was about to step out of the trees when Daniel walked out the front door of the house. His damp hair glistened in the evening sun, and he looked especially attractive in a light-blue button down and dark jeans. Her smile faded when he jumped in his truck and drove down the lane with a squeal of rubber as though he was late for an important date.

Date.

Was Daniel seeing someone? The thought made her stomach sink faster than a rock and her heart hurt a little. She may have walked away from Daniel three years ago, but she'd never stopped loving him.

CHAPTER 8

*T*he next morning, a knock sounded on Riley's bedroom door five minutes before her alarm was set to go off.

"Come in." Her voice came out muffled by her pillow because she lay on her stomach.

Jake opened her door. "Sorry to wake you up so early."

She flopped onto her back with a groan. "You and I both know it's only early for me. I bet you've been up for hours."

"Yes, I have, and I need to leave soon to take a load of cattle to Missoula."

"Missoula?" Riley sat up now. "So you'll be gone all day?"

"Yes, and Zane worked the calving sheds last night, so he's out of commission this morning. Which means I need Daniel to feed the cattle and you—"

"I'll be cleaning the stables by myself," she finished for him.

"Yes, sorry to dump that on you, but..." His words died off.

"But what?"

"I'm beginning to get the feeling you'd prefer to work alone, even though we usually pair up the ranch hands for safety and man-power reasons."

"I know." Her gaze dropped to the blue and tan comforter that covered her legs. She'd never enjoyed working alone but working with Daniel seemed to keep setting her off.

Did he tell everyone how she attacked him yesterday?

Does Jake regret letting me come home?

A surge of sadness shot through her as she realized she didn't have anywhere else to go. She supposed she could always go stay with her mom and Aunt Charity in town, but she didn't think she could handle her mom's coddling. A cold chill swept over her as she considered returning to Seattle.

"I'm sorry I'm being so difficult, Jake. I don't mean to be. I just..." She couldn't find the words to express her frustrations with herself and what she'd been through.

"I know, Ri, and I'm sorry I keep saying the wrong things." He looked down at the floor for a moment before speaking again. "Please don't take this the wrong way, but...maybe you need to talk to someone."

Riley tensed, her defenses rising.

He must have sensed a change in her because he raised a hand in surrender. "I know Emily would be happy to talk through things with you...or maybe even Mom."

Just the thought of talking about what happened to her made her tremble and bile rise in her throat. The last thing she wanted to do was explain the details to her mom.

"I'm not trying to force you to do something you don't want to do, but think about it, okay?"

She nodded, but she couldn't bring herself to look at him. She didn't want him to see the tears in her eyes.

Her door closed then opened again and Jake poked his head back in. "By the way, Daniel said he'd take care of the calving sheds tonight, so you don't need to worry about it."

"I'll help him." The words were out before she could stop herself. She wasn't sure why she said them other than she still owed him an apology for assaulting him yesterday, and she felt bad that he had to do all the mowing and weed whacking by himself.

"Are you sure? You don't have to."

"I want to." Much to Riley's surprise the words were true. As she'd reminisced about her childhood with Daniel in the orchard, she realized how much she missed her best friend.

Jake nodded. "Try to squeeze in a little nap this afternoon then."

She wouldn't argue with that. Even though she'd spent an hour in Daniel's gym before going to bed, she'd still had a nightmare last night that caused her to lose sleep. Which meant she was awake when Daniel drove down the lane just before midnight.

Forty minutes later, Riley stood alone in the stables after turning out the horses. She'd always hated having to clean the stables alone when she was young. Sharing the task with Daniel had always made it much faster and more enjoyable because they joked and laughed about anything and everything.

She hadn't worked that closely with him since she came home, which was a good thing, considering how his presence seemed to keep sparking a panic attack in her.

Cleaning all the stalls by herself was every bit as exhausting as Riley expected it to be. She developed a new empathy for Daniel, knowing he often had to do it by himself.

Not for the first time, she wondered why he was home on the ranch. When they were young, he always talked about becoming an architect. He wanted to design houses and big hotels, hospitals and apartment complexes, and even sports arenas.

By the time she finished the stables and was ready for lunch, Zane was awake and had sent Daniel to the Tri-Cities area to pick up a part for one of the tractors. He gave her a couple small tasks to do, then told her to rest up if she planned to help at the calving sheds tonight.

"Hey, Riley, come watch this," Emily said when Riley walked into the family room that afternoon. "Adam's got the cutest little giggles."

Riley sat down on the couch near them and watched Emily tickle Adam's chubby little thighs. The giggles that erupted from Adam turned to squeals, and Riley found herself laughing right alongside mother and son.

She'd never been one of those women who were eager to get married at a young age and start having babies right away because she had goals she wanted to accomplish. She'd gotten her degree two years ago, though. Marriage seemed like the logical next step, but she hadn't met anyone she could care about like she had Daniel.

Emily repeated the tickling until little Adam could hardly breathe. Eventually, she gave the baby a break and held up a toy for him to bat. "So how are you adjusting to life on the ranch again?"

"Good. I hardly get saddle sore when I ride now." Riley relaxed back on the couch.

"How are you and Daniel getting along?"

Tension filled Riley's body. "Fine."

"That's good. I know it can be hard to work with someone you have history with." Emily cast a casual glance her way, but Riley felt like her sister-in-law could read every emotion on her face—the ones she showed and the ones she tried to hide. "Didn't you two used to date?"

"Yeah, only for a couple of months though."

Two amazing, blissful months.

But they ended abruptly when Daniel suggested she transfer to Oregon Health and Science University to finish her nursing degree so they could be together while he did his internship with an architectural firm. Then they would get married.

But Riley had just been accepted into the Nurse Practitioner program at University of Washington, and it felt like too much of a sacrifice to walk away from her goals. So, she'd ended the relationship. And regretted it ever since.

"Two months is long enough to form a solid relationship after being life-long friends."

Not solid enough to keep me from panicking at the mention of marriage.

Riley didn't bother responding. She didn't want to admit how heartbroken she'd been to walk away from Daniel or acknowledge how badly she'd hurt him.

Emily must have decided to change the subject because she said, "Are you sleeping any better than you did that first night?"

Additional tension hit Riley, and she sat up. She wasn't sure how to answer. She didn't want to tell Emily the truth, but she feared the other woman would see right through her if she lied. For all she knew, Emily had been up with Adam again when Riley sneaked out to the stables the past few nights or heard her return and take a hot shower.

She recalled Jake's words that morning, encouraging her to talk to Emily, but she couldn't make her mouth form the words to tell her sister-in-law what happened to her. Besides not wanting to relive the assault, she didn't want to tell anyone how violated and filthy she felt. Shame ate at her for getting herself in that position, and she felt weak for not being able to protect herself better.

Riley pushed to her feet. "I'm fine. Speaking of sleep, I should rest a little since I'm working the calving sheds tonight."

She hurried to her room and closed the door. She hated being rude, but she wasn't ready to face the demons Emily wanted her to face.

Riley laid on her bed and tried to rest but she couldn't shut her mind off.

Would she ever be able to talk about what happened to her? How long would it take her to get over the sense of panic that seized her every time a man got close? Why was Daniel still here on the ranch? Did he have a girlfriend?

The lack of an answer to all these questions left her feeling heavy and exhausted, but she wasn't sure she truly wanted to know the answer to that last question.

RILEY WAS surprised when Jake made it home from Missoula in time for dinner. She was also stunned and a little disappointed when Lottie announced that Daniel wouldn't be joining them for dinner.

"He's having dinner with a friend in Pasco, so he won't be home until late. But he promised he'd take his shift at the calving sheds tonight."

Friend?

Riley couldn't recall Daniel having any friends in Pasco, so again, she had to wonder if he had a girlfriend.

Is that why he's sticking around the ranch now?

Both Emily and Jake's heads popped up at Lottie's news. But Emily spoke first. "Who is he having dinner with?" Tension filled her voice, and Riley didn't miss the hitch in both hers and Jake's shoulders.

"Tom." Lottie said the single word like everyone knew who that was.

Apparently, everyone did—well, everyone except her—because Jake and Emily relaxed and nodded their heads, like Daniel having dinner with Tom was a good thing. Even Zane looked pleased.

Tom didn't sound like a girl's name though. So who was Tom? And how did Daniel become such good friends with him?

Daniel hadn't returned home by the time it grew dark, so Jake walked with Riley to the calving sheds. Even though a large open shelter sat at the back of each field, what they called the calving sheds were really massive, fenced corrals.

He pointed at the small camp trailer parked in the middle of the lane near the two large fields that months ago were probably bursting with expecting mothers, but now only held ten or so cows each. "I don't mind if you catch a little shut eye in the trailer, but make sure you set an alarm and check on every cow every hour." He opened the door of the trailer and grabbed a flashlight off the small counter. "Watch their stomachs carefully to see if they're in labor. Watch for signs of distress, labored or faint breathing—"

"I know. I remember Dad teaching me all of this." It had come in handy with some of her medical courses as she worked on her nursing degree.

"Right, of course." He turned to the right and shined the flashlight across the field. "These are the first timers. Most of them should be fine but keep an eye on them." Then he crossed the lane to the field on the left and shone the light on the only cow that lay down. "This one has been laboring for a while now. She'll probably deliver within the next two hours. If she doesn't get up and clean the calf off within the hour of it being born, grab some of the old rags in the trailer."

"I know what to do Jake." Riley put a hand on her brother's arm. "I've been gone a long time, but some experiences stick with you." She looked out toward the western hills where the final rays of sun glowed orange on the horizon. "It's times like these that I miss dad, though."

"I know. Me too."

Jake left a short time later, and Riley found herself alone.

So far, they'd enjoyed pleasant weather this spring, but the sun took all its warmth with it when it went down, and the night grew chillier by the minute. She debated trying to light the propane heater that stood several yards away from the trailer with a couple camp chairs but couldn't justify it yet. Instead, she zipped her jacket a little higher and checked all the cows carefully before going into the trailer.

Using the flashlight, she located the light switch and flipped it on. Unease twisted her stomach as she looked around her cramped confines. A small bedroom sat at the back of the trailer, and the table and bench seats had been made down into another bed.

Two beds in such a tiny space.

Riley's breaths came a little faster. When she'd volunteered to help Daniel tonight, she'd forgotten that the men often took turns sleeping in the trailer.

It's okay. We'll take turns. I won't have to be in here with him.

She examined both beds, trying to determine whether either one was clean enough to sleep in. Finally, she decided she'd take the one where the table usually sat. It was smaller, and Daniel needed the bigger bed. She doubted she'd sleep tonight anyway.

She was still staring at the smaller bed and stewing over the closed confines when the door behind her burst open. Heart in her throat and hand pressed to her chest, she spun around.

"Aah!" A scream erupted from her before she could stop it.

"Good gravy!" Daniel pressed a hand to his own chest. "You scared me to death."

"Me? You just took ten years off my life! Y-you should have knocked or something."

"Why would I knock? I told Jake I'd cover the night shift by myself."

Riley propped her hands on her hips. "And I told him I'd help you."

"Well, he forgot to mention that to me." Daniel stepped up the single step, bringing him closer. His tall broad frame blocked the doorway.

Riley's heart jerked in her chest, bolting like that demonic stallion named Zeus that Jake used to own. Her stomach hardened as her knees grew weak. She grabbed the counter with one and held the other one out.

"Stop! Please. Don't come any closer." Her voice wasn't nearly as strong as she'd meant it to be.

Daniel froze, a flash of fear flitted through his eyes before they narrowed, and he studied her face. Ever so slowly he lowered himself from the step and moved back.

"I—I'm sorry." She pressed a hand to her stomach. "I—I'm feeling really claustrophobic all of a sudden. A—and there's not room for both of us in here."

After Daniel backed away another step, she darted through the door and squeezed past him. She didn't stop moving until she stood nearly six feet away.

Daniel shook his head as he rubbed a hand over his jaw. "You shouldn't have volunteered to help tonight if you find me that repulsive." His words were sharp and defensive.

"I don't!" Riley wrapped her arms around herself to try to calm her trembling limbs. "I don't find you repulsive."

"That's not what your actions say." His voice was still hard.

"I know. I'm sorry, I overreacted yesterday. I never should have shouted at you and...and...done what I did to you. I just..."

She stopped talking, unsure of how to finish her sentence. She couldn't bring herself to tell him what she was going through.

"Just what?"

"I—I'm dealing with...some stuff, okay?"

He scoffed. "You're dealing with some stuff? Blowing up at everyone who tries to talk to you and assaulting me? You call that dealing with it?"

She spun away so Daniel wouldn't see the tears that flooded her eyes. She'd been treating everybody, especially Daniel, horribly. She knew that, but she couldn't seem to stop. She felt so defenseless, so powerless. So, she did the only thing she could do; she lashed out at everyone.

Daniel let out a heavy sigh that sounded like it was full of regret. Gravel crunched under his boots as he stepped closer, and she braced herself, expecting him to touch her.

But he didn't.

She turned and looked at him.

He stood, hands on his hips, staring at the sky, lips moving as though silently praying. Even after his lips stopped moving, he continued to stare at the heavens as though searching for words of wisdom in the stars. When he finally lowered his head, it was to stare at his boots.

"It's obvious you're dealing with...some serious stuff. I'm sorry for whatever happened to you to make you so... jumpy and defensive and angry." He shifted his gaze to the dark pasture now. "But we're all dealing with stuff, Ri." He rubbed his hand over his jaw again and swallowed hard. "When you turn us into your punching bag, you make our...garbage harder to deal with."

A lump filled Riley's throat, and a heaviness settled over her like an oppressive, weighted blanket. The kind that made her too hot and claustrophobic. "I'm sorry, Daniel." Her words were little more than a whisper. "And I'm so sorry for the way I lashed out at you yesterday. You didn't deserve that."

She really wanted to know what "garbage" Daniel was dealing with, but she was afraid to ask because then he would want to know her "garbage." She couldn't help but wonder if his had something to do with the reason he worked here on the ranch instead of at an architectural firm in some big city.

"Sometimes..." Daniel's words were stilted. "Sometimes it...helps to talk about your... 'stuff' with someone."

She hugged her arms tighter around herself and shook her head. "I can't."

Would she ever be able to talk about it without crying hysterically like she did with the police or nearly hyperventilating like she did when she told Dr. Nelson what happened to her?

"Not yet."

"Well, when you're ready, Emily is a great listener. And she's smart. She knows her stuff."

Daniel was the second person to tell her that today, but it didn't make the thought of telling Emily what she went through any easier.

They both stood there—only a few feet apart—staring silently into the darkness.

A mournful moo filled the quiet night.

They turned toward the sound.

"That heifer Jake said to keep an eye on must be ready to deliver." Riley grabbed the flashlight from the trailer and walked over to the corner nearest to the laboring cow. She shined the light on the back end to check the cow's progress.

The tips of two little white hooves poked out.

"Do you think she needs help?" Riley asked.

"I don't know. Let's wait a minute and see."

Riley shifted the light to the cow's stomach. She could tell when the next contraction started by the way the muscles squeezed inward. The cow let out a low huff then seemed to stop breathing for the duration of the contraction.

Riley shifted the light to the back end again. More of the hooves showed now.

She propped her arms on the wooden fence and watched, waiting for one of the most miraculous experiences of her life to unfold. Daniel bent and leaned his arms on the fence too. His elbow brushed hers, and surprisingly, she didn't feel the need to pull away.

"It never gets old, does it?" His voice was quiet, almost reverent.

"Never. Although, I have to say watching a human birth is a bit more exhilarating."

"I can imagine."

Thirty minutes later, they turned away from the fence as the new momma continued to clean her baby. The little guy was already trying to figure out how to get his legs under him.

Daniel and Riley walked side by side, checking all the other cows.

Only one other cow lay down, but she lazily chewed her cud and showed no signs of being in labor.

They both came to a stop outside the door to the trailer.

"I'll take the first shift," Riley said at the same moment Daniel motioned over his shoulder and said, "You can sleep first."

"I don't think I'll be able to sleep, so you may as well go ahead." She waved toward the door. "I rested a little bit today, so I should be good for a few hours."

"There's plenty of room inside the trailer for both of us." He watched her carefully as though wary of how she might react.

She backed up a step and wrapped her arms around herself as she shook her head. "I can't...be in there...with you."

Daniel's gaze went heavenward again for a long moment. Then he walked over to the propane heater and went through the steps of lighting it.

It's just as well Riley never tried to light it. It was considerably more complicated than she'd thought.

Daniel stopped when he reached the trailer door again. "Is it...is it insomnia or...nightmares that drive you to the punching bag in the middle of the night?"

Riley drew in a sharp breath. Had he seen her in his little gym? Or did he figure it out because she didn't put his gloves away in the right spot.

"How...?"

His gaze dropped to his boots again. "I sometimes have trouble sleeping too."

So he had seen her. But why did he have trouble sleeping?

Again, Riley wondered what Daniel's "garbage" was.

Daniel lifted his gaze to her face. "So, which is it?"

Riley licked dry lips. "Nightmares." The word was barely audible.

"I'm sorry." Daniel rubbed his jaw again, this time swiping his hand over his mouth too. "Me too." He squeezed his eyes shut. "Sometimes I wish it could just be insomnia." He reached for the doorknob.

"Daniel, wait." Riley rubbed her hands on her arms to combat the chill that swept over her. "What... What causes your—"

The ringtone of Riley's cell phone split the night air, cutting off her words.

"Who the devil is calling you at this hour?"

Riley pulled her phone from her back pocket to find Paige's goofy grin from her contacts on her screen. "It's Paige."

"It figures. Tell her 'Hi' for me." He turned back toward the door once again.

Riley swiped up. "Hi, Paige."

"Guess again, Riley Darling." The deep menacing voice that came over the phone did not match Paige's bright, bubbly voice.

Riley's audible gasp came out as a cry of alarm. A cold chill hit her as she felt the blood drain from her face and the hair on the nape of her neck stand up. Her mind scrambled to process how Collin's call had gotten through. She'd blocked him.

But the caller ID showed Paige's face.

Then it hit her. Collin had Paige's phone which meant he must have done something to her.

A band tightened around her chest. So tight she could hardly breathe. Riley's hand shook so badly she nearly dropped the phone. A lump filled her throat as she struggled to draw air into her lungs.

"You—" She let loose a swear word she'd only ever used one other time in her life. The night Collin Ainsworth attacked her. "What have you done to Paige? Where is she?"

At her initial outburst, Daniel spun around to face her. He now stared wide-eyed, and slack jawed, getting a front row seat to Riley's "garbage" but she didn't care. She had to know where Paige was. Had Collin hurt her?

"Did you really think I wouldn't figure out where you were, darling?"

"Where is Paige?" Riley screamed into the phone. "If you've hurt her, I'll swear I'll ki—"

Deep, mocking laughter cut off Riley's threat. "Enjoy playing cowgirl on that little ranch of yours. What was it called? The Double Diamond? Don't worry, I'll be waiting for you when you get back."

Riley gasped again and threw her phone on the ground as though it had burned her. She pressed her hands to her face.

He knows where I am. And he's done something—probably something unspeakable—to Paige.

"I never should have left her alone in Seattle." Riley paced away from Daniel who stared at her.

"Ri."

"I should have insisted she come home with me." She changed directions. "She could have gotten a sub for the last six weeks of school."

"Riley." Daniel stepped in front of her, forcing her to change directions again.

"I can't believe I just left her behind. And now, Collin has...done something to her." Her stomach churned and she feared she might be sick.

"Riley Jo Winters." Daniel's voice was loud and stern. "What in the blue blazes is going on?"

Riley stopped pacing and stared at Daniel. His face blurred when tears filled her eyes. She shook her head.

"What happened to Paige?"

Now the tears cascaded down her face. "I don't know."

A CHILL SETTLED OVER DANIEL, and a sense of dread made every beat of his heart hard and sluggish.

Had something bad happened to Paige? And who was that man on the phone? Daniel couldn't hear the words he'd said to Riley, but he'd heard enough to know it wasn't Paige on the other end. And Riley's ashen face and frantic movements told him she was either terrified or very worried. Maybe both.

He grabbed Riley's shoulders, and immediately, she tensed up, her eyes wide and full of panic. He released her just as fast but stayed standing in front of her.

"Where is Paige?"

"Sh-she's supposed to be staying with our n-neighbors."

"What neighbors?"

"Jen and Shaylee." Riley sidestepped him and began pacing again with her arms wrapped tightly around her body. "They live next door to us."

"Why would Paige stay with them?"

"Because I refused to leave her alone when I decided to come home. I was afraid he would hurt her." She swore under her breath then pressed one hand to her stomach and the other to her face. "And he has. Oh, why did I leave her? I should have known—"

"Known what?" Daniel stepped in front of her again. "Riley, I can't make sense of what you're saying. Why do you think something has happened to Paige?"

"He has her phone. That means he's done something bad to her."

"Who?" Daniel's stomach sank. He hated the idea of something bad happening to one of Riley's cousins and his childhood friend.

"Collin Ainsworth." Again, Riley swore, fury filling her eyes.

Daniel had no idea who Collin Ainsworth was, but he hated him immediately. He must be a terrible man to evoke such hatred in Riley. Daniel couldn't recall ever hearing her swear before, but she'd done it three times now in a matter of a few minutes in reference to that man.

He hurried to where Riley had dropped her phone on the ground and picked it up. "Hello?"

No response.

He walked back over to where Riley stood shivering. "Call your friends."

"What?"

He held the phone out to her. "Call your friends. The ones Paige is supposed to be staying with. Let's find out what's going on."

"Right. Okay." Her hand shook as she took the phone and searched her contacts. Finally, she pressed a button and lifted the phone to her ear. "Jen? Where's Paige?"

Daniel couldn't hear the response on the other end of the line, so he watched Riley's face carefully, looking for clues of Jen's response. Each breath he drew in seemed to echo in his ears as he waited.

"Are you sure?" Relief mingled with skepticism in Riley's voice. "I need to talk to her." A pause. "Yes, I know it's after midnight, but I need you to wake her up. Please."

After a short wait during which he and Riley stared at each other, gazes locked, both of them holding their breaths, Paige must have answered the phone because Riley nearly collapsed with relief.

"Oh, thank goodness you're okay." When her knees buckled, he caught her and guided her over to a camp chair under the warmth of the propane heater. "Please tell me that scumbag didn't hurt you."

The tension inside him relaxed, and he breathed more easily as he dropped into the other chair. He continued to study Riley's face, attempting to glean more information about Collin Ainsworth and why he had such a debilitating effect on Riley.

Tears once again filled her eyes as she said, "Collin called me with your phone."

Daniel only grasped snippets of the conversation from Riley's end after that, but apparently, Paige's purse had been stolen while she was at a restaurant with her friends earlier that evening.

"I can't believe he walked right past you and took it." Indignation filled Riley's voice now that she knew her cousin and best friend was safe. "He probably wore a hoodie or something so you wouldn't recognize him."

Daniel relaxed back into his chair and crossed one ankle over his knee as Riley and Paige talked a little longer, during which Riley lowered her voice and assured her cousin multiple times that she was fine. She stopped meeting Daniel's gaze about that same time, however. Which meant she was anything but fine.

When Riley ended the call, Daniel waited for her to fill him in.

It felt like an eternity before she looked at him. "I guess you figured out that Paige is fine. Her phone was stolen along with her purse."

He dipped his chin, trying hard to be patient and put it all in the Lord's hands like Tom had reminded him to do during dinner.

Daniel silently repeated the words he'd whispered to the heavens earlier.

God grant me the serenity to accept the things I cannot change, courage to change the things I can, and the wisdom to know the difference.

When Riley didn't offer more information, he cleared his throat. "Who is Collin Ainsworth?"

Riley's arms again wrapped around her body, and she rocked back and forth as she stared at a spot on the ground near the base of the propane heater.

Does she realize what she's doing?

When she didn't speak, he lost his patience and ventured a guess. "Is he stalking you? Is that why you're so jumpy?"

"Yeah, something like that." Relief crossed Riley's face. "H-he knows where I live, and he k-keeps coming to the clinic."

"Is that why Dr. Nelson suggested you take a leave of absence?"

She nodded. "We're hoping Collin will lose interest when I'm no longer around to...harass."

"It doesn't appear to be working...yet."

"No, it doesn't." She continued to rock.

Tension curled tight in Daniel's gut. He wanted to wrap Riley in his arms and protect her. That's what he did when it came to Riley. It had always been his responsibility to keep her safe, and he wanted to protect her now from everything that frightened her.

The problem was: he didn't dare touch her.

CHAPTER 9

"*B*eat you!" Daniel slid into his seat at the dinner table only moments before Riley arrived.

She smirked at him as she combed fingers through her damp hair. "Only because my hair takes longer to wash than yours."

"Yeah, but I have more body mass to scrub."

"Yes, you do." Her gaze raked over him, lingering momentarily on his shoulders. A rosy tint colored her cheeks, and a matching warmth heated his body.

They'd worked well together this past week. Daniel was careful to give Riley the space she needed, and he could tell she tried not to overreact any time he got too close to her. Which he'd done a lot over the past few days as they delivered the last of the calves—three this afternoon in drizzling rain.

Working with Riley had almost been like old times, and his attraction for her had settled right back into place, like a comfortable pair of old boots. Except he felt anything but comfortable. His dreams were still haunted by images of him holding an unresponsive Riley in his arms or trying to save her from a faceless man who wanted to hurt her. One night, he even became the man who chased her.

Ever since Riley admitted to having a stalker, Daniel had wondered exactly what the man had done to strike the kind of fear in her that he saw during the phone call out by the calving sheds. She refused to talk more about it, so he hadn't pushed her, but judging by the shadows under her eyes, she wasn't sleeping any better than he was.

The guttural sound of someone clearing their throat filled the room and Daniel tore his eyes away from Riley to find Jake smirking at him. He turned his grin on Riley next. Her cheeks only grew rosier.

After Daniel's father said grace, talk quickly turned to the need to check the fence lines, so they could move the herds to the summer grazing pastures.

"The new ranch hands arrived this afternoon," his dad said. "I'll orient them tomorrow and make sure they know what they're doing, then we'll get to work on the fence lines soon."

Would working with Riley, riding the fence line, be like old times? He didn't mind spending all day in the saddle when Riley was by his side, especially when they talked, laughed, and ate lunch at their favorite swimming hole.

Jake pulled Daniel from his thoughts when he stood. "Oh, Riley, I forgot. You got a letter in the mail today." He hurried to his office, returning moments later with an envelope.

"Am I still getting junk mail here? I haven't lived here for seven years."

"It doesn't look like junk mail." Jake handed over the envelope with a shrug. "But there's no return address either."

Riley took it and studied the front for a moment before sliding a finger under the flap and tearing it open. She'd barely pulled out the pale blue paper before she gasped and dropped the envelope and letter as though it had burned her. All color drained from her face.

A sinking sensation hit Daniel's stomach.

Riley's stalker knows where she is.

"Is something wrong?" Emily asked, her eyes glued to Riley's face.

Riley forced a smile that couldn't have been more fake and

scooped up the paper and envelope with trembling hands. "No, everything's fine." She stood and walked to the kitchen.

Before the door swung closed behind her, Daniel saw her frantically tearing the paper and envelope to pieces. His first instinct was to go after her, but he had no idea what to say.

"That was odd." His mom shook her head.

"I'll say." Jake scratched the back of his neck. "What was that all about?"

Emily didn't say anything, but Daniel sensed the wheels turning in her head, analyzing Riley's behavior.

The back door of the mud room slammed, reverberating through the house, and they all jumped.

Daniel couldn't stand it anymore. He sprang to his feet. "I'm going to talk to her."

"Do you know what's going on with Riley?" His mom's question caused him to pause before opening the back door.

"Sort of."

He'd purposefully made his answer vague because it wasn't his place to tell them, but also because he feared there was a whole lot more going on with Riley's stalker than she'd let on the other night, and the thought sickened him.

He'd expected to find Riley saddling Misty, intent on taking a long ride, like she'd done so many times since coming home. He was determined to take Rebel and join her. She shouldn't have to go through whatever she was dealing with alone.

But Riley was nowhere to be seen, and Misty stood in the nearby corral, looking bored.

Faint drumming reached his ears, and Daniel knew she was much more unsettled than he'd originally thought. Riley rode Misty when she was upset, but she went to the punching bag when something triggered her.

Riley's back was to him when he walked into the small gym at the back of the stables, so he quietly wandered over and picked up a fifteen-pound dumbbell and started doing bicep curls, waiting for her to notice him.

Her pounding paused momentarily when she spotted him, but then she picked up the pace again.

Daniel waited for what felt like an eternity before her actions slowed and she slumped back against the wall, a sheen of perspiration glistening on her brow.

"It was from him, wasn't it?" When she didn't respond, he tried again. "That Collin guy wrote the letter, didn't he?"

This time she winced and nodded. Her mouth opened but no words came out. The tears flooding her eyes expressed the things she couldn't seem to voice, and Daniel hated that he'd brought up that man's name.

The silence in the small room was deafening, especially since Daniel wanted answers.

"What did he say?"

Stupid question. She didn't even read it before tearing it up.

"I don't know, and I don't care. I just want him to leave me alone." She hugged herself now, the boxing gloves making the task awkward.

Daniel ached to cross the small room and pull her into his arms, but he didn't dare get close to her for fear of upsetting her even further. He should be glad they'd been able to work closely together delivering the calves without her going ballistic on him, but he could tell by the guarded look on her face now that getting close to her would only make things worse.

"Is it possible the letter was an apology for scaring you with his phone call the other night?"

She shook her head so hard he was surprised he didn't hear rattling. "No, he's trying to torment me."

"Playing mind games?"

"Exactly."

"Mind games can only have power over you if you let them." He put the dumbbell down and leaned against the opposite wall mimicking her posture. "Maybe if you talk about it, you can get it all out of your head, and it will have less of an effect on you."

"I can't." She shook her head again and her arms tightened around herself. Her gaze dropped to the wooden floor.

"You don't have to talk to me, but you should talk to someone." She didn't look up so he went on. "All you have to do is ask Emily if you can have some lemonade."

Her head popped up at this.

"It lets her know you want to talk about something personal." He rubbed his jaw as he realized what he was admitting to. "She's incredibly patient when you struggle to find the words you want to say. She doesn't judge or criticize." Riley continued to stare at him, so he kept talking. "She's got some great coping techniques to use when you get...triggered."

"Do you...have you...asked Emily for lemonade before?"

Now Daniel was the one to look away. He swiped his hand over his mouth and jaw as a sudden urge for a stiff drink hit him. "More times than I can count."

Her brow furrowed. "Why?"

A tense chuckle escaped his throat before he could stop it. He wasn't ready to bare his soul to Riley, but maybe if she realized she wasn't the only one dealing with difficult things, she'd be willing to talk to Emily. He couldn't bring himself to look at her as he spoke though.

"Two and a half years ago, I was involved in..." His stomach clenched, and the familiar tightness settled around his chest as he recalled hitting little Isaac Russell with his truck. "...something that...screwed me up."

"But Jake only married Emily a year and a half ago."

"Yeah, I was pretty messed up by the time I started talking to Emily." He gave a self-deprecating chuckle that sounded flat even to his own ears. "Talk about baggage."

Riley continued to stare at him through narrowed eyes. "Was it... Was it because I broke up with you?"

Daniel let out a genuine laugh this time. "Not going to lie, Pockets, it hurt when you dumped me, but that wasn't what derailed my life."

"Nobody has called me Pockets since..."

He raised an eyebrow at her and hazarded a guess. "Since you broke up with me?"

"Yeah." A sheepish look crossed her face. "I think we should be allowed to outgrow childhood nicknames."

"Normally I'd agree with you, but you still tuck your hands in your back pockets and rock up on your toes when you're nervous or excited."

"I do not."

"You did it the day you arrived home after we let our horses into the corral." A small frown marred her face, and Daniel grinned. "At least I didn't call you Princess Sparkle Pockets."

Riley burst out laughing at this. "Those pants with the bedazzled pockets were my favorite."

"I know, and you refused to take them off, so your mom had to buy four pairs. You even slept in those things."

"I threw such a fit the first time your mom washed them. I was so afraid it would make the little rhinestones fall off."

He chuckled. "I remember that time you got mad at your dad when he called you Princess like he usually did, and you stomped your foot, put your hands on your hips, and demanded he call you Princess Sparkle Pockets."

Her laughter joined his, and warmth seeped over Daniel. He'd forgotten how much he loved laughing with Riley.

"I was only six. I outgrew sparkly-pocket pants a long time ago."

"I don't know. I recall you wearing them for a lot of years. You wore a more mature version all through your rodeo royalty days."

Riley scoffed as she pulled off the boxing gloves and threw them on the shelf. She headed for the door. "I was expected to wear them when I did rodeo stuff."

Daniel followed her. "Yes, but I think you enjoyed it more than the average cowgirl."

Riley spun around and glared at him. "Don't call me that!"

Daniel fell back a step. "Call you what?"

"That word. Don't call me that!"

Daniel scrambled to recall what he'd been saying before she turned on him. "What word? Cow—"

"Don't!" She clapped a hand over his mouth, then quickly jerked it back again and wrapped her arms around herself. She squeezed her eyes shut and sucked in a deep breath.

What just happened?

Daniel took an additional step back, giving Riley the space she apparently needed and waited for her trembling and ragged breathing to subside. He had no idea why calling her "cowgirl" set her off, but the simple fact that it did, meant Riley had issues.

She didn't meet his eyes when she finally spoke. "I'm sorry... I... I..." She stopped trying to explain her behavior and walked out of the stables.

Daniel followed her again, keeping his distance. "Seriously, Ri, you need to talk to someone."

"I told you, I can't."

"Well, you can't let it keep eating at you."

She spun around again. "You have no idea what I've been through, so don't tell me what I can and can't do."

And there was that sinking feeling in his stomach again, deeper, and heavier this time. He hated to think of what happened to Riley to make her act like this.

"You're right, I don't." He let out a heavy sigh. "But I do know you're only as sick as your secrets."

She glared at him. "What's that supposed to mean?"

It was a term he'd heard many times in AA meetings, and he'd never really understood it until now.

He looked her in the eye. "It's the things you keep hidden that hurt you the most." The words hit too close to home, and he rubbed at his jaw to fight the tension they triggered in him. "As long as you keep denying you have a problem, it will keep doing its damage."

Daniel paused at his own words.

Was that why he still struggled so much with his own addiction? Because he'd tried to keep it hidden from everyone? Sure, he'd been sober for seven months, but every day had been a constant battle. It was also the reason he drove to Pasco to attend meetings. He didn't want the locals—the people he went to church with—to know he had a problem.

While he and Riley had been laughing together in the gym, he'd considered skipping tonight's AA meeting and inviting her to go for a ride. He figured it would be a worthwhile use of his time, especially if it meant they could work on their relationship so they didn't keep experiencing conflicts like this.

But now, Daniel knew he needed to attend his regular Friday night meeting. And for the first time, he would speak up and share his story. He was done keeping secrets.

RILEY STOPPED SHORT the next morning outside the kitchen door when she heard Jake say her name.

"Daniel, I want you to continue to partner with Riley. I don't want these new ranch hands anywhere near her."

"Are you sure you want me working with her? I mean, it doesn't matter what I do or say, I somehow manage to set her off every time I turn around."

"You let me know if working with her becomes a problem for you." Jake's voice was low and serious. "I know she's being difficult, but just do the best you can."

Difficult?

Riley's mouth dropped open. How dare Jake talk about her like that?

She was about to push open the door and give him a piece of her mind when he spoke again. "Zane, I'm serious about keeping these new ranch hands as far away from Riley as possible. She's too fragile right now."

Fragile?

Heat filled Riley's chest. Sure, her emotions had been all over the place since she came home, but fragile? She hated being called weak. It made her feel powerless and vulnerable. She put her hand on the door, but once again his words stopped her.

"They've both got records."

Daniel made a snorting sound. "Like I don't?"

Riley's head shot up. She must have heard wrong because she would have known if he'd been arrested. Wouldn't she?

What was it he said last night?

You're only as sick as your secrets.

What kind of secrets was Daniel keeping? Did they have something to do with his life being derailed and the nightmares he had?

It was Zane's voice that came through the door next. "Yes, you've made mistakes, son. We all have. But you've done your penance. Now you need to let it go and move on."

Penance?

"Move on?" Sarcasm filled Daniel's voice. "How do I do that when I can't leave the ranch?"

What did Daniel mean? He left the ranch all the time. In fact, he left again last night and didn't come home until late.

"Give it time," Lottie said. "You'll be strong enough someday."

Another snort.

Quiet fell in the kitchen then Riley heard the closing of the back door. She wasn't sure who had walked out, but she didn't want to face any of the occupants of the kitchen after eavesdropping on that conversation.

She walked back to her bedroom. Known for being a sleepy head, she decided to take advantage of everyone's low expectations today. Not so she could get some extra sleep, but so she could think. So many questions frequently tumbled around inside her head concerning Daniel, but now there were even more.

When Riley walked into the stables forty minutes later and found Zane talking to two rough-looking, muscle-bound men covered in tattoos, the hairs on her neck stood up. Her heart rate kicked into overdrive, making her chest tight. She sucked in a deep breath, doing her best to keep herself from panicking.

She'd always admired her father for the program he started over thirty years ago with his brother, Dawson, who was in law-enforcement. They helped rehabilitate former inmates by providing them with a stable job and a place to live—for the summer anyway. Robert and Jake now continued the program. Even though most of the men they'd hired over the years had been nice despite their gruff and intimidating appearances, a few of them made her skin crawl with the way they leered at her. That was why she was always assigned to work with Daniel.

The shorter and stockier of the two men with Zane let out a low wolf whistle. "Well, hello, gorgeous." He jabbed his buddy with his elbow. "This job just got a whole lot more interesting, eh Brody?"

"You got that right." Brody's eyes raked over her from head to toe. An appreciative grin filled his face, and nausea filled Riley's stomach.

Zane's hand flew out and smacked the back of the shorter man's head. "Keep your thoughts and hands to yourself, Crew. You'll show respect to *everyone* who works on this ranch regardless of their gender." Now Zane's finger was in the guy's face. "You got that?"

"Sure thing, Boss," Crew said, but his eyes roved over Riley again.

She repressed a shudder and resisted the urge to run from the stables. Instead, she forced herself to study first Brody, then Crew, before giving them a look of dismissal. "What happened, Zane? Couldn't Jake find any real men to hire this summer?"

Crew made a groaning sound as he pressed a hand to his chest. Brody hooted with laughter then made a sizzling sound.

Zane grinned as he wrapped an arm around her shoulders. "That's my girl." He pressed a quick kiss to her temple that reminded her of her dad, then he released her and nudged her toward the door. "You're working with Daniel in the equipment shed today."

She'd barely stepped out the double doors when Crew started mouthing off again. "Whose backside do I need to kiss to be assigned to work with the dame?"

"Mine," Zane's voice came sharp and fast. "But save the wooing, Romeo, 'cuz it ain't never gonna happen. The big boss would sooner shoot you than let you touch his sister. And with a ranch this size, there are plenty of places to bury a body."

Riley's lips turned up. She appreciated Zane's protectiveness. Once she'd distanced herself from the things she overheard in the kitchen, she realized Jake had only been trying to protect her. But poor Daniel. He kept getting saddled with her. And all she did was lash out at him.

Speaking of Daniel, she spotted him half bent over, reaching into the engine of one of the tractors. His worn denim shirt stretched across the taut muscles of his back, and again, Riley was struck by how much he'd filled out over the past few years. He'd lost his gangling, boyish looks in his early twenties, but even then, he'd been slender like his dad. But now...

He wasn't as bulky as Crew and Brody because he was taller, but the definition of muscle on Daniel was sheer perfection. Like watching the muscles on a racehorse flex and ripple; Riley had a hard time looking away.

"We get mechanic duty today, huh?" She said in greeting, her voice dry and flat, showing how much she disliked this task.

Daniel straightened and grinned. "Anything to keep us away from the stables while my dad breaks in the new ranch hands. At least we don't have to muck out the stalls anymore."

"Yeah, I had the displeasure of meeting Crew and Brody." Riley wrinkled her nose.

Daniel looked down at the wrench in his hand, slapping it against his open palm. "Quite the pair, huh?"

Her thoughts turned to the things she'd overheard that morning. Did Daniel really say he had a record? What on earth could he have possibly done that would have gotten him arrested?

Daniel cleared his throat. "I'll work on gaskets and seals where needed, if you want to start with the oil changes. Then we can work together to sharpen the blades on the swather."

In a few weeks, they would cut the first crop of hay. Because the weather forecast often dictated when they cut the alfalfa, leaving the sharpening of the blades on the sickle bar of the swather until the last minute was never a good idea.

"Aye aye, captain." Riley saluted.

Daniel gave her a sharp look, then shook his head and rolled his eyes.

Riley laughed as she walked away. She liked keeping Daniel on his toes.

By the time they took a break for lunch, Riley's back ached, and she was covered from head to toe in grease and grime. All she wanted was a hot shower and a nap.

She and Daniel had changed the oil, filters, gaskets, and seals on just about every motor and engine in the equipment shed. They'd prepared six tractors, two balers, half a dozen four-wheelers, a dirt bike, two side by sides, and a golf cart, plus a dump truck, a flat bed, and two old pickup trucks for the upcoming summer season. Riley had even gone the extra mile and cleaned inside the tractors and trucks, something she was certain hadn't been done in years.

The kitchen was empty when they arrived for lunch, but Lottie had left a note stating that there was chili and cornbread in the fridge and cookies in the pantry.

They were mostly quiet while they ate because Daniel looked as exhausted as she felt.

Was his exhaustion due to nightmares or his late nights with a girl-friend? Riley couldn't deny the little surge of jealousy and disappoint-ment that weighed heavy in her stomach last night when he drove up the lane after eleven, like he did last Friday night and again on Monday.

Riley turned to Daniel after loading her dirty dishes into the dish-washer. "What's on the agenda for the afternoon?"

"Cleaning and repairing tack."

"Ahhh." She sighed. "At least we can sit while doing that."

"Thank goodness. I don't know about you, but my back is killing me."

"Same." Riley rubbed at the sore muscles in her lower back as she crossed the yard to the tack room located at the side of the stables.

The overpowering scent of leather and dust hit Riley as she entered the tack room. This room smelled like it could use a good cleaning too. There was always so much work to do on a ranch that chores like cleaning and repairs were often put on the back burner until they became a necessity.

When Daniel didn't follow her into the tack room, she walked out to find him staring at the back deck of the main house. Her gaze followed his to where Emily sat in a chaise lounge reading a book.

Adam must be down for a nap.

"Is something wrong?"

Daniel jumped. "No, everything's fine. Um...are you okay cleaning the tack by yourself for a few minutes?"

"Sure."

"Thanks. I need to talk to Emily for a minute." He started walking away then looked back over his shoulder. "I'll try not to take too long."

Riley watched him go, wondering what he needed to talk to Emily about. She pondered his words from last night about secrets eating at her and causing more damage and realized Daniel was right. She'd kept what happened to her quiet because she didn't want to relive it and didn't want people to criticize her for not being able to stop Collin's attack. But her attempt to bury it hadn't made it affect her any less. She still had nightmares. She still got angry and irritated. She still tensed any time Daniel got close. She was just getting better at hiding it.

But I shouldn't have to hide it.

They often took the tack outside to clean it because of the strong smell of saddle soap. Riley appreciated that habit today as she carried a wooden chair and two bridles outside. Hopefully, her actions didn't look too calculated.

From her vantage point, Riley couldn't hear what Daniel said but she could see both him and Emily.

Riley's brow lifted in surprise when Emily got up and walked away from Daniel, leaving him alone on the back deck. Daniel didn't act upset, however. He simply sat on the side of the other chaise lounge and waited, elbows on his knees.

A few minutes later, Emily walked out the back door carrying a pitcher of lemonade and two glasses.

Apparently, asking Emily for a glass of lemonade wasn't just a euphemism.

Riley tried not to appear too nosy as she discreetly watched Daniel talk to his therapist. Early in their conversation, Emily leaned forward and clapped Daniel on the shoulder, a smile on her face. But after a while, Daniel hung his head much like he did in church on Sundays as though shame, grief, or guilt weighed him down.

At one point Riley looked up to find both Daniel and Emily watching her. She quickly looked away but couldn't keep her gaze from darting back to them. They still stared at her.

Are they talking about me?

Heat filled her chest, and she ground her teeth together. Recalling how Jake called her difficult and fragile this morning only amplified the anger building in her. But then she remembered what Daniel said at the calving sheds a few nights ago.

"When you turn us into your punching bag, you make our garbage harder to deal with."

Then Jake's words to Daniel this morning echoed in her head: "You let me know if working with her becomes a problem for you."

Riley hung her own head. She had no idea what Daniel was going through, yet she'd made it harder for him by repeatedly taking her frustrations out on him.

She'd just carried out a sawhorse in preparation to clean the saddles when Daniel returned.

He stared at her for a long moment before opening his mouth, but no words came out.

"Is everything okay?" Riley asked cautiously.

"Everything's great." He sucked in a deep breath then let it out again. His lips turned up. "Best it's been in a long time." He stepped into the tack room then right back out again. He tilted his head toward the house. "If you're thirsty, Emily has some lemonade." Then he disappeared inside the tack room.

When he reappeared with a saddle in his arms a few moments later, Riley still sat where he left her, not moving a muscle.

"It's okay, Pockets. You can do it."

Riley didn't know if it was his use of her childhood nickname or the gentleness of his voice, but she found herself standing. She couldn't manage to get her feet to move though.

Daniel stepped a little closer. "You can tell her as much or as little as you want." Then he grinned. "If you want, you can tell her how

Damon and I used to torment you and Paige by sneaking frogs into your sleeping bags when we had sleepovers and how that traumatized you for life."

This brought a smile to her face, and she smacked his shoulder. "You guys were awful."

"We really were." He chuckled. "You should go tell Emily how horrible we were." He put a hand on her shoulder and gently nudged her toward the back deck.

That set her in motion, and Riley concentrated on putting one foot in front of the other as she walked toward the house. If she stopped and thought about what she was about to do, she'd chicken out because by the time she'd crossed the lawn to the house, she could barely draw in a full breath.

Her boots felt like they were encased in concrete as she climbed the three steps up to the deck. Her heart pounded so heavily in her chest she hardly heard Emily's greeting.

"Hi, Riley." Her sister-in-law didn't seem at all surprised to see her.

"Hey." Riley slipped her hands into her back pockets and rocked forward on her toes, searching for the words she was supposed to say.

How did one admit they were so screwed up they couldn't make it through the day without getting triggered and feeling like they were on the verge of panicking every time they turned around?

When Riley didn't speak, Emily smiled again. "Would you like a glass of lemonade?"

"Yes!" The word exploded out of her before she could stop it, and she hurried over and perched on the second chaise lounge like Daniel had done.

"Great. Let me get another glass." Emily shifted to stand up.

"No, it's fine. I'll just use Daniel's." Riley was afraid if Emily walked away—even for a second—she would chicken out and bolt.

If Emily was surprised by Riley's words, she didn't show it. It's not like Riley had never shared germs with Daniel before. They did it all the time as kids. Then, when they dated three years ago, they'd made out plenty of times.

Emily looked amused as she refilled Daniel's glass with lemonade.

"You can sit back and relax, Riley. I know Jake and Zane can be slave drivers sometimes, but I have a little sway there. Don't worry, they won't give you a hard time for taking a break with me."

Riley sat back and put her legs up on the chair, but it didn't help her relax at all. There was simply no comfortable way to say the things she needed to say. She scooted forward again, taking up Daniel's pose again. She rubbed her hands on her dirty jeans, trying to figure out how to get the lump out of her throat.

"What kind of horse is Misty?" Emily asked.

"What?" How could Emily think about horses at a time like this?

"Her smoky gray coat with the black mane and tail are beautiful. What breed is she?"

"She's...uh...she's an Arabian."

"Jake said you got her when she was a filly and you named her. Misty is the perfect name."

Riley nodded, still trying to figure out why Emily was talking about horses.

Emily must have seen her confusion because she said. "You didn't come over here to talk about horses, did you?"

Riley shook her head.

"Is there something specific you'd like to talk about?"

Riley nodded, but she couldn't open her mouth. Her heart pounded so hard, she feared it might burst through her ribcage any second. A cold chill swept over her as she tried to formulate the words she needed to say in her head. They felt too oppressive, heavy, and dark.

She stared intently at the wooden slats of the decking, as she focused on bringing air into her lungs and out again. In. Out. She brought her hands together, intending to rub her clammy palms together, but found herself wringing them instead.

She shot Emily an apologetic glance.

Her sister-in-law smiled. "It's okay. Take your time."

Tears blurred Riley's vision and nausea filled her stomach as she replayed in her mind the things Collin had done to her. The way he'd touched her. The crude things he'd said.

Emily's warm hand settled around her clasped ones.

Riley blinked the tears from her eyes and looked up to see Emily's sympathetic gaze on her face.

"How long ago did it happen?"

The gentle and compassionate tone of Emily's voice opened a floodgate Riley couldn't close. Not until she'd purged every obscene and repulsive thing inside.

CHAPTER 10

*J*ake and Lottie were the only ones in the kitchen when Riley pushed open the kitchen door a few days later. "Good morning."

Jake's brows shot up. "Aren't you chipper this morning?" He made a show of checking his non-existent watch. "And it's only a quarter after six."

"Just eager to start the workday." She poured herself a glass of orange juice.

"You're eager to dig post holes and wrestle barbed wire?" His gaze narrowed on her face, scrutinizing her. "Are you sure you're not excited about not having to clean the stables?"

She tipped her glass toward him and grinned. "That too."

Fixing fences was not her favorite job, but it meant she got to spend the day in the saddle. She and Daniel would ride more than twenty miles of the prettiest scenery on the ranch, stopping occasionally to repair patches of fence. It was a small price to pay to get to ride all day.

"I hope you and Daniel can cover the whole northern fence line today, but there's a good chance a storm front will move in this afternoon. If that happens, hightail it home. Or get to the north cabin and wait out the storm there."

"We'll do our best."

If they finished the northern fence line today, they wouldn't get back until dark. That was assuming they only had to make minor repairs. Bigger repairs would require more time.

Jake darted a glance at Lottie's back then stepped closer and lowered his voice. "How are you and Daniel getting along?"

Riley's stomach hardened as she recalled overhearing Jake call her difficult and fragile last week. But then she remembered the way she broke down in front of Emily later that afternoon and realized just how fragile she was.

"Good." She downed the rest of her juice "We're fine." She turned away from him to take her glass to the sink, signifying that she was done with that topic.

Not that it was any of Jake's business, but at least she'd finally stopped jumping and getting defensive every time Daniel got close. They'd been able to work well together lately. It wasn't the same as it used to be, though.

She hated the invisible barriers between them, but she wasn't sure what to do about it, not while she still struggled to put Collin's assault behind her. Talking to Emily had helped to a degree, but healing was going to take time, and Riley was not a patient person.

"Let me know if you need anything, okay?" Jake said from beside her.

His concern made Riley wonder if Emily had told him the things she'd shared with her.

No, she wouldn't do that.

He'd stepped out on the back deck looking for Emily the other day and caught sight of Riley in full-blown meltdown. He'd apologized and disappeared quickly, but all he had to do was add that scene to the times she'd stormed away from the dinner table, and it was obvious there was something wrong with her.

"Thanks." She gave him a curt smile. "I appreciate that."

He leaned closer and lowered his voice even more. "And if you and

Daniel decide you want to...get back together, know that you have my blessing."

Riley's mouth dropped open. "What? We...we're not..."

"I know." Grinning, Jake backed away from her, his hands up in surrender. "I'm just saying...it wouldn't be a bad thing." He winked before heading toward the back door. Before it closed, he called, "Think about it, Ri."

Warmth filled her face. Then a small surge of a different kind of warmth ignited in her abdomen as she recalled how happy she had been with Daniel three years ago.

No, it wouldn't be a bad thing.

But she needed to deal with her trauma first, and she had a feeling Daniel was keeping secrets of his own.

Lottie pushed two gallon-sized bags across the island. "Okay, here are yours and Daniel's lunches. It's going to be a long day for you two, so I put plenty of snacks in there for this afternoon." She slid two more smaller, foil-wrapped packages toward Riley. "And here's your breakfast."

A grin covered Riley's face as she picked up the warm, heavy, foil packages. "Your breakfast burritos are the best, Lottie."

The housekeeper reached out and grabbed one of the lunch bags as Riley prepared to stack them in her arms.

Riley's gaze jumped to her face, questioning.

"Zane and I approve too."

"What?" Riley's eyes flew open.

"I heard what Jake said to you even though he tried to be sneaky, and I want you to know, we—Zane and I—wholeheartedly approve of you and Daniel getting back together. I think it would be good for both of you."

For some silly reason, hearing this from Lottie, who could be rather strict at times, brought tears to Riley's eyes. She tried to blink them away before the older woman noticed, but Lottie was too astute.

She rounded the counter and wrapped her arm around Riley. "Hey, we're not going to push you into something you don't want."

"It's not that." Riley sniffled. "I'm just not in a very good place right now."

Lottie's embrace tightened. "I know, honey, but sometimes a friend can help guide you to a better place."

A friend.

Riley wasn't sure she could classify her relationship with Daniel as friends yet. But Jake and Lottie wanted them to be more? She liked the idea, but she wasn't ready to consider anything more than friendship right now.

"I'll keep that in mind." Riley set down the burritos and returned Lottie's side hug. "Thanks for everything."

When she walked out the back door a few minutes later with her arms loaded, she found Daniel near the stables with three horses tied to the hitching post. Samson, a strong black Morgan horse, was loaded with fencing materials. Misty and Rebel waited to be saddled.

Before long, they were on their way. They talked as they rode, making casual conversation that was impersonal and superficial. Riley wanted the comfortable, easy-going friendship they used to have, but it felt like there was a gulf between them, physically and emotionally. She could tell he often censored his words and went out of his way to avoid getting too close to her. He also had a habit of rubbing his jaw and swiping his hand over his mouth as though he'd developed a nervous tic.

They rode a full two miles before they had to stop and make a minor repair, tightening and reattaching the strand of barbed wire that ran along the top. Despite the chill that lingered in the early morning air, Daniel shed his flannel shirt as soon as he slid down from the saddle.

Thanks to Jake and Lottie's comments, Riley couldn't help noticing the flexing of Daniel's biceps and forearms as he twisted thick wire strands together. A little curl of desire warmed her stomach as she watched the way the sunlight danced on his skin. She even caught herself admiring the fit of his Wranglers.

By mid-morning, the day had grown warm enough that she shed her flannel shirt and stuffed it in her saddle bag. When lunch time neared, they guided their horses to the river. This area was one of the prettiest spots on the ranch, and Riley's favorite. The fresh air became crisper and more refreshing near the river, and thanks to the shade of the trees, the rising temperatures stayed bearable.

After letting their horses drink, they tethered them in a small meadow near a copse of trees and pulled their lunches from the saddlebags. They sat on the riverbank where it widened, creating a small swimming hole. She and Daniel swam here countless times when they were young.

While they ate, Riley searched for a way to break down the barriers between them. She wanted her friend back. Even if they never got back together, she didn't want to continue to feel like she worked with an almost stranger. It was going to be a long enough summer as it was.

"Do you remember how we used to come swimming here when we were kids?"

"Of course, I remember." Daniel tossed his apple up in the air then caught it. "We came at least once a week during the summers. I also recall the summer after you turned eleven. You suddenly started demanding I turn around and close my eyes while you undressed and darted into the water."

Riley smiled at the memory. "My dad had started calling me his little lady. I knew that meant I was supposed to act differently even though I hadn't started to develop yet. But I definitely wasn't ready to give up swimming in the river." She laughed. "You on the other hand at thirteen, didn't bat an eye at stripping down in front of a girl. You simply pulled off your shirt and jeans and walked into the water like it was no big deal."

He shrugged. "It wasn't at the time. You'd seen me in my under-wear loads of times. It wasn't like something had changed overnight. Besides, I didn't think of you as *a girl*. You were just Riley back then. You were my best friend, when Paige wasn't around."

Riley laughed. Daniel and Paige had always fought over the title of Riley's Best Friend, which made her feel special. She loved hanging out with Daniel every day on the ranch, but Paige was her only female cousin on her mom's side. They were only a month apart in age, so they often dressed alike and told people they were twins even though Paige's hair was blond. They even got away with it a time or two because they both looked like their mothers, who were triplets, along with their Aunt Charity.

They continued to reminisce about their childhood while they ate, and Riley's longing for the friendship they used to have grew stronger.

"We used to be so close. What happened to us?" she asked as she nibbled on the chocolate chip cookies Lottie had packed.

The smile Daniel had worn for the last twenty minutes disappeared, and he picked up a small rock and threw it into the river. "You insisted we date, then after you became the center of my whole world, you decided you didn't want anything to do with me."

Her stomach bottomed out. She dropped her gaze to her hands as she fought to breathe around the thickness that suddenly filled her throat. She knew she hurt Daniel when she broke up with him, but she didn't realize he had taken it so hard.

"It wasn't like that." The words were quiet and full of regret.

"It felt like that to me." His posture was stiff now.

"I know. I'm sorry." She set her cookie aside as a heavy sense of sadness consumed her. Walking away from Daniel had been the hardest thing she'd ever done. She'd regretted it every day for that first year, but she had goals she wanted to achieve, and she was afraid if she interrupted her schooling to help him chase his dreams, she'd never achieve hers. "I thought I wanted a serious relationship, but it turned out I wasn't ready to get married."

Her instant attraction to him and longing to spend time with him despite their history when she came home for Jake and Emily's wedding a year and a half ago confirmed that she'd never stopped loving Daniel. Even though there was a gulf between them now, she still cared for him more than she'd ever cared for any other man.

They lapsed into silence for a few minutes, but Riley wasn't ready to give up on trying to revive their friendship.

"We've changed so much. I feel like we hardly know each other anymore."

"Ditto." Daniel's voice was quiet.

Riley plucked a long blade of grass and tore it into little pieces. "Can we work on getting to know each other again and becoming friends since we'll be working together all summer?"

Daniel studied her for a long moment before giving a slow nod.

A spark of hope ignited her chest. She'd half expected him to say no or ask, "What's the point?"

His lips turned up. "You might want to warn Paige that I intend to take back the best friend title before the summer is over."

Riley laughed, a sudden lightness filling her. There were a lot of things she could ask Daniel to get reacquainted, but she couldn't resist diving in and asking the questions she really wanted to know.

"Why do you... drink lemonade with Emily?"

For the second time in less than a minute, Daniel's smile faded. He did that thing where he rubbed his jaw then swiped his hand over his mouth.

When he didn't speak, she pressed on. "Two weeks ago at the calving sheds, you mentioned your...'garbage.'" She made finger quotes. "That's why you talk to Emily, isn't it?" Without waiting for a response, she simply plowed on. "Will you...will you tell me why you sometimes have nightmares?"

She hated putting him on the spot, but she hoped if she could understand what his issues were and how he dealt with them, then maybe she could figure out how to deal with her own. The breathing techniques and tapping Emily had taught her hadn't been very effective yet in helping with her anxiety and panic attacks.

Daniel pushed the bag containing the remainder of his lunch aside and stared out across the water. The muscle in his jaw repeatedly jumped as he propped his elbows on his knees and clasped his hands together. He shook his head, but his lips lifted in a tight smile.

A BAND TIGHTENED around Daniel's chest. He picked up a small rock and threw it into the river. "Wow, Pockets, you don't pull any punches, do you?"

"I'm sorry. I imagine it's not something you want to talk about, but..." Her words died off before an imploring look filled her eyes. "I want to understand what's going on with you. Why are you back here on the ranch again this summer instead of working for an architectural firm in the city?"

He filled his lungs with the crisp spring air and tilted his head upward. Closing his eyes, he listened to the sound of the trickling water as he mouthed a silent prayer.

God, grant me the serenity to accept the things I cannot change, courage to change the things I can, and the wisdom to know the difference. And give me the courage to tell Riley about all my faults.

He'd told himself he was done keeping secrets, but that didn't make it any easier to tell people what he'd done. What he'd become. And Riley wasn't just anyone. She used to be his best friend, and he wanted her to be again. She was the woman he'd been sure he'd spend the rest of his life with. The one he'd never stopped loving.

"It's okay. You don't have to tell me if you don't want to."

Daniel's eyes flew open at the dejected tone of her voice. "No, it's not—" He shook his head. "I haven't told many people what I've done and why I'm back on the ranch." He picked up a small twig and snapped it into little pieces.

"Why not?"

"I don't...want people to think less of me or see me as a monster."

Riley frowned. "You are not a monster. Believe me."

The fervor in her voice didn't convince him. It only raised questions about what she thought constituted a monster, but he couldn't allow himself to be sidetracked by that right now. He needed to tell Riley everything.

"After you hear why I talk to Emily you might think differently."

She scoffed. "I doubt that."

Feeling fidgety and anxious, he got to his feet and searched the ground for a stick while he pulled his knife from his pocket.

"What are you doing?"

He found a branch—too thick and not the best wood for whittling —but it would help take his mind off the urge for a drink while he told Riley how he'd become addicted to alcohol.

Riley waited patiently, her brow furrowed as he sat beside her again and began stripping the bark off the branch. He kept his gaze on the stick. It would be easier to tell her if he didn't look at her. His stomach knotted as he pressed the blade of his knife into the hard wood. "You never met my grandfathers. I barely knew them myself, but do you know why my parents never let us spend much time around them?"

"Weren't they both alcoholics?"

"Yes, and do you know the risks children and grandchildren of alcoholics face?"

"They can have a genetic predisposition to develop an alcohol use disorder."

Trust Nurse Practitioner Riley to know the technical terms.

"Why are we discussing this?" Riley's words were careful, guarded.

He sighed and met her gaze. "Because I inherited that predisposition and developed that disorder."

"But you don't drink."

He cocked his head and grimaced.

Deep furrows formed between her brows. "When did you start drinking?" Before he could respond, she went on. "And why? Your parents warned you repeatedly about alcohol, of the dangers of taking that first drink. I remember being there for some of those lectures."

"You're right, they did. I knew I should stay away from the stuff. When I was young, I promised myself I would. But...sometimes life doesn't turn out like you expect it to." Daniel stopped whittling and squeezed his eyes shut as images of that fateful day flashed through his mind.

If I'd only made different choices!

Riley's hand landed on his arm, warm and soft. "What happened to make you start drinking?"

He wanted to take her hand in both of his and hold on for dear life, but he feared if he even acknowledged her touch, she'd realize what she was doing and pull away.

He let out another long sigh and started whittling again. "After we broke up at the end of that summer, it was harder than ever to return to school for my final semester and prepare for an internship. My heart wasn't in it. I missed you and the ranch like crazy." He darted a glance in her direction.

A look of contrition filled her face, and she ducked her head, withdrawing her hand with the motion.

"One day, I saw a listing for a dirt bike for sale. I figured it would be the next best thing to going back to the ranch, so I arranged to test drive it." His knife cut deeper into the wood now. "When I drove through the neighborhood, looking for the seller's house, a teenage driver came barreling out of his driveway, way too fast, right at me."

Daniel's knife moved faster now in short, deep strokes, matching the hammering of his heart. It didn't matter how many times he told people what happened, it always made his heart race, his gut clench, and his hands shake. He probably shouldn't be holding a knife right now, but he couldn't stop. If he did, his hands would start itching to pick up a bottle, and he'd get even thirstier than he already was.

"I wasn't even going that fast. I had been driving the speed limit, but I sped up a little, so the kid wouldn't T-bone me. And I... swerved to the other side of the street." He dropped his knife and swiped a hand over his jaw as he swallowed the lump in his throat. "At that moment, a four-year-old boy, who had just learned to ride his bike, came flying down his sloped driveway. I had been watching the teen driver to make sure he didn't hit me, so I didn't see the little boy in time." His next words squeezed out through a tight throat as a tsunami of guilt washed over him. "I hit him, Ri."

"Oh, Daniel." Her hand was back on his arm now, gently squeezing, pulling him from the dark place his mind always went when he recalled what he'd done.

Once again, he wanted to take her hand in his and soak up her comfort. Her acceptance would likely change when she learned how weak he was.

Daniel watched the ripples in the water, wishing it could wash away the memories that drove him to drink. Memories that made him crave a double shot of Jack Daniel's whisky right now.

"I didn't run over him, but I knocked him off his bike. He wasn't wearing a helmet, so when his head hit the ground..." Daniel swiped a hand over his mouth at the memory of the blood that flowed from that small head wound. But that wasn't the worst part. "He just lay there. So still." He swallowed again to alleviate the tightness that clogged his throat, but that did nothing for the jumble of knots in his stomach. "After the police finished their report, I drove to the hospital. I had to know if he was going to be okay."

He propped his elbows on his knees and plunged his hands into his hair. "Isaac never woke up. I heard the doctor tell his parents they couldn't stop the swelling in his brain." Daniel cleared his throat yet again before continuing. "I watched his mom collapse, and his father was so overcome with his own grief he was powerless to help her."

That was one of the images that haunted his dreams for months. He pressed the heels of his hands to his eyes to combat the sting of tears.

"I can't imagine how difficult that must have been for you."

And still is.

He lifted his head to see tears on Riley's cheeks. She made no move to wipe them away.

"For weeks, I couldn't eat, couldn't sleep. Every time I closed my eyes I saw his lifeless body, and I watched his mother collapse all over again. I couldn't help thinking about all the things little Isaac would never get to experience. Drive a car. Go on his first date. Kiss a girl. Fall in love."

"Daniel, don't do that to yourself."

"Do what? Acknowledge all I took away from Isaac and his family?" He shook his head as he picked up his knife and stick again. "Too late. I did that for two months. Every day, I relived that accident over and over. I thought of the things I robbed those parents of. I went to the funeral, but I stayed in the background. I didn't want to upset them even more than they already were. I even went to their house a couple weeks later."

Again, Daniel's knife cut deep scars into the wood. "The mother broke down on the doorstep when she saw me. Then her husband came out. I tried to apologize, but there weren't words adequate enough to express how truly sorry I was. The father was gracious. He told me he didn't hold me responsible, but he asked me to never come again because it upset his wife too much."

"I'm so sorry." Riley squeezed his arm.

"Everyone tells me I shouldn't blame myself, but I do. I should have just let that teenage driver hit me. And if I hadn't gone to buy that motorcycle in the first place, Isaac would still be alive." He shook his head in disgust. "I bought it anyway and developed a death wish. I spent hours riding at extreme speeds on back roads, but it didn't help."

"Is that how you broke your leg? By wrecking the dirt bike?"

"Not exactly." He stared out across the water again as he shook his head. "I don't know if I ever told you about my roommate..."

"The one who kept his shelf in the fridge full of beer?" Riley's tone showed her disapproval.

"That's the one. A couple months after the accident, I was as messed up as the night it happened. He convinced me to have a beer. Said it would make it all go away."

Riley snorted, but Daniel kept talking. "It tasted disgusting, but I kept drinking. First one, then a second and a third. After a few beers, I couldn't picture little Isaac's face so clearly anymore. So, I drank until I puked, then I drank some more. I kept going until I passed out. I had a horrible hangover the next morning, but I didn't mind, because I felt like I was getting the punishment I deserved."

"You didn't deserve to be punished." This time Riley's hand landed on his shoulder.

"Guilt ate at me for turning to alcohol, but the following week, images of that little boy kept coming back to me, and by the weekend, I couldn't wait to have a few beers to help me forget again. It wasn't long before drinking became my coping mechanism, but beer was no longer strong enough to dull the pain." His cuts against the wood grew more rapid. "Alcohol masked the pain, made me numb. It made me forget and not care. About anything."

"I blew off most of my classes the last half of that term. Barely managed to graduate. I lost my job, but I was fortunate to secure an internship with a prestigious architectural firm. I told myself I needed to stop drinking or I'd screw it up, and I tried. I tried so hard. I managed to stay high functioning for a while, but when the internship got stressful, I began drinking more heavily. Within six months of that first drink, I was well on my way to becoming addicted."

"I'm sorry you went through that alone, Daniel. I wish you'd called me. I would have done my best to talk you through those difficult nights or helped you find someone—a professional—you could talk to."

"I thought about calling you all the time, but I couldn't bring myself to dial your number. We made the break final, so naturally, I felt like I'd lost my best friend."

"I'm sorry."

"It's not your fault. I'm the one who was weak. The one who made all the wrong choices."

"But you were dealing with so much."

He held up his hand. "There is no justification for my actions. Actions have consequences. Lasting consequences. I have to live with mine. Some of them are painful and lifelong. I have a record now. That will never go away."

"A record?"

He picked up his knife and stick yet again. "One day, I made the mistake of getting on my motorcycle after having a couple drinks." He shook his head at himself. "I caused an accident. Fortunately, no one was hurt besides me, but it totaled their car."

"That's when you broke your leg."

"Yes. It hurt like crazy, but I welcomed the pain because I knew I deserved it. My parents came to get me from the hospital, but I couldn't leave Portland, because I was under arrest for drunk driving. Eventually, they were allowed to post bail for me and bring me home. I almost became addicted to my pain meds as a replacement for the alcohol. Fortunately, Emily saw the warning signs and helped me through it all."

"Wow," Riley said, "I had no idea you were dealing with so much that summer. When you acted so distant, I thought it was because you didn't want anything to do with me after our breakup."

He turned to face her. "It was the opposite, Ri. I wanted so badly to spend time with you, but I was ashamed of what I had done, of what I had become. I didn't want to see the disappointment in your eyes that I saw in my parents' eyes and in Jake's when I first came home."

The disappointment I see in my own eyes every time I look in the mirror.

"I know how much you always looked up to Jake and Robert." Riley's voice was gentle, compassionate.

He didn't deserve her compassion. He'd made too many mistakes.

"They were there for me when I went to court. The judge went easy on me because it was my first offense and I plead guilty, but I think Jake and Robert's presence made the judge give me a relatively light sentence. Robert convinced the judge to let me fulfill my sentence here in Providence where I would have the help of family and friends to stay sober. In addition to losing my license and having to attend a sobriety program, I was hit with a hefty fine, a bunch of service hours, and fifteen days in jail. Thanks to the rehabilitation program your dad and uncle started years ago, Jake had no problem persuading the judge to let me do my service here at the Double Diamond, and Robert..." Daniel gave a small smile. "He let me serve my jail time on the weekends from Friday night to Sunday evening. Of course, he dragged my butt to church every Sunday morning. Without the handcuffs, thank goodness."

Two birds that had been flitting through the trees above them darted down to grab small twigs then back up to the treetops.

Daniel lifted his chin and watched them for a moment.

They're building a nest. Planning for the future.

He wished he knew what his future held.

"Until last Saturday, my parents, Jake, Emily, and Robert were the only ones who knew about the accident and my subsequent drinking. Robert may have told Jessie, but I don't think they've told any of the rest of your family. I don't think my parents have even told my older siblings. They live so far away, it doesn't really affect them."

"Who did you tell last Saturday?"

"My Alcoholics Anonymous group."

"That's where you go on Saturdays? To AA meetings?"

Had Riley noticed his absence at the ranch? A spark of warmth lit in his chest.

"Yes." He narrowed his gaze on her. "Where did you think I went?"

She shrugged, but the rosy tint in her cheeks piqued his interest.

"Come on, Pockets, tell me where you thought I went."

She plucked a blade of grass. "I thought maybe you had a girlfriend."

Daniel laughed. "Were you jealous?"

"Of course not." More color flooded her cheeks, belying her words.

"Liar."

"Okay, maybe I was a little jealous."

He laughed again. He loved the idea of Riley noticing his absence and being jealous.

As though full of nervous energy, Riley began gathering up the remnants of their lunch, but he wasn't done. He needed to tell her everything.

If there was a possibility of a second chance for them—and he wanted there to be, even though he didn't feel like he deserved it—she needed to know all his secrets, all his bad choices, all his faults and shortcomings. He wouldn't jeopardize a second chance with Riley by keeping things from her.

He put a hand on her arm then quickly withdrew it before she went ballistic. "There's more I need to tell you."

She stilled and her brows lifted in surprise. "Okay." Despite the encouragement in her words, that guarded tone filled her voice again. "Tell me."

Daniel stared at the water again so he wouldn't see the disappointment in her eyes. "After that summer here at the ranch with my broken leg, I thought I was ready to go back to Portland. By some miracle, the architectural firm agreed to let me come back and finish my internship." He hung his head. "But I fell off the wagon less than six months later. Right after Jake and Emily's wedding."

Riley's cousins Damon and Paige had come home for the wedding, and it was like old times having the four of them together again. Their presence eased the awkwardness between him and Riley, and it made Daniel long for a second chance with her. That longing triggered something in him, and he started seeing her face on Isaac's lifeless body in his dreams. Sometimes, it was Riley who collapsed in despair and disappointment instead of Isaac's mom.

Emily had told him the reason he kept seeing Riley's face was because of his unresolved feelings for her. He knew she was right, even though he didn't want to admit it. But now that she had come home, he was quickly reaching a point where he could no longer deny it.

"What happened to cause you to start drinking again?"

He wasn't ready to admit the whole truth to her yet. "I'd started hanging out with some of my old friends who kept inviting me to have a drink with them. I resisted for a while, but after the wedding, I saw Isaac's mom in the grocery store." He paused his whittling. "She didn't see me, but it was enough to bring back the guilt. I caved and started going out drinking with my friends. It didn't take long for the alcohol to take control of my life."

"Why didn't you call Emily?"

"She was on her honeymoon." The words came out sharp and curt. "By the time she came home, I was so ashamed of myself for giving in to the alcohol again that I couldn't face her. So, I drowned my guilt with more alcohol." He lifted his chin and studied the green leaves above him. "I spiraled out of control with my drinking and did so many stupid things. Things that I had little to no recollection of the next day. Things that can't be undone. I turned into one of the ranch hands that your father always warned you to keep your distance from."

She snorted in disbelief. "You were arrested for a DUI. That hardly puts you in the same class as the ex-convicts we've had over the years."

"I've been arrested more than once, Ri," he said quietly, hanging his head again. "I was arrested again last fall in a drunken brawl. The charges ended up getting dropped the next day when the waitress I was trying to protect told her boss why I attacked that biker guy and started a brawl in his bar, but the problem was, I'd made another wrong choice in a long line of bad choices." He rubbed his jaw again. "I've screwed up so many times I've lost the trust of the people I care about."

"That's not true." Her hand was back on his arm again. "Your parents love you and trust you. And I know Jake trusts you. If he didn't, we wouldn't be working together."

Daniel rolled his eyes. "I'm just the lesser of two evils."

"Stop it!" She smacked his shoulder. "Stop talking like you're such a horrible person because you've made a few bad choices."

"A few? I can't count the number of times I woke up with no recall of the things I did the night before. I turned my back on all the values I was raised with and did so many things I'm ashamed of."

"What kind of things?" Her tone was quiet and guarded again.

Is she really that naive?

He thought he wanted to come completely clean with Riley and tell her everything, but he had no desire to admit to the woman he'd loved all his life how many times he'd taken other women home from the bar. Not that he could recall exactly how many there were, thanks to the alcohol.

He may as well show her one of his biggest regrets. She was likely to see it at some point anyway. He pulled the tail of his t-shirt from the waistband of his jeans, then he reached behind his head and tugged his shirt up by the collar, dragging it over his head. He rotated toward her, showing her the monstrosity on his chest. "This is bigger than any of the tattoos the hired ranch hands ever had."

He held his breath and braced himself, waiting for Riley to freak out. Good thing he'd set his knife on the opposite side of him, out of her reach.

TIGHTNESS SEIZED Riley's chest the moment it became apparent Daniel intended to take off his shirt. She struggled to draw air into her lungs at the sight of his bare midriff.

Warning bells rang in her head, screaming louder the higher his shirt lifted. Her fight or flight instincts kicked in, but because she sat on the ground, she felt incapable of doing either.

She gave herself a mental shake.

It's only Daniel. One of my oldest and dearest friends.

She tapped her fingers against her thighs to give herself something else to focus on besides the panic raging through her body.

When he pulled his shirt over his head, she couldn't keep from gasping. Her eyes widened in surprise as she studied his chest. Not because of his toned pectoral and abdominal muscles, but rather because a magnificent, colorful tattoo of an eagle in flight covered his upper torso. The bird was splendid with a white head, golden beak, and talons. Detailed feathers in shades from light brown to dark brown and even black fanned out across Daniel's skin.

Riley couldn't help herself; she burst out laughing. "You think you're a bad person because you got a tattoo?"

"It's not funny, Pockets. Look at the size of this thing." He pointed at his chest. Each of the eagle's wings was at least as big as her palm. "This is permanent. It's just one of the many choices I made while I was drunk that will stick with me for the rest of my life."

She continued to giggle. "It's a good thing you found a reputable artist, considering you were drunk when you got this. As far as tattoos go, you picked a good one. The colors are absolutely breathtaking."

Still grinning, she reached her hand out to touch his torso, but then a chill shot through her veins, reminding her how intimate this situation was and how quickly it could go south. She jerked her hand back.

Disappointment filled Daniel's eyes, and he pulled his shirt back over his head.

"That large of a tattoo in those colors must have cost a small fortune."

"Yeah, and it was money I didn't have because I had just lost my job thanks to my drinking." He shook his head in disgust. Self-loathing filled his voice when he spoke again. "I threw my life away for booze."

"You're changing, though. For the better. You'll get your life back on track."

"I don't know. I have a degree I'm not sure I'll ever use, because I don't dare leave the ranch."

"Why?"

"I have a great support system here that I wouldn't have anywhere else. I'm not sure I could stay sober if I left. It's a battle I fight every single day as it is."

Her heart went out to him. She understood fighting battles, but she hoped with time, hers would get easier. She wasn't sure Daniel's ever would.

His parents and Jake and Emily probably feared he'd relapse if he left the ranch again. Was that why they wanted her and Daniel to get back together? Did they expect her to stay here forever?

Although she wasn't opposed to a second chance with Daniel—when she was ready—she wasn't sure she wanted to stay here on the ranch indefinitely.

Such thoughts continued to dance around inside her head as they got back to work. If she and Daniel were ever going to become friends again, Riley knew she needed to trust him with her garbage. Like he did with her.

The temperature grew warmer over the next hour as they continued to ride the fence line, stopping occasionally to make repairs. By four o'clock, however, a heavy cloud cover blew in and the wind picked up so much Riley had a hard time keeping her hat on her head. The temperature dropped rapidly, going from pleasant to downright chilly within the course of an hour.

She tugged her hat low on her head, pulled her flannel shirt from her saddle bag, and put it on as the first drops of rain began to fall.

"What do you think?" Daniel studied the sky as he buttoned his long-sleeved shirt. "Do we stick it out and try to finish the last few miles of fence line? Or do we call it a day and head home?"

Riley pointed at the darker clouds to the southwest. "That's headed our way. No matter what we do, we're going to get soaked. I don't want to ride fifteen miles in that."

The rain came faster even as she spoke, pelting and stinging despite her layered shirts and thick jeans.

Daniel grimaced as he tugged his hat low on his head. "We'd better head to the cabin then."

After Riley's parents got caught in a sudden rainstorm when they were dating and had to spend the night in a tiny cave not far from here, her dad built two small emergency cabins: one near the northeast property line and the other near the southeast border.

"That's still almost two miles away by the time we skirt around this rocky ridge."

"Then we'd better get moving." Daniel kicked his horse in the flanks.

As she gave Misty enough rein to follow Rebel and Samson, Riley couldn't help recalling in vivid detail what happened the last time she and Daniel got stuck at the north emergency cabin three years ago.

The small cabin was a far cry better than a cramped cave, but she didn't look forward to having to spend the night there with Daniel this time. What if being stuck there with him triggered her?

I haven't learned enough coping skills from Emily yet.

CHAPTER 11

*D*aniel ducked his head against the onslaught of rain and checked over his shoulder to see if Riley followed him and to ensure Samson kept up with Rebel.

His midsection tightened as he recalled the last time he and Riley raced to the emergency cabin, trying to outrun a storm. That had been three years ago, but he found himself experiencing the same mixture of excitement and anxiety as he had back then.

Excitement because he'd fallen head over heels for Riley while working with her that summer, and he looked forward to spending the evening alone with her. He'd been dying for over a month to move their relationship out of the friend zone, but he feared how she might react. The last thing he wanted to do was ruin his relationship with his best friend.

Keeping tempo with Rebel's pounding hooves, memories filled his head of that night three years ago.

Daniel slammed the door behind him and pulled his hat from his head, flinging water across the wood floor that was already splattered with droplets from Riley. "Talk about a downpour!"

"I know, I'm soaked." She took off her own hat and hung it on a hook

near the door. Her wet denim shirt quickly followed. The tank top she wore underneath was equally as wet and clung to her curves like a second skin.

A surge of desire rushed through him. He swallowed hard and pulled his mind from the gutter. It had been harder and harder this summer to think of Riley as a friend. She was like a sister to him, so keeping their relationship friendly shouldn't be that hard. But he wanted to be so much more than friends, and his thoughts lately were far from brotherly.

Her cousin Paige had conceded the title of Riley's best friend to him for the summer while she was away on the east coast, working as a nanny, and he didn't want to do anything to screw it up. But he could no longer deny how much Riley's hardworking and spunky nature had grown on him. She challenged him and made him laugh. She also made him want to be a better person.

He couldn't imagine life without her. He wanted her by his side forever.

"I'll get a fire going." Riley crouched near the large, rock fireplace. "Will you text Jake and tell him we'll most likely spend the night here?"

Daniel's heart rate kicked into overdrive. He spent practically every evening with Riley anyway, so the thought of spending the night sleeping in this small cabin with her shouldn't get him all worked up, but it did.

He looked to the left where two barely-bigger-than-a-cot twin beds sat, only a few feet apart. The cabin was so much smaller than he remembered, and with the dim light coming through the single, small window, the whole setting looked intimate and cozy.

"Daniel? Did you hear me?" Riley stared at him from across the narrow room. "We don't have very good service out here, but will you try to call or at least text Jake or your dad?"

"Yeah, sorry."

"And for Pete's sake take your wet shirt off. You're going to get chilled."

He peeled off his long-sleeved shirt, then stopped himself from pulling off the muscle shirt he wore underneath. Riley had seen him shirtless many times, but with the direction his mind kept traveling lately in regard to her, it was best he keep a shirt on for the evening.

He sent Jake and his dad a quick text, hoping one bar of service was enough to get the job done, then he went to the small kitchenette—if you could call it that—and searched the handful of second-hand cabinets for the tea *kettle. By the time he located it and filled it with water, Riley had a fire blazing, making the cabin look downright romantic.*

She stood near the fireplace undoing her braid and running her fingers through her wet hair. The thick, disheveled waves only added to her attractiveness, and another surge of desire filled him. She was a tomboy through and through, but she had feminine assets that were anything but boyish.

"Are you going to put the kettle on the hearth?" She laughed, sending a little jolt through Daniel's system. "Or are you just going to stand there, staring at me?"

He loved hearing her laugh, even if it was at his expense. He dropped the kettle on the brick hearth, spilling a little. Heat rushed up his neck as he returned to the cabinets for mugs.

"Do you want apple cider or hot chocolate?" His voice was half an octave higher than usual, and additional heat filled his face.

"Chocolate of course." She clicked her tongue in disappointment. "You should know that by now."

"I do know that. I just wanted you to know you have options." He bit his tongue before saying something incredibly stupid and cheesy like I'm an option. Pick me.

Riley walked over to the window. "So much for our plans to go to the movies tonight." She crossed the few feet to the kitchenette and opened a cabinet. "It's a good thing we've got some games to play." She pulled out Scrabble, Yahtzee, and Uno. "I'd hate to think how we'd entertain ourselves all evening with nothing to do."

Daniel could think of a few things they could do to entertain themselves. Things like snuggling in front of the fire and talking about a future together.

Within the hour, they had heated canned beef stew and eaten it with crackers and canned peaches. They now nursed their second mug of hot chocolate as they settled around the small table to play scrabble.

Riley was good at word games, so Daniel anticipated losing. It didn't help that he seemed to have a one-track mind tonight; a track that revolved around dating, kissing, and hugging because those were the kinds of words that kept popping up in his tiles until he finally used the I-N-G to spell STING.

When Riley added G-I-R-L to the word FRIEND that he'd previously laid down, Daniel's blood warmed and pumped a little faster through his veins. He kept telling himself to ask her to be his girlfriend, but he couldn't seem to spit the words out.

When she spelled HEART, his own beat a little harder against his ribcage. He must have been imagining things because he swore she looked at him through her lashes after laying down the tiles. Bedroom eyes. He'd heard that term and seen actresses do that with their eyes in the movies, but he'd never seen that look on Riley's face before.

He loved it, but he feared he was reading too much into a single look.

When she laid down K-I-S-S a few minutes later, he sucked in a sharp breath. Was she on the same wavelength he was on?

"Do you remember giving me my first kiss?" Her big blue eyes looked at him full of innocence with a glint of something mischievous in them.

Yep, they were bedroom eyes alright, and it did all kinds of crazy things to his insides.

He cleared his throat before trusting himself to speak. "Like it was yesterday."

It was true. He could still hear the fire crackling in the fireplace of the big ranch house, like tonight, and smell her subtle floral perfume, the feel of his hands encircling her waist, and the softness of her lips yielding to his.

Her mouth curved upward. "I can't believe you drove half the night to take me to my senior prom."

"Like I could stay away. You called me in tears, crying over how Jaxon had broken his leg and wouldn't be able to take you." He gestured toward her. "I knew how excited you were about wearing that dress." A ripple of warmth coursed through him as he recalled how mature and feminine the tomboy he'd grown up with had looked in that elegant satin dress that fit her like a glove. The burgundy color had complimented her complexion in the best way possible. "No way could I let you miss your senior prom."

"It was the most amazing day." She pretended to scowl. "Even the part where you woke me up before dawn to watch the sunrise."

"I was just glad it turned out to be a beautiful one."

"The prettiest." She grinned, then her smile faded, and she looked down and ran a fingernail along the edge of the Scrabble board. "Did you think I was a total idiot when I kissed you that night?"

"An idiot? No." He gave a tight laugh. "Sure, I was shocked, especially with the way you grabbed my shirt and swooped in and attacked me."

Her mouth dropped open. "I did not attack you."

"What you did could hardly be called a kiss. That's why I had to give you a real one."

A sheepish look crossed her face. "Do you know why I kissed you?"

"You told me you didn't want to graduate from high school, never having been kissed."

"That was true but..."

"But what?" Daniel ducked his head to meet her lowered gaze. When she finally made eye contact with him, he asked, "Why did you really kiss me?"

"I was...jealous."

His head reared back. "Jealous? Of whom?"

"You'd spent all day talking about all the college girls you'd dated and hung out with, and I got jealous. I knew I wasn't as pretty and sophisticated as them, but I wanted to...stake my claim."

He held up a hand in protest. "First of all, you are plenty pretty, Pockets. Gorgeous, in fact. But what do you mean by 'stake your claim'?" Daniel's mouth hung open in disbelief. "Did you want to be more than friends? Or were you afraid I'd quit being your friend if I started dating someone seriously?"

His heartbeat pulsed loud and strong in his ears as he waited for her response.

She shrugged. "Before you kissed me, you made me promise not to tell anyone, especially not my family. I assumed you didn't want anyone to know because you didn't like me like that."

"I said that because I didn't want Robert and Jake to beat the crap out of me. They would have killed me if they found out I took advantage of their little sister."

She rolled her eyes. "You didn't take advantage of me."

"Maybe not, but you have to admit the kiss I gave you wasn't exactly a peck on the lips."

He'd planned on making a quick getaway that night after the dance because he was finding it so hard to fight his attraction to Riley, but when she admitted she'd never been kissed, no way could he walk away and let her down. He'd gotten a little carried away, though. Not only did Riley get her first kiss, she also got a taste of French kissing.

"I never told anyone. Not even Paige."

"Really?" Daniel thought for sure she'd told Paige first thing the next morning. He'd always wondered why Riley's cousin never said anything to him.

"Four years later, and it's still one of the best kisses I've ever had." She gave a soft smile, but her gaze remained on the table where she continued to trace the edge of the Scrabble board.

Daniel sucked in a sharp breath. "That's a shame, because I've learned a lot about kissing since then."

Her gaze jumped to his, and they stared at each other for a long moment. Then without breaking eye contact, he reached out and took her hand. "You didn't answer my question. Did you want to be more than friends back then?"

She ducked her head again. "I kept telling myself it was just a silly teenage crush, but—"

"You're not a teenager anymore, Ri."

She was twenty-two now. Had she really had a crush on him for four years?

Was that why she always came up with things for them to do in the evenings, even though they'd spent all day working together? Dancing at Scooters, riding four-wheelers, target practicing, watching a movie. He assumed she was bored because Paige was gone for the summer, playing nanny on the East coast, but each evening he spent with her made him fall a little harder.

We've wasted so much time.

"No, I'm not a teenager." Finally, she lifted her head. "And after spending sixteen to eighteen hours a day with you every day this summer, I'm pretty sure it's a whole lot more than a crush."

Daniel's chest expanded with a hopeful yet anxious feeling. He scooted his chair around the table until his leg pressed against hers. "I feel the same way. Question is: what do we do about it?"

"I don't want to ruin our friendship." Her hand tightened around his.

"Me either."

"But I want to date you. I want you to kiss me again, like you did four years ago." She pulled their clasped hands toward her.

He couldn't help but follow. *"Me too."*

"So kiss me."

Daniel wanted nothing more than to do exactly that, but the rational part of his brain cried, *"Wait!"*

"What will your family think?" He forced the words out through a dry mouth.

"I don't care. I'm an adult, I can choose who I date. Besides, you're practically family, so it's not like they won't like you."

"Yeah, but—"

"No buts." She leaned toward him. *"You need to kiss me now before I take matters into my own hands."* She grabbed a fistful of his shirt and tugged. *"I should probably warn you... I haven't learned that much over the past four years when it comes to kissing."*

He grinned as he cupped a hand to her face. *"Just keep your teeth out of it, Pockets."* Then he winked. *"For now, anyway."*

Before she could close the gap between them, he stroked his thumb over her bottom lip. He'd waited four years to kiss these lips again, and the last thing he wanted to do was rush it. He wanted to commit the feel of her soft skin to memory, along with her floral perfume mixed with the fresh scent of rain and pine.

Her warm breath caressed his thumb, and a surge of desire jolted through him.

Bag it. I've got the rest of my life to memorize everything about her.

He leaned the final few inches and pressed his lips to hers. Hers parted almost immediately, and he found himself unable to continue the kiss through his smile. He quickly recovered, however, and accepted all that she offered and gave to her in return.

The taste of hot chocolate and peaches on her mouth was rich and tantalizing. His hand slid into her hair, his fingers tangling in her damp locks. Flames crackled in the fireplace, and he couldn't help thinking that he couldn't have picked a more perfect setting for their second kiss if he'd tried.

Riley's chin jutted out then dipped, playing a game of cat and mouse with his lips. The ebb and flow of her mouth against his was sheer perfection, and he quickly realized, contrary to her words, she'd learned a thing or two about kissing.

Instead of being jealous of the man who taught her such teasing tactics, he counted himself lucky to be on the receiving end of her kisses. He reached out to wrap his arm around her waist so he could pull her closer, but met the spindles on the back of her chair. With a soft growl, he pulled her chair toward him with one hand and shoved the table away with the other. Scrabble tiles clattered to the floor.

Oh well, I was losing anyway.

But he sure felt like the victor at that moment.

Not even Riley's giggle was enough to deter him from claiming her lips again. This time when he wrapped his arms around her, hers encircled his neck, and before he knew it, she sat on his lap. He continued to caress her lips for several long moments, doing a little teasing of his own, before ending the kiss.

He pressed his forehead to her temple and sucked in several deep breaths. "Promise me you'll come visit me in the hospital after your brothers rearrange my face."

Riley burst into laughter.

Rebel stumbled, abruptly jerking Daniel from his memories. He nearly pitched over the horse's neck before Rebel righted himself.

Speaking of the hospital...he'd better pay attention, or he'd land himself there tonight.

Relief flooded Daniel when the cabin finally came into view, but he didn't experience the release of tension that he'd hoped to feel. Tonight, wouldn't be anything like that night three years ago. He was sure of it.

He and Riley had found a way to work together peaceably, but they were both so different from the veritable kids who'd made out behind those walls three years ago. Deep down, he sensed this night could turn out miserable—and perhaps painful for him—if Riley decided to go ballistic like she had so many times.

~

RILEY WAS THOROUGHLY SOAKED by the time they reached the small northern cabin. The shelter for the horses was little more than a lean-to and was barely big enough for the three animals. Despite wanting to get inside and get warm and dry, Riley stuck by Daniel's side, getting the horses unsaddled and the fencing materials unloaded.

While she fed the horses from the small stash of dry hay kept under a tarp in the corner of the lean-to, Daniel cranked the pump to water the horses from the well. Once they finished caring for the horses, they darted to the cabin.

Daniel opened the door for her and waved her in.

She stepped inside and froze. It was so much smaller and darker than she remembered. Almost claustrophobic. Barely a few feet separated the two twin beds to the left, and the round table that sat in the center of the room was so small, with only two chairs.

Images of the last time she was stuck here overnight with Daniel filled her head. That was the night she'd convinced him they should date. They'd kissed a lot that night.

The thought of spending the night with Daniel in this tiny cabin again, let alone kissing him, caused her heart to race in a way that made her blood pressure skyrocket. Her breathing came faster, yet her chest grew so tight, she feared she might suffocate.

She turned toward the door, looking to escape, and ran right into Daniel's solid chest.

"Careful, Pockets." He braced her with a hand on her shoulder so she didn't topple over and nudged her to the side. "Let me in so I can close the door."

Riley didn't want the door closed. She didn't want to be here. Trapped with a man. Her mind went straight back to the night Collin walked into her apartment, like he owned the place.

"Wow! It's really coming down out there!" Daniel walked farther into the one-room cabin, but Riley couldn't make her feet move.

Wrapping her arms around her trembling body, she stared out the small window. The sky grew darker by the second, and the rain came down in sheets now. That was the only thing keeping her from bolting out the door.

They'd gotten there just in time before the worst of the storm hit, but the panicked voice inside her head told her it could be more dangerous inside the cabin than outside. She took several deep breaths, following the breathing exercises Emily suggested, but she couldn't focus well enough for them to be effective.

Daniel said something about building a fire so they could dry out, but the blood pumping in her ears muted his voice, making it sound like it came from far away. The more she told herself to calm down, the more her body shivered and the harder she found it to breathe.

"You okay, Ri?"

She ignored Daniel's question. She couldn't have answered if she'd wanted to because her teeth chattered so hard, but also because she was definitely not okay. It was all she could do not to scream and burst into hysterics.

"Hey."

The word came from right beside her ear, and Riley jumped, certain she'd felt the rush of his hot breath across her cheek. Or maybe that was just her overactive imagination. Suppressing the urge to scream, she dug her fingernails into the palms of her hands to keep from striking him.

"Here wrap up in a blanket until the fire warms up the cabin."

Riley turned enough to see that he held up a blanket from one of the beds. She reached for it, but he pulled back.

"You should probably shed at least the outer layer of wet clothing first."

Too shaky to even nod, she stepped further away and turned her back to him as her cold fingers fumbled with the buttons of her flannel shirt. His proximity made it harder to breathe, and she couldn't seem to make her fingers work.

A clap of thunder sounded at the same moment a flash of lightning lit up the cabin. An additional dose of fear and anxiety surged through her, making her whole body tremble.

"Riley?"

She looked over her shoulder at him. He hadn't come any closer, thank goodness, but concern lined his face.

"I can tell you don't want to be in this cabin...with me, but I promise, I'm not going to hurt you." He swiped a hand over his jaw and mouth. "I need you to believe that."

He'd done that several times this afternoon when he talked about his alcohol addiction, and Riley couldn't help wondering if it meant he was craving a drink. She hated that he thought he was the problem, when really, it was all her.

"I-I know that. I do. B-but I just..." She pressed a hand to her racing heart.

"But your PTSD has kicked in." It was a statement, not a question, but she nodded anyway.

He laid the blanket over the chair and took a small step toward her. "How can I help?"

"I don't know."

For the first time, Riley noticed he had shed his hat and his wet denim shirt and even built a fire while she did nothing but stand there trembling and freaking out. She attempted to unbutton her shirt again, but her heart still raced, her lungs still struggled to draw in a full breath, and her hands still shook so badly she couldn't grasp the buttons let alone push them through a little hole.

"W-will you...h-help me." She balled her shaky hands into fists. "With my b-buttons?"

"Sure." He swiped a hand over his jaw again before stepping toward her.

She squeezed her eyes shut. If she didn't see how close he stood or the way his wet t-shirt clung to his sculpted chest, maybe she could keep from freaking out on him.

His boots shifted on the wooden floor, and his quiet voice came from directly in front of her. "Please don't knee me in the groin again."

"No promises." The muttered words came out through clenched teeth.

The heel of her right boot bounced against the floor, tapping a steady staccato. She flexed her fingers then balled them into fists at her sides again. Anything to distract herself from the fact that Daniel touched her.

Even though she hardly felt any contact, she sensed movement in front of her, and she tensed. Her mind screamed at her to fight or run.

"Deep breaths, Pockets." Daniel's use of her childhood nickname reminded her that she could trust him. "In through your nose, out through your mouth."

Riley did as he instructed, keeping her eyes closed tight. She managed three breaths, but then his knuckles grazed against her abdomen, and panic rose in her throat again, clogging it, making breathing impossible.

Daniel must have noticed the change in her because he asked, "Do you remember that time I cut myself with my pocketknife?" Without waiting for her to respond, he went on. "You insisted on being the one to play nurse and bandage my hand, using your mother's first aid kit." He let out a little chuckle. "I walked out of that bathroom with my whole hand bandaged even though I only had a little cut on my index finger."

Riley's lips turned up unexpectedly as she recalled her mom's instructions before walking out of the bathroom. "Put a butterfly bandage on it nice and tight, then wrap a little gauze around it to keep it clean."

She had done as her mother instructed, but a simple butterfly bandage and a little gauze hadn't been satisfying enough. So she kept wrapping. Despite protesting, Daniel let her wrap until she ran out of gauze. That was the day she realized she wanted to follow in her mother's footsteps and become a nurse.

"You kept that big bandage on for a whole week." The mumbled words were barely audible.

"Yeah, because it got me out of work." Daniel chuckled again. Then his voice came from farther away. "I'm done. You can open your eyes now."

Her eyes sprang open. She'd hardly felt him touch her except for that one brush that she was sure had been accidental. He'd been masterful at distracting her from the fact that he unbuttoned her shirt.

She drew in a deep breath, realizing that her chest was no longer tight, and her heart rate had slowed considerably. She continued to shiver because the rest of her clothing was soaked, and she was freezing, but she'd survived Daniel's proximity.

He held up the blanket again.

She hung her hat on the hook beside the door and peeled off her flannel shirt. Then, exercising every ounce of trust she could muster, she stepped close and turned her back to him so he could lay the blanket across her shoulders.

"Have a seat by the fire and I'll find us something to eat." When she didn't move, he stepped in front of her. "Would you like me to help you to a chair?"

Riley shook her head so hard her neck spasmed.

What is wrong with me? It's only Daniel.

"Well, whenever you're ready, it'll be warmer by the fire."

She stood warily by the door, watching from the corner of her eye as he moved around the room, searching the small kitchenette that consisted of a single counter and a row of cabinets. Locating a kettle in one cupboard, he filled it at the small wash basin then took it to the fireplace and set it on the hearth.

"By the way, while I was waiting for the fire to take off, I sent a text to Jake and my dad, letting them know we'll likely spend the night here."

Riley recalled asking him to do that exact thing three years ago, but boy, the emotions besieging her tonight were sure different than the ones she experienced last time. She didn't want to admit that the thought of spending the night here with Daniel terrified her.

He returned to the kitchen and rummaged around again until he located a lantern and a flashlight. He tested both to make sure they worked. They'd need them later when it got dark outside.

Drilling a well to have water was one thing. Figuring out how to get power out to the cabins was more work than her dad wanted to deal with. That's why they had to pump the water by hand.

Riley still stood near the door shivering when the kettle whistled.

Shooting her a concerned glance, Daniel used a hot pad to take the kettle to the counter. "Hot chocolate or apple cider?" Before Riley could answer, he spoke again. "I don't know why I even bothered to ask. Chocolate of course. Double serving."

Daniel remembering her preferences caused a glimmer of warmth to settle in her chest. Oh, how she wished they could forget all that had happened to them and return to that night three years ago when they were both all too eager to be stuck in the cabin together.

He set a steaming mug on the table and gave her an expectant look that held a challenge. "It's warmer by the fire, Ri."

Nodding her head much longer than necessary, she walked toward the table. But only because Daniel returned to the kitchen. He continued to search the cabinets as he sipped from his mug. "Looks like our options are beef stew or chili. There's a box of crackers here and some canned pears and mandarin oranges. Then we have oatmeal and granola bars for breakfast."

He turned and looked at her, brows raised.

"Chili." She forced the word out.

He nodded and set to work.

She remained silent, sipping her hot chocolate, and watching every move he made. Gradually, she warmed up, and her shivering subsided. She wished she could take her wet jeans off and hang them over a chair to dry without feeling like it would make her a target.

When he placed two steaming bowls of chili on the table, she still sat in a near stupor. Silently berating herself for not helping him fix dinner, she reached for her spoon.

"Shall I pray first?" Daniel dropped into his chair after placing crackers and canned oranges on the table as well.

Riley nodded and bowed her head.

Daniel's heartfelt prayer brought tears to her eyes. The thanks he gave for their safety and the comforts of the cabin and the food they were about to eat were sweet, but it was the words he said on her behalf that were her undoing. "Father, please bless Riley that she can have peace and comfort here tonight. Bless her in her struggles to trust the people around her, and help her recognize that they care about her. Help her to heal from the things she's experienced and feel your love for her."

Riley couldn't even say, "amen" when Daniel ended the prayer, because a golf-ball-sized lump filled her throat. Blinking away the tears, she kept her eyes downcast as she ate, but she could feel his gaze on her.

He tried a couple times to make conversation, but when she didn't respond, he went quiet too.

She appreciated that he didn't feel the need to fill the silence in the small cabin with chatter. He deserved an explanation for why she'd treated him so horribly these past few weeks, and after everything he'd shared with her this afternoon, she wanted to give him one, but she didn't want to relive the ordeal with Collin.

She was almost done eating when he said her name.

"Riley?" His quiet voice brought her head up. "I don't want to be pushy, but..." He jerked a hand through his hair. "I could be a lot more supportive if you help me understand what you're going through."

A small smile lifted her lips. "You're very supportive, considering you don't know."

"Unfortunately, I think I have an inkling, but I'm trying not to jump to conclusions."

Of course, he knows. How could he not with the way I freak out every time he gets close?

Like Emily, he probably thought she'd been raped. Which wasn't far from the truth, but wasn't it better to tell him the truth than to let him wonder and worry? No matter how much she hated talking about it.

She looked out the window. The rain had slowed to a drizzle, but it was almost dark now. No way could they safely make their way home. She was stuck here for the night with Daniel. Wasn't it best to prepare him in case she had a nightmare tonight?

She shoved the last of her oranges into her mouth then picked up her bowl and Daniel's empty one. "You cooked, so I'll wash the dishes."

"Riley." Frustration and disappointment filled Daniel's voice.

Turning to face him, she braced her hands on the counter behind her. "I want to tell you, Daniel. No, I don't want to tell you, but I will. I need a few minutes. Please?" Unable to look at him any longer, she grabbed the hot pad to fetch the kettle of water from the hearth to wash the dishes.

A few minutes later, Daniel stood from the table. "I'm going to check on the horses and bring in more firewood." He slipped out the door.

CHAPTER 12

$\mathcal{R}$iley sucked in a deep breath.

I can do this. I can tell Daniel what happened, and I can spend the night here with him.

If there was anyone she could trust, it was Daniel. Her mind flashed back three years ago. Even though they'd admitted their feelings for each other and shared several passionate kisses here in this cabin, Daniel had been the perfect gentleman that night.

As soon as she finished the dishes, she made a quick trip to the tiny bathroom off the kitchen that consisted of a toilet and a sink. She expected to find Daniel back in the cabin when she came out of the bathroom, but the room was empty.

She loaded more wood on the fire, kicked her wet pants off, and hung them over a chair to dry. Then she darted to the bed on the left, straightened the blanket Daniel had pulled from it, and climbed in. She sat with her back against the wall with her legs hugged to her chest and waited for Daneil to return.

She jumped when the door finally opened.

Daniel set the firewood near the hearth, then froze when he spotted her jeans hanging over the chair. His gaze darted to the open bathroom door.

"I thought maybe you'd decided not to come back," she said quietly from her corner of the room.

He jumped and turned her direction. He must not have seen her when he glanced around the room.

"To be honest, I wasn't sure if I should." He shrugged, but there was a slight tremble in his hands as he wiped them on his jeans. "Thought it might be easier for you if I spent the night with the horses."

She gave a tight smile that could be mistaken for a grimace. "There's no room out there."

"Hence the reason I came back." He stepped closer to her bed, hesitant and slow.

One side of her mouth lifted before dropping again. He wasn't there because he wanted to be. He was only there because he didn't have another option. While a small part of her wished she didn't have to spend the night in this small cabin with him, she was grateful that if she had to be stuck with someone, at least it was Daniel.

She sucked in a deep breath. "Thank you."

"For coming back?" His brows drew together.

"For dinner and your help and...patience earlier." She grabbed a lock of hair and twisted it around her finger. "I should probably warn you...my...PTSD may get a lot worse before the night is over."

"Tell me what you need from me, Ri." Daniel's narrowed eyes and pinched lips showed his wariness as he took another hesitant step closer.

She leaned forward and patted the middle of her bed. "I need you to sit and listen."

Relief filled his face, but it took longer than it should have for his long legs to close the short distance between them. When he sat, it was in a perched position on the edge of the bed, as though prepared to dart away at a moment's notice.

"I'll always be here for you." He reached out a hand, hesitated, then pulled it back.

She hated that he didn't even dare touch her anymore. Even worse, she hated that she wasn't sure she wanted him to touch her.

"I know you will." She gave him another weak smile. "In my heart, I know you'd never hurt me, but my head..." She didn't bother finishing the sentence. She simply shook her head and balled her fists as her stomach hardened. Once again, she cursed Collin for what he took from her.

"Can you tell me what happened that sends you...into a panic any time I get close?"

She stared at the alternating glimmers of light and dark cast across the table by the dancing flames and swallowed the fear that clogged her throat. "Six weeks ago..." Her voice was quiet but steady, and she wanted to applaud herself. "A pharmaceutical rep who frequently visits our clinic asked me out. He was good looking and charming, and I was flattered, but I wasn't interested in going out with him. I could tell he was a player by the way he flirted with all the women in the office. He was everyone's favorite rep. All the nurses loved him." She tucked the lock of hair she'd been playing with behind her ear. "He asked me out in front of half the office staff, so I didn't feel like I could say no."

"We went to dinner and a play, then he invited me back to his place." She shook her head. "I told him I wasn't that kind of girl. He joked about changing my mind someday, but let it go and drove me home, where we talked for another hour in his car." She shrugged now. "I had a nice time, but I didn't expect him to ask me out again. It was obvious he wanted a physical relationship, but I'd made it clear I didn't."

"However, he came into the clinic a few days later and insisted on buying me lunch. Again, I didn't feel like I could refuse, because he asked in front of all the nurses who would love to be in my shoes. We ended up in the hospital cafeteria because I didn't have much time. He kissed my cheek before leaving and said he couldn't wait to see me again." Her voice grew louder and steadier, even though she wished she didn't feel compelled to tell Daniel all of this.

"The following week, Collin asked me out again—"

"Collin? As in the guy who's stalking you?"

"Yes." Riley finally looked at Daniel now.

"So, your stalker isn't some random guy off the street?" He scrubbed his hands over his face and shook his head.

"No."

"I'm sorry. Please continue."

"He asked me out again in front of several nurses, and while I searched for an excuse to say no, my medical assistant spoke for me and told him I'd love to go out with him again." Riley grabbed the pillow behind her and hugged it to her chest as though it could somehow alleviate the tightness there.

"The night we talked in his car, we talked about how I grew up on a ranch and I loved swing dancing. He told me he wanted to take me swing dancing and couldn't wait to see me dressed like a true cowgirl. He kept calling me his c-cowgirl all night."

Daniel's brows inched upward, and his jaw dropped. "That's why you got angry when I called you a cow—" He stopped himself.

She cringed as she nodded. "No matter how many times I tell myself it's stupid to let these little things affect me, they still do."

"It's not stupid. Triggers aren't something you can control."

"I know, but according to Emily, I can learn to control how I react to them."

"You can." Confidence filled his voice.

"I might need you to teach me how to whittle," she joked, but couldn't force enough lightness in her voice for him to take her seriously. However, a certain sense of comfort filled her at the thought of carrying a pocketknife around.

The smile on Daniel's face looked more conciliatory than humorous, but she appreciated it nonetheless.

"Anyway." She shrugged one shoulder. "I had fun on the date, I guess."

"You guess?"

"I enjoyed swing dancing, even though I had to teach him how, but..."

"But?" Daniel prompted, his voice curious.

Her gaze locked on the bobbing flames in the fireplace. "He made me uncomfortable with how touchy-feely he was. He kept putting his hand on my leg during dinner and playing with my hair and caressing my neck." She shuddered. "He kept saying things that were full of innuendos that made me uncomfortable. I was anxious for the evening to end and relieved when he finally took me home. I got out of his car as soon as he stopped, telling him he didn't need to walk me to the door. But he insisted on being a gentleman and seeing me inside."

She bunched the pillow between her fists. "I had no intention of inviting him in, but he took the key from my hand and opened the door for me. Then he walked inside before I could stop him." The more she talked, the more tension sharpened her words. "He wandered around my apartment, making small talk the whole time. He asked which bedroom was mine, and when I told him, he joked about finding out all my childhood secrets and walked into my room. I didn't follow him, because the whole situation made me extremely uncomfortable. He kept asking questions from inside my room, but I stayed in the doorway as I answered them." She scratched her neck and tugged at the ribbing of her t-shirt that suddenly felt too tight. Trying to follow Emily's counsel, she tapped her fingers against her collar bone.

"He finally came back out and sat on the couch. He patted the cushion beside him and said he wanted to have another stimulating conversation with me, like we had in his car the week before." Her chest continued to grow tight despite her tapping, so she gave up and wrapped another lock of hair around her finger and gently tugged. Just hard enough to keep her grounded in the cabin. "So I sat down, leaving a cushion between us, and we talked. During our conversation, he gradually scooted closer until his leg pressed against mine. When I told him it was getting late, and it was time for him to leave, he asked if he could have a goodnight k-kiss."

"Riley," Daniel said in a hoarse whisper, "you don't have to tell me this." He rubbed a trembling hand over his jaw.

"I think I do." Tears filled her eyes, and she swallowed the lump that filled her throat. "I need you to understand why I freak out like I do." She gave a tight chuckle and motioned toward the window where she had stood frozen this afternoon. "It's obvious I'm not coping well. If you know what happened, then maybe it'll be easier to talk about it when I get...triggered."

He nodded, but his face looked grim. "I want to help you any way I can."

Sucking in a deep breath, she picked up her story again. She needed to get it all out now. "I told Collin he was a nice guy, but I wasn't interested in kissing him, because I didn't like him like that. I just wanted to be friends."

"I assume he didn't like that answer?" Daniel's voice was gruff and full of tension now.

"No. He accused me of leading him on by going out with him repeatedly. Then he said I owed him a little something for the expensive dinner he'd bought me."

Daniel snorted, but Riley ignored him and pressed on. "He forced himself on me." She squeezed the pillow tighter, digging her fingernails into the soft batting. "I tried to shove him away, but somehow, he trapped me against the corner of the sofa." She curled her hands tighter until her nails dug into her palms, attempting to focus on the here and now. It was all she could do to keep from scratching at the crawling sensations that raced across her skin. "The way he kissed and t-touched me were barbaric. He kept accusing me of coming onto him all night and saying, 'You know you want it.'"

"Riley," Daniel's strained whisper was barely audible.

"The harder I fought, the more insistent he became." The tears now spilled down her cheeks. She didn't bother wiping them away. More would only follow. "I panicked and froze when I realized he didn't intend to take no for an answer. I couldn't believe such a horrible thing was happening to me." She shuddered and swallowed hard to dislodge another lump from her throat, then pushed on. "I finally snapped out of it and began to fight him again. But he'd gained the advantage and had me fully pinned against the couch at that point, straddling me." She rubbed absently at her cheek, recalling how coarse the fabric of their cheap couch was.

She gave a self-deprecating chuckle as feelings of being powerless swamped her. "You know, I grew up working hard and always thought of myself as a strong woman."

"You are strong, Ri!" Daniel's hand covered hers, then he tensed. Slowly, he relaxed his hold and pulled back. "I'm sorry. I didn't mean to touch you."

Appreciating his attempt to comfort her and realizing that she hadn't panicked at his touch this time, she reached out and grabbed his hand before he could fully retreat. Holding his hand might ground her better than inflicting pain on herself. She held tight, sandwiching his hand between her palms.

"I wasn't strong enough." She shook her head. "He wasn't that much bigger than me, but he was so strong." Her voice grew a little louder. "The harder I fought, the more excited he became. It was like an adrenaline rush to him. I must have hurt him at one point in my attempt to fight him off because he swore and backhanded me so hard I nearly blacked out..." Her voice trailed off as she brought her left hand to her temple, recalling the splitting pain of that blow. "I was stunned enough that I stopped fighting for a while, and he used that to his advantage. He ripped my shir—"

A low growl erupted from Daniel, and he bolted to his feet, jerking his hand from hers. "I'm sorry. I know I said I'd help you any way I can, but I can't...sit here and listen to what that bast—"

"He didn't succeed."

"What?" Daniel spun around. Despite his wide defensive stance, she saw how badly his hands trembled.

"Collin didn't succeed in raping me."

For Daniel's sake she would gloss over how close Collin had actually come to achieving his goal. She'd spare him the graphic details of that scumbag's savage assault. Details, that when she shared them with Emily last week had made her physically ill to the point that she vomited over the deck railing onto the grass.

"Paige came home before Collin could—" Riley stopped, not wanting to spell out the repugnant details any more than Daniel wanted to hear them.

"Thank goodness." Exhaling abruptly, Daniel dropped down onto the bed again. "I'm sorry. I don't mean to make light of what you went through. I'm just glad..." His words trailed off.

"Me too."

"That should never have happened to you, though."

He propped his elbows on his knees and scrubbed his hands over his face, then shoved them into his hair. It was the same posture he had at church each Sunday.

"No, it shouldn't have. But because it did, I find myself analyzing every little thing that I said and did, asking myself if I'd sent the wrong message."

"No. That man's a—" Daniel lowered his voice before letting loose the swear word.

"That's exactly what I called him while he was attacking me."

He lifted his head. "Please tell me you went to the police."

"I did, and I filed a restraining order. He was questioned but not arrested."

"What?" Daniel's brow lowered.

"He comes from a very influential family. Collin's last name is Ainsworth." Riley let Daniel put the pieces together.

His head jerked back. "As in Senator Ainsworth?"

"Yes, Collin is the senator's son." Riley nodded. "He managed to convince the police that we were just making out and that things got a little...steamy and rowdy."

Daniel swore under his breath again.

"He showed up at my work the following week and convinced my medical assistant to let him wait in an exam room so he could surprise me."

Daniel's brows dropped even lower, and a dangerous look filled his eyes. "Let me guess, you hadn't told anyone at work what he'd done to you?"

"No, I didn't think they'd believe me, because they all loved Collin." She shook her head. "As soon as I entered the exam room, he blocked the door, so I couldn't get out. I should have screamed, but I froze in fear again. And he assaulted me again, though not to the extent that he did the first time. He also threatened me and told me he wasn't done with me."

"So, you decided to come home." It was more of a statement than a question. He shook his head again. "And it's only been a month? No wonder you're so easily jumpy and anxious."

"Emily told me it would take time to feel normal again, but a simple phone call or a letter from him sends me right back to my apartment where I'm pinned against the couch." Her hands and voice trembled again as she thought about how trapped and powerless she'd felt.

Daniel took her hands in both of his. "Tell me how I can help, Pockets."

She gave him a watery smile. "Believe it or not, when you call me Pockets, it takes me back to a happier time in my life when Collin didn't exist. It reminds me I don't need to fear you."

"You don't." He leaned toward her until they locked gazes. "I promise I will never hurt you, Princess Sparkle Pockets."

Riley laughed. "Just Pockets. Lose the princess and the sparkles, Tarzan." She leaned toward him until her forehead rested against his shoulder.

Daniel sucked in a sharp breath as though bracing himself for an attack, then gradually relaxed. When she didn't pull away, he released her hand and brought his up to caress the back of her head.

The hesitancy and gentleness of his touch brought fresh tears to her eyes, and she sniffled. She hated that what Collin did to her made her fear every man around, even the one whose touch she used to crave.

DANIEL HOPED Riley couldn't feel the tremble in his hand. He wanted to wrap her in his arms and promise to never let anyone hurt her again, but he didn't dare touch her any more than he already did. He also wanted to punch something, or rather, a certain someone. And boy, did he ache for a drink. Better yet, a whole bottle.

Riley had censored her story after his outburst, he was sure of it, but he was grateful. He didn't need to hear every sordid detail to know she endured something horrible. No wonder she had nightmares and was so easily triggered.

He felt ill thinking about how that man had hurt the woman he'd loved for so many years.

"You really are a strong woman, Ri. You're courageous and brave."

"I don't feel brave at all." She lifted her head and swiped the tears from one cheek with the back of her hand. "I mean, the thought of spending the night here with you had me cowering by the window this afternoon."

"It takes a lot of courage to tell people what you've been through." He reached up and gently wiped the tears from her other cheek. "What do I need to do to make this more bearable for you? It's been a while since I've slept under the stars, but I'll do it, if you want me to."

"No. It's way too wet and cold out there." She looked down to their clasped hands. "I should probably let you distract me with card games, but I'm exhausted." Right on cue, she covered her mouth as a yawn took over.

"You still aren't sleeping well, are you?"

"No. You?"

He shrugged. He wouldn't tell her his nightmares had only gotten worse since she came home.

"Thank you for listening." She put her free hand on his arm, sending warmth radiating through him. "And for telling me about your struggles. I know it wasn't easy for you to tell me, but I'm glad you told me."

"I've kept it hidden long enough." He let out a heavy sigh. "I think you're right about getting it out there. It makes it easier to talk about now that you know." He swiped a hand across his mouth. "I may as well be honest with you, I'm really thirsty at the moment. Hearing what you went through has made the cravings stronger than they've been in a long time."

"I'm sorry." She squeezed his hand. "What can I do to help you? Do we need to find you a stick to whittle?" Her gaze darted to the logs near the fireplace.

He let his gaze follow hers. "Nah, I'll get through it. Just don't be surprised if I suddenly drop and start doing pushups."

Understanding lit her eyes. "That's why you put the gym in that extra room at the stables. You work out when you're craving alcohol?"

"Working out, whittling, riding Rebel, and playing guitar. Those are my coping strategies now."

"Robert mentioned a few weeks ago that you'd learned to play the guitar. You'll have to play for me sometime."

"I'm really not that good. But it keeps my fingers busy and gives my mind something to focus on besides...well, you know." He let go of her hand and stood. "If you help me, we can lift my bunk up and over the table and set it in front of the cabinets over there. This cabin is so small it won't put much distance between us, but—"

"No. It's fine where it is. I want you close by."

"Are you sure?"

"Yes. Your presence actually helps ground me."

"Okay then." He shuffled his feet, trying to figure out how to take his damp jeans off and hang them over the other chair to dry without making Riley uncomfortable. He pointed over his shoulder. "I need to use the bathroom before I turn in for the night."

Nodding, she shifted and plumped her pillow.

Praying the night didn't turn out to be a disaster for both of them, he grabbed the lantern off the table and retreated to the bathroom. He'd barely had time to use the facility before a noise in the cabin startled him. The scraping of the bed frame reverberated across the wood floor.

She must have decided she doesn't want me sleeping close to her after all.

He stared at himself in the small circular mirror above the sink. He didn't look any different, but he felt different. Lighter somehow. He'd kept his secrets hidden for so long they had become a heavy burden. One he didn't need to carry alone anymore.

Okay, I haven't exactly been carrying them alone, but I'm glad Riley knows.

Did she feel better after telling him her secrets? As much as it sickened him, it was good to finally understand what she was going through.

The thump of a chair on the floor pulled his attention away from his reflection, and he decided there was no point in delaying the inevitable. He may as well get some sleep while he could in case he or Riley ended up having nightmares tonight.

He turned the wick down on the lantern and doused the flame as he came out of the bathroom, but Riley had loaded more wood on the fire, and firelight illuminated the small cabin. She hadn't moved his bed across the room like he'd thought, she'd pushed the beds together, leaving only a narrow walkway on the outside of each.

He froze. Did she really want him sleeping that close to her? He doubted he'd sleep at all with her in arm's reach.

She lay in her bed facing the wall, her back to him.

Riley lifted her head and looked over her shoulder. "If your jeans are still damp like mine, you can hang them over the other chair. Don't worry I won't peek." She grinned and winked before laying back down, giving him a glimpse of the old Riley.

He cleared his throat. "Are you sure you want the beds so close?"

"I meant it when I said your presence grounds me." The glimpse of the old Riley was gone, and her voice was once again hesitant and meek. "I want to be able to touch you if I have a bad dream."

A spark of warmth filled his chest momentarily taking his breath away.

Good Gravy! This woman sure wove her way back into my heart fast.

He set the lantern on the table and unbuckled his belt. Sending up another little prayer that his heart didn't get broken again, he pulled off his jeans and threw them over the chair. Not wanting to make any sudden movements that would startle or frighten Riley, he took his time settling into the too small bed.

"Is it safe to roll over?"

"Yes." Daniel's voice croaked, and heat filled his face.

Riley shifted until she faced him. Their eyes met, and in the firelight, he saw something there he hadn't seen since she came home. A measure of peace, perhaps?

She laid her arm out with her hand resting at the edge of her mattress, palm up. It looked so much like an invitation he couldn't resist.

Moving slowly so as not to startle her—or make her regret her decision—he slid his palm across the sheet and into hers. He hooked his thumb against hers and curled his fingers around her hand.

He'd held Riley's hand so many times throughout his life. When they were young it was so he could guide her up a tree or across the creek. As a teenager, it was to drag her out to drive the four-wheeler so he could practice roping the fake steer tied behind it. Then three summers ago, he'd held her hand in a much different way.

Tonight, however, the connection felt monumental. She was the piece he'd been searching the whole ranch for over the past seven months. It wasn't the ranch he missed when he was away. It was Riley.

Her fingers curled around his hand, and a small smile graced her lips. Then her lashes fluttered closed.

It wasn't only peace he'd seen in her eyes. He'd seen trust. Despite everything she'd been through and everything she knew about him, Riley trusted him.

His heart swelled in his chest, filling him with contentment. He closed his eyes and let his mind once again replay that night three years ago.

CHAPTER 13

*I*t was early afternoon when they arrived back at the ranch. Riley longed for a hot bath, but knowing Jake and Zane, they probably had a list a mile long of things they needed her and Daniel to do.

"There they are," Jake rounded the stables as Daniel and Riley dismounted their horses. "Glad you two didn't get swept away in the storm. I prayed you'd make it to the cabin okay. Imagine my relief when I finally got your text around nine last night." He studied each of their faces, no doubt searching for ill effects of being forced to spend the night together.

Grateful Riley didn't feel the need to force it, she gave Jake her biggest smile. "We were soaked by the time we reached the cabin, but we made it before the worst of the storm hit."

"Glad to hear it." Jake continued to eye them. "And you're both okay?" He spoke slowly, deliberately.

"I'm fine," Riley assured her brother.

She was better than fine. She was great. For the first time in a month, she'd slept through the night. No nightmares. No restlessness. It was all because of Daniel's presence. She was sure of it. She'd felt safe and secure with him next to her.

Jake's eyes shifted to Daniel.

"I'm good, man." He too smiled, but it was the cheerfulness with which he said the words that made Riley grin again.

For the second time in their lives, something significant happened for Riley and Daniel in that small cabin. She couldn't wait to ride back there with him again—maybe to replenish the supplies they'd used.

Jake gave an approving nod, then changed the subject. "How far did you make it on the fence?"

"We finished up the last five miles this morning before riding back," Daniel said as he set to work unsaddling Rebel.

"Excellent. I might have to give you two a raise."

Daniel said, "I could go for that," at the same moment Riley said, "I won't argue with that."

Riley laughed. She'd forgotten how she and Daniel often thought alike after spending a little time together. Back when they had dated, her brother Robert often joked about them becoming the same person.

She locked gazes with Daniel. A spark of warmth ignited in her abdomen. He winked before looking away, and the warmth spread through her body. A fluttering sensation in her stomach quickly followed the warmth, morphing into attraction for the man sporting a three-day stubble.

After the way they'd talked and joked all morning and shared more about their individual struggles, she felt they were well on their way to being best friends again.

Jake helped unload Samson and brush the horses down, then followed them into the house for lunch. The scent of hot oil and bread dough hit Riley the moment she opened the back door.

Scones.

Riley had been known to eat Lottie's scones with whipped honey butter until she was physically ill.

Will Jake give me the afternoon off if I eat myself into a food coma? Then I could take a hot bath.

Emily entered the kitchen through the swinging door as they walked through the mud room. Like Jake, she searched Riley's and

Daniel's faces, her eyes full of concern. "How did you two fare last night?"

Daniel grinned and gave her two thumbs up.

Riley settled for a genuine smile. "We had a good night."

Emily studied their faces a little longer before her own lips turned up. "I'm glad."

Riley had just finished washing her hands when Lottie got her attention. "Look what arrived for you about ten minutes ago." The housekeeper pulled a small card from a massive arrangement of red roses and baby's breath in a crystal vase. She held it out to Riley.

A cold chill swept over Riley as the blood drained from her face. Her good mood plummeted right alongside her stomach. She grabbed the counter behind her to steady herself.

They're from him. Why won't that scumbag leave me alone?

She didn't need to read the card to know the flowers were from Collin.

Lottie wiggled the card when Riley made no move to take it. "I think you have a secret admirer."

"Who delivered them?" Her words were sharp enough to cause Lottie to fall back a step.

Lottie frowned as she shrugged her shoulders. "A delivery guy from the florist in town."

Riley tamped down the fear that reared its ugly head every time Collin intruded into her life. Anger rushed in on its heels, and she fanned the flames. She was sick and tired of letting that man intrude in her life.

Swearing out loud, she grabbed the bouquet—vase and all—and shoved it into the trash can, sending a few errant leaves and rose petals flying.

"Why did you do that?" Lottie's mouth dropped open, and her eyebrows shot up almost to her hairline.

Riley spun around and found Daniel wearing a sympathetic expression. "Tell her! Tell all of them!" She waved a hand encompassing everyone in the kitchen. "Call my mom and Robert. I want everyone to know. I don't want anyone to accept a delivery like this again." Then she turned and stormed out of the house, slamming the door behind her.

She'd barely hit the lane when Daniel raced out of the house behind her. "Riley, wait!"

"What are you doing?"

"I'm coming with you."

She stomped her foot on the pavement. "I don't even know where I'm going."

"Well, wherever it is, I'm going with you. You shouldn't have to be alone right now."

"What if I want to be alone?"

She didn't. It allowed her to get too much inside her own head where she second guessed every interaction with Collin and made her question, "Why me?" It also made her feel bad for being so affected by what happened to her when it wasn't nearly as bad as what some women experienced.

"You don't."

"How can you tell?"

"Because you stopped walking when I called your name."

Huffing, she folded her arms and turned away from him. Deep down, she'd been hoping he would follow her, even though she'd told him to tell the others what happened to her.

"But I need you to tell the others." She shook her head in frustration. "I can't keep reliving it over and over, but I think I want everyone to know."

"You think?"

"I don't want people to look at me differently. What if they don't believe me, or think I'm seeking attention? They might think I brought it on myself."

"This is your family, Pockets. Of course, they'll believe you." He stepped closer and took her hand. "They all know if you wanted attention, you would do it in some loud, sensational way. Not with something like this."

"You're right, but will you tell them for me, please? I meant it when I said I don't want to keep reliving it."

He tilted his head toward the house. "Emily said she'd tell them."

Her eyes widened. She'd explained everything to Emily in great detail, hoping if she got it out, it wouldn't have so much of an effect on her. Judging by her reaction to the flowers, it hadn't helped as much as she'd hoped.

"Don't worry, she'll give them the edited version you gave me last night. Not the full, graphic explanation you shared with your therapist."

Riley stomped her foot again and let out a little growl. "I need a distraction. But I don't want to go to the punching bag still wearing yesterday's clothes." She pointed toward the house. "And I definitely don't want to go back in there right now."

"So, let's go for a ride."

"Ugh, I've just spent two days in the saddle."

"I know, so let's ride four-wheelers."

She hadn't ridden a four-wheeler much since she'd come home. Not for pleasure anyway. A good long ride would do her some good, but a ride alone wasn't enough to blow off the kind of steam that she needed to vent.

"Okay, let's do it." She grabbed his arm as he turned toward the equipment shed. "But I'm in the mood to be destructive. Go in the house and get a couple rifles."

"That's what I mean about loud and sensational." Daniel laughed. "I'll be right back. Make sure the four-wheelers have plenty of gas to make it out to the shooting range and back."

Riley wanted to kiss Daniel ten minutes later when he arrived at the equipment shed carrying two rifles slung over his shoulder and a heaping plate full of scones dripping with Lottie's whipped honey butter. She settled for stealing the plate from him and lavishing her attention on the scones.

"Hey, you'd better save me a couple of those, Pockets."

"No promitheth," she said around a mouthful of fried dough.

Racing across the ranch and shooting were exactly what Riley needed, and after beating Daniel in a friendly target practice competition, she felt even better.

Her euphoria quickly dissipated, however, when they returned to the ranch house to find her mother's and Robert's vehicles parked out front.

Daniel must have noticed that her gait slowed because he put a hand on her shoulder. "It's okay, Pockets. They are your family. They're here because they love you."

"I know. I just…" She stopped talking when she struggled to find a valid reason to explain her hesitancy.

"Do you want me to go in with you?"

"Yes." She grabbed his hand and walked toward the back door of the house. She released it again less than a minute later when she found herself enveloped in her mother's arms seconds after walking into the house.

"Oh, my dear, sweet girl." Faith Winters was a small woman, but she gave the most amazing hugs. "I'm so sorry you went through that."

Riley caught sight of the love and concern on the faces of everyone in the room; her protective older brothers, her sweet and caring sisters-in-law, Zane and Lottie, her second parents. She squeezed her eyes closed, fighting the emotion that clogged her throat. A few tears managed to leak from the corner of her eyes.

Why had she thought keeping what happened to her a secret was the best way to protect herself and everyone around her? She'd isolated herself because of shame and fear, but it had only made it all worse. Pride kept her from admitting she wasn't strong enough to stop Collin, but now, she realized real strength came from trusting others. She'd treated everyone around her horribly, and she felt terrible about that.

"I wish you'd felt like you could tell me," Mom said as she continued to hold her.

Riley sniffled. "It wasn't just you mom. Except for Dr. Nelson, I didn't tell anyone until last week."

"But Emily said you went to the police." Robert stepped close.

Mom released her, and they turned to face her oldest brother.

"A lot of good it did me. Collin managed to talk his way out of even being charged."

"You should have called Uncle Lincoln."

"Why?" Riley could count on one hand the number of times she'd met their mom's much older brother.

When Faith and her sisters settled in Providence, Grandpa and Grandma Whittaker bought land out by the lake and built a cabin on it. Most of the Whittaker Family get-togethers took place at that cabin. Uncle Lincoln rarely made it.

"He was appointed to the state supreme court a few years ago."

Riley had forgotten that. Probably because they didn't associate with Uncle Lincoln's family very often.

"I don't know that it would have done any good. Collin made the police believe that we'd only been having a passionate make-out session."

Jessie stepped forward. "With Collin's father being a senator, it would have become very public. I'm not sure Riley would have wanted that."

"No, I wouldn't have."

"I suppose you're right." Robert gave her a gentle look. "Can I give you a hug, Sis?"

"I'd like that."

Once again, Riley found herself enveloped in an accepting and comforting hug, and she chided herself for not telling her family sooner.

"I'm so proud of you, Ri. It takes a lot of courage to stand tall in the face of something like this."

And here came the tears again. "I don't feel very courageous."

"But you are. Emily told us how you fought off Ainsworth."

"I didn't fight hard enough."

"Sh…" Robert's arms tightened around her. "You did the best you could under the circumstances."

When Robert released her, Jake waited with open arms. The moment she stepped into them, he apologized. "I'm sorry for being so hard on you. I had no idea what you were going through."

"It's not your fault. I should have told you all sooner." She gave a tearful chuckle. "I'm the one who needs to apologize for repeatedly blowing up at you."

Jake chuckled. "I'm just glad to know you didn't revert back to your hormonal teenage years."

Riley shoved his shoulder as she left his embrace. She soon found herself wrapped in one hug after another until she'd made the rounds that brought her back to Daniel. Everyone thought of Daniel as family, but because of their shared history, he was so much more than that to Riley.

The way he held her hand last night comforted her in ways nothing else could, but was she ready to hug him?

He took a small step back, clasping his hands in front of him, letting her know he didn't expect her to hug him. Or maybe he was protecting himself, in case she suddenly freaked out.

She wanted her best friend back. The one whose shoulder she cried on after her dad died, and the one who picked her up and swung her around when he won first place in steer wrestling at the state high school rodeo championship.

Before she could change her mind or give her brain a chance to come up with a reason why hugging Daniel wasn't a good idea, she stepped forward and wrapped her arms around him.

He tensed, like she expected him to, but then he relaxed and slid his arms around her. He rested his chin on top of her head and let out a deep sigh.

Something inside Riley melted, and a strange sensation of expansion filled her chest. She let go of the belief that to protect herself she needed to keep everyone at a distance. Then she chided herself for believing Daniel wanted her to walk away from her dreams so he could follow his all those years ago. She should have known Daniel would do anything for her and that he would have made sure she reached all her goals.

They were good for each other. They always had been. And they could be again. Warmth flooded over her as she considered a second chance with Daniel. One thing was for sure; she wouldn't walk away this time.

She clung a little tighter when his arms loosened, not ready to let go yet. "Thank you."

"For what?" His whispered words tickled her scalp.

"For being you." She released him finally and turned around to see a mixture of pleased and surprised expressions on everyone's faces.

Robert recovered first, his sly grin disappearing as he clapped his hands. "Alright, starting next week, the sheriff's office will be holding self-defense classes. I need all of you to help me spread the word."

CHAPTER 14

*R*iley walked out of the tack room carrying a lead rope for Misty, but stopped short when Crew and Brody rounded the corner of the stables. She'd been fortunate not to have to cross paths with the other ranch hands very often. When she did, Zane, Jake, or Daniel were usually nearby, so the two wannabe cowboys stayed on their best behavior.

That didn't stop her stomach from sinking and her heart from racing every time their gazes raked over her like she was a juicy steak.

"Whooee!" Crew took off his cowboy hat and fanned himself. "Today's our lucky day, Brody. We get to work with the babe."

Riley's skin crawled, and excess saliva filled her mouth. She schooled her features the best she could despite the turmoil raging inside her. "Work with me?" She forced a laugh and shook her head. "As if you could keep up with me." Refusing to be intimidated, she pushed her way between the two men.

Daniel rounded the corner of the stables just then, and she wanted to run into his arms to let him shield her, but she held her head high and walked toward the corral where Jake checked over one of the horses.

"Playing hard to get, huh?" Crew's words followed her. "I'll play any game you want, darlin'."

"Leave her alone." Tension filled Daniel's sharp voice.

Riley looked back in time to see Daniel bump Crew's shoulder as he passed.

"Being possessive, huh, Slim?" Crew laughed. "Can't say I blame you, but the girl needs to know she has options." He raised his voice. "Come on, sexy cowgirl, I'll take you for a ride you'll never forget."

Furious, Riley spun on her heel, intent on lashing out at Crew, but Daniel beat her to him.

He grabbed Crew by the front of his shirt and slammed him up against the stables. "Watch your mouth!"

"Daniel!" Both Riley and Jake shouted at the same time.

Jake sprang into action, however, whereas Riley simply stared, stunned. He darted to the fence, stepped on the bottom pole, and vaulted himself up and over like a lithe teenager. He pulled Daniel off Crew and shoved him away. "Go cool off."

Crew sneered and started laughing. "Yeah, man, chill ou—"

His words were cut off by Jake slamming him up against the wall even harder than Daniel had. "Don't you ever talk to my sister like that again. One more crude and inappropriate word out of your mouth and I'll call your case worker. I'm sure he'd love to hear how you lost this job too."

Jake pulled Crew away from the wall and shoved him toward the front of the stables. "Now, go get the stalls cleaned out so we can start the real work." He shot Brody a glare next, daring him to argue.

As soon as Crew and Brody were out of sight, Jake turned to Daniel, who fingered his new eight-month, black and gold sobriety chip. "You okay?"

"I'm fine." The words were little more than a grunt.

"They're not worth it." Jake put his hand on Daniel's shoulder and gave him a shake.

"Did you hear what they said to Riley?" Daniel's voice turned defensive.

"It's called posturing. He doesn't have the social skills to realize

Riley's not impressed by that garbage. She's smarter than that. And so are you." Jake wrapped his fist around Daniel's hand that held the chip. "Don't let a couple blow-hards ruin what you've worked so hard for."

When Daniel nodded his head and slipped his chip back into his pocket, Jake released his shoulder. "You two get your horses saddled. We've got to get the herd separated."

After Jake walked away, Riley stepped up beside Daniel. "Are you sure you're okay?"

"Yes." He nodded but he didn't meet her gaze, and the muscle in his jaw ticked.

She thought about asking him if he wanted a hug, but she figured he was too proud for that. Instead, she stepped in front of him, rocked up on her toes and pressed a kiss to his cheek.

He startled and stared at her, wide-eyed.

"Thanks for coming to my rescue." She squeezed his hand. "But Jake's right. We—and I mean me more than you—need to not let stupid things like that bother us."

"You can shake it off just like that?" Daniel caught her hand as she was about to let go.

"No, not just like that. But I'm trying to choose not to let what happened to me control my life."

Daniel sighed. "Right, because our thoughts and actions are the only things we can control."

Riley nodded as she stepped away. "I see Emily gave you the same counsel she gave me."

"Yeah, but I think you're picking up on it quicker than I am."

DANIEL WAS FILTHY, sun-burned, and exhausted by the time they finished branding, vaccinating, and dehorning hundreds of calves. It had been a grueling day, but working alongside Riley made all the hard work worth it.

She was still by his side as they turned their horses back into the corral after reuniting the calves with their mothers. She'd worked as hard as any of the rest of them today, and she was filthy too, but she looked radiant and beautiful. He'd had a hard time taking his eyes off her most of the day, especially while she and Misty separated the calves from their mothers. She knew how to handle a horse, and she did it with grace and poise.

He hadn't stopped thinking about that kiss all day. Sure, it was only a peck on the cheek, but what did she mean by it? He suspected she did it simply to distract him. And boy, did it work.

The little thoughts he'd had here and there about possibly getting back together with Riley blossomed into full-blown fantasies. He had to keep reminding himself not to get carried away. She deserved a better man than him. She shouldn't saddle herself to a recovering alcoholic who had a sordid past.

He fell into step beside her as they walked toward the back of the big house. All he wanted was a hot shower, food, and his bed. And a few minutes alone with Riley.

Their steps slowed as they approached the back of the house.

She tucked her hands into her back pockets. "So...I guess I'll see you at dinner in a little bit?"

He looked more closely at her. Why was she suddenly acting nervous?

"Yeah, I'll be over after I get cleaned up."

"Okay, do you...uh...do you want to maybe do something tonight?"

He recalled how she'd repeatedly invited him to hang out in the evenings three years ago and how that had led to them dating.

"Something...like what?" He said the words slowly, with caution.

She rocked up on her toes as she shrugged. "Maybe we could watch a movie or something."

He'd probably fall asleep on her, but he couldn't think of a better way to spend the evening than by Riley's side, even though he shouldn't encourage a relationship between them.

Before he could answer, however, Crew and Brody stepped out of the stables and walked their direction.

"Riley." Crew stopped a few yards away and kicked at a rock with the toe of his boot.

Daniel stepped forward, half blocking Riley, fists balled.

"Relax, Slim." Crew held his hands out in a pacifying gesture. "I just want to apologize to Riley for what I said this morning." He looked back at Riley. "I should never have disrespected you like that."

"No, you shouldn't have." Daniel's tone was hard.

Riley put a hand on his arm. "Thank you, Crew."

"I've never seen anyone handle a horse like you do. Or work as hard as you. You're something else."

He turned to walk away, but Brody put his hand out. "Crew and me are going to Scooter's tonight. You guys wanna join us?"

"No thanks." Daniel didn't even need to think twice about the invitation.

He avoided Scooters like the plague nowadays. He used to love going to the modern-day diner and dance hall with old-west saloon vibes, but most people went there for the alcohol and dancing rather than the food. It was too much of a temptation for him.

Riley grabbed Daniel's arm and grinned at him. A glimmer of light filled her eyes, causing his breath to hitch. It was the first real glimpse he'd seen of the old Riley since she came home.

"We should go. It's been ages since we've been dancing together."

It had been years since they'd danced together, and he wanted nothing more than to dance with Riley again, even in his exhausted state. He'd felt horrible for refusing when she, Paige, and Damon begged him to go dancing with them when they were all home for Jake and Emily's wedding last year. He'd only been sober for a couple of months and knew he couldn't tempt himself that way.

And I fell off the wagon less than a month later anyway.

He cleared the tightness from his throat and lowered his voice so only she could hear. "I'm not sure I dare go to Scooters."

Her face fell and concern flitted through her eyes. "Oh right. Sorry, I forgot about your..." She let her words die off and gave the other ranch hands a weak smile. "Not tonight, guys. We're wiped out. Thanks for the invitation though."

"Your loss," Brody said as they turned and walked away.

It killed him to see that light die from her eyes. Would it always be that way between them? Would he always be the thief of her joy because of his weakness?

Riley stepped up the first stair of the back deck, but he caught her hand.

"I'm sorry, Ri. You know I would go if..."

"I know." She squeezed his hand. "It's okay."

No. It's not. I hate stealing your happiness.

"You know what? Maybe we should go." His mouth went dry even as he said the words, but he wanted Riley to be happy again. If dancing would help her move beyond what happened to her, then he would take her dancing.

Riley put a hand on his shoulder. "I understand how difficult it is for you to go there. So, it's probably best if we stay home and watch a movie."

He searched her face, looking for that little spark of light in her eyes. The prospect of spending time with him didn't bring the same light as the thought of dancing.

He squeezed her hand. "I want to take you dancing, Ri. If you promise to stay by my side, I think I can handle it."

"Really?" Her eyes lit up, sparkling and bright. She rocked up on her toes, bouncing with excitement. "Are you sure?"

"Yes, I'm sure. Just don't expect me to do many lifts, my arms feel like jelly after all the work we did today."

"That's okay." She let out a little squeal. "I promise I will not let you out of my sight."

Daniel hoped that was enough. If he couldn't keep it together for the woman he'd always loved, he feared he'd never succeed in staying sober.

"I'm going to get showered." She patted his shoulder before pulling her hand back. "Do we want to eat here or at Scooters?"

His mom's cooking was much better than anything they served at Scooters, but he could go for one of their pulled pork sandwiches with their sweet and spicy barbecue sauce. It was the only decent thing on the menu.

"You decide," he said as he stepped back.

"I haven't had their pulled pork and steak fries in ages." She grinned again and the light in her eyes intensified. "Let's eat out."

"Sounds good, as long as I get to pay."

Her grin grew. "Like a date?"

He locked gazes with her for a long moment; the air between them charged with electricity. "I want to take you on a date, Pockets."

She shoved her hands into her back pockets again as her lips lifted in a shy smile. Then she rocked up on her toes. "Good because I would love to go on a date with you, Tarzan."

Daniel rubbed the back of his neck as Riley darted into the house. He turned to walk down the lane, sending up a little prayer that this night didn't turn into a disaster.

CHAPTER 15

*R*iley collided with Jake when she came out of her room.

He caught her by the shoulders. "Whoa there. Slow down." His brows hiked up as he took in her fancy white shirt with a ruffled V neck and lacy sleeves, indigo jeans with silver stitching and rhinestone accents on the pockets in the shape of a butterfly, and even more expensive white boots. "Where are you going all dolled up?"

She may have gone a little overboard, but she was so excited about going out with Daniel that not even the memory of what happened the last time she went swing dancing was enough to dampen her spirits.

"Daniel and I are going to Scooters." She stepped away from him, intent on not keeping her date waiting.

"Hold up. Scooters?" When she nodded, he shook his head. "That's not a good idea."

"He's taking me on a date." She propped her hands on her hips. "You said you'd be okay with us getting back together. This is the first step."

"But Daniel shouldn't go to Scooters or any other place that serves alcohol. The temptation will be too much for him."

She'd seen Daniel's hesitation when Brody invited them to join them at Scooter's, but when he insisted they should go after all, she assumed he figured he could handle it. "He's a lot stronger than everyone thinks. He needs the chance to prove that to himself."

"You might be right." Jake let out a sigh, but then he scowled and pointed a finger at her. "Keep a close eye on him. Get him out of there if it looks like he's struggling. The last thing we want is for him to relapse."

"I will." Because she was in such a good mood, Riley rocked up on her toes and planted a quick kiss on Jake's cheek even though they weren't the demonstrative type. "Don't be a worry wart." Then she headed to the door. "And don't wait up."

Daniel's wide eyes tracked her progress down the front steps, and Riley couldn't help the smile that covered her face. He was so stunned he almost forgot to get out and open the truck door for her. A faux pas that would have had his mother lecturing him.

"You look...incredible." The breathless quality of his voice made all the effort she'd gone to worth it.

"You don't look so bad yourself." She brushed an imaginary speck of lint from the chest of his smoky-gray button down. The red and white design across the shoulders made them look broader than ever. "You clean up quite nicely."

She caught a whiff of his woodsy cologne as she climbed into his truck. It was the one she gave him for Christmas years ago. She loved how it smelled on him.

They made casual conversation as they drove, but Riley couldn't keep her mind from wandering.

A bond had been growing between them since that night at the cabin. One that became stronger every day. Her attraction to him had grown right along with it. She knew she could trust him in ways she couldn't trust other men. She trusted him to do more than hold her hand.

The idea of asking Daniel to kiss her to see if she could handle it had been playing in her mind all week, and she couldn't seem to shake it. She didn't want to.

Riley had ample opportunity during the lengthy drive to contemplate ways to convince Daniel to kiss her. It was quickly becoming less of a desire to see if she could tolerate it, and more of something she wanted. Badly.

~

RILEY TOOK Daniel's breath away. From her brilliant smile to her fancy boots, and from her dark wavy hair to her rhinestone-studded pockets.

She was stunning. The light in her eyes when she smiled reflected the old carefree Riley who enjoyed having a good time. He hoped he didn't do something to dim that light by the time the night was over.

The lengthy drive to Scooters out by the county line passed much too fast, with the knot that formed in his stomach when he told her he wanted to take her dancing growing the entire time.

Riley had no idea the turmoil raging inside him, and he wasn't about to tell her.

The moment they turned into the parking lot of Scooters, his throat went as dry as the Sahara, and the knot in his stomach clenched tighter. His grip on the steering wheel tightened as he searched for a parking spot.

As soon as he put the truck into park, Riley turned troubled eyes on him. "Are you sure you want to do this?"

No, but I want to make you happy.

He nodded instead of speaking because his tongue felt like it was made of sandpaper. Then he opened his door.

Riley's face still registered concern when she slid down from the truck seat. She grabbed his hand before he could even close her door. "If this becomes too much, say the word and we'll leave, okay?" When he didn't respond, she squeezed his hand. "Promise me you'll tell me if you need to leave."

"I promise." The words sounded flat around the dryness of his mouth. Determined to face and slay this demon, he repeated the words to the serenity prayer as he led her through the crowded parking lot to the front door of the dance hall and bar.

Daniel had expected an extreme thirst to hit him the moment he stepped through the door. What he didn't expect was the overwhelming sense of nostalgia the moment his gaze landed on the polished wooden dance floor in the center of the massive room. He couldn't count the number of hours he'd spent on that floor with Riley and Paige.

Upbeat country music accompanied by the tapping of boots, laughter, and even the clank of silverware and dishes filled the space. The smell of fried foods, grilled meats, and body odor permeated the air. But above it all, the pungent smell of hops and barley, and the fruity yet fermented scent of wine teased Daniel's senses.

His mouth watered. The sudden urge for a double shot of whiskey hit him like a semi-truck. He imagined the burn of alcohol sliding down his throat, warming him from the inside out.

Riley tugged his arm in the opposite direction of the bar. "Come on, I see a table near the back."

Even though alcohol was served on the restaurant side of Scooters as well, the smell of liquor decreased as the aroma of fried foods intensified.

Riley dropped into a chair. "Doesn't that greasy, fried food smell make your mouth water?"

Daniel gave her a tight smile. "No. It smells kind of gross actually."

Her gaze zeroed in on his face. "Are you okay?"

He chewed on his lip for a moment before answering. "You want the truth?" When she nodded, he said, "Not really."

"Do we need to leave?" Her face fell, extinguishing the light in her eyes. "We can drive to the Tri-Cities area and catch a movie if you want."

He caught her hand as she started to stand. "We're not leaving. Yes, I'm struggling, but with your help, I'll be fine."

I hope.

She leaned close. "I won't think any less of you if you decide you need to leave."

Her warm breath caressed his cheek, and a surge of desire shot through him. His gaze dropped to her glossy red lips. Now there was a distraction that erased all thoughts of alcohol from his mind. Too bad Riley wouldn't welcome a kiss from him or any man for a long time.

"Good to know." He squeezed her hand. "I'm not leaving without dancing with you. So let's track down a server and get some food."

She grinned. "Sounds good."

The third best thing about Scooters—besides the dancing and the pulled pork sandwiches—was the fast service, provided you ordered the right thing. Once their food arrived, Daniel found it easier to ignore the fact that he was surrounded by alcohol, and when Riley pulled him out onto the dance floor, the rest of the world faded away.

He was swept back in time as they effortlessly danced together, shifting seamlessly from one move to another. Dancing with Riley was pure bliss. She was graceful and athletic, and every time he swung her out and she returned to his arms, he sighed in contentment.

She's what I've been searching for these past few years.

When the first slow song played, Riley didn't hesitate to step into his arms. His heart pounded in his chest as he pulled her close and they slowly swayed. This woman was quickly coming to mean the world to him. Again. With all she'd been through, she wouldn't be ready for a relationship for a long time, but he didn't think he could ever let her go again.

If she chose to leave the ranch at the end of the summer, it would crush him. His sobriety wouldn't stand a chance.

I could go with her.

Even as the thought filled his head, he feared he wouldn't be able to stay sober if he left the ranch. Riley deserved a man who wasn't weak and packing baggage. A man whose past wasn't likely to come back and haunt them years down the road.

She looked up at him through her lashes. "You're the best I've ever danced with."

His heart swelled in his chest, and a curl of desire snaked through his stomach. Her blue eyes were so bright and trusting. The light that shone in them was simply radiant. Now that the spark had returned to her eyes, he never wanted to do anything to extinguish it.

Her lips were no longer glossy, but they were full and red, and the flush on her cheeks made her even more attractive. The urge to kiss her hit him even harder than the craving for a drink when they first arrived. Now his mouth watered in a whole new way. A way that wouldn't be satisfied until he'd tasted her kiss again. But then he feared, he'd never want to stop, and Riley wouldn't appreciate that.

"I could say the same about you." He caressed her cheek. "But I think we're both biased. We learned to dance together, so we prefer each other's style."

"Maybe." She blinked, fluttering her lashes. "All I know is I enjoy dancing with you more than any other man I've ever danced with."

Good gravy!

If she kept talking like that he was going to break down and kiss her. Right here on the dance floor. Then she'd probably go ballistic and end up laying him out. Right here on the dance floor. In front of dozens of people.

It would be best if he kept his hands and lips to himself.

Fortunately, the song changed, and a popular, upbeat country song filled the room. Riley seemed as reluctant to leave his arms as he was to let her go.

They danced another long song set, working up a sweat and even doing a few lifts, before returning to their table and ordering another round of sodas.

"I need to go to the restroom." Concern again filled Riley's face. "Will you be okay while I'm gone?"

"I'll be fine." Surprisingly, the words were true. Despite being surrounded by alcohol, he hadn't thought about having a drink since he stepped onto the dance floor with Riley.

"You're sure?"

He hated that she felt the need to babysit him, but he appreciated her vigilance.

"Yes. Go."

"Okay, I'll hurry back."

"Take your time. I'm fine."

He couldn't help grinning at the way the butterflies on her pockets sparkled and reflected the light with the gentle sway of her hips as she walked away. He had a feeling she'd worn those jeans just for him, and he loved it. For the dozenth time since telling her he wanted to take her dancing, he wondered if there was really a possibility of him and Riley getting a second chance.

Even though he didn't deserve it, he wanted it more than anything. But if it was ever going to happen, he'd need to be patient.

He finished his soda shortly after Riley left and decided he should probably hit the restroom too before they danced again. He was about to get to his feet when he saw a large cowboy block Riley's path out of the hallway that led to the bathrooms.

Sudden heat shot through his veins, much as it had that morning when Crew aimed his crass words at Riley, and Daniel shot to his feet.

CHAPTER 16

*R*iley paused for a moment after washing her hands and studied her reflection in the mirror. The flush in her cheeks provided better blush than she could apply. She pulled her lip gloss from her pocket and applied it.

She could have sworn Daniel wanted to kiss her when they were dancing that slow dance. And she'd wanted him to. Once again, she contemplated asking him to kiss her before the night was over.

She pulled open the bathroom door and walked out. Hopefully, she could convince Daniel to dance another set with her before they went home, and if she was lucky, that set would include another slow song.

A large cowboy with broad shoulders, no neck, and thick thighs blocked the end of the narrow hallway where it opened onto the dance floor. Three open buttons exposed a wide swath of hairy chest.

Warning bells sounded in Riley's head, and a chill swept over her. She tried to convince herself everything was fine, but her feet slowed of their own accord.

"Hey there, little lady." He smiled around the bulge in his cheek that was undoubtedly a wad of chewing tobacco. "How about spending a little time on the dance floor with me?"

She repressed a shudder and gave him a tight but polite smile. "No thank you. I'm here with someone." She tried to sidestep him, but he shifted and blocked her path again.

"That tall feller? You two look real good dancin' together, but you need a real cowboy." He hooked his thumbs in his belt loops and puffed out his chest.

A crawling sensation skittered across her skin.

Ugh. Do guys really think women find such cockiness attractive?

He stepped a little closer and dropped his voice in pitch. "I can show you a real good time, darlin'."

The stench of alcohol on his breath made her stomach churn.

The drawl of the endearment reminded her of Collin, sending another chill racing down her spine as she felt the blood drain from her face. Her stomach turned rock-hard. She retreated a step, putting distance between them and held up her hand.

"I said no thank you." Her voice was as tense as the muscles bunched in her shoulders.

Nonplussed, he stepped closer still until her outstretched hand pressed against his chest. "Come on, I bet a pretty little cowgirl like you enjoys a good time."

On shaky legs, she retreated another step but found herself with her back pressed against the wall. The sound of blood pumping through her veins reverberated in her ears, and shadows filled the edges of her vision.

Not again! I refuse to be the victim again!

Channeling the fear coursing through her body, she turned it into anger.

The nerve of this man.

Taking the single small step the space between them allowed, she brought her knee up hard and fast into the cocky cowboy's groin. "I said I'm not interested!"

The man doubled over with a grunt and Riley shoved him out of her way. He fell against the wall, cursing her.

She'd only taken a few steps out of the dim hallway when she ran into another rock-hard chest. Her defenses rose and she prepared to fight again until she recognized the red design across Daniel's shoulders.

He grabbed her shoulders to support her. "Are you okay?"

"I'm fine." She pulled away from him and headed toward the door. "I just want to get out of here." She was halfway across the dance floor before she realized he wasn't following her. Turning, she spotted him blocking the hallway now, shoulders hunched, fists balled.

Oh no!

"Daniel, stop!" She hurried back to the hall and grabbed his arm from behind just as he was about to throw a punch at the cocky cowboy. "He's not worth it." With considerable effort she managed to turn him to face her. "Let's leave, please."

He relaxed only a margin, but it was enough that she managed to pull him toward the door.

Brody and Crew rushed toward them before they made it out. They both spoke at once.

"Are you okay?"

"Did that man hurt you, Riley?"

She and Daniel had seen them over the course of the evening, but the ranch hands had been too busy flirting with all the pretty women to pay them any attention. It wasn't lost on her, however, that a little over twelve hours ago, she'd felt toward Crew exactly as she had toward the cocky cowboy.

Crew was lucky Daniel and then Jake had intervened, otherwise he'd be nursing the family jewels just like Cocky Cowboy over there.

"Yes, everything is fine." She spoke through clenched teeth. "Like I'd let him have the chance to hurt me." She nudged Daniel toward the door. "We're going to get some air."

She let go of Daniel as soon as they stepped outside. "Why do guys have to be such jerks?" With adrenaline still warming her veins, she stomped several paces down the wooden boardwalk that ran the length of the building. "Is there some sort of flashing sign over my head that says Easy Victim?"

When Daniel didn't respond, she turned back to find him hunched over, gripping the wooden railing that skirted the boardwalk. She hurried back to his side. "Are you okay?"

"I'm sorry, Ri."

"Why are you sorry? You're the only guy who hasn't treated me like some sort of object to be conquered since I came home. Well, you and my brothers."

He straightened. "I'm sorry I wasn't there to protect you."

"It's not your job to protect me. Besides, I think I did a pretty good job of protecting myself."

Too bad she hadn't been able to defend herself against Collin six weeks ago.

Daniel gave a tight smile. "Yeah, being on the receiving end of your wrath isn't pleasant."

"Sorry again about that." Embarrassment swept over her as she recalled the way she kneed Daniel in the groin a few weeks ago.

He rubbed a hand over his mouth then shoved shaky hands into his hair. Riley looked more closely at his face. His tan complexion had turned a whitish-gray color.

"What's wrong?" She grabbed the front of his shirt as he tried to turn away. "You look like you're going to be sick."

"Nah, just thirsty." The words were clipped and tight.

He'd downed a full glass of water before they got their sodas, so why was he thirsty?

He rubbed a shaky hand over his jaw and mouth again, and it hit her. He was craving alcohol.

"It's time for us to go home." She took his hand and led him toward his truck.

He resisted. "I don't want to be a killjoy."

"You're not a killjoy." She pointed back at the building. "That cocky cowboy was the one who put an end to our fun." She started walking again, dragging him along with her. "I just want to go home now."

"Are you sure?"

"I'm sure." She let go of his hand once she was sure he intended to follow her and walked straight to his truck.

So much for another slow song. Daniel was struggling; this probably wasn't the best time to convince him to kiss her.

They rode in silence for some time before Riley attempted conversation. "This morning, you were ready to beat Crew up for what he said, and Jake had to tell you to cool off. Then you were ready to punch that guy tonight. Do you...do you have anger issues?"

"I have issues with men who don't treat women with the respect they deserve." His grip tightened on the steering wheel, turning his knuckles white in the dim light. "That's why I was arrested last fall. I stood up to some biker guy who kept harassing a waitress and ended up starting a bar room brawl." He shook his head. "I get triggered and the cravings for a drink always intensify when my emotions run high. It doesn't only happen when I'm angry."

She reached out and took his hand. "Thank you for being ready to rush to my rescue."

He looked at their hands then briefly at her before shifting his eyes back to the road. His fingers curled tighter around hers, and the corners of his lips lifted in a small smile.

And she was right back to wanting him to kiss her. She needed to know if the disgust she felt at Crew's words this morning and the cocky cowboy's advances tonight was her new norm, or if she could overcome the feelings of repugnance and defensiveness with the right guy. One who respected and cared about her. One who was willing to defend her.

The remainder of the drive passed in comfortable silence, and her hand remained in his. The contact encouraged Riley, and she promised herself she would ask him to kiss her when they got home.

As soon as they pulled up beside the ranch house, however, Daniel pulled his hand from hers and got out of the truck. He hurried around to her door and opened it for her. He left his truck running while he walked her to the door.

The closer they got to the porch, the more her pace slowed.

"Is something wrong?" Daniel stopped at the bottom of the steps and waited for her to join him. "Are you still upset about that guy at Scooters?"

"No. I'm fine."

"Good." He shuffled his feet and shoved his hands into his pockets. "Thanks for going dancing with me."

"Thanks for taking me." She smiled up at him. "Seriously, I appreciate it. I know how hard it was for you to go to Scooters. But you did great tonight. I'm proud of you."

"Thanks." He returned her smile. "Too bad the evening had to end the way it did."

"We both managed to walk away without any serious repercussions, so we should applaud ourselves."

He gave a slow nod as his gaze slid over her face and settled on her mouth.

Encouraged, she stepped a little closer to him.

He blinked several times, then his gaze dropped to the ground. He let out a little huff and balled his fists. "Good night, Pockets." And then he walked away.

Riley's stomach dropped. "Daniel, wait!"

He stopped at the edge of the illumination from the porch light and turned to look at her. A shadow covered half of his face.

Butterflies filled her abdomen as she took a step toward him. She wiped suddenly clammy hands on her jeans.

"Is something wrong?"

"No...uh...I just need you to..." Her mouth went dry, and she scrambled to find the words she needed.

He stepped a little closer. "What do you need me to do?" His brow lowered in concern.

"I need a favor." Her voice came out tight and higher than usual. She pulled her gaze away from his chiseled features and studied her white boots.

"Sure, what is it?"

She shoved her hands into her back pockets and dug the toe of her boot into the dirt of the flower bed beside the sidewalk.

"Are you okay, Ri?" He stepped a little closer. Small lines fanned out around his eyes showing his growing concern.

"I want you to kiss me!" The words came out much louder and faster than she intended.

"What?" His mouth dropped open, and he fell back a step.

"I need to know.... If I'm ever going to be able to handle....physical touch and...any kind of intimacy again."

He scrubbed a hand over his jaw, his stubble making a rasping sound. "Wow. I was not expecting that."

"I'm afraid I'm always going to be repulsed by advances from men." She rubbed at her arms, recalling the way her skin had crawled when the cocky cowboy propositioned her.

"It's not something you should rush into, Ri. It's only been a little over a month since..." He let his words die off. "Give yourself more time to heal, and I'm sure you'll be fine."

"But what if I'm not? What if I always freak out any time a man gets close?"

"You don't freak out anymore when I get close." To prove his point, he stepped a little closer.

Riley's breath hitched in a good way.

"You held my hand last week at the cabin and tonight in my truck without freaking out. And you hugged me last Saturday. You're making progress. Someday, when you've had more time to heal, you'll have the opportunity to build trust as you grow into a relationship with someone." Tension deepened his voice. "When that happens, I'm sure you'll be able to handle the physical stuff just fine."

But I want that man to be you.

She couldn't convince Daniel to give them a second chance if she couldn't stand to be kissed by him. Knowing how he struggled, she didn't want to make things harder for him, but she wanted to start building a relationship with him now. This time, she wouldn't walk away.

"That's why it has to be you." She inched closer to him and took his hand. "We've known each other forever. I trust you like I've never trusted another man. I know you'd never hurt me."

He let out a tense chuckle. "I kind of walked into that one, didn't I?" He ran his fingers through his hair. "What I meant was—"

"I know this is asking a lot of you, but you gave me my first kiss."

Amusement lit his face, and he pointed a finger at her. "No, *you* gave me your first kiss. You practically attacked me."

She punched his arm. "I did not."

"You did too."

"But you kissed me back." Her voice softened. "You gave me my first kiss..." She lowered her gaze to their interlocked fingers. "And I need you to kiss me now to show me I'm not permanently damaged and broken. That I'm capable of having a relationship."

Daniel sucked in a sharp breath. "Riley." The husky timber of his voice sent a shiver down her spine.

"Three years ago, I welcomed your kisses and your touch. If I can't.... tolerate that from you again, I'm not sure I'll ever feel comfortable with any man." She added that last bit so Daniel wouldn't feel like she put too many expectations on him.

"It has taken us a long time to get to this level of...comfort with each other this summer." His voice was gentle and warm as he ran his thumb over her knuckles. "If I kiss you and you're...repulsed by it..." He rubbed his free hand over his jaw again. "I don't think my sobriety can handle a repeat of what we went through earlier this summer. Especially if you knee me in the groin again."

"I won't, I promise." She leaned toward him a little. "Just one kiss. Please."

"For the record, I think this is a bad idea. But heaven help me, I do want to kiss you." The low and rumbling words were a soft caress against her cheek. He shifted, closing the gap between them.

He lifted a hand and caressed her cheek then gently tucked a lock of hair behind her ear. Ever so slowly, he slid his fingers into her hair and brought them to rest at the nape of her neck.

Tingles raced across her scalp, and her lungs seized. Each beat of her heart pounded a little harder as though trying to push too much blood through her veins. A momentary flash of panic filled her mind until she reminded herself that her breathlessness and racing heartbeat were caused by desire, not fear.

His other hand gently settled on her waist as he slowly tilted his head toward hers.

Her eyes drifted closed, and moisture filled her mouth in anticipation of his kiss.

"How are you doing, Pockets?"

Her eyes flew open. "Fine." The single word was breathy and shallow.

He dipped his head a little lower until his warm breath caressed her lips. "Are you sure about this?" The low rumbling tone of his voice heightened her anticipation in an almost torturous way.

Gah. Just kiss me already.

She gave a curt nod before closing her eyes again. She'd forgotten how much she loved kissing him years ago, but it was all coming back to her now, the giddiness, the pleasure, the euphoria. She couldn't wait to feel his lips on hers once again.

Finally, the painfully slow descent of his lips ended, meeting hers in a gentle kiss. Tiny electrical sparks radiated out from her lips, spreading rapidly throughout her body, making her feel so alive. A melting sensation filled her as the anxiety drained away, leaving her blanketed in a comfortable warmth.

Daniel's kiss remained light, tenderly caressing, yet his lips were firm and confident. A tension radiated from him as though reading her reaction, preparing to make a full retreat at the slightest sign of distress from her.

She leaned closer to him, letting him know she was okay. In fact, she was better than okay.

Daniel is kissing me, and I'm not panicking.

A spark of triumph ignited in her chest. Not only was she not panicking, she was enjoying every second of his kiss.

All too soon his lips started to withdraw without ever taking the opportunity to deepen the kiss. Not ready for it to end yet, she grabbed the front of his shirt to prevent him from retreating and rocked up on her toes.

His lips pulled away momentarily in a grin, but then he claimed hers in a kiss that was a little less gentle and considerably more passionate. His arms slid around her, pulling her tight against him, and for the first time this summer, Riley felt like she'd found home.

Her hands glided over his shoulders until she could tangle her fingers in the hair at the nape of his neck. She reveled in the feel of his lips on hers and his arms holding her close. She had forgotten how amazing it felt to be held by him. Her breathing quickened and her heart rate kicked up a few notches as desire built in her.

Daniel's arms tightened around her, and a low moan erupted from him. The soft guttural sound set off warning bells in her head.

Riley was suddenly transported back to her apartment in Seattle where Collin's strong arms pinned her down, his kisses becoming more demanding and invasive by the second. His throaty laugh and passionate groans grew louder the more he violated her.

She tried to push the horrible memory from her mind by reminding herself she was safe with Daniel, but the rasp of his stubble that she'd found pleasant at first suddenly dug into the tender skin of her face.

Her chest tightened to the point where her lungs struggled to bring in sufficient air. An unpleasant quivering sensation filled her, sending a prickly feeling to her fingertips. She pulled her hands from his hair as warning bells continued to sound in her head. The curl of desire in her abdomen hardened into stone.

She gasped and shoved him away.

Wide-eyed, Daniel fell back a step. "Are you okay?"

"I'm fine." She gave a jerky nod and retreated a step. She sucked in a deep breath. "I've—I've got to go."

She spun on her heel and practically raced up the porch steps.

"Riley? Are you sure you're okay?" Daniel's concerned voice followed her.

She turned back when she reached the door. "I'm fine, really. It was just...a lot of...sensations." She pressed a hand to her chest to still her racing heart. "My mind went a little haywire there at the end, but I'm okay. I promise."

Pushing open the door, she went inside. She closed the door behind her and leaned back against it. Her eyes closed as she processed the emotions coursing through her. Yes, the panic had set in, but she'd enjoyed Daniel's kiss and touch for several long, glorious moments before it did.

She'd anticipated having to endure the kiss in order to prove to herself she could handle it. She hadn't expected to enjoy it as much as she did. A hint of the desire she'd felt while in his arms continued to linger now that she'd distanced herself from him. Her lips turned up. With time and a little practice, she was confident she'd be able to overcome the panic that had ended the kiss so abruptly.

Would Daniel be game for more practice? No, practice wasn't the right word, but she definitely wanted to experiment more with Daniel.

"Looks like the night was either a success or a disaster."

She jumped at the sound of Jake's voice. Her eyes flew open and searched the dimly lit room to find him lying in the recliner with little Adam on his chest.

"I didn't expect you to still be up."

"I wish I wasn't, but this little guy..." Jake's large hand gently stroked Adam's back. "...needs to learn his days from his nights." He studied her face. "So...how did Daniel do tonight?"

"He did really well. I'm proud of him. There were moments where I could tell he was struggling, but he didn't have a single drop of alcohol." She plopped down on the end of the couch closest to the recliner and pulled her boots off. "We were having a good time until some guy —a cocky cowboy with an over-inflated ego—stopped me in the hall outside the bathrooms and propositioned me."

Jake swore under his breath.

"I told him I wasn't interested and tried to walk away, but he trapped me against the wall. Daniel saw it all happen and rushed over to help me. I had already taken care of the guy by the time he got there, but that didn't keep Daniel from trying to punch him."

Jake grimaced and shook his head.

"Luckily, I was able to stop him."

"I was afraid something like that might happen."

"Me getting propositioned or Daniel getting in another bar fight?"

"Both. Emily and Jessie have had run-ins at Scooters with brash cowboys who don't want to take no for an answer. But I also worried that being surrounded by alcohol might be too much for Daniel."

"He shouldn't make a habit of going there very often, which is unfortunate because it's the only place to swing dance." She stood and picked up her boots. "But he's stronger than you all think."

She picked up her boots, told Jake goodnight, and headed to bed. It had been a long day and she was exhausted. When she plugged her cell phone in for the night, she noticed a text from Daniel.

Are you sure you're okay?

After the way she pushed him away and rushed into the house then ignored his text, the poor man probably thought she was having a major meltdown.

I'm okay, I promise.

Better than okay actually. Grinning, she sent a second text. *Thanks for a fun date.*

She waited for a response from him, but when none came, she quickly drifted off to sleep, dreaming about a future with Daniel.

CHAPTER 17

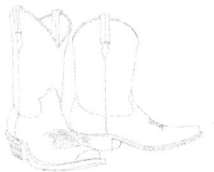

*a*n annoying sound somewhere between a buzz and roar pierced Daniel's consciousness. He lifted his head and looked toward the window. A gray pre-dawn light shown through the crack in the curtains. He looked at his clock next.

5:30

His alarm wasn't set to go off for another fifteen minutes.

Who on earth is running a...chainsaw at this time of the morning?

A loud crack followed by a booming crash rattled the house.

Daniel bolted upright and threw back the covers. He jumped out of bed. Barely taking time to pull on a pair of jeans, he hurried from his room to find his parents coming out of their room.

"What in tarnation is going on?" His dad's gruff voice was deeper than usual.

"Sounds like someone cut down a tree." His mom tied the sash of her robe.

Daniel nodded. That's what it sounded like to him too.

Without further discussion, the three of them pulled on boots and followed the sound outside.

The buzz continued, and another loud splintering crash split the air just as they stepped out of their small yard. An unspoken urgency pushed them all into a jog down the lane.

Halfway to the big house they met Riley and Emily coming from the opposite direction, wearing equally puzzled looks. Emily gripped a baby monitor in her hand. Her frantic gaze locked on Jake, who wielded a chainsaw. She yelled his name, but he didn't hear her over the roar of the saw.

Finally, she managed to get close enough to tap his shoulder.

Jake killed the motor on the chainsaw before spinning around to find a crowd gathered behind him. Hank, Brody, and Crew hurried from the direction of the bunkhouse.

Jake cleared his throat. "Sorry everyone. I know it's still early, but I couldn't wait any longer."

"What are you doing?" Emily's brow creased.

"I'm tired of it, Em." Jake wiped perspiration from his brow with his arm.

"Tired of the trees?"

"No, I'm tired of having to take our wives and girlfriends to places like Scooters so we can dance and have a little fun, only to have drunk men proposition them. You ladies shouldn't have to be subjected to that."

Riley must have told her brother what happened last night at Scooters. Daniel studied her face looking for signs of a difficult night but didn't find any. He was relieved when she responded to his text last night, saying she was okay, but it was easy to lie in a text. He'd done it dozens of times with his parents and Emily after he fell off the wagon.

When Riley darted away like that, he feared kissing her had been a mistake. It was too soon after her assault. He'd never been good at saying no to Riley, though, especially when he'd been thinking about kissing her all evening.

He shouldn't let himself get attached to her, though. She deserved someone better than him. Now that he'd kissed her and held her in his arms again, however, the last thing he wanted was to let her walk away from him again.

He tuned back into Emily and Jake's conversation, trying to ignore the fact that Riley wore one of his old T-shirts from high school and short shorts.

"I agree that we shouldn't have to be subjected to drunken come-ons at Scooters, but what does that have to do with you cutting down trees?"

"I'm building a dance floor."

"A dance floor?" Emily's brows hiked up.

"Well, I'm going to build a recreation center of sorts, where we can dance and play basketball and maybe volleyball. We'll put in a sound system and a bathroom and maybe even a small kitchen."

"A kitchen? Of course, because every gymnasium needs a kitchen." Sarcasm laced Emily's words. "Don't you think you're going a little overboard, just so we can dance?"

"No, I'm not." Jake pulled Emily into his arms, "You know how we were discussing that the ranch house, as big as it is, is getting too small for family gatherings, especially with another generation coming along? This building will give us the space we need for all our family parties, regardless of the weather."

Emily shook her head, skepticism covering her face. "Did you sleep at all last night?"

"I don't think so. I went to bed, but then I started thinking, and I had to get up." He looked directly at Daniel now. "There are some crude sketches on my desk I want you to develop. I need you to draw up the plans for this." He waved his arm in a broad circle.

A spark of excitement filled Daniel's abdomen and radiated up through his chest. Images filled his head of ways he could make Jake's ramblings come to life. Maybe they could use the wood from the trees Jake cut down for the dance floor. He'd have to do some research to see if white oak, Oregon ash, and maple would make good flooring.

Emily clipped the baby monitor onto the waistband of her pajama pants and put a hand on either side of Jake's face as though to rein him in. "You realize this is going to be a very costly project?"

He grimaced, but Daniel could tell it was fake. "I might run the ranch into bankruptcy." Then he winked as he pulled her close. He lowered his voice, but Daniel stood close enough to hear him. "Good thing I married into money." He pressed a brief kiss to Emily's lips.

Her mouth curved up and she gave a little nod. "I can't think of a better project to spend some of that money on."

Two years ago, Emily inherited a massive fortune after her dad and brother were murdered. Despite the numerous scholarships they funded and their generous donations to dozens of charities, Daniel figured they'd hardly made a dent in the billions she inherited after the sale of her father's tech company.

Jake started gesturing and explaining his plans to Emily, but everyone gathered listened intently. For the first time, Daniel noticed three-foot stakes in the ground with orange ribbons tied around them, marking out what Jake intended to be the boundaries of the building.

He let out a low whistle. This was going to be a major project. The excitement building inside him amplified, taking his breath away. He couldn't wait to take on this challenge. Designing buildings like this was what he was meant to do.

When Jake finished gesturing and explaining, Daniel grinned. "Where's the swimming pool supposed to go?"

Jake spun around, the crazed look in his eyes growing more intense. He studied the line of trees he'd marked.

"Zane, we're going to need to push the fence to the north another hundred fifty feet."

"I was kidding, man." Daniel put a hand on Jake's shoulder as though to hold him back.

"I'm not. Our children shouldn't have to swim in the creek and mud holes that leave them covered in leeches like we did."

"I agree, but don't you think you're going a little overboard?" Daniel quirked a brow at Jake.

"I agree." Emily propped a hand on her hip.

"Why not go overboard?" Jake turned to Emily. "We've got the space. We can afford it."

Emily gave a reluctant nod and smiled. "You're right. Don't you dare tear down the tree house, though. I still want our kids to have the kind of childhood you had."

"I won't. In fact, I have plans to make it bigger and better."

"Of course you do." Emily rolled her eyes.

Jake surveyed the gathered group. "Anyone willing to work on..." His words died off as he turned to wave his hand in the direction of the trees he'd already cut. He paused, as though realizing how crazy this whole thing was, and chuckled. "Anyone willing to help with my insanity will get time and a half."

Crew whooped and hollered. "Are we helping you go insane?"

"Or keeping you from going?" Brody finished.

"Maybe both." Jake chuckled again.

"You heard the boss," Zane called out. "Time and a half for anyone willing to help build Jake's Rec Center. But first, get some breakfast and do your regular chores."

Jake picked up the chainsaw, but Emily caught his arm before he could pull the cord to start it. "Oh no you don't. You need some sleep."

Jake's face fell. "You're probably right."

"I know I'm right." She held out a hand to him. "Come on."

"Let me put the chainsaw back in the shed for now." He headed toward the equipment shed while Emily headed to the house. "I'll be right in."

Daniel's parents were already almost back to their house, and Hank and the ranch hands had disappeared. That left Daniel and Riley standing alone in the trees. The sun, barely cresting the distant hills, cast a golden glow over the ranch and the gentle light made Riley look as beautiful as ever despite her sleep-tousled hair.

Perfect. Now I can find out how our kiss really affected her.

She quickly looked away after glancing in his direction and finding him staring at her.

He stepped toward her. "Are you sure you're okay after last night?"

"Yes, I'm good."

"Then why did you rush away? Did the kiss trigger you?" He raked a hand through his hair. The last thing he wanted to hear was that his touch and kiss repulsed her.

"The kiss was fine."

"Fine?" He cocked his head. "I'm not sure whether to be relieved or offended." He gave a tight chuckle. "So, you really didn't feel anything?"

"I didn't say that." She shifted her hands behind her as though to tuck them into her pockets, but her shorts didn't have pockets. After fidgeting for a moment, she finally ended up folding her arms across her chest.

"So you did feel something?" A spark of warmth fueled by hope ignited in his chest.

"Yes, I felt something." She shifted from one foot to the other. "Initially, it was good things, then the panic set in."

"That's when you pushed me away?"

She nodded but didn't meet his gaze.

They were tucked mostly under a giant oak tree, so he stepped a little closer to her. "But you were okay until the panic hit?"

"Yes, it didn't hit immediately, like I thought it would." A small smile played at the edges of her lips, and she finally met his gaze.

"But the first part of the kiss was good?" He needed clarification. Needed to know she had enjoyed their kiss as much as he did.

"Yes." She tried to hide a smile but Daniel knew her too well.

"How good?" He crept a little closer.

"Very good." She took a step back, but the smile she gave him and the flirty gleam in her eyes couldn't be mistaken as anything other than an invitation.

And smitten sap that he was, he wanted to accept.

"Good enough that I'd like to experiment a little more." An impish grin covered her face.

"Experiment?" He stopped advancing on her.

The word was like cold water in his face. He didn't want to experiment with her. He wanted to pick up where they left off three years ago. He wanted a promise of forever, even though he didn't warrant it, because Riley deserved better than him.

She gave a stiff shrug. "I figure with a little practice, I can handle longer, more passionate kisses."

Practice? Habitually doing something to become perfect at it.

He and Riley didn't need to practice kissing to become perfect at it. They'd mastered that skill years ago, but he liked the idea of long, passionate kisses with Riley. Maybe experimenting wasn't such a bad idea after all. He'd hate himself if his kiss ever triggered her though.

"What kind of experiment do you have in mind?" He stepped toward her again.

She grinned as she retreated another step. "Last night you thought kissing me was a bad idea."

"I still do, but it turns out..." He took another step. "I like kissing you, Pockets."

Her next step back brought her up against the trunk of a decades-old oak tree. She jerked a shoulder forward when the rough bark pressed into it.

He closed the gap between them and brought his hands to her waist.

"I like kissing you too, Tarzan." Her hands came up to rest on his bare chest, sending all kinds of warm and fluttering sensations shooting through him.

He leaned in, tilting his head.

Her whole body went rigid before he could press his lips to hers. Her smile vanished, and her eyes widened. She sucked in a sharp breath. Then suddenly, she tapped repeatedly against his chest.

"Wait! I can't!" She barely got the words out before pushing him with both hands.

He took two steps away and swore under his breath. He should have known better. Just because they'd shared one good kiss didn't mean she was ready to make out under the oak tree.

"I'm sorry, Ri." He scrubbed at his jaw. "I didn't mean to pressure you."

She pushed away from the tree, pressed a hand to her stomach, and took several deep breaths.

"I knew this was a bad idea." He shook his head. "I'm such a selfish jerk."

"Daniel, it's all right." Riley turned toward him. "I'm fine. Really."

He studied her face, looking for the panic that was there a moment ago. Nothing. Her face was as beautiful as ever.

"I felt a little trapped there for a moment with my back up against the tree, but it has passed." Her lips curved up. "The fact you were about to kiss me wasn't the problem, believe me." Now she was the one who advanced on him.

He retreated a step, still certain this was a bad idea, but wanting more than anything to hold and kiss her.

"We're making progress already." Her smile grew. "We've learned that I can't handle being pinned against anything so...." She advanced again. "We just need to find a different approach."

He stepped back again, suddenly finding himself in the position Riley was moments ago, with his back against the oak tree. "You should give yourself more time."

She shook her head. "I want to kiss you now. Here. Under this maple tree."

"It's an oak tree."

"I don't care. I still want to kiss you." She stepped closer, planting both slippered-feet between the narrow stance of his boots.

Unable to resist her, he widened his stance. The movement brought his back down lower against the tree and his face down to her level. "I don't think—"

"Let's try again, please," she whispered as she leaned into him.

Her warm lips grazed against his in a feather-light kiss that was little more than a whisper. The contact sent a ripple of sweet pleasure cascading through him. An energizing sensation that didn't stop until it reached his toes.

He should push her away and put an end to the kiss, but making the right choice was not one of his strengths, and he sure didn't want it to be now. Not when Riley's lips were on his. Besides, he'd never been good at telling her no. She was his weakness. Well, his first weakness, alcohol had become his second.

Her lips pressed more fully against his as she leaned against his bare chest and slid her hands over his shoulders. Desire ignited in him, and he ached to pull her closer—to crush her against him—and claim her mouth in a kiss that was far less sweet and much more passionate. But the last thing he wanted was to upset her and put an abrupt end to this delicious torment.

Exercising every ounce of self-control he possessed, he settled his hands on her waist. He couldn't afford to let them roam no matter how badly he wanted to. It didn't take but a moment, however, for them to gather the fabric of her oversized t-shirt into his balled fists as her mouth continued to nip and nuzzle at his in a tantalizing dance of want and need with a sprinkling of pent-up emotion.

He had the potential to break her heart in more ways than one, so he shouldn't be enjoying the kiss so much, but he felt powerless to stop. To lose contact with her. Because now that he'd experienced her kiss again, he knew the craving for more would never go away. It would make his battle with alcohol feel like a walk in the park.

The rough bark digging into his back only emphasized the softness of her lips and the teasing tangle of her fingers in his hair. It would be so easy to lose himself so completely with this woman.

A loud guttural sound filled the air, and Riley jerked away.

Struggling to catch his breath, Daniel looked up to find Jake standing only a few feet away, a grin as big as the Joker's on his face.

"Sorry to interrupt, but I left my hat in that tree." He stepped close and reached over Daniel's head to pull his cowboy hat from a V in the branches.

He and Riley shared a surprised look. Her lips pinched as though she held back a laugh.

Jake paused before walking away. "I'm glad to see you guys are working things out, but tread lightly." He motioned to them with his cowboy hat. "You're both dealing with your own trauma. Trauma that can quickly grow worse if this goes south." He looked directly at Daniel now. "Take it slow." Then he turned to Riley. "And don't play games with him by starting something you aren't willing to see through."

Her mouth dropped open. "I am willing."

"Good. I'm worried about both of you." He looked back and forth between them. "Keep a perspective on each other's struggles as well as your own." Then he looked at Riley again. "I understand that Daniel is a safe space for you, but don't toy with his emotions." He focused his attention back on Daniel now. "Just because Riley can tolerate a kiss doesn't mean she's ready for a serious relationship yet."

Riley slapped Jake's shoulder. "You told me you'd be okay with us getting back together. And now you're saying you don't think I'm ready for a relationship?"

When did Jake tell her that?

"I am okay with you getting back together, but you two have been down this road before. It didn't end well last time, and you were both hurt. I don't want that to happen to either of you again. You're both carrying additional baggage you didn't have last time, so take it slow. Don't start something that you aren't prepared to see through."

Baggage.

Daniel had baggage alright. Baggage that could come knocking on his door someday and destroy the happiness he hoped to find with Riley. It wasn't fair to her to saddle her with the mistakes of his past.

Jake took a deep breath, then let out a sigh. "Okay, lecture over. For what it's worth I hope things work out between you two. You both deserve to be happy." He wrapped an arm around each of them and pulled them in for a quick hug.

Riley's face registered the surprise Daniel felt.

Jake released them then smothered a yawn as he walked away.

"Jake's right," Riley said, shifting from one foot to the other again. "We should probably discuss what we both want before we 'experiment.'" She made finger quotes when she said experiment.

"Jake is absolutely right." Daniel backed away from her. "We have a lot of baggage we didn't have before. I should never have kissed you last night or this morning." He turned and walked away.

"Now who's the one playing games?" Hurt laced her words.

He spun around. "It's never been a game for me, Ri. Never."

"Then why are you walking away?"

"To protect you."

"From what?"

"From me. You deserve a better man than me."

"You think that because you're a recovering alcoholic that I shouldn't want to be with you? That you don't deserve a chance at happiness?"

The fact that she wanted to be with him made his heart soar, but he reined it in. He would only bring her heartache down the road when his past caught up to him in the form of a teenager on his doorstep, declaring Daniel was his dad. People who made the kind of mistakes he had didn't deserve the happiness he wanted for Riley.

"I think because of the choices I've made, you'd be wise to stay away from me." This time when he walked away, he didn't stop. Not even when she called his name.

Now he had two weaknesses to deal with: Riley and alcohol. Staying on the ranch helped with the alcohol cravings, but as long as Riley was here, he'd never escape that temptation.

CHAPTER 18

Five days later, Daniel groaned when his alarm went off.

He'd stayed up late again working on the designs for Jake's Rec Center after yesterday's cattle drive, and he was not ready to face another long day already. He stumbled from his bed, heading for the bathroom.

"Oh good, you're up." His mom, suitcase in hand, stopped him in the hallway. "I just left you a note in the kitchen. Dad and I are leaving soon, but don't worry, Emily will make sure you're fed. I left plenty of meals stockpiled in the fridge and freezer for her to prepare."

His older sister Mandy just had her third baby, and Mom insisted she and Dad needed to go to Denver to help her for a while. Knowing Mom, Mandy would have enough frozen meals to last three months by the time they returned. And Brian and Mandy's yard would be immaculate because his father wasn't the sit-around-and-do-nothing type. They might even get the rest of the basement finished.

"Thanks, Mom. I'll be fine."

If worse came to worse, he'd go mooch off Hank.

She pulled him down to plant a quick kiss on his cheek. "Dad and I will only be a phone call away if you need anything. And remember,

Emily and Jake are always happy to talk if you find yourself struggling."

"I'll be fine," he insisted again.

"I know you will." Mom patted his arm. "See you in two weeks."

The only thing he struggled with now was the desire to pull Riley into his arms every time he turned around. She'd given him the cold shoulder all day Saturday, as expected, but then she did a one-eighty on Monday and had been as friendly as could be ever since, acting like he hadn't rejected her.

Daniel tried to do the same, but he couldn't forget the amazing kisses they'd shared. The more he tried to block them out and the feelings they evoked in him, the more persistent the memories became. He thanked his lucky stars each evening that he had an excuse to hole up in his room and think about something other than Riley. Well, mostly. Unfortunately, sketching designs for the rec center didn't require his full concentration.

It gave him plenty of time to wonder how RIley's second self-defense class went last night. Last week, she was eager to show him what she'd learned in her first class. Thankfully, she hadn't hurt him, even though she could have if she wanted to.

An hour later, Daniel swung himself back into the saddle without the use of a stirrup after closing the final gate behind the herd of two-year-old steers and heifers—their third and final herd to drive to summer grazing pastures—and the cowboys driving them. He couldn't think of Riley as the lone cowgirl, because of the way that word bothered her, so he lumped her in with the rest of the cowboys, even though she was much more attractive than them.

"Show off." Riley rolled her eyes then nudged her horse in the flanks.

Daniel flicked Rebel's reins and followed her. "You're just jealous because you've never been able to swing yourself up like that."

"I'm not tall enough. Nor do I have the upper body strength you do."

She was the perfect height for him to pull into his arms and rest his chin on her head.

Stop it.

Ever since he walked away from her last week, he felt like he'd made the biggest mistake of his life. Well, maybe not the biggest, because he was pretty sure he'd already made those mistakes. He couldn't stop obsessing over her, though. Her smile. Her gracefulness when they danced together. The way she fit in his arms. The feel of his lips on hers.

And here I go again.

He was surprised when she stayed near his side at the back of the herd, instead of flanking one side or the other, like she had the past two days. She made casual conversation about the weather and the terrain then talked about how she missed her job back in Seattle. He kept expecting her to blow up at him, accusing him of leading her on only to reject her, but she didn't. She simply talked about the kind of things they'd always discussed. The things that made being with her so comfortable.

Three hours later, the sun beat down on them as they pushed the herd over a rocky ridge. Because of the steepness and height of the rock face, they took the easiest, yet longest, route for the cattle, keeping them as far away from the precipice as possible, but it still brought the herd closer to the edge than any of them liked.

Jake guided his horse to where Daniel and Riley rode at the back of the herd. "I want you two to take the right side and keep the cattle away from the edge of the ridge." He turned his horse away before calling over his shoulder. "And keep an eye on L-218."

Steer L-218, or Flash—as Daniel had come to think of him today— had been giving them fits all morning. He'd repeatedly broken loose and bolted any time he saw an opening. The wily thing was fast. He was one of the few they'd left the horns on since they planned to sell him to the rodeo circuit later this summer along with half a dozen other steers. He'd give the team ropers a run for their money.

Riley had ended up roping him last time he broke loose and dragged him back to the herd.

It reminded Daniel of how she used to rope and barrel race back in high school. He couldn't believe she still had it after seven years. She looked as beautiful and graceful as ever in the saddle. He hadn't tested his own rodeo skills of steer wrestling and team roping for years, but he'd been pretty good back in the day.

Twenty minutes later, Flash made a break for it again, bolting straight toward the edge of the steep rocky slope. If he made it over, he'd end up at the bottom of the thirty-foot drop with multiple broken bones. They'd have to put him down.

Riley unstrapped her rope and kicked Misty in the flanks, racing after the steer.

Daniel followed, in case she wasn't successful in roping the runaway. They would need to head him off before he got too close to the edge.

When Riley threw her rope, she only managed to snag a single horn, which Flash promptly shook off with a flick of his head before increasing his speed. He headed straight for the veritable cliff.

Daniel swore and urged Rebel to run faster. He'd never seen a seven-to-eight-hundred-pound steer move so fast.

"Be careful, Daniel!" Riley shouted, following him. "If you don't turn him soon, all three of you will go over."

Daniel judged the distance to the steer—just over ten yards—then he checked the distance to the edge of the precipice—roughly thirty yards. His stomach clenched. Riley was right. If he didn't turn this steer soon, they were all in trouble.

Getting beyond Flash would bring him and Rebel much closer to the cliff's edge than he wanted. That left only one option. Take Flash down.

He hadn't wrestled a steer in ten years, but he knew what needed to be done, and he was a lot stronger now than he used to be.

He guided Rebel up beside the steer. "You know what to do, boy."

Daniel took a deep breath, focused on both Rebel's and Flash's movements, ignored whatever it was that Riley shouted at him, and let go of the reins. He kicked his feet from the stirrups and with a final glance at the edge of the cliff that was less than twenty yards away now, he launched himself off Rebel's back, doing his best to divert the horse's direction as he dropped onto the steer's neck.

Although he landed where he needed to, his right hand slipped off Flash's horn initially. Laying on the steer's neck, he scrambled and managed to hook his left arm around the horn in the proper hold. He was harder to shake off than Riley's rope and the steer's momentum slowed considerably. Slowed, but didn't stop.

Daniel pulled his right arm in as tight as he could and lifted his left elbow, wrenching the steer's neck down and to the side. He dug in his heels. The wily animal was not only faster than he looked but he was stronger too. Which was saying something because he looked plenty strong.

Daniel renewed his efforts as the edge of the cliff drew closer. Engaging his core, he curled his right shoulder forward, pulled his left elbow back a little farther, and brought the steer to the ground with a thud.

When the bovine finally dropped, an audible pop sounded next to Daniel's ear and splitting pain pierced his shoulder. Groaning in agony, he kept Flash down until Riley rode Misty between them and the cliff. It felt like an eternity, but probably wasn't more than a few seconds.

"Are you crazy?" Her voice was high-pitched and so loud it echoed off the rock walls below them. "I can't believe you did that."

Daniel released Flash's horns and rolled away, attempting to cradle his arm by his side, but the slightest movement intensified the excruciating pain in his shoulder. He was vaguely aware of Riley pushing Flash toward the herd and Jake yelling something at them, but it all felt muddled and disjointed in his head, overpowered by the sound of the blood pulsing in his ears. The throbbing in his left shoulder kept time with the pounding in his head.

Hoof beats vibrated the ground beside him, and Riley slid down from Misty's back before the horse even came to a stop. "What's wrong? Why are you still laying there?" She dropped to her knees.

"I wrecked my shoulder." The words came out through clenched teeth.

"Let me see." She cupped her hand under his elbow and began gently probing up his arm.

The closer she got to his shoulder, the more her gentle touch hurt. He groaned and flinched.

"Sorry," she said.

Not sorry enough to stop probing, however.

More hoof beats drew near as Riley hit the shoulder joint. Daniel sucked in a sharp breath then let it out in a hiss. It was all he could do to keep from letting loose a string of swear words.

Jake reined in Thor on Daniel's other side. "What happened?"

"Daniel dislocated his shoulder when he wrestled that stupid steer to the ground."

"I knew that beast was going to give us trouble again." Jake shook his head. "I'll be glad to get rid of that one." Jake took a knee beside Daniel. "Are you going to try to set it out here?"

Riley chewed on her bottom lip for a moment before answering. "I'd love to be able to give him some pain meds before I do, but riding back to the ranch will be extremely painful if we don't set it first."

"You can say that again." Daniel pushed himself upright then regretted the movement as another sharp wave of pain pierced his shoulder. He groaned, again biting back curse words.

Riley scooted a little closer. "I can set it for you, but I need you to relax and trust me, okay?"

"Relax? Yeah right."

"Daniel, look at me. Look at my eyes."

He did as she instructed, zeroing in on her beautiful blue irises. He loved how they were dark around the edges and lighter—almost a silvery blue—close to the pupils.

She lifted his hand to rest on her shoulder, sending another wave of pain shooting through his. "Take deep breaths. In through your nose, out through your mouth." Her voice was calm and steady.

It reminded him of how he'd instructed her to do the same thing when he unbuttoned her shirt at the cabin two weeks ago. At the time, his only goal was to make her feel as comfortable as possible, so she didn't knee him in the groin again. But she'd trusted him. Now he needed to trust her.

"We're going to take this nice and slow. It'll be easier and go faster if you relax."

"I'm trying." The words came out akin to a growl.

"Jake, kneel behind Daniel, so he can lean back against you yet stay upright."

"Got it." Jake shifted, and though it was the strangest thing Daniel had ever done with his boss, he leaned back.

"Good, now remember to take deep breaths," Riley's soothing voice pulled him in again as she gently massaged his bicep, slowly working her way up his shoulder.

Her soft touch set off an awareness in him that distracted him from the pain in his shoulder. His fingers itched to reach up and pull the elastic from her braid so he could run his fingers through her hair.

"Do you remember back when that old blind mare we used to have stepped on my foot, breaking two of the bones?"

He gave a small smile. "Yeah. You were what...ten?"

"Eleven." Her fingers inched up his arm as she slowly rotated his elbow away from his body. "You were my hero that spring."

He frowned at her. "How so?"

"You carried me everywhere when I got sick of the crutches and complained about them hurting my hands."

Ah yes. He remembered now. He'd felt guilty that she got stepped on because she was helping him do his chores so they could go for a ride on the four-wheelers.

It dawned on him that she was trying to distract him, just like he'd done for her at the cabin when she had her panic attack. He appreciated the effort, but he really wanted to go back to daydreaming about the silkiness of her hair.

Her fingers continued their tender ministering as she shifted his elbow to an awkward angle. The joint and muscles grew so tight and uncomfortable he was ready to swear. Then with a small pop, his shoulder slipped back into place. The noise wasn't nearly as loud as when it popped out, and the discomfort he expected to feel with the movement ended up being a release of pain rather than an additional burst.

"Thank you." He sank back even farther against Jake, letting out a sigh of relief.

Riley continued to gently probe his shoulder joint, and he couldn't help wincing when she hit an especially tender spot. She frowned. "It's possible you've torn your rotator cuff."

"Nah, I'm sure it's just sore muscles."

She shifted her fingers and pressed again.

He winced again.

"We'd better get you to the hospital and get an MRI done."

"I'm fine." Cradling his arm to his side because his shoulder still throbbed, he managed to get to his feet. "We have work to do." He picked up his hat that had fallen on the ground and settled it on his head.

Jake rose also. "Riley's right. We shouldn't take any chances." He rubbed at the back of his neck as he scowled first at the herd that was growing more distant by the second then at his sister. "You'd better ride back to the house with him and drive him to the hospital."

"No way." Daniel looked around in search of Rebel. He found him not far away patiently waiting to get back to work, which is what Daniel needed to do because if he didn't, he'd seek out a stiff drink to dull the pain in his shoulder. "We need to drive this herd another five or six miles. It's going to take all of us to get them to their summer pastures safely."

"No, you're done for the day," Jake said, stepping in front of him.

"Come on, man," he said, his voice tight. "Don't sideline me. I need to keep busy."

Jake's eyes narrowed as he studied Daniel's face. "Pushing yourself won't make the situation better if you've got an injury that needs medical attention."

"I'll be fine." It was a lie, but he didn't want to admit how much a little pain—okay, a lot of pain—had brought the cravings back with such intensity that he feared if he drove into town, he'd head straight to a bar. Or maybe the liquor store since it wasn't even noon yet. He sidestepped Jake and reached for Rebel's saddle horn.

"Daniel Evan Hamilton, don't you dare get on that horse yet." Riley pulled a pink and gray flannel shirt from her saddle bag. "That arm needs to be kept immobile for at least a week, maybe longer."

"Don't worry, I won't use it." It hurt too bad to even think about moving it.

"I know you won't, because I'm going to make you a sling." Without giving him an opportunity to argue, she stepped close and used her shirt to create a sling by tying the ends of the sleeves behind his neck. Then she tied the bottom front corners of the shirt behind his elbow.

It looked funny, but it cradled his arm close enough that he didn't need to use the muscles in his shoulder to keep it immobile. He relaxed his arm. The throbbing in his shoulder settled to a dull ache. It was going to be a long day, but no matter what it took, he'd keep working.

"You look good in pink." She grinned and patted his chest. "Are you sure you're okay?"

"I'll be fine." Turning away from her, he swung himself up into the saddle. Without the use of his left arm for leverage and momentum, he almost didn't make it. He caught himself, however, and maneuvered into the saddle, but not before jarring his shoulder. He bit his lip to keep from grimacing and swallowed the groan that wanted out. "We'd better hurry and catch up to the herd before Brody and Crew drive them the wrong direction."

After nudging Rebel in the flanks, he sent up a prayer that this injury wouldn't cause greater temptation than he could bear. Because even though they weren't together, the fear of falling off the wagon and disappointing Riley was so much worse than the thought of letting down his parents or Jake.

THE KITCHEN FELT EERILY quiet the next morning when Riley pushed through the swinging door. Only Emily sat at the counter with a book and a glass of juice.

"Where is everyone?" Riley asked.

"Jake just walked out the back door, Lottie and Zane are gone, of course, and Adam is still sleeping." She motioned to the baby monitor on the counter.

Riley grabbed a plate and served herself some of the breakfast casserole on the stove. "Has Daniel come and gone already?"

"No, I haven't seen him yet this morning."

Riley's actions slowed as her stomach tightened. He was always here around six. She looked at the clock on the stove. It was six-thirty now.

Had his shoulder kept him up last night?

She'd tried to convince him to let her take him to the hospital when they finally arrived back at the ranch house late yesterday afternoon, but he'd refused. He insisted he just needed a hot shower, some ibuprofen, and a good night's sleep. He'd looked miserable at dinner though, despite the pain meds.

And if he tore his rotator cuff, a good night's sleep would be impossible.

"I'd better go check on him." She shoved a bite of breakfast casserole in her mouth and chewed. "I may have to get forceful about taking him to the hospital." Then she frowned. "I hate to leave Jake short-handed, especially with Zane gone."

Emily waved a hand. "There's always plenty of work to do, but he was commenting this morning that with all the herds out at the summer grazing pastures the hands would have more time to work on the rec center. Until you all start cutting hay next week, that is. I'm sure they will manage without you and Daniel."

Between bites, Riley put a hearty serving of the breakfast casserole in a container for Daniel, and as soon as she'd finished eating, she headed down the lane. She couldn't ignore the niggling fear in the back of her mind that Daniel might have sought out some alcohol last night to help manage his pain.

She sent up a little prayer that wasn't the case.

When she reached the smaller cottage-style house, she knocked then walked in without waiting for a response, like she'd always done. She'd expected to find Daniel in bed, but he sat in his dad's recliner.

His head popped up, and he rubbed his eyes. "What time is it?" He flipped the lever that dropped his legs and propped him upright with a jerk. His face scrunched into a wince.

He still wore last night's shirt, but it was unbuttoned as though he'd attempted to take it off but decided it required too much effort. At least he wore the sling she'd found at home and wasn't trying to tough it out.

"Let me guess, you didn't sleep well, because your shoulder hurt?"

He rubbed the back of his neck while rotating it from side to side. "Yeah, I couldn't find a comfortable position."

"That's what I was afraid of." She grimaced. "I'm afraid you tore your rotator cuff." She shoved the food storage container into his hands. "Here, eat your breakfast. Then we're going to the hospital."

"I'll be fine. I just need to rest it for a few days."

"Yes, you need to rest it, but you might also need surgery."

Daniel's face blanched. "No, I can't go through surgery."

Riley propped her hands on her hips. "Well, you may not have a choice." She softened her tone. "Why are you so averse to getting medical attention?" When he didn't respond, she knelt beside his chair. "Is this about your alcohol addiction?"

"A couple of strong drinks could dull the pain in no time." He looked away, not meeting her gaze. He shook his head. "If I have to have surgery, they'll prescribe narcotics to help with the pain. I don't want to become dependent on them."

"Not all rotator cuff tears require surgery." She put a hand on his good arm. "Let me take you to see Uncle James so we can find out what we're dealing with at least."

"Okay." He grimaced again as he stood, and Riley prayed she hadn't given him false hope about not needing surgery.

Impatient as she was to get him to the hospital before he changed his mind, she let him eat his breakfast and get dressed before hurrying him out the door. When he asked for her help to button his shirt, warmth spread through her body as she admired the magnificent eagle spread across his broad chest.

A twinge of disappointment hit her with each button that she closed, and the eagle slowly disappeared. She was still trying to figure out how to get Daniel to give them a chance. She understood his hesitation to get involved in a relationship when he felt he was too damaged and would end up letting her down some day. But he was stronger than he thought.

Clearing her throat, she stepped back. "I'll go grab my Jeep and be back in a jiffy."

"Let's take my truck."

"No, you shouldn't be driving."

He picked up the keys off the counter and tossed them in her direction. "So you drive."

Three hours later, after waiting for a full hour in the waiting room, then another thirty minutes for Uncle James to see Daniel, followed by a forty-five-minute wait to be taken to radiology for the MRI, Riley was tired, grumpy, and impatient. She was about to push to her feet to go in search of answers when the curtain opened again.

"I have good and bad news." Uncle James moved the rolling stool directly in front of them and took a seat. "The bad news is you do indeed have a small tear in the rotator cuff." He raised a finger as Daniel let out a soft groan. "But since it's such a small tear, it won't require surgery."

Daniel heaved a sigh of relief beside her.

"Here's the catch though..." Uncle James gave Daniel a stern look. "If you don't rest it, it won't heal." He picked up the sling that hung over Daniel's knee. "That means this is your most important accessory for the next four to six weeks. More so than even your hat, belt, and boots combined. Got it?"

Daniel nodded, a small smile lifting his lips.

Uncle James rolled the stool back and stood but Riley stopped him. "I think Daniel could use something for the pain. Something a little stronger than over the counter pain relievers."

She hated even suggesting it because there really weren't any great alternatives to opioid pain relievers, but she feared as long as Daniel was in pain, he'd crave the alcohol.

"No," Daniel said. "I'll make do."

"You don't have to make do." She turned to her uncle again. "Perhaps an NSAID like Diclofenac or maybe even a Cortisone shot?"

"Both are great options." Uncle James nodded. "If we go with the cortisone shot, I fear he'll feel better right away and use that arm too much. Then that tear will never heal." He turned to Daniel. "It's your choice, however."

"I don't want anything that could be addictive."

"Neither are addictive. As far as side effects go, it's a wash." He shrugged then looked at Daniel with raised eyebrows.

Daniel looked at Riley. "What do you think I should do?"

"The shot will give you faster relief, once the pain of the injection subsides."

"Okay, let's go with the shot."

"Sounds good. I'll be back in a few minutes with an ultrasound machine and a Cortisone shot."

Judging by the noise out in the hall, the ER was still busy, so Riley anticipated having to wait at least another thirty minutes, but Uncle James returned only a few minutes later, rolling a cart with an ultrasound machine.

"This is a little unorthodox, but we're short-staffed today, so Riley, if you could assist me, we can finally get the two of you out of here."

Riley's eyes widened, and she stared at her uncle until Daniel elbowed her in the ribs with his good arm.

"Uh, yeah, sure." She sprang to her feet. "Let me wash up."

Uncle James alternately explained to Daniel how he would use the ultrasound to guide the needle into the shoulder joint and to Riley what he needed her to do to assist him. Her job was mainly to hand him different syringes as he injected Lidocaine first then the Cortisone.

Once he was finished, he turned to Riley. "Excellent work, thank you." He cleaned up the garbage and rolled the ultrasound machine through the curtained partition then stepped back inside. "Remember,

Daniel, rest it for at least four weeks. I don't care how good it feels."
He turned to Riley again. "After you're done helping Daniel get put
back together, I'd like to talk to you before you leave."

"Okay."

She quickly stepped out of the role of nurse to help Daniel button
his shirt and set his sling properly. He grabbed her hand as she was
about to step away. "Thank you. I probably should have listened to
you and let you bring me in last night."

"Yes, you should have." She smiled as she patted his good shoulder.
"Hopefully, the cortisone will do its job, and you'll be relatively pain
and craving free soon."

"I don't think there is an injection strong enough to make that
happen, but it will be nice to be out of pain." He stood and stepped
into the hallway. "I'll be in the waiting room."

"Okay, I have no idea what Uncle James wants to talk to me about,
but I don't think I'll be very long."

It didn't take her long to find her uncle, who was busy giving
instructions to a nurse, so she hung back and waited for him to
finish.

Smiling, he put a hand on her shoulder, playing the part of caring
uncle and guided her to an empty cubicle. "Your mother told Hope
and I what happened to you. Let me say how terribly sorry I am that
you had to go through that."

Riley's gaze dropped to the floor as she blinked away the tears that
suddenly filled her eyes. "Thank you."

"I hope you're utilizing Emily's expertise to help you deal with it."

She nodded. "I am."

"Good." He patted her shoulder. "Okay, the real reason I asked to
speak with you is this: I'd like to offer you a job."

"What?" Her mouth dropped open.

"You have skills that we desperately need. Both here in the hospital
and at the clinic."

"But I'm not—"

"I know you aren't—or rather weren't—planning on sticking
around, but I'm pretty sure I'm not the only one who would like you

to make your move back to Providence permanent." He cast a glance toward the door that led to the waiting room.

Mixed emotions swamped Riley. She loved working with Dr. Nelson, but she'd already had the thought multiple times over the past few weeks that if Daniel was willing to take a chance on them again, she'd do whatever it took to make things work. Even if it meant moving back to this small town that she was so eager to leave seven years ago.

Coming home wasn't as bad as she thought it would be.

Besides, if she went back to Seattle, she risked running into Collin again. She hadn't received any more phone calls, letters, or flowers over the last two weeks, but she didn't dare hope he had given up.

"Can I think about it?"

"Sure, but if you're interested, I'd like you to start as soon as possible." He stepped out of the cubicle and waited for her to follow.

Riley laughed. "A little desperate, are you?"

"Extremely, but I'm confident your skills would be a great asset to the hospital."

She couldn't help grinning at the praise. Setting Daniel's shoulder and helping Uncle James had made her realize how much she missed nursing. Riding horses and working with cows was enjoyable, but it was also exhausting and dirty work. Helping someone feel better and occasionally even saving a life was much more rewarding.

"I'll let you know in the next day or two."

"Great. I look forward to your call."

Riley's steps slowed as she walked toward the door to the waiting room. She glanced around. People in small towns got sick too and accidents happened everywhere. She could make a difference here like she did in Seattle.

The deciding factor, though, would be if there was a possibility of a future with Daniel. So how did she convince him to take a chance on them?

CHAPTER 19

*D*aniel had been sitting in the waiting room for less than a minute when his phone rang. He pulled it from his pocket, surprised to see Robert's name on his screen.

"Hello."

"Are you with Riley?" Robert's terse question surprised Daniel even further. He only spoke like that when he was in full-on sheriff mode.

"Yes."

"Good. Keep her away from the ranch."

"Why?"

"Collin Ainsworth just showed up at the Double Diamond."

"What?!" Daniel bolted to his feet.

His stomach bottomed out. He should have known after the flowers arrived two weeks ago, Riley's stalker wasn't going to give up. He couldn't believe the man was bold enough to show up at the ranch. He wished he was there right now, so he could deck the man who hurt Riley.

"Jake called me. He's trying to stall him until I get there." Robert's voice pulled him from his fantasies of beating up Collin Ainsworth. "But I need you to keep Riley away for a while. It might be best not to tell her why yet."

Daniel looked up to see Riley coming through the door that led to the exam rooms. "Got it. Keep me posted."

He ended the call and got to his feet, falling into step beside her as they headed for the door.

"Who were you talking to?"

"Uh...Jake." He hated lying, but he figured it was the best way to protect her. "Told him we probably wouldn't be back for a while, because I'm taking you to lunch."

She looked at him with wide eyes, her lips turning up. "Oh, you are, are you?"

"It's the least I can do to thank you for all your help yesterday and today."

"Oh." Her face fell.

Shoot.

He shouldn't have made it sound like he was doing it out of gratitude, but rather because he wanted to spend more time with her.

"Did you also tell Jake that you are out of commission for the next few weeks?"

"Not yet, but I will. Maybe now, I'll be able to spend the kind of time that I'd like on the designs for the rec center."

"That's one positive thing about your injury, I guess. You're still going to be plenty busy." After they climbed into the truck, she asked, "So, where are we going to lunch?"

"Charity's, of course." He gave her a look that said she'd obviously been away too long, if she thought he'd eat anywhere other than at her Aunt Charity's diner.

"Right. It's not like there's anywhere else to eat."

"Except for the Tasty Freeze."

She shuddered. "That grease pit? No thanks."

Before long, they were seated in the back corner at Charity's and had placed their orders with Riley's cousin-in-law, Amy Young. The lunchtime rush hadn't started yet, so the diner was quiet.

Riley placed her hands on the table, fingers clasped.

Daniel couldn't help studying the delicate hands with slender, yet strong and skilled fingers that massaged his shoulder yesterday and buttoned his shirt twice today. He ached to pull her hands into his and press his lips to her knuckles.

Instead, he grabbed his water glass and took a long drink.

"Uncle James offered me a job."

It was all he could do to not spit water all over the table and Riley. Finally, he managed to swallow it all and clear his throat. "He did? That's great." He pressed a napkin to his mouth before crumpling it into a tight ball. "Are you going to take it?"

"I want to. I'll feel bad leaving Dr. Nelson, but your injury has made me realize how much I've missed practicing medicine."

"So, you're planning on staying here long term?" He held his breath, waiting for her answer.

A rosy tint covered her cheeks as she smiled. "I'm not as opposed to the idea as I was years ago."

"Why not?"

"You're here." She shrugged as though that said it all, and the light that he loved to see filled her eyes.

Daniel's heart leaped in his chest. Did he dare hope there could be a future for them? Here in Providence. Together.

But she deserves better than you.

Two voices had warred in his head all week. One, telling him he was an idiot for walking away from Riley, and the other constantly reminding him he wasn't good enough for her.

On one hand, he felt if he had Riley by his side, it wouldn't be difficult to stay sober. On the other hand, he knew his past could come back to haunt them at any moment. And not just the addiction part of his past.

They'd talked in depth at last week's AA meeting about making restitution for their wrongs. It was something Daniel couldn't do, no matter how badly he wished he could. He couldn't bring back little Isaac, nor could he track down the women he'd slept with—women whose names he didn't even remember—to make sure they weren't bearing a burden he should share. He mentally kicked himself again for all the poor choices he'd made over the past two and a half years.

Riley locked gazes with him. "I think I'd be willing to stick around if there was more than a job for me here." Her voice was heavy with innuendo as she blinked, fluttering her lashes.

Daniel's mouth went dry. "You think?"

"I'd love to stay in Providence if I could convince a certain someone to give us a chance."

He wanted to give them a chance. More than he wanted a stiff drink, which was saying something. Because just like that craving never went away, he knew he'd never stop loving Riley. But this was not the time or the place to discuss his reservations with her.

"Alright, here we are." Amy stepped up to their table, arms loaded.

Daniel sighed. Amy's timely arrival saved him from having to respond, but it also put a scowl on Riley's face.

No, I'm the one who disappointed Riley. Not Amy.

"I have a turkey bacon club for you, Riley." Amy placed a plate in front of Riley. "And here's your BLT, Daniel." She stepped back and smoothed her hands down the front of her apron. "Is there anything else you need?"

"Not at the moment." Riley gave Amy a tight smile. "Thanks."

"I'll let you enjoy your lunch then." Instead of walking away, however, she put her hands on the table and leaned down. "Can I just say how happy I am that the two of you are back together again? You make a very attractive couple." Then she smiled, winked, and walked away.

It was just as well she didn't wait around to hear that they weren't actually back together, because by the way Riley kept blinking, he figured she was seconds away from bursting into tears.

He felt like such a heel for not being able to give her what she wanted. Especially when he wanted it too. He reached across the table and grabbed her hand as she went for her sandwich. Leaning as close as the table allowed, he glanced around before speaking to make sure there weren't any eavesdroppers.

"I would love to give us a chance Riley, but I'm no good for you. You deserve—"

"Stop saying that!" Her words came out as a hiss. "You don't get to decide what I do and do not deserve." Her voice had risen by the time she finished speaking.

An older couple in the process of sitting at a nearby table stared at them.

Daniel released her hand and sat back in his chair. "You're right. But I don't think you understand the full ramifications of getting mixed up with me."

Riley must have noticed the older couple too, because she lowered her voice and pitched forward in her seat. "Like it or not, I'm already mixed up with you." Her voice grew more fervent. "Because I have never stopped loving you, Daniel."

Hearing Riley echo his sentiments caused his chest to swell, which was good because his heart raced so fast he could have powered his truck with it. He wanted to drag her out of the diner right now and have a heart to heart with her. He needed to know she wouldn't change her mind when he spelled out to her all the ways his past could catch up to him.

He leaned forward again, bringing his face within inches of hers. "There are things you need to understand about me—about my past— before you make declarations like that."

"I doubt there's anything you can say that will change my mind."

"Don't be so sure."

"Tell me then."

He glanced around again. The diner was starting to fill up with the lunchtime rush. "Not here."

Riley looked around too, then slowly nodded. She sat back in her seat. "Fine, but we are going to talk about this." She picked up a French fry and pointed it at him. "I need to let Uncle James know my answer soon. And like it or not, it all depends on you."

Great! As if I'm not worried enough about how she'll react when I tell her of my indiscretions, now her future rests in my hands.

Thirty minutes later, after Amy walked away with Daniel's credit card, Riley stood. "I need to go to the restroom before we head home."

As soon as she was out of sight, Daniel pulled his phone from his pocket and called Robert.

"What's going on?" he asked as soon as Robert answered. He could be as abrupt as Riley's oldest brother when it came to her well-being.

"Jake and I finally managed to convince Ainsworth Riley wasn't at the ranch—despite her Jeep being here—and that he needed to leave. I'm not sure we were as successful at convincing him to leave her alone, however."

"You let him leave? You didn't arrest him?"

"Couldn't. Yes, the restraining order states that he can't come within three hundred feet of Riley. Technically, he didn't—since she isn't here—so I couldn't arrest him."

"But he didn't know she wasn't there when he showed up on her doorstep."

"No, he didn't, and I pointed out that had she been there, I would have arrested him. As it is, I just followed him to the motel on the south end of town."

"What's he doing there?"

"My guess? Renting a room." Robert's voice was grim. "It doesn't look like he plans to leave town any time soon."

Daniel cursed under his breath.

"My sentiments exactly. This means you can't let Riley go home."

"What am I supposed to do with her? We're done with lunch and we're about to head back to the ranch. I'm not sure I can come up with a good enough excuse to convince her to stay at my house for the rest of the day and night."

His thoughts turned to the north cabin where he and Riley spent the night a few weeks ago. They hadn't taken supplies out to replace the ones they'd used yet. It would be the perfect place to hide away for a while, but he wasn't sure he could stand spending hours in the saddle again in his condition.

"No, your house is too close. I don't want her anywhere near the ranch." Robert stopped talking for a moment and Daniel was about to ask again how he was supposed to keep Riley away, when Robert spoke again. "Take her out to the lake."

"The lake?"

"Yes, take her to my mom's family's cabin at the lake. Riley knows the door code. Spend the night there, then check in with me in the morning, and I'll fill you in on Ainsworth's whereabouts."

Daniel wanted to argue. Taking Riley out to the lake would trigger all kinds of memories. Fun, carefree ones from their youth and romantic ones from the two evenings they spent there during the summer they dated.

"How am I supposed to convince her to stay there without telling her why?"

Robert laughed, sounding less like the sheriff and more like the big brother Daniel knew. "Flirt with her. Convince her you've been dying to spend more time with her."

"What?" Daiel balled up his used napkin.

Robert's chuckle cut him off. "Come on, I saw the way you hugged each other a couple weeks ago, and Jake told me he caught you guys kissing under the oak tree. You can't tell me nothing's going on between you and Riley."

He definitely couldn't tell Robert now, because Riley walked out of the bathroom.

"Ri's coming. Gotta go. Let Jake know we won't be home until tomorrow." He hung up on another peal of laughter from Robert.

Amy arrived back at the table with his credit card at the same moment Riley did.

Daniel quickly added a tip, signed the receipt, and thanked Amy before getting to his feet.

"Bye you two. I hope you enjoy the rest of your date." Amy collected their dirty plates.

"We're not—"

Daniel grabbed Riley's arm, cutting her off. He hurried her toward the door. "Don't bother."

Everyone knew Amy said things without thinking them through first. Setting her straight would only draw more attention to them, and Daniel didn't want that right now.

Silence filled the cab of the truck as they drove back toward the Double Diamond. He'd expected Riley to demand he tell her about his past as soon as they got into his truck, but she didn't. Either she didn't want to hear the things he had to say, or she didn't want to be distracted while driving.

Daniel was more than happy to put off their discussion. However, the wide gates of the Double Diamond came into view all too soon, and Riley started to slow the truck.

"Keep driving."

"What? Why?"

"I'm not ready to go home yet. We need to talk, and I'd rather not do it here." He motioned out the window toward the ranch.

"Where do you want to go?"

"Out to the lake."

"The lake? That's twenty minutes away. Jake will be expecting us back soon."

"No, he won't. I told him I was kidnapping you for the day." Another lie.

"You're kidnapping me?" Her lips quirked. "How exactly does that work when I'm the one driving?"

Daniel reached across his body and took her hand that rested on the console and pressed his lips to the back of it. "Please, Pockets, keep driving."

He swore he heard her breath hitch before she grinned. "Well, when you ask like that, I can't possibly say no."

Daniel wished persuading her was truly that easy. He feared she wouldn't have a problem saying, "no," after he explained all the reasons she didn't belong with him.

CHAPTER 20

*R*iley's stomach grew increasingly tighter the closer they got to the lake, making her nauseous. Her turkey, bacon club sandwich and fries sat in her stomach like concrete. Not even the majestic view of towering trees, emerald water, or the weathered dock that held so many memories could soothe her fears.

She didn't know what Daniel needed to tell her, but it was serious enough to make him repeatedly swipe a hand across his jaw and mouth. He hadn't said a word since kissing her hand and begging her to keep driving, but his posture grew more and more rigid.

As soon as she brought the truck to a stop beside the cabin her grandpa and grandma Whittaker bought decades ago, Daniel opened his door and jumped out as though he'd been fighting claustrophobia for the last twenty minutes.

Riley slid down from the truck at a much slower pace and followed him across the small clearing to the water's edge. She doubted there was anything he could tell her that would change the way she felt about him. She loved him. She always had, and she always would. Despite all the horrible things he felt he'd done, he deserved to be loved. He needed someone by his side who could see beyond his weaknesses and faults to the amazing, hardworking, patient man he was.

She didn't want that someone to be anyone but her. So that meant accepting the bad with the good. And because she grew up with Daniel, she knew how good life could be with him. Sure, he was damaged, but so was she.

He kept talking about how he wished he'd made different choices. Well, so did she. The way she saw it, if she hadn't walked away three years ago, Daniel might never have been in that accident and started drinking. At the very least, she would have been there to help him through the difficult times. And she wouldn't have accepted a date with Collin if she was married to Daniel.

She stood beside him at the water's edge, waiting for him to speak. When he didn't, she found several smooth, flat rocks, perfect for skipping. Handing one to him, she squinted out across the still lake, studied the size of the rock in her hand, and said, "Six."

Daniel snorted. "No way you're getting more than five skips with that rock."

"Make your bet." She nodded toward the rock in his hand.

She couldn't remember how old she was when they first started playing this game where they'd created a complicated scoring system for predicting how many skips they would get with each rock, including extra points for whoever got the most skips each round. The loser had to do a favor for the winner. One summer, she saved up her favors until she had enough to make Daniel her servant for a whole day.

He had to do everything she asked. He hated it. She loved it.

Daniel studied the rock in his hand. "Four."

Riley coughed into her hand. "Wimp."

He cocked an eyebrow at her. "Overachiever."

She simply grinned and threw her rock from hip level. It hit the water with a soft plink, skipped once, then twice and promptly sank after the third skip. She let out a little groan.

He laughed. "I haven't done this in years, so I doubt I'll be any better." He angled his body away from the lake and pitched his rock.

It bounced six times before sinking.

"Show off." She selected another rock from her handful and handed it to Daniel. "Okay, you have two points, and I'm negative one."

Instead of taking the rock, he grabbed her hand, letting the small stone fall to the ground.

"Thank you for trying to distract me, but delaying what I need to say won't make it any easier to get out."

Riley dropped the rest of the rocks, dreading the words that might come from his mouth.

He released her hand then lifted his baseball cap and raked his fingers through his hair before replacing his hat. He turned toward the lake again. "I promise myself every day that I will never drink again, but I can't guarantee I won't fall off the wagon at some point."

She leaned against his good arm and laced her fingers with his. "I know staying sober will always be a challenge for you, but I promise I will be there to help you through your struggles. Every. Single. Day."

"Do you remember that day at the river when I said I turned my back on all the values I was raised with?" He pulled his hand from hers and stepped away.

"Yes." The single word came out through a tight throat.

She'd thought about the possible implications behind those words many times over the past two weeks and concluded that besides drinking and getting a tattoo, there were likely other things in Daniel's past that he felt were inappropriate, considering their Christian upbringing. Which gave her a pretty good idea of what those things were.

She'd be lying if she said they didn't bother her, mostly because the thought of Daniel with another woman pierced her heart. But she knew that the man who did those things while under the influence of alcohol was not the penitent man who stood before her now, refusing to forgive himself.

"I mean all of my values." He placed heavy emphasis on the word all.

Even though she didn't want to discuss this, she decided to make it easier for him. "If you're trying to tell me that you've...been with other women..." The words were harder to spit out than she thought they would be. "I know, and it doesn't change the way I feel about you."

He turned and looked at her, his eyes wide. "You're saying it doesn't bother you at all that I've slept with... a lot of women?"

She tried not to flinch when he said *a lot*. "Of course, it bothers me, but I'm not going to hold something against you that's in the past." She sucked in a deep breath. "I know you feel horrible about the choices you've made. You've beat yourself up plenty over them. You don't need me to do it too."

"You're missing the point, Ri." He scrubbed a hand over his face and let out a small growl. "What happens if we get married, then ten years down the road, some teenager shows up on our doorstep claiming I'm his dad?"

A sharp pain shot through Riley's chest, causing her to fall back a step. An oppressive weight settled over her, making the early June day feel much hotter than it was.

When Daniel told her he'd turned his back on the values he'd been raised with, she'd considered all kinds of scenarios, even to the point of thinking he could have an STD, but she hadn't thought about him fathering children.

Why didn't I consider that?

Probably because she'd dreamed many times over the years of Daniel being the father of her children. She'd pictured their sons having his prominent brow and strong jawline and their daughters having his expressive brown eyes. She didn't want to consider that some other woman had carried his child.

"In my drunken state, I can't guarantee I always took measures to prevent that from happening." Daniel shook his head in disgust.

A band tightened around Riley's chest, making it difficult to breathe, and for a moment, she feared her lunch might come back up. She wrapped her arms around herself in a protective gesture.

"I can tell by the look on your face that you're second guessing giving us a second chance now." Derision filled his voice. "Like I said, you deserve someone better than me. You shouldn't have to be saddled with my baggage." He spun around and walked away.

Riley wanted to go after him, but she needed to catch her breath first. She needed to come to terms with the fact that life with Daniel may not be exactly what she'd dreamed it would be.

But life with Daniel would be good, of that she was certain. He had always put her and her needs first—from helping her study for her history test to driving four hours to take her to prom. He would treat her right, and he would work hard to support their family.

The sun moved out from behind the clouds and warmed her face. She closed her eyes and lifted her face toward the sky. Warmth filled Riley.

Would it be such a bad thing if someone showed up on our doorstep claiming Daniel was their father?

As long as they prepared themselves for that possibility, she felt like they could handle it. They would have some explaining to do to their own children, but the simple fact that Riley still imagined having a family with Daniel meant that she could get beyond this, even though it felt like a huge betrayal at the moment.

She took a few minutes to let the emotions surging through her settle as she watched Daniel walk down the length of the dock. When she went to talk to him again, she wanted to make sure he knew she meant it when she said she loved him, no matter what.

He didn't turn when she finally walked up behind him, even though her boots made plenty of noise on the wooden planks. He simply stood with the hand of his good arm shoved deep into his pocket, his shoulders hunched.

She paused behind him, still struggling to find the words she needed to say to put Daniel's demons to rest. Ever so slowly, she slid her arms around him, locking her fingers together against his abdomen.

His already tensed body tightened, and she feared for a moment he might jerk away. She held fast, waiting for him to relax. It took much longer than she expected, but finally he pulled his hand from his pocket and covered her hands.

"I don't want to hurt you, Ri. Now or in the future."

She kept her cheek pressed to his back when she spoke. "I won't lie and say that your past doesn't bother me, but I mean it when I say, 'It doesn't change how I feel about you.'"

"That's easy to say now but when the day comes that there's a stranger standing on our doorstep—"

Riley released him and quickly stepped around him to press her fingers to his lips. "We'll prepare ourselves for that day now by praying that if you do indeed have a child—or children—somewhere out there that they have a mother who is taking good care of them until we have the opportunity to get to know them."

Daniel's brow creased. Little lines formed at the corners of his eyes as he studied her face. "Do you mean it?"

"Yes." The word came out as a fervent whisper.

He squeezed his eyes closed and sucked in a deep breath.

She leaned into him. "I love you, Daniel. I always have and I always will. Nothing will ever change that."

His good arm wrapped around her so fast and so tightly it took her breath away. He buried his face against her neck. "Good, because I'm so in love with you, Pockets. I've loved you my whole life, and I promise I will never stop loving you. I want to spend the rest of my life with you."

She melted against him, wishing he didn't have an injured arm sandwiched between them.

Then Daniel's lips were on hers, stealing her breath in a whole new way. The pressure of his kiss didn't stay gentle for very long, but Riley didn't mind. If he felt anything like her, they had three years to make up for. She parted her lips, inviting him to deepen the kiss.

As his mouth mingled with hers, Riley's senses went on high alert, making the kiss an all-consuming experience. From the taste of bacon that lingered in his mouth to the fresh, pine-scented air tainted with the algae smell of the lake that surrounded them. The feel of his strong hand splayed across her back only added to the warmth and contentment enveloping her. Even the lapping of the water against the shore seemed to keep rhythm with his mouth on hers.

Resisting the urge to rip his sling off so he could hold her closer, she settled for pushing his hat off his head and tangling her fingers in his thick hair. Kissing Daniel had always been amazing, but she'd forgotten how utterly perfect they were together. As though they were created solely for this purpose—to enjoy each other's kiss.

It wasn't long before she started to feel light-headed—whether for lack of oxygen or because Daniel's kiss was that incredible—and she found herself clinging to his broad shoulders to keep herself upright.

He groaned and tightened his arm around her until it felt almost like a vice.

Warning bells sounded in her head, and her difficulty in drawing in a full breath was no longer due to Daniel's kiss, but rather to his presence in general. She stiffened in his arms and almost of its own accord, her right hand tapped three times against his shoulder before she shoved against him.

He released her immediately, a look of alarm filling his face, then his expression quickly morphed into one of concern. "Riley, I'm so sorry. I shouldn't have been so...aggressive."

"No, don't apologize. It's not your fault. It's all me. I just...I need a second."

She stepped away from him and focused on the breathing techniques Emily had taught her. Either she did them wrong or she couldn't focus well, because they never seemed to work fast enough for her.

Or I'm just too impatient. And angry.

She hadn't seen Collin Ainsworth for over six weeks, yet he still affected her, controlling her life. She faced Daniel again when her breathing finally settled down. "I'm so sorry. I didn't mean for that to happen."

"It's not your fault." He took her hand. "You need to give yourself a little more time. It might be best if we don't kiss anymore for a while."

"No!" She clung to his hand and stepped close to him again. "I love you. I want to kiss you. I want you to hold me in your arms." Her voice rose with each sentence. The panic attack had subsided, but the anger hadn't yet. "I love kissing you, so I don't know why my brain does this to me."

He released her hand and swiped back a lock of hair that the breeze had blown across her face. His calloused fingers were so soft and gentle against her cheek, it brought tears to her eyes. She didn't need to fear Daniel. She knew that, so why did her mind try to convince her otherwise every time they kissed.

"Our emotions are processed in the same part of the brain as our memories," he said. "When emotions run high, the amygdala can go a little haywire, especially where trauma is involved."

Riley knew that. Well, she recalled learning something about that in one of her classes in nursing school. She was surprised Daniel knew that information though.

"Did Emily teach you that?"

He nodded as he traced his finger along her jaw. "Don't worry, Pockets, I'm not going anywhere. We have all the time in the world." Then he wrapped his arm around her and held her close. But not tight.

Riley appreciated his tenderness, but she wished he didn't need to coddle her.

They stood there for several long minutes looking out across the lake, and gradually her ping ponging emotions settled down, and she relished the feeling of being held by the man she loved. This was what love was all about: being there for the one you loved in the ways they needed. No matter what.

It's what she'd vowed to do for Daniel if he struggled, so she needed to graciously accept that he was willing to do the same for her.

She looked up at him and smiled. "Are we really going to give this a try?"

"No, Pockets, we're not trying." He cupped her cheek and locked eyes with her. "We're doing this. You and me. Forever."

"Deal."

He leaned in for another kiss that was sweet, gentle, and way too brief.

She put a hand on his chest. "Promise me if you're ever struggling, for any reason, that you will tell me, so I can do my best to help you. I don't want us keeping secrets from each other."

"I promise."

Riley stirred, becoming aware of the stiffness in her neck. Pushing her elbow into the couch beneath her, she lifted her head from Daniel's chest. She blinked to focus her eyes in the muted golden light that filled the main room of the cabin.

"Good, you're awake." Daniel stroked her arm, raising goosebumps across her skin. "I was afraid you were going to miss this amazing sunset."

She shifted enough to look out the floor to ceiling windows that overlooked the lake but not so much that she had to leave the comfort of Daniel's embrace.

Golden rays of sun arced through scattered clouds making the horizon look like a glowing pot of gold with puffy pink blobs of cotton candy. The reflection of the sunset across the lake only made the scene more spectacular.

"It's beautiful!" She ran her hand across Daniel's chest, feeling the definition of the muscles beneath his shirt. She looked forward to an opportunity to examine his eagle tattoo more carefully. "How long have I been asleep?"

"I'm not sure, because I'm pretty sure I fell asleep before you did. I didn't even make it to the part where the Spaniard keeps asking Westley to climb the cliff faster."

"I remember that part, but I don't remember the fire swamp."

Riley couldn't think of a better way to spend the afternoon than in Daniel's arms watching *The Princess Bride*, unless it was sleeping in his arms while said movie played in the background.

They'd spent an hour sitting on the dock this afternoon, kissing and talking then kissing some more, before going on a short hike. They would have hiked longer if Daniel's pain and exhaustion hadn't been so apparent on his face.

When they returned to the cabin, Riley found him some ibuprofen and a bag of frozen peas that had been in the freezer for who knows how long and tried to convince him to lay down and rest. He agreed, but only if she cuddled with him. She couldn't argue with that, since he needed the rest.

"How long have you been awake?"

"Long enough to know I'm not dreaming." His arm tightened around her. "I'm convinced I've died and gone to heaven."

She snuggled in closer to him to watch the sunset. "Feels heavenly to me."

They stayed on the couch until her stomach growled, sounding like some type of wild animal.

Daniel laughed. "We'd better feed the beast."

As much as she hated to leave his arms, she pushed to her feet and went to search the kitchen for food.

"What are our chances of finding something to eat here?" Daniel asked as he followed her.

"We always keep a few staples in the cupboards, but then we always bring more food with us when we come to stay. Anything that doesn't expire right away usually gets left behind." She pulled open the freezer. "The scary part is not knowing how long some of this stuff has been here." She rummaged around until she found a one-dish meal, consisting of chicken, veggies, and pasta that was simple enough to fix.

While they ate, they talked more about what their future looked like. Even though Daniel encouraged her to work at the hospital, she saw an emotion on his face that looked like disappointment.

Riley set down her fork. "Are you sure you don't mind me working with my Uncle James?"

"Of course not. Why would I mind?"

"I don't know, you seem...disappointed."

"I'm happy for you, I promise. I love that you're planning to stay in Providence so we can settle down together, but..." The disappointment lingered on his face.

"But what?" She leaned across the table and looked in his eyes.

"I'm disappointed in myself for derailing my life." He shook his head. "I can do so much more than muck out stalls. I'm excited about designing Jake's rec center, but then what?"

"Maybe you should look for a job with an architectural firm in the Tri-Cities area."

"I'm not sure I dare leave the ranch."

"It's not like you'd be leaving forever. You'd still come home every evening." She reached across the table and put a hand on his arm. "If you want to stay on the ranch, I could ask Jake if he'd sell us an acre or two of land to build a house on."

A thoughtful look filled his face before he slowly nodded, then his lips turned up. "I could design our house."

Now she smiled. "You could, but I don't want to wait until we have a house built to get married."

"Me either." He laid down his fork and took her hand. "We'll have to look for a place in town to rent, which could be difficult."

Her face fell. "I heard my mom and brothers talking about the housing shortage in Providence."

"We'll figure something out. My parents will be so glad we're back together, they'd let us live with them, if we need to until we get a house built."

Riley grimaced. "I love your parents, but I hope we don't have to do that."

"Me too."

Thirty minutes later, Riley dried the last plate and put it back in the cupboard. She looked around to make sure she'd taken care of everything they needed to do before leaving. "I hate to have this day come to an end, but I suppose we should head home before it gets even later."

Daniel caught her hand as she headed toward the door. "Let's stay here tonight."

"I'd love that, but Jake and Emily will be worried about us."

"No, they won't." Daniel's whole body tensed. "I mean, I'm sure it'll be fine."

"Let me guess, you told Jake you were keeping me away overnight too?" She propped her hands on her hips, both pleased and perturbed that Daniel and her brother thought they could plan her whole day for her.

Daniel scratched the back of his neck. "Something like that."

"What's going on?" Her gaze narrowed on his face. "What are you hiding?"

He shuffled his feet and looked away.

She shifted to hold his gaze. "We promised each other this afternoon there would be no secrets between us, remember? So, tell me what's going on."

He scratched his neck again. "You're right. It's probably best you know anyway. Robert didn't think I should tell—"

"Robert? What does he have to do with this?"

Daniel let out a heavy sigh. "Collin Ainsworth showed up at the ranch today."

Riley fell back a step, a cold chill sweeping over her. Daniel may as well have struck her. She couldn't possibly be more stunned. She knew Collin wouldn't give up easily, but to show up at the ranch, knowing he was breaking the restraining order...

Why am I surprised? He showed up at the clinic five days after attacking me despite the restraining order.

Riley's heart rate took off, bolting like a racehorse out of the starting gate. She struggled to draw in a full breath around the tightness in her chest. Pressing a trembling hand to her stomach, she fought the sudden urge to vomit.

Until her little anxiety attack this afternoon while kissing Daniel, she'd thought she was getting better. The nightmares were much less frequent now. But she was never going to be able to leave it all behind her if Collin kept taunting her with letters and flowers and showing up on her doorstep...

All she had to do was hear Collin's name and she reverted to a frightened victim again. She closed her eyes and sucked in several deep breaths, like Emily taught her to do, but her chest remained tight, and her whole body quivered on the inside.

"Hey, Pockets, are you okay?" Daniel touched her shoulder, and she flinched.

It was all she could do to not strike him. She'd learned some useful skills in the self-defense class the past couple weeks and was eager to put them to use. The only thing that kept her from punching him was his use of her nickname.

"No, I am not okay." She turned away from him and stomped over to the wall of windows. She focused on redirecting the anxiety coursing through her into anger. "I'm sick and tired of that man wreaking havoc on my life. Why won't he leave me alone?"

"He seems to be obsessed with you." Daniel took a step closer.

She scowled at him. "Please tell me that lunch at the diner and all this..." She motioned to the cabin. "Wasn't just a diversion tactic to keep me away from the ranch."

Daniel slipped an arm around her waist. "Yes it was a diversion, but one that I eagerly participated in. I've enjoyed having you to myself all day" When she didn't resist, he pulled her a little closer. "The only thing that kept me from getting in my truck last night and driving into town to find some booze to dull the pain in my shoulder was you."

"Me?" RIley's irritation melted away as she leaned into him.

"Yes. Even though I didn't feel like I deserved a second chance with you, I wanted it more than anything, and I didn't want to screw that up."

"Awe, you're kind of romantic in a twisted way." She planted a quick kiss on his lips then pulled away. "Now, give me your knife."

She still had some adrenaline and anger pulsing through her and she refused to let herself be distracted until she'd properly exhausted it.

"What?"

"Give me your pocketknife."

"Why?" He let go of her and took a step back.

"Because I need you to teach me to whittle."

CHAPTER 21

*D*aniel straightened from where he was hunched over his drawing table when a car drove down the lane. He let out a groan as he stretched his right arm.

I need to exercise more.

He'd slacked off on his weightlifting since injuring his shoulder, but he really needed to move more often. He was so over wearing the sling already because his shoulder felt much better, but Riley hounded him every day about it.

Speaking of Riley, he looked out his bedroom window and watched her climb from her Jeep.

Man, she's beautiful.

He'd always found her attractive, but the twinkle—that was so uniquely Riley—manifested itself in her eyes more often lately, making her prettier than ever. He could always tell when thoughts of Collin plagued her, though, because the twinkle disappeared.

She looked up and caught him watching her through his window. She smiled and waved, setting his heart to racing.

Good gravy. The woman does crazy things to my blood pressure.

If she rejected him again, it would crush him.

He shook the thought from his head. That wasn't going to happen this time. They were finally getting their happily ever after. He was determined not to do anything to mess it up.

Daniel felt like a heel for not getting up and greeting her at the door, but she always insisted on checking out his progress on the blueprints for the rec center, so he waited for her to come to him. He rolled his chair back from his drafting table as she stepped into his bedroom.

"Hi, handsome." Riley walked over and slid onto his lap.

When she first started working at the hospital a week and a half ago, she stood behind him while he showed her the plans, but then she often bent over and started kissing him. She always ended up on his lap. So now, it had become part of their standard greeting for her to sit on his lap.

"I missed working with you today." He nuzzled her neck.

Another part of their standard greeting. They were both doing what they loved, but they missed spending all day together.

"Me too."

They shared several long, breathtaking kisses, before Daniel backed off. Riley often tensed up when their kisses became passionate. It was a subtle shift, but he felt the change in her and was determined to end the kissing before she could get triggered again. They were usually both breathless by that point anyway.

"How was your day?" he asked as he tucked a lock of hair behind her ear.

"Good. I saw a male patient without feeling the need to have a nurse accompany me into the exam room."

"That's great! It's progress."

She scrunched her nose. "He was eighty years old."

"Not much of a threat, huh?" Daniel laughed, then quickly sobered. "Are you still working with Emily?"

"Yes. I thought I was making progress, but after that scumbag showed up here last week, I feel anxious and panicky all the time."

Riley always referred to her attacker as that scumbag. Daniel called him something much worse in his head.

Collin Ainsworth had some gall. He ended up showing up at the ranch again later that evening, looking for Riley, while she and Daniel were still at the lake. In an effort to dissuade him, Jake told him she'd gone away for the weekend with her boyfriend. He'd also told Ainsworth if he showed up at the ranch again, he'd have him arrested for trespassing.

According to Jake, anger had been evident in Ainsworth's face, but he left without further argument. Robert followed him to the county line the next morning.

They all hoped that if Ainsworth thought Riley was in a relationship, he'd leave her alone. Judging by the tension he sensed in Riley, she didn't think that was the case.

Daniel stroked her hair. "You'll get beyond it eventually."

If we can ever get this guy to leave her alone.

He wanted to take Riley to the courthouse and marry her right now, thinking it might stop Collin Ainsworth from harassing her, but also so he could better protect her. However, Riley wasn't ready for that level of commitment and intimacy yet.

"I'm sure you're right. But patience isn't one of my strengths."

Daniel chuckled. "No, it's not."

Then her lips were on his again, and as much as he wanted to lose himself in her kiss, he was careful to take it slow and not push it too far.

"I'm going to miss this," Riley said when the kiss ended.

He frowned. "Why?"

"Your parents come home tomorrow. I don't think they'd appreciate me coming into your room and making out with you."

"Probably not. But at this hour, my mom is usually at the big house, fixing dinner. And my dad is either working or hanging out in the kitchen with my mom."

"You mean we're not going to have to give up our afternoon make out sessions?"

"I hope not." Instead of allowing himself to be tempted to kiss her again, he asked, "Do you want to see what I accomplished today?"

Several minutes later, they were still discussing the plans for the rec center when a knock sounded on the front door. He looked at

Riley in surprise. Few people ever came to his parents' house that sat so far down the lane that it wasn't visible from the highway. Her expression looked every bit as confused and surprised as he felt.

He looked out the window and found a gleaming red Porsche parked beside Riley's Jeep. No wonder they didn't hear another car drive up. "Is that Debbie Wheeler's car?"

Riley vacated his lap and looked out the window. "Looks like it. I wonder why she's here."

"I guess we'd better go find out."

A second knock sounded just as they reached the front entry.

Daniel opened the door to find not only Debbie but a tall dark-haired man.

"Hi, Daniel," Debbie gave a broad smile. "And Riley. I heard you were home for a while. How are you doing?"

"I'm good, and you?"

"I'm doing fantastic." Debbie put a hand that sported a flashy engagement ring on the man's chest. "This is my fiancé, Austin Reed."

Daniel couldn't help it; his jaw dropped. He quickly snapped it closed to hide his surprise. The rich widow who had been after many of Providence's bachelors for years, including Robert and Jake and their cousin Ben, had finally found a man.

"C-congratulations," Riley sputtered, and Daniel nodded.

"Thank you." Debbie beamed. She looked happier than Daniel had ever seen her.

Riley remembered her manners enough to shake Austin's hand, and Daniel followed.

"Word has it that you're an architect," Austin said as he shook Daniel's hand in a firm grip.

"Yes."

"Good. Then we're in need of your services."

"Excuse me?"

Debbie already owned a mansion. Daniel couldn't think of a single thing they would need design help with.

"We have a job proposal for you," Austin said. "Could we come in and discuss it with you?"

"Sure, uh, yeah. Come in." Daniel swung the door open wider and waved them in, belatedly realizing the front room wasn't all that tidy. He planned to do something about that tonight before his parents came home tomorrow.

Riley quickly snatched one of his shirts off the couch and his ice cream bowl from the coffee table. "Have a seat."

In less than a minute, he and Riley were settled on the love seat, her hand in his. Debbie and Austin sat on the sofa, also holding hands.

Debbie looked at her fiancé and nodded. "Go ahead."

Austin cleared his throat. "Debbie and I have set a wedding date for mid-August. As soon as we are married, we plan to go into business together. We want to provide more affordable housing here in Providence."

Daniel's ears perked up. "Housing?"

"Apartment buildings, small homes for low-income families, as well as larger homes."

"That's great! Providence definitely needs more housing."

"It does, and we're hoping you can help us."

"Me? How?"

Riley nudged him with her elbow and rolled her eyes at the same moment Austin replied, "Sorry, I thought that was obvious. We need an architect to design not only the apartment buildings and houses but also the layout of the subdivisions. Although we can find another contractor to do the latter, if you're not comfortable with that."

"No, no, no." Daniel's chest swelled, cutting off his air supply. "I can design the subdivisions no problem. Tell me what you have in mind."

Austin continued to talk about his and Debbie's plans to build three separate subdivisions and how they wanted to have the designs in place by the time they were married and kicked off their partnership.

Austin finished with, "If you're interested in working with us, I'd like to see your portfolio and maybe get a few references."

Daniel's stomach clenched. He had an impressive resume for the short time that he'd worked in the architecture field, but considering he got fired from the prestigious firm he worked for in Portland, finding references could be difficult.

"He's designing plans for a recreation center for Jake right now. Would you like to see them?" Riley got to her feet.

Daniel wanted to kiss her.

As he led the group into his bedroom, he prayed his work would be proof enough for Debbie and Austin to show he was a competent architect. His eyes scanned his room, trying to decide if he should be embarrassed. It wasn't immaculate, but at least he'd taken the time to make his bed this morning and throw his dirty laundry in the washer.

Austin stepped right up to the drafting table and studied the designs for the rec center. Then he started pointing and asking questions. Daniel answered every question in detail, and the older man frequently nodded, looking suitably impressed. Talk shifted to some of the things Austin had in mind for the subdivisions and the apartment complexes, and Daniel laid out a fresh paper on his table and began some rudimentary sketches.

Austin continued to nod and point, talking much faster than Daniel could sketch.

He jumped when the other man's hand clapped him on the shoulder. "I think you're seeing our vision. Would you be available for lunch this Saturday so we can discuss more details and a contract?"

For the second time in less than an hour, Daniel's mouth dropped open. His heart raced as though he'd run a hundred-yard dash—something he hadn't done since high school.

Is this for real?

Not only was Jake paying him an obscene amount of money to draw up blueprints for the rec center, but Daniel also now had the possibility of a long-term job that could very well set him up with his own business here in Providence. A flush of dopamine zinged through his body, raising his temperature.

Riley nudged his arm.

"S-sure. I'd love to talk with you more." Daniel nodded so aggressively he felt like a bobblehead on the dash of a truck driving over a wash-board road.

"Excellent," Debbie said. "Why don't you and Riley come to the house on Saturday at one for lunch? That way, I'll have someone to visit with while you men talk business."

Daniel's grin grew so big, his cheeks cramped, and he caught himself nodding again. He couldn't believe this was really happening.

Finally, everything in his life was falling into place.

CHAPTER 22

*R*iley pushed open the door to exam room two. "Good news, Clint. I don't see a break."

She sat down on the stool and handed Clint—the older brother of one of her high school friends—the boot that he'd be wearing for the next four weeks. Then she explained the need for rest, ice, and elevation as well as the possible need for physical therapy down the road.

After helping Clint put on his new footwear, she opened the door for him and showed him out of the office. Then she heaved a sigh of relief.

I did it!

Vera, her medical assistant, had offered to accompany her into the exam room, but Riley had declined. She was tired of being afraid.

Last night in the self-defense class, she took down Rudy Wheeler, one of the sheriff's deputies. Judging by the look of surprise followed by pain in his eyes, he wasn't just going easy on her. Surely, she could defend herself against a man who hobbled in on his son's too small crutches.

As she made some final notes in Clint's chart, her thoughts quickly turned to Daniel as they did every time she had a few free moments. The last three weeks since they made up and made out at the lake had been amazing. Daniel was happier than she'd ever seen him. He hardly ever scrubbed his hand over his jaw and mouth anymore.

They both still whittled, though. It had become one of the many new things they did together. She now carried his small pocketknife with her all the time like he carried his sobriety chip in his pocket. It reminded her she could face her fears and do hard things.

She patted the knife in her pocket again, just as she did before going in to examine Clint's ankle.

"Are you okay, Riley?" Vera's voice pulled her from her musings.

She grinned at her medical assistant. "I'm great!"

Vera's smile matched her own. "Glad to hear it."

They chatted for a few minutes about work, then family, and finally their plans for the weekend before Riley went to her office and finished dictating her notes for the day. Vera and Lisa, the other medical assistant, were gone by the time she walked out of her office.

Riley's phone rang as she was about to push open the door to the rear parking lot. Juggling her purse, lunch bag, and water bottle she pulled her phone from her pocket. Warmth filled her when she saw Daniel's name on her phone.

"Well, hello, Tarzan."

"Hey, Pockets." A sultry tone filled his voice, and her heart did a series of backflips. "I was sitting here thinking that something was missing from my day when I noticed how late it was, and I realized I'm missing your pockets. On my lap." His voice took on a seductive quality, making her heart do more crazy gymnastics. Her stomach even dipped, joining in on the action.

"I'm sorry. I got caught up talking to Vera." Riley pushed through the door and squinted when the bright sunlight hit her full in the face. She brought the arm carrying her empty lunch back up to shield her face as she walked to her car. "But I'm headed home right now."

"Glad to hear it. Would you like to drive to Pasco tonight to catch a movie? Or would you rather go for a ride?"

Because of the time of day, only a handful of cars remained in the parking lot, so Riley didn't have to watch too carefully where she walked. Which was a good thing because the late-afternoon sun was blinding.

"I bet Misty and Rebel are missing us, but I'm not sure you should ride until your shoulder is completely healed."

"That's right, I'd better hurry and put my sling on before my girl-friend gets home. She can be such a tyrant."

Riley laughed. "Very funny."

She knew Daniel well enough, however, to know that he wasn't kidding. She'd caught him without it twice in the past two weeks. Other times, judging by his bunched collar, she was certain he slipped it on after he heard her park beside the house. At least his work was not physically taxing on his shoulder.

When she reached her Jeep, she turned her back to the sun, held her phone against her shoulder, and did more juggling as she fished in her purse for her keys. The door of the car next to hers opened, so she shifted closer to her car to get out of the person's way.

"Hello, Riley Darling," a familiar voice said behind her.

A sudden cold chill hit Riley with the speed of lightning. Every muscle in her body seized up, including her lungs. Alarm bells rang so loud in her head, she could no longer hear Daniel's voice.

No. No. No.

Why did she have to freeze at the mere sound of that scumbag's voice when she had no problem taking down Rudy or kneeing Daniel in the groin?

Because deep down I knew they weren't real threats. But Collin is.

Hands settled on her shoulders before she managed to mobilize her body. The contact caused her to snap out of it. Dropping every-thing she held, including her phone, she brought her elbow back hard and fast.

Collin grunted and swore. Then his arms closed around her in a vice-like grip. "You're such a spitfire. I've been looking forward to taming you."

Full of disgust, Riley lifted her right foot and stomped her heel down on what should have been his instep, but she missed her mark, and her soft soled shoe didn't do the damage that her cowboy boots would have.

"I was counting on a struggle, but this is even better than I imagined." He pinned her against her Jeep as he pressed his cheek close to her ear. "And believe me, I've had plenty of time to imagine how this moment would play out after you got me fired from my job." His voice grew more menacing and strained as she continued to squirm and fight against him. "I was hoping we could do this without the use of my little weapon, but you leave me no choice."

Weapon?

Additional alarm bells blared in her head.

"Help! Help me!" She screamed at the top of her lungs, knowing it was in vain. There was no one else in the nearly empty rear parking lot. And it wasn't likely someone in the front parking lot would hear her.

One of Collin's arms released her, so she spun, intending to deliver the fist-to-the-throat death blow they'd only talked about but never practiced in self-defense class. But Collin slammed her up against her Jeep so hard she saw stars. Then something sharp pierced her neck.

"I secured a little Ketamine and Ativan from a veterinarian friend of mine." Collin's breath was hot against her ear. "I've been saving this special little cocktail just for you."

Sedatives?

Her already-racing heart beat so fast her vision blurred. Fighting against the new level of panic that surged through her, she tried to shove away from her car to defend herself before they took effect. But already her limbs felt heavy and disjointed. Or maybe it was the knowledge that what he'd given her would totally incapacitate her, allowing him to do whatever he wanted to her.

A sinking sensation swooped downward through her chest and abdomen, simultaneously filling her with dread and nausea. Her hands shook so badly, she could hardly fight against him.

Collin's laughter rang in her ears, drowning out the alarm bells. "Oh, I'm going to have fun with you, my little cowgirl." Then his voice turned hard. "You're the only woman who refused to give in to me, and you're going to pay for that. Then I'll make your cousin pay for interrupting our little party."

Fueled by anger and contempt, she kicked and clawed at Collin, anything to protect herself. She screamed and swore as she swung her arms and fists wildly with every ounce of energy she could muster, but he withstood her blows, laughing the whole time.

All too soon her limbs lost their strength and darkness closed in. A bizarre sense of calm that didn't fit her circumstances settled over her.

It's the drugs.

Her thoughts turned to Daniel as the blackness claimed her. What would this do to him?

"RILEY? WHAT'S GOING ON?" Daniel shouted into his phone as he bolted to his feet, nearly knocking his drafting table over.

A muffled man's voice filled his ear, followed by the sounds of a struggle and a cry of alarm. Daniel was already halfway to his front door when Riley's scream for help came through his phone.

His gut clenched so hard it sent hot bile shooting up his throat.

"Riley!"

The only response was more muted voices and scuffling sounds, then Riley screamed again.

This time, his stomach plummeted.

Collin Ainsworth found Riley.

He was sure of it and the thought of what the man intended to do to her sickened him. He yelled Riley's name again but was greeted by what sounded like the slamming of a car door. He swore and ended the call then grabbed his keys. He had Robert on the phone by the time he reached his truck.

"Something's happened to Riley," he said as soon as Robert answered.

"What's happened?"

"I don't know. I was on the phone with her when suddenly there was a muffled man's voice, the sound of a struggle, and Riley screaming for help."

Robert swore on the other end of the phone. "Where is she?"

"She was just leaving the hospital."

"I'll head over there."

"I'm coming too." Staying on the line with Robert, he started his truck and took off down the lane with a squeal of rubber on pavement.

Daniel was almost halfway to town when Robert reported that he'd arrived at the hospital. More swear words came over the line. "I need to call this in." Then the line went dead.

Daniel echoed Robert's swear words. He lifted his phone again to call Jake. He should know something was going on with Riley.

A loud honk sounded, pulling his attention away from his phone.

Daniel looked up to see that he'd strayed from his lane, heading straight toward a dark red car. He jerked his wheel to the right, over correcting. Now he headed for a reflector post. He braked hard and corrected his steering again. Once he had his truck under control, he sucked in a deep breath, he found Jake's contact, then picked up his speed again.

Daniel made it to town in half the time it usually took. His tires screeched when he brought his truck to a stop just outside the back parking lot where Riley usually parked. He would have pulled into the lot, but a police cruiser blocked the entrance. Robert's Tahoe and another police car were parked near Riley's gray Jeep.

He jumped from his truck and raced toward Robert. "Where's Riley?"

Robert gripped Daniel by the shoulders, making him realize his left shoulder wasn't as healed as he thought. "She's gone, but we're going to find her."

Daniel's stomach hardened. "Gone? Gone where?"

"We don't know, but a witness came out of the hospital and saw a maroon car drive away a few minutes before I arrived." Robert shook his head in disgust. "Ainsworth drives a maroon Dodge Charger."

Daniel shoved his hands into his hair. "How? How did he manage to get her to go with him? Knowing Riley, she would have fought him tooth and nail."

"I'm sure she did, but he must have overpowered her or incapacitated her in some way."

"Incapacitated? How?" A band tightened around Daniel's chest, stealing his breath.

Robert's jaw clenched, his face grim. "I don't know. My only hope is that she has the opportunity to defend herself again at some point."

Ainsworth wouldn't have ki — No, he couldn't even think that.

He shoved both hands into his hair as a feeling of hopelessness swept over Daniel, making him crave a shot of whiskey. "Where would he have taken her?"

"I don't know, but I've put a BOLO out on Ainsworth's car. I've got Dale inside checking the security cameras to verify that it was indeed Ainsworth and to make sure he was alone."

"And we're supposed to just wait?" Anger deepened Daniel's voice. He turned and kicked the tire of Robert's SUV, then spun back around. "Hold on! You said Ainsworth drives a maroon Charger?"

"That's right."

Daniel remembered the car he nearly hit on the highway. He slapped his forehead. "I nearly hit them."

"What do you mean?"

"I passed a charger on my way into town."

"Headed toward the ranch?"

"Maybe. I don't know." Tension coiled in Daniel's gut like a snake ready to strike,

That didn't make sense though. Why would Ainsworth take Riley to her own home?

"Could he be taking her out to the lake?" He frowned at Robert.

There were a lot of properties out there. It could take days to search them all.

"It's possible." Robert turned and barked orders to Brady, the other deputy at the scene. Then he smacked Daniel's bad shoulder, sending a jolt of pain though him. "Let's go."

He climbed into Robert's Tahoe. "I'll call Jake."

It only took a brief conversation with Jake, who had been pacing the front porch since Daniel's last phone call, to know they hadn't come to the ranch. Daniel didn't think his stomach could plummet any lower, but it did. If Ainsworth took Riley to the ranch, she might have a chance. But if she was unconscious…

Daniel couldn't let himself consider all the horrible things Ainsworth intended to do to Riley.

Robert called Rudy, another deputy with the sheriff's department who happened to be a computer genius, while they drove. "See if you can connect this Ainsworth guy to any properties near the lake and call the ranger station out at the state park and have them keep an eye out for Ainsworth's car."

"His dad is Senator Ainsworth," Daniel said. "If he's taking her to the lake, it's probably to a property his dad owns."

The liquor store came into view, and Daniel's mouth watered so intensely he had to swallow twice. They drove so fast the store was little more than a blur, but the intense thirst sparked by the fear of what might happen to Riley stayed with him until long after they'd passed the ranch again.

CHAPTER 23

A sensation of cold seeped into Riley's body. But that didn't make sense. The last thing she remembered was walking out of the hospital into the blazing sunshine.

The hospital.

Her head throbbed as she struggled to recall what happened when she left work.

Hazy images danced through her mind that didn't make sense. Collin's voice behind her while Daniel flirted with her on her phone.

Strong arms.

A sharp pain in her neck.

She heard her own voice call for help.

Why did I call for help?

Flashes of what transpired in the hospital parking lot filled her head, quickening her heart rate, and making her breathing suddenly feel labored yet disconnected from her own body.

Fighting to keep her breathing slow and steady, she resisted the urge to open her eyes and alert Collin to her consciousness. She had no idea where he was—or where she was, for that matter—but she refused to let herself panic. Instead, she concentrated on one of her breathing techniques. If she had any chance of survival, she needed to collect her wits that seemed to be scattered from here to Canada.

But where is here?

She attempted to discern what she could of her surroundings without sight. Softness. She lay on her side on something soft. A couch or a bed?

Quiet rustling noises came from a distance. Indiscernible noises. Then another farther away. A droning motor that gradually grew louder then faded away, followed by a faint, rhythmic, lapping sound.

Water?

Were they near the lake? How long had she been unconscious?

She detected light behind her eyelids, but not a bright light. Still, she kept her eyes closed.

She continued to mentally take stock of her faculties while remaining motionless. She tested her limbs by slowly flexing each muscle one at a time. She sensed the tightness of the waistband of her slacks around her stomach and the softness of her rayon shirt against her arm. Her heart sank when she realized her hands were tied behind her back, and lifted only slightly when she discovered her legs were free.

She managed to cling to one positive thought —Collin hadn't yet done the horrible things he intended to do to her. So how did she keep him from succeeding in his goal?

Panic spiked again, and once more she focused on her breathing. Thinking clearly came a little easier now. She recalled the small pocketknife she'd carried everywhere for the last three weeks. If she could manage to get it from her pocket, maybe she could cut whatever bound her wrists.

She slowly pressed against her restraints. Not narrow and sharp like zip ties. Nor thick like a rope.

She strained again.

Duct tape?

Slowly, she peeked her eyes open to see if she was alone. Did she dare try to break the tape?

The blurry blue, gray, and white designs of the bedspread beneath her slowly came into focus. Paisley print. She let her gaze wander around the large bedroom as far as she could without moving, spotting a chest of drawers in a rich, dark mahogany color.

No Collin, thank goodness.

More rustling noises came through an open door.

But he's here.

She strained against her bands again.

Definitely tape, but not something she could tear. She quickly blinked against the onslaught of the tears that flooded her eyes.

Getting emotional won't help.

Footsteps drew closer.

Riley closed her eyes again and tensed, steeling herself for what was to come. She wished she'd had an opportunity to get her knife out, but she feared even if she had, she wouldn't have strength enough to defend herself with the small blade.

"Riley Darling," Collin's voice was soft, cooing. "It's time to wake up."

A wave of nausea swept through her stomach and filled her mouth with excess saliva.

The bed sank beside her causing her to pitch forward. It was all she could do to not jerk away from the solid body that sat so close.

Don't react.

Fingers touched her skin, caressing from her shoulder to her elbow.

She shuddered internally, willing herself not to flinch. She refused to give Collin the satisfaction of a reaction. Especially a negative one. That would only excite him.

"It didn't have to be like this, you know." Now his fingers caressed her cheek. "If you'd only given me what I've wanted for years, it would have satisfied my obsession with you. Then I would have walked away. Maybe."

Years!

She'd only known Collin for a few months. Hadn't she? Was it possible he had been stalking her since before they actually met?

So many questions tumbled around inside her head, but she

couldn't focus on any of them, because Collin's words and touch caused bile to rise in her throat. She clenched her jaw, hoping to avoid throwing up on him and alerting him to consciousness. She needed to buy herself time.

It was clear he wanted to have his way with her, but then what? Surely, he wasn't delusional enough to think Daddy's lawyers could get him out of abduction and rape charges. Although if he'd been obsessing over her for years—the thought still baffled her—maybe he was that delusional.

Would he silence her after he accomplished his goal?

Her heart rate took off again.

Calm down. Panicking won't do any good.

"I have something special planned for you. Or rather for us." His voice was low and seductive as his palm stroked her back from her shoulder to her hip and up again.

She felt her shirt pull from the back of her waistband with the motion, and she cringed inwardly.

"A candlelight dinner, roses, romantic music, and champagne. I even have a pretty dress for you to wear." Thankfully, he ignored the patch of exposed skin at her back, but the way his hand now slid over her thigh intensified the urge to vomit and lash out at him.

Except I can't lash out with my hands bound.

"You'll have such a good time with me. Of course, when my father finds out what I've done, I might have to leave the country for a while until he can make all of this go away."

Leave the country?

Riley's mind reeled. There was so much packed into Collin's words that she couldn't make sense of. She focused on not giving away the fact that she was conscious, knowing she'd eventually have to unpack and process it all.

"You need to wake up soon, or you're going to ruin my plans." His voice turned hard as he shook her shoulder.

Riley tensed inside, but she did her best to remain limp and unresponsive.

A timer went off somewhere in the other room, and the bed lifted when he stood.

Riley sent up a silent prayer of gratitude.

"Time's running out, Darling." He touched her cheek one more time then walked out of the room, whistling.

Does he mean that literally?

Riley breathed a sigh of relief as soon as he was gone, then she set to work trying to retrieve the knife from the pocket of her slacks. She moved as little as possible to avoid making noise but found it impossible to contort her body the way she needed to pull out the knife. Just as she feared she might dislocate her right shoulder, the fingers of her left hand finally connected with the cool metal and smooth stained wood.

She let out a soft swear word when it fell from her fingers once free of her pocket. Rolling and twisting, she wiggled until she retrieved it again.

Soft music came from the other room, and Riley sent up another prayer of thanks that she didn't have to be so careful about making noise. Once she got the blade out, she made quick work of the tape, only nicking herself a little. As far as she was concerned, leaving behind evidence wasn't a bad thing.

Once her hands were free, she rolled off the side of the bed farthest from the door and stayed crouched on the floor while she came up with a plan. She couldn't let Collin get the upper hand again. She searched the room for a weapon bigger than her small knife, but the room was sparsely decorated. Even the lamp on the bedside table was too short and thick to make a good weapon.

I'll have to use my knife.

She shuddered at the thought, but the sensation quickly passed. If she didn't incapacitate him in some way, who knew what he would do to her.

The blade was small, but in the right spot, it could do serious damage. She'd avoid major arteries because then she'd feel obligated to save his life. She hated him too much right now to have to do that. But she needed to slow him down enough to get away.

Strengthening her resolve and forming a plan, she crawled across the room until she was in front of the dresser near the door. Gratefully, her limbs responded like they should, and most of her strength had returned.

Then she waited.

"Riley Darling! Dinner's ready!"

Riley jumped when Collin called from just outside the room. The way he called her "Darling" made her skin crawl.

"Time to wake up, sweet—" He stepped through the door and cut his words off when he spotted the empty bed.

A surge of adrenaline shot through her, raising her body temperature.

Now or never!

Riley sprang from where she'd been crouching near the dresser and rammed the blade of her small knife into the center of the quadricep muscle of his left thigh.

"What the—" He stumbled against the dresser, nearly falling on her.

Keeping hold of her knife she pulled it from his leg and darted out of his reach, remaining crouched and wary. He stood between her and the door.

"You little—"

Ignoring the foul words that flew from his mouth, she sneered at him. In a mocking tone, she said, "It didn't have to be this way."

He pressed a hand to his thigh, blood quickly seeped through his fingers. He cursed again, and slowly advanced on her.

Breathing heavily from the adrenaline surging through her body, she circled in an arc toward the bed, hoping to get around him and closer to the door. "I won't hesitate to stab you again."

"Like that little thing could actually hurt me." Judging by the strain in his voice, she had indeed hurt him.

They continued their little dance for several long moments, but unfortunately, he remained between her and the door.

With a guttural growl, he dove at her, tackling her to the floor.

She went down hard, but the carpet was soft. Thankfully, she kept a hold of her knife. With little time to think and assess her situation, she reacted, bringing the blade down hard into the back of his shoulder joint.

He let out an animalistic roar and reared backward, nearly ripping the knife from her hand. She tightened her grip and pulled the blade from his shoulder. He'd likely end up with some tendon damage from that blow, but she refused to feel bad.

She managed to push him off her and spring to her feet. She darted toward the door. She'd just found her momentum when a hand grabbed her ankle, sending her sprawling onto the floor.

There was no soft landing this time as her body connected with the hardwood outside the bedroom. The air rushed from her lungs in a loud oomph. Her knees and elbows throbbed from the contact. The knife flew from her hand and clattered across the floor.

She kicked at Collin's hand on her ankle, and his hold loosened enough that she managed to combat-crawl to her knife. As she grasped it, a vice-like grip clamped down on her other ankle. With sweat stinging her forehead, she twisted and sat up.

Collin's face was beet red. A continuous string of curse words mingled with threats flowed from his mouth. If there was any doubt in her mind earlier whether he planned to let her live, it was gone now.

The knowledge was incentive enough to do what needed to be done. Letting out a growl of her own, she rammed the knife into his body for the third time. This time into the back of his hand.

Another roar came from him as he released her ankle.

Riley didn't hesitate. She sprang to her feet. And ran.

The short hallway ended abruptly in a large great room. Her eyes darted, searching for the door. She needed to get out of this cabin. It was her only chance at surviving.

Finally, she spotted a door across the room. She bolted toward it as more verbal threats followed her. She grasped the large knob and twisted, but it didn't turn. Wasting precious moments—moments, in which Collin drew ever nearer—she unlocked the dead bolt and the lock.

She swung the door open as Collin reached for her. Ducking his arm, she darted out the door, running for all she was worth. If she could just get into the trees beyond the small clearing, maybe she could evade him, especially with his limp slowing him down.

She prayed as she ran, relishing the feel of the cool breeze on her face.

A flash of blinding sunlight reflecting off the water hit her in the eyes just before she entered the trees. She turned and ran toward the water, staying in the cover of the trees. If she could figure out exactly where she was, then she could figure out how to get out of here.

At first, Collin's voice followed her, but then his cursing and threats grew fainter and fainter. She didn't slow, however. She could never put enough distance between her and that vile man.

She burst out of the trees onto a narrow, paved road.

Tires squealed, and she looked up to see an SUV coming right at her. She raised her arms in front of her face and squeezed her eyes shut, bracing for impact.

The heel of Daniel's boot bounced against the floor of Robert's Tahoe. They were so close, assuming Ainsworth took Riley to his father's lake house. He refused to even consider that Collin might have taken Riley somewhere else. If he did, he'd lose hope of finding her, and then he really would spiral.

A large animal darted into the road in front of them, and Daniel slapped his hands on the dash, bracing himself. "Robert, stop!"

Brakes squealed, and the SUV skidded to a stop, but Daniel's mind kept racing. Images of a small boy on a bike darting into the road filled his head. An unresponsive body. Screaming sirens. Flashing lights. Distraught parents. Daniel's heart rate spiked, and a band squeezed around his chest, making it difficult to breathe. Shadows danced around the edges of his vision, threatening to drag him down into the darkness that had consumed him for so long.

He sucked in a deep breath, fighting against the darkness and the guilt that accompanied it. The incredible thirst that hit him almost an hour ago—that he'd almost managed to tamp down—reared its ugly head.

Stop. Breathe. Focus. Riley needs your help. You can't spiral right now.

Robert pitched forward in his seat. "Is that—"

Daniel stared at the creature in the middle of the road.

Wait! That's not an animal.

He'd recognize that figure anywhere.

"Riley!" He and Robert said the word in unison and threw their doors open at the same time.

He reached Riley first and threw his arms around her. Robert wrapped his arms around both of them.

"Thank heavens." The words came from Robert, but Daniel felt them to his core.

Riley let out a cry of alarm then jerked and squirmed in his arms.

He backed off when he caught sight of a bloody knife in her hand. Robert was quicker than Daniel and caught her wrist as she swung wildly, thrashing around.

"Relax, Sis. It's me." Robert gently relieved her of the knife. "You're okay. You're safe now."

My knife. Covered in blood.

Daniel's chest tightened again as he considered what Riley had gone through. He took in her wild eyes, disheveled state, and blood-smeared clothing. Studying her carefully, he determined none of it was hers, except maybe the small cut on her wrist.

Relief filled him, making him almost light-headed. He wanted to pull her into his arms and never let her go, but he could tell she was running scared and possibly in shock.

He reached for her hand, but Robert stepped in front of her and gently cupped her face, so he pulled back. "Are you hurt, Riley?"

She started to shake her head in the negative then paused and nodded as she rubbed her neck with one hand and her elbow with the other. A look of confusion filled her eyes.

Daniel saw the exact moment she realized she was safe, because her face crumpled, and so did her body. He and Robert each grabbed an arm, keeping her from going down.

"It's okay," Robert said softly. "We've got you."

A twig snapped somewhere in the trees in the direction from which Riley had come, and she jerked upright, her eyes taking on that frantic look again.

"He's s-still out there."

Daniel pulled her close, gently cradling her in his arms. He shot Robert a look that said you'd-better-take-care-of-this-guy-once-and-for-all-before-I-do.

"Where's Ainsworth, Ri?" Robert's hand hovered over his gun.

"He was several yards behind me." She stared at the blood on her hands. "I-I stabbed him."

"Good." Daniel couldn't help the outburst. He was glad Riley had the courage to defend herself and managed to inflict a little pain on her attacker.

"Is he armed?" Robert asked.

"No, I don't think so."

"Don't let her out of your sight." Riley's brother gave him a hard look then took off into the trees.

Daniel's heart rate finally settled down as Riley buried her face against his chest. He cupped the back of her head. "Where are you hurt, Pockets?"

"I'm...I'm not injured," she whispered into his shirt.

Daniel didn't miss the way she changed his words. She may not be hurt physically, but he doubted she could say the same about her mental and emotional state.

"Are you sure?" He pressed his cheek to her temple. "Did he— Did he ra—" Bile filled his mouth, and he couldn't say the word that made his stomach churn.

"No."

Oh, thank you, Lord!

It wouldn't have affected how he felt about her, but that kind of trauma could take Riley years to overcome.

A shout came from the woods, followed by scuffling noises and more shouting.

Daniel and Riley both froze, listening intently.

"On your feet, Ainsworth!" Robert's voice carried clearly through the trees. "You've racked up quite the list of felonies today. Don't even think Daddy's money and influence is going to get you off this time."

Daniel continued to hold Riley right there in the middle of the road, waiting for Robert to bring Riley's attacker into view. Powerful emotions built in his chest, stealing his breath again, anger and contempt, disgust and hatred.

Did Robert have more than one set of handcuffs? He'd need them after he dragged Daniel off Ainsworth.

"Daniel," Robert's voice again came from the trees. "I don't want Riley to have to face this jerk again. Take her down the road about fifty yards to that path that cuts over to the south side of the lake. My family's cabin is only about a quarter of a mile away. I need to call for backup to help process Ainsworth's house. Then I'll tell Jake to bring my mom to come meet you guys at the cabin."

A flash of disappointment shot through Daniel, but it was probably best that he not face Ainsworth today. "Okay."

Without speaking, he and Riley turned and walked down the road. He kept an arm around her shoulders, and thankfully, she stayed close to his side. A deep-seated need to comfort her filled him, but her quiet, stoic expression told him she either didn't need comforting or she didn't want him to be the one to do it. He feared it was the latter.

They made the trek along the algae and pine scented trail in silence. Daniel kept wishing she would talk to him, but Riley had a lot of processing to do, so he stayed quiet, waiting until she was ready. When they finally reached the cabin, Riley pulled away from him and huddled in the corner of the sofa, her arms wrapped around her knees.

He recalled how the two of them snuggled on that very sofa only a few weeks ago, watching a movie. The woman who fell asleep in his arms that afternoon looked so very different from the frightened victim who sat there now.

Daniel sat near her yet was careful to give her the space she seemed to need. "What can I do for you, Pockets?"

"Nothing." She shook her head, then rubbed her forehead with trembling fingers. "Did you know the Ainsworth's cabin was so close to ours? Did we know Collin when we were kids?"

Daniel's eyes widened.

Did we?

Even though they weren't related, the Winters, Youngs, and Knights were always generous to include his family in their get-togethers. Daniel hadn't spent as much time here when he was a kid as Riley and her cousins did, but he'd spent enough time to know that the families who owned the cabins often hung out together. Their kids swam, canoed, and camped out together all the time.

Daniel couldn't recall ever meeting the Ainsworths, but it was entirely possible that Collin had been obsessing over Riley much longer than any of them realized.

Riley must have come to the same conclusion because she shuddered then covered her face with both hands. Whimpering and squeaking sounds came from her, then suddenly her shoulders shook with great wracking sobs.

He scooted closer and pulled her into his arms. Gratefully she came, but her body remained tense and rigid. He held her for a long time until her hiccupping sniffles finally subsided. When she pulled away to go to the bathroom, he had no choice but to let her go. She may have let him hold and comfort her, but there was an emotional barrier between them as tall and as thick as the great wall of China.

He couldn't force her to trust him, so he focused on finding them food. By the time she came out of the bathroom, he had toast from a loaf of bread he found in the freezer and a mug of herbal tea on the table. He also had water boiling on the stove for macaroni and cheese.

Her mumbled, "Thanks," did little to ease his concerns.

He'd just placed a bowl of macaroni in front of her when the door burst open, and Faith Winters rushed in. Within seconds, she'd swept Riley, who'd started crying hysterically at the sight of her mother, into her arms. The two of them ended up on the couch again exactly where he'd held Riley a short time ago, but Riley's posture was different now.

She wilted into her mother, practically curling up on her lap, never mind that she was taller than her mom.

Jake stepped over to Daniel. "How did you and Robert find Riley?"

"She found us." He spoke in hushed tones. "She managed to escape Ainsworth and ran into the road right in front of us. We almost hit her."

Daniel's chest swelled with pride as he told Jake that Riley had stabbed Ainsworth with the whittling knife he'd given her. He was so proud of her for standing up to and triumphing over Ainsworth. Unfortunately, overcoming the fear this new assault triggered would take a lot longer.

The rest of the evening passed in a blur of high tension on Daniel's part and even higher emotions on Riley's part. She babbled to her mother as she cried, making her sentences either incoherent or disjointed. Then Robert arrived to get a full statement from her.

Attempting to stay out of the way, but mostly because he was so keyed up, Daniel stood near the table, gripping the top two rungs of a ladder-back chair while Robert questioned Riley.

She rubbed at a spot on the side of her neck as she struggled to recall the details of what happened in the hospital parking lot. "I think he drugged me."

Jake bolted to his feet at her words and joined Daniel in the kitchen gripping a second chair.

Robert shot his younger brother a look that was a combination of I-hear-you and cool-it, then turned back to Riley. "We found a syringe in his car. I'll have the lab at the hospital analyze it to figure out exactly what he gave you. I had Dale pull the security footage. He'll fill in the details at the hospital." He consulted his notebook. "Do you remember anything about the car ride to Ainsworth's lake house?"

Riley shook her head. "No, I just gradually came-to on a bed."

Daniel's blood grew hot and his grip on the chair tightened as he listened to Riley describe her disturbing interactions with Ainsworth. Pretending to still be unconscious was genius. It was no secret what

Ainsworth's end goal was, so Daniel appreciated that the man planned an elaborate seduction if for no other reason than it delayed the inevitable and gave Riley an opportunity to escape.

When she described how he tackled her and the way he grabbed her ankle, sending her sprawling, his grip on the chair tightened.

Crack! The second slat snapped, breaking in two. Splintered wood dug into his fingers.

"Dude!" Jake scowled at him, then he looked down at his own white-knuckle grip and loosened the hold he had on his chair.

This time, Daniel got the look of empathy and warning from Robert.

Robert shared a few minor details that he'd learned with the rest of them, but Daniel could tell he knew more than he was divulging.

The drive back to the ranch passed quietly with Faith in the back seat holding Riley, and Daniel sitting up front with Jake. He hoped to have an opportunity to talk with Riley more when they got home or at least hold her to confirm to himself that she was really okay, but Faith talked her into going into town to stay with her at her Aunt Charity's house.

Daniel suspected the part that swayed Riley the most was the promise of her uncle James prescribing something that would help her sleep tonight. But what hurt the most was that Riley didn't even say goodbye.

Less than ten minutes after arriving back at the ranch, he stood in the darkness under a tree near the big house with the breeze rifling his hair as he watched Faith's car drive away. The smaller the taillights became, the larger the hole in his chest grew.

He was tempted to ask Jake to drive him into town to get his truck, but he feared if he did, he wouldn't make it back home without stopping at one of the two bars in town or the liquor store. Because unfortunately, despite Riley being safe, the urge for a stiff drink hadn't diminished one bit from this afternoon.

CHAPTER 24

Faith grimaced as she walked back into Charity's living room. "I'm sorry Daniel, Riley doesn't want to see you right now."

Again.

It had been three days since Riley was abducted, and he'd come every day, multiple times a day, and every time, she refused to talk to him. She hadn't responded to any of the dozens of texts he'd sent her either.

Three long days that he'd been fighting the cravings.

"How is she doing?"

"Honestly, I don't know. She says she's fine, but she hardly comes out of her room. Emily did manage to convince her to sit with her under the maple tree yesterday. They were out there for two hours."

"Can you help me understand what she's going through?" He leaned forward, propping his elbows on his knees. "I want to be supportive, and I can be patient. I don't know how to help her, though, especially when she won't even talk to me."

"I wish I had answers for you. Being drugged and abducted are plenty traumatic and knowing what that man intended to do to her..." Faith's eyes filled with tears that she quickly blinked away. "Then there's the physical fight she went through to escape and the fear that she might die in that cabin. All of that is too much for one person, but I think what bothers her is that this man has obsessed over her since she was a teenager and she had no idea."

Faith shifted in her seat as though getting more comfortable. "His family didn't spend as much time at the lake as ours did, but he admitted to Robert on Friday night that he's had a thing for Riley since she was fourteen and he was seventeen. She doesn't remember him very well, because not only was he a scrawny kid and his hair much lighter back then but he was also a socially-awkward, only-child. She, Paige, and Damon didn't like hanging out with him, because he always threatened to tell on them if they didn't play the games he wanted to play. I can't help but wonder if he's been harboring resentment over being rejected by Riley for over a decade."

Daniel recalled Riley telling him that Ainsworth was all the nurses' favorite pharmaceutical rep because he was so charming. He must have learned some social skills at some point. And once he discovered Riley working at a clinic his company sold to, he turned on the charm as part of an elaborate plan to win her over.

"Robert also told us that Collin intended to keep Riley a hostage at the cabin with him for as long as possible. If she cooperated..." She made air quotes as she continued, her voice heavy with disgust. "They'd have a great life together. He hoped to persuade her to leave the country with him."

"And if she refused?" Dread filled Daniel's gut at realizing how twisted this man was.

Faith frowned. "Collin admitted to having a lethal dose of horse tranquilizer that he planned to give her before dumping her body in the lake and fleeing the country, if necessary."

Daniel sat back in his seat as a powerful wave of nausea swept over him. He knew the man was sick and demented, but he assumed his motives were passion driven, not carefully calculated and psychotic.

"Sickening, isn't it?"

"I'll say." He scrubbed his hands over his face. "So how do I help Riley?"

"Be patient. I wonder if the reason she's pulling away from you is because all of this actually ties back to her childhood in which you played such a big part, and she's having a hard time separating it all."

It wasn't the answer Daniel wanted to hear, but it made sense.

A door opened down the hall, and Daniel bolted to his feet.

Riley stopped in her tracks when she saw him standing there. "What are you still doing here?"

"I came to see you." He swiped his sweaty palms on his jeans. "I thought you might like to go for a walk."

She retreated a step, wrapping her arms around herself, and shook her head.

"I could drive you out to the ranch to ride Misty."

"No thanks."

Unwilling to give up yet, he pulled the new pocketknife he'd bought for her that afternoon from his pocket. "Would you like to go out back and whittle?"

Riley shuddered and shook her head so vigorously he feared she'd snap a vertebra.

"Please leave."

"Come on, Pockets," He hoped the use of his nickname for her would help soften her—or ground her, as she put it—but then belatedly remembered when she frowned that much of what she was dealing with was tied to the past.

"I don't want to be around you right now. Why can't you understand that?" A heavy and deadly serious tone filled her voice.

In all the years he and Riley had spent together, he'd never heard her use that tone. Exasperation and frustration, sure. Annoyance and even anger. But this... This was...contempt? Disgust?

Whatever it was, it was aimed directly at him. This was personal.

Daniel spun on the heel of his boot and walked out the door. Riley had ripped his heart to shreds once. He wouldn't stay here and let her do it all over again.

Except she already has.

He climbed in his truck and drove away. When he hit the entrance to the subdivision, instead of turning left to head back out to the ranch, he turned right. He didn't know where he was even headed until he found himself pulling into the parking lot of the liquor store.

A sharp pang of disappointment filled him. Disappointment in himself.

Riley would be disappointed in him too.

But what does she care right now?

His parents, Jake, and Emily. Ever since he came home, he'd been afraid he'd let them down again someday.

So why not today?

Emily always encouraged him to choose faith over fear. *"Instead of being afraid you will fail again someday, have faith that you will stay sober for the rest of your life."*

He'd already committed to turn his life over to God months ago, knowing He could make more of it than Daniel could. So why was he contemplating turning his back on God now?

He put his truck into park and stared at the small gray building.

Do I really want to do this?

He reminded himself of the steps he hadn't had to use for some time to deal with a craving.

1. Acknowledge the craving.

Oh, I've acknowledged it, alright. For the past three days!

Wiping the perspiration from his brow, he shut off the engine and pulled the keys from the ignition. Once again, he looked at the liquor store. Only twenty yards away.

2. Recognize that it will pass.

Except it hasn't!

Swiping a hand over his mouth, his gaze zeroed in on the front door of the store. The heel of his right boot bounced against the floor as he gripped the steering wheel with both hands, twisting against the leather.

3. Distract yourself.

This is where he got hung up every time. He couldn't work out in the weight room in the stables, because it reminded him of Riley nowadays. He couldn't whittle, because it had become a tie to Riley.

Riding?

Riley.

Shooting?

Riley.

His life was so wrapped up in Riley, her withdrawal—and now rejection—made him feel completely lost without her. Alcohol would make him not feel so lost and alone. He imagined the burn of whiskey sliding down his throat then had to swallow the saliva that filled his mouth.

With a trembling hand, he unbuckled his seat belt. Instead of opening his door like he was tempted to do, he pulled the sobriety chip from his pocket. He ran his thumb across the black and bronze surface, then around the edge where the words Unity, Service, and Recovery were etched. He pressed his thumb against the number eight in the center until the flesh under his nail turned white.

He considered calling Tom, his mentor from the AA group in Pasco. But he'd stopped attending there, and even though he'd gone to a handful of meetings here in Providence, he hadn't yet been assigned a sponsor. In fact, they'd asked him to be a sponsor.

Daniel wasn't ready for that, so he'd declined and hadn't gone back. He hadn't needed to while he and Riley were together. When he was with her, he had no desire to drink.

He could call Emily, or better yet, drive home and talk to her, which would distance him from the temptation of the liquor store or a bar. But it wasn't fair to Emily to tell her how much Riley's behavior affected him while she was trying to help Riley through her problems.

Then he remembered it was Monday night. Providence held AA meetings on Mondays and Thursdays, as opposed to Pasco's Tuesday and Friday meetings.

Go to the meeting.

Going to the meeting might help him through today's cravings, but it wouldn't fix the issues with Riley. He had to do that himself. It would take patience. He'd told Faith he could be patient, so why was he here trying to justify going into the liquor store and buying a bottle of Johnny Walker Red?

He looked at the chip in his hand again and read the words written below the number eight. To thine own self be true. Letting Riley and his loved ones down wasn't being true to himself.

Riley may have given up on them for the time being, but he refused to give up on her. She was his best friend and forever love. He couldn't lose that.

He stared at the black and bronze chip in his hand again. Eight months.

I've been sober for eight months. I won't throw that away.

No, wait. He paused and did a few mental calculations. He'd hit his nine-month mark two weeks ago, right after he and Riley got back together.

He put the key back in the ignition and started his truck.

I want my nine-month chip.

He'd go to tonight's meeting. And Thursday's meeting. Then next week's meetings. Because even though he was strong enough to drive away tonight, he recognized didn't have to do it all on his own.

Maybe I'll even sign up to be a sponsor.

He wasn't simply choosing faith over fear. He was choosing love.

Love for Riley, but more importantly, love for himself.

CHAPTER 25

*R*iley lowered the book she'd been attempting to read all week and rolled her eyes when a knock sounded on her bedroom door.

No, this isn't my bedroom.

It was simply the guest room at Aunt Charity's house. A room she'd occupied for far too long. She should go back to her room at the ranch.

Funny how two months ago, she didn't consider that guest room hers either. But now she did.

The knock was probably her mom trying to coax her from her room yet again. Riley loved her mother, but she was tired of being smothered.

She cringed when the door creaked as it opened. Steven or Matt, one of Charity's two oldest sons, should do something about that for her. If Damon was here, he would have taken care of it already. He was always good about things like that.

"There's my favorite cousin." Paige stepped into the room sporting a smile that lifted Riley's spirits immediately.

She let out a little squeal and sprang to her feet. Paige always gave the best hugs, and today was no exception.

Her cousin spent the day with her last Saturday, the day following Riley's abduction, and they'd talked for hours about what happened. Paige helped her remember the awkward, scrawny, blond boy who sometimes wanted to hang out with them at the lake. They hadn't intentionally snubbed him; they'd simply been more interested in hanging out with their own cousins rather than wanting to play with an awkward stranger.

"I stopped by the ranch, thinking you'd gone home." Paige pulled back and studied Riley's face. "Why are you still here?"

"I don't know." Riley shrugged as she stepped away from the embrace. "I just can't..."

She dropped down on the bed as she struggled to find the words to explain how messed up she felt inside. She'd promised Uncle James she would return to work on Monday, even though he insisted she take all the time she needed. She was tired of sitting around feeling sorry for herself, though, so she needed to get herself figured out quickly.

Paige sat beside her. "Can't what?"

"I can't be around Daniel right now, which sounds so stupid because I miss him like crazy."

And here came the tears again. Riley didn't know one person could create so much water.

"He misses you too."

"Did you see him when you stopped at the ranch?" She paused in the process of wiping her tears.

"Of course, I did. He showed me the completed designs for the rec center. It's going to be so amazing." Paige gently rubbed Riley's back. "Is it hard to be around Daniel because of the physical stuff?"

Why did it not bother her when Paige or her mom rubbed her back, but made her want to crawl out of her skin when Daniel did it at the cabin to console her? Why couldn't she separate Daniel's touch from Collin's?

"Yes, but it's more than that."

"Like what?"

"I feel so mixed up inside. There are so many powerful emotions raging through me. They surge to the surface without warning, and I react, usually in negative ways." She pointed to the sad-looking throw pillows behind her. "Those poor pillows have taken a lot of beatings."

Paige grimaced and rubbed Riley's back again. "That's okay. It takes time to process and heal. We all understand that."

"But I take my anger, sadness, and repulsion out on those around me. Even my mom has learned it's best to give me space." Riley sighed and brushed her hair back from her face. How did she explain why she felt the need to avoid Daniel without giving away things he didn't want others to know? "When I came home from Seattle, I felt damaged, and I'd finally started to heal from it all, but now...I feel shattered."

"You deserve to feel that way. You've been through so much. Are you talking with Emily?"

"Yes, she came over on Sunday, then again on Tuesday and Thursday."

On Tuesday, Riley had been so stir crazy, she told Emily if they were going to talk, she needed to take her for a walk because Riley didn't dare go out alone anymore, even in broad daylight. Emily had been more than willing to walk with her. They walked and talked again on Thursday.

"She's helping me process everything, but I have a long way to go."

"No one expects you to heal overnight."

"I know, but I don't want Daniel to see me like this."

Paige's blond hair fell forward when she leaned down to look Riley in the eye. "He understands you're dealing with some really heavy stuff right now. He doesn't expect anything from you."

"I know, but when I came home from Seattle feeling so violated, I took it all out on him. I overreacted anytime he got too close and I...I hurt him." Riley sniffled. "It's all so much worse this time."

Daniel would probably rather Paige not know how she assaulted him by kneeing him in the groin. It was not one of her finer moments. Nor could she explain to Paige that while she'd struggled to deal with her baggage, she made Daniel's garbage harder to handle.

"I'm afraid if I'm around him, I'll take all these crazy and irrational emotions out on him again. He doesn't deserve that."

A surge of guilt twisted her stomach. He didn't deserve the icy-cold shoulder she'd given him either.

"They are not irrational." Paige's voice was forceful, then her face grew serious. "He told me what he's been through. About hitting that little boy and his subsequent drinking problem." She pressed her hands to her chest. "I feel so bad. I had no idea he was going through that. I feel like the worst friend ever."

"You and me both." Riley swiped away a tear that leaked out at the thought of the turmoil Daniel must have gone through after the accident. "I know we'd just broken up, but I wish he would have called me."

"That's exactly how he feels right now." Paige's hand landed on her back again. "He wants to help you through this."

Riley's head popped up. "Did he tell you that?"

"He didn't have to. It was all over his face." Paige grimaced. "He did mention what a struggle it's been this week to stay sober."

Riley's heart ached. By trying to protect him from her emotional outbursts, she'd made things harder for him. She knew that was a possibility, so she prayed every day that he'd stay strong. She was thrilled when she received a text from him Monday night with a picture of his nine-month sobriety chip.

He'd texted her multiple times every day this week. Most of them simply said, "I miss you" or "I love you." Sometimes he shared inspirational quotes or a funny story with her. Once, he recounted a memory from their childhood that made her miss him that much more.

She cherished each text, but she didn't always respond. Riley couldn't make him any promises and give him false hope while she was so screwed up. She wanted to go back to the ranch so badly. Not just to see Daniel but so she could ride Misty. She needed to start feeling normal again.

But could she open herself up to him again so soon? What if being around him made her long to be held by him, but then she felt repulsed by his touch?

"Hey," Paige must have noticed Riley over-thinking things because she grasped her hand. "He understands. He knows it's going to take time for you to feel normal again. He wants to be there for you, but he'll respect any boundaries you set. You know that, right?"

"I do." Tears again flooded Riley's eyes. "I just can't stop feeling anxious."

Her breath quickened, and her heart hammered against her rib cage at the mere thought of seeing Daniel again. The emotions flooding through her were a lot more than anxiety.

She'd stood up to Collin, surely she was brave enough to talk to Daniel?

DANIEL STOPPED SHORT when he pushed through the kitchen door of the ranch house to find Riley sitting at the dining table surrounded by Jake, Emily, and his parents. His lungs seized at the same moment his heart rate skyrocketed, making him feel like one or the other—or maybe both—might burst any second.

Riley's long, dark hair that was usually pulled back in a ponytail or a braid hung down, framing her face in gentle waves. Her beautiful blue eyes held his gaze for a moment, before lowering. The light that he loved to see there—the one he'd come to associate with the woman he loved—was absent. Her hunched shoulders curled forward, her whole demeanor guarded. She reminded him of a skittish colt, but she looked absolutely beautiful.

His stomach sank. Riley may be home, but she wasn't truly back yet. Would she let him help her find herself again? Did he even dare try?

Everyone else must have known she was coming home, or at least had a chance to greet her already, because he seemed to be the only one surprised to see her. He ached to walk around the table and pull her into his arms, but something told him if he did, she'd run straight back to her Aunt Charity's house. Or maybe even Seattle now that Collin was in jail.

He gave her a gentle smile across the table as he took his seat. "Welcome home, Riley."

A small nod accompanied her hesitant smile.

Either Emily had warned everyone not to talk about things that might upset Riley, or they all understood, as he did, that a certain name and subject were off limits, because conversation was stilted.

"So, how are the plans for the rec center coming?" Riley finally asked, and it felt as if a collective exhale circled around the table.

"Great." Jake beamed. "Daniel finished them this week. They're amazing."

Riley asked the right question because the conversation concerning the rec center lasted the entirety of the meal.

They all chipped in to clear the table when dinner was over. Daniel made sure not to crowd Riley as he followed her to the kitchen, but he couldn't take his eyes off her. He kept hoping for a signal of some sort. Some indication that she wanted to spend a little time with him or a hint that they were going to be able to work through this.

When she looked at him over her shoulder and tilted her head toward the backyard before pushing through the swinging door, he wanted to cheer and hive-five everyone in the kitchen. He resisted for fear of looking like an idiot.

Jake elbowed Daniel in the side. "Well, if that isn't an invitation that says, 'Follow me,' I don't know what is."

"You think?" A sudden flood of uncertainty swamped Daniel.

What if I say or do the wrong thing?

Emily stepped close. "Take it slow. Let her set the pace." She handed baby Adam to Jake and put a hand on Daniel's shoulder. "Let her decide what you talk about, how close you sit. Don't touch her unless she touches you first. Respect the boundaries she sets." Then her hand shifted to his back, and the next thing he knew he was being pushed through the swinging door. "Just be yourself."

Daniel quickly scanned the family and dining room to make sure Riley wasn't there before walking to the back door. He swiped sweaty palms on his jeans before grabbing the knob. His heart skipped a beat when he stepped out and spotted her sitting on the porch swing.

She sat sideways with her bare feet on the seat, arms wrapped around her knees. It was a protective gesture that prevented him from sitting too close, but he was grateful she left him any space at all on the swing, otherwise he'd have to sit in a lounge chair several feet away.

"May I?" he motioned to the end of the swing near her feet.

"Please."

That sounds encouraging.

Careful not to move too quickly or sit too closely, he took a seat.

They sat in silence for almost a full minute, during which Daniel grew more and more tense, before she finally spoke. "I've missed you."

The corner of his mouth hitched up as he sucked in a deep breath. A part of him still feared she would tell him to take a hike, so those three words elated him.

"I've missed you too." Careful not to touch her, he shifted slightly to face her. "I've prayed for you every day."

"Thank you." She lowered her gaze. "I prayed for you too. I worried that pushing you away would make staying sober harder, but I was afraid I would hurt you worse if I was around you."

"Not gonna lie, Pockets, staying sober this week has been a challenge."

"I know. I'm sorry I pushed you away. I knew you could do it though. You are so much stronger than you think."

"You are too," he said without hesitation.

Her lips curved in a small smile, but she didn't speak.

He lifted his hat and ran his fingers through his hair. "Why did you think it would hurt me worse if you were around me?"

Her eyebrows rose as a look of surprise crossed her face. "Have you forgotten how I kneed you in the groin because you made the mistake of touching me when I first came home?" She motioned toward the spot in the yard where it happened. "The emotional roller coaster I'm on now is so much worse than last time."

"No, I haven't forgotten. But that physical pain was nothing compared to the emotional turmoil I've been through this week."

She winced and lowered her gaze again.

"Not only because you pushed me away but because I was worried sick about you. I honestly had no idea how you were doing. I had to rely on reports from your mom—which weren't positive—and Emily who couldn't divulge anything."

"I know. I'm sorry." Tears filled her eyes, and when she reached out and took his hand, he hung on for dear life. "I told myself I was protecting you from my emotional outbursts, but I was trying to protect myself too. From expectations. From feeling the need to make promises I wasn't sure I could keep."

"I'm not asking you to make me any promises, Ri. Not yet anyway."

"But what if I can't get beyond all of this?" She waved a hand, encompassing her body. "What if I can't handle a normal relationship ever again?"

"You can. You'll see. You just need to give yourself time." He locked gazes with her and squeezed the hand he still held, grateful for the connection. "I'm not going anywhere, Pockets. You take all the time you need."

"Thank you." Her grip tightened, and more tears filled her eyes, spilling onto her cheeks. "I'm trying, but it's so much harder than I thought it would be. Knowing Collin obsessed over me for years and was plotting every time he came into the clinic, has me questioning everyone's motives and fearing every interaction."

"There's no rush." He grazed his thumb across her knuckles. "You know, after you turned me away Monday evening, I found myself parked outside the liquor store." He sensed her body tensing, but he kept talking. "I was so tempted to go inside and buy some booze, but I decided to choose love over fear."

"What?"

"Emily always encourages me to choose faith over fear. Faith that I'll stay sober, instead of fear that I'll fail someday. But the other day outside the liquor store, I decided to choose love over fear." He locked gazes with her. "Our love is strong enough to overcome all of our fears if we let it." Feeling brave, he lifted Riley's hand and pressed a lingering kiss to the back of it. He was almost afraid to open his eyes again after lowering her hand, but the sigh he heard escaping her lips gave him the encouragement he needed.

Additional tears streamed down her cheeks. "I wish I could show you how much I love you."

"Me too." He squeezed her hand again. "What do you say we take a rain check on that display of affection and go for a ride? I think Misty and Rebel have missed us."

She grinned, a hint of that old spark lighting her eyes. "Sounds perfect."

CHAPTER 26

*a*t the sound of hooves on the nearly frozen ground, Riley straightened from the hearth in the small north cabin. She hurried over to the window and looked out to see Daniel and Rebel cresting the hill.

The mid-November landscape was barren, but this small cabin was warm and cozy.

Her heart did that funny little tap dance thing it did every time she saw him. The man was handsome, sure, but he was so much more than that. He was patient and gentle, understanding and encouraging. She loved him more than she ever thought possible.

She spun around and double-checked the room. A fire blazed in the fireplace and two small dutch ovens sat on either side of the hearth, keeping warm. One contained lasagna, the other peach cobbler. It had been a chilly four-wheeler ride to get here, but since it hadn't snowed yet, she absolutely wanted to do this in the small cabin where she'd experienced two life-changing events.

Her eyes darted to the candles on the table, then to the Scrabble game on the counter of the small kitchenette. She patted her pocket, reminding herself she'd placed all the necessary tiles there earlier. She couldn't rely on luck this time. She'd have to cheat if she wanted Daniel to believe she was ready for a serious relationship.

It had been almost five months since her abduction. It had taken her a long time to process that transpired with Collin, but once she did, she found it easier to separate it from her life with Daniel. She'd been telling him for months that she was no longer bothered by his touch and kisses, but the man was so afraid of triggering her, he often held back.

Hopefully, that would change after tonight. She was ready to start her life with Daniel, and she needed to make sure he knew that. She pulled the lip gloss from her pocket and quickly coated her lips then fluffed her hair, knowing the knit cap she wore on the ride up here had probably flattened her curls.

Her heart beat a little faster in her chest as the hoof beats sounded right outside the cabin. Grabbing the lighter off the counter, she hurried to light the candles on the table.

The door opened just as she straightened.

"Pockets?" Surprise filled Daniel's voice. He blocked the small doorway, holding saddlebags filled with canned goods. "What are you doing here?"

She gave him her biggest smile. "Fancy meeting you here, Tarzan."

"Wait. Did you plan this?" His brow furrowed as his eyes darted around the room before settling on the candles on the table. "This is why Jake insisted I needed to ride out today to replenish the food we used this summer?"

She set the lighter on the table and tucked her hands into her back pockets. "It was either this or I get my brothers to help me kidnap you so I could whisk you away to the cabin at the lake."

She hadn't been able to bring herself to return to the lake for a few months. But thanks to all the hard work she'd put in with Emily, Labor Day at the lake —surrounded by family —had been a blast. She now made it a point to choose love over fear every chance she got.

Daniel grinned as he closed the door and let the saddlebags drop to the floor. "What makes you think you'd have to kidnap me? You could have simply invited me."

"Considering the panic attack I had the last time we were here, I was afraid you'd refuse to come."

He locked gazes with her as he took off his coat. "You seem to be doing okay today."

"I'm better than okay." She grinned. "I'm doing great." She rounded the table, bringing her within a few feet of him. "I haven't been triggered for a long time, and I'm eager to get on with my life." She placed heavy emphasis on the last few words but wasn't sure her meaning came across like she intended.

"I'm glad to hear it. I knew you'd eventually get beyond what happened to you."

"Do you really believe I'm beyond it?" She took another step toward him.

"Only you can decide that. Though I imagine there will still be difficult moments now and then."

"But you agree that I shouldn't let what happened to me continue to dictate how I live my life?"

"Of course not. You should live your life however you want."

"I'm glad you agree." Taking the final step toward him, she closed the gap between them. "I want to live my life with you. Starting now." She rocked up on her toes and wrapped her arms around his neck. She leaned in to kiss him, but he pulled back.

"Right now?" Surprise filled his face.

"Yes, starting right now. I want you to kiss me like you did the last time we were in this cabin." She tugged him toward her again, but he resisted.

"The last time we were in this cabin, you had a panic attack. I didn't kiss you that night."

"Right, sorry. I meant that night three and a half years ago."

It was so vivid in her mind, it felt like only last week.

His hands finally settled on her waist and his lips turned up. "You want me to kiss you like I did the night we both admitted we'd been pining for each other for four years?"

"Exactly like that." She closed her eyes, expecting him to lean in and kiss her. They popped back open when nothing happened.

"Three and a half years is a long time." A teasing glint filled his eyes. "I'm not sure I remember exactly how I kissed you back then."

She grabbed his ear and twisted. "Daniel Evan Hamilton, you'd better kiss me right now, or you're not getting dinner tonight."

"Ouch!" He pulled her hand away. "Sheesh, such a bossy woman." The words sounded harsh, but he said them with a chuckle.

She reached for the other ear, but he grabbed her hands and pinned them behind her back.

"Careful, Pockets. You might get more than you bargained for." His voice took on a husky timber that sent a wave of warmth flooding over her.

Finally!

She bit back a smile and let her eyes drift closed as she leaned into him. His lips didn't meet hers, however. Instead, his cold lips pressed first to one eyelid then the other before grazing her temple. Then his lips drifted lower. His warm breath —a contrast to his cold lips — tickled her ear when he spoke. "You need to learn a little patience, Pockets."

"Patience is for losers." The words came out with a shuddery breath as she struggled to fill her lungs with all the fluttering sensations swarming her chest.

Daniel gave a soft chuckle as he kissed the hollow below her ear. "This feels like winning to me."

"Mmm..hmm..." Riley melted into him.

When he released her arms to delve one hand into her hair and pull her closer with the other, she wasted no time in wrapping her arms around his neck. As soon as his mouth drew close to hers, she turned her head and claimed his lips in the long awaited kiss she'd dreamed of all day.

Daniel's kisses never failed to take her breath away. They made her feel complete and whole. Every time she was in his arms, she knew she was where she was meant to be. He was her best friend and better half.

She loved everything about kissing Daniel. The rasp of his whiskers when he went a few days without shaving. The confidence of his strong hands in her hair, on her hips, or splayed across her back. The warmth that flooded over her every time she was in his arms.

They were both breathless by the time the kiss ended, so when he continued to hold her in his embrace for several long moments, she gratefully lingered.

"You're not mad at me for asking Jake to make you ride out here in the cold are you?"

He chuckled. "Did that kiss feel like I was mad?"

"No."

Between his kiss and the fire that finally warmed the cabin, she feared she might combust. She anticipated a lot more kissing throughout the evening, but it was best to put a little distance between them for now.

She smiled up at him before stepping out of his embrace. "Have a seat, and I'll dish up dinner."

"Dinner?" He pulled out his phone. "It's only three in the afternoon."

"Yeah." She grimaced. "I didn't plan all of this in a very timely manner, did I?" She shrugged, then turned in a half circle. "If you want, we can play Scrabble before dinner."

"Scrabble." His eyebrows rose, and she hoped he was remembering the last time they played Scrabble together in this little cabin. He looked around, his gaze landing on the extra blankets on the beds. He cleared his throat. "Are you planning on us spending the night here again?"

"It's up to you. If you don't want to spend the night, we can hurry and eat then pack up so we can make it home before dark." She'd looked forward to a quiet evening with just the two of them, but now, a sudden onset of nerves hit her, filling her with self-doubt. Had she overstepped in assuming he'd want to spend the night here with her?

He reached out and slowly pulled her back into his arms. "Do I get to hold your hand again while we sleep?"

"Depends."

"On what?"

"Whether you can beat me at Scrabble."

He groaned. "I never beat you at Scrabble. You're better with words than I am."

She rocked up on her toes and planted a kiss on his cheek. "I promise I'll go easy on you."

"Fat chance of that. You're as competitive as you are impatient."

Her mouth dropped open as she pretended to take offense, then she smiled and shrugged. "You're right."

"Fine. Let's do this." He picked up his coat. "I'm going to go unsaddle Rebel and put him in the lean-to. I'll be back in a few minutes."

Riley barely had time to clear away the candles and the place settings from the table and lay out the Scrabble board before he returned.

Daniel clapped his hands as he took his seat. "Hope the food will keep for a bit because I'm about to beat you at Scrabble."

"Give it your best shot cowboy." Riley bit back a smile. No matter who got the most points, she was sure to win tonight.

Although she was eager to use the tiles she'd stashed in her pocket, Riley decided to take her time and play the tiles she drew for the first few rounds. She almost laughed out loud when she drew the letters necessary to spell family. Maybe she'd get lucky and be able to spell the words she wanted without having to cheat.

She sucked in a sharp breath two turns later when Daniel added O-V-E to the L in family. Her gaze jumped to his. Was he playing the same kind of not-so-hidden messages game she was?

He smiled and winked at her.

She studied her tiles, searching for letters to form the perfect word. The best she could come up with was to add T-R-U to the E in love.

"Good one." Daniel's low voice sent a shiver of awareness shooting through her.

After another couple rounds of lame three-letter words, Riley grew impatient. Every time Daniel studied his tiles, deep in thought, she pulled a few more tiles from her right pocket and slipped a few from her tray into her left. Once she had all the necessary tiles in front of her, she couldn't wait to make her move. She needed to utilize the spaces between the M in family and the R in true before she lost her chance.

Sucking in a deep breath, she laid down an A below the M, then added another R before the R in true. Her Y came next, then before Daniel could read the letters she'd laid down, she tacked M and E onto the end.

MARRY ME.

"That's two words. You can't—" His words died off when he looked up and found her staring at him with raised eyebrows. He looked back down at the board, his brows drawing together. "Wait. Is this serious?" He shook his head. "Are you...proposing to me?"

She laughed at the way the surprise in his voice made it rise in pitch. She didn't blame him for being shocked. "I know it's not traditional, and I don't have a ring or anything. There aren't clear guidelines for how a woman should do this, but..." She slipped from her chair, took the single step necessary to bring her to his side of the small table, and dropped to one knee. "Daniel, I love you. I always have, and I always will." She put a hand on his knee. "We've lost out on so much time together because I walked away from you three years ago. We could have both been saved so much hearta—"

His fingers pressed against her lips, cutting off her words. "Don't ruin this moment with regrets and 'should haves.'"

"You're right." She'd worked with Emily long enough to know there were some things that weren't worth devoting time and emotional energy to, and the past was one of them. She took his hand in hers. "I don't want to waste another moment. I want to marry you and start the life we were always meant to have together."

She stopped speaking, expecting him to say something. A goofy grin covered his face, but he didn't speak.

"You have been so patient and gentle with me while I worked through my issues, and it's convinced me more than ever that I want you by my side through all of life's ups and downs."

She didn't think it was possible for his grin to grow any bigger, but it did. Still, he didn't speak.

"Well, are you going to say something?" She nudged his knee.

"Oh, I have lots of things to say. I was anticipating answering a certain question, but you haven't actually asked it, so now I'm floundering for exactly how I'm supposed to respond." The twinkle in his eyes let her know he was teasing her and enjoying every minute of it.

She folded her arms and tilted her head toward the Scrabble board. "I did ask you."

"Ah, that's right." He studied his tiles, then promptly grabbed two. He placed a Y in front of the E in me and an S after it. "Yes, Pockets, I will marry you. You and me forever." He pulled her up and onto his lap. Her hip bumped the table hard enough that half the tiles fell on the floor.

They both laughed.

"I believe it's my turn to tell you what an amazing woman you are and how much I love you, but first..." His fingers slid into her hair and cupped the back of her head, guiding it down until her lips met his. His other arm snaked around her, pulling her tight against him.

He kissed her with so much emotion, it brought tears to her eyes. The kiss was passionate and probing yet gentle and sweet. Heady yet tender. It was sheer perfection.

EPILOGUE

*P*aige jumped when a knock sounded on the door behind her. She opened the door of the small classroom that doubled as a bride's room today and peered out.

"Faith said it's time to get this show on the road." Zane tugged on the collar of his white button-down shirt above the knot of his sage green tie.

Paige had never seen him wear anything other than a bolo tie and knew he must be incredibly uncomfortable in his suit. She laughed. "Are you sure that's what Aunt Faith said?"

He waved a hand in dismissal. "She said some nonsense about how if I didn't escort Riley down the aisle exactly at one o'clock, then it will throw off the schedule for the whole day."

"Yep, that sounds like Aunt Faith alright." She opened the door a little wider and beckoned to Riley. "Zane said it's time to get this show on the road."

"It sure is. I've waited long enough to marry the love of my life." Excitement filled Riley's voice.

"You've only been engaged for a little over two months." Their cousin Damon Knight stepped up beside Zane in the hallway. He looked handsome in his full-dress uniform, identifying him as a sergeant first class in the Army.

"Yes, but I should have married him years ago."

"You did. Don't you remember that time I married the two of you in the orchard back when we were ten?" He looked up at the ceiling. "You would have been eight at the time."

"I remember." Riley laughed. "Daniel has sure learned a lot about kissing since then." A flush of pink colored her cheeks.

Zane cleared his throat and tapped his watch-less wrist. "I'm going to have Faith breathing down my neck if we don't get you girls down that aisle ASAP."

Damon held his arm out to Paige. "I think we're supposed to lead off this procession."

Paige took his arm and fell into step beside him. It wasn't much of a procession, since Riley chose not to have bridesmaids, only Paige as a maid of honor. And Daniel asked Damon to be his best man. Paige was tickled pink to have her cousin home for a few days, especially since she was losing her best friend. Good thing she'd always have Riley—and now Daniel—as a cousin.

"So, I hear you have a serious boyfriend. When do I get to meet him?" Damon arrived in town late last night, and they hadn't had a chance to catch up with each other properly yet. "If you want me to take leave to attend your wedding, I need to approve of this guy first."

A thrill of excitement shot through her at the mention of Phillip, the businessman she'd been dating for the past six months, but it was quickly followed by a stab of disappointment. He'd planned to come to Providence with her for the wedding, but he'd had an urgent business trip pop up at the last minute.

"He couldn't make it this weekend after all, so you're going to have to come home again soon so you can meet him."

There always seemed to be something that drew Phillip away on the weekends, leaving Paige feeling neglected. He was such a fun and charismatic guy, and he was a total gentleman, which was difficult to find nowadays. But even though she was certain she was in love with him, there were things about their relationship that made her question whether he was as committed as she was.

He'd only had time to squeeze in lunch with her family last month, but at least, he'd met her parents. He hadn't bothered to introduce her to his family yet.

She and Damon stepped into the doorway of the sanctuary and waited for the organist to start playing the wedding march. She scanned the gathered crowd spotting many familiar faces, but not the one she really wanted to see. Shaking off her melancholy, she determined she would be happy for her cousin and friend today.

No more pining over Phillip.

She and Damon made their slow walk down the aisle followed by a positively radiant Riley. Daniel's eyes never left his bride, and Paige knew her relationship with Riley was about to change forever. But in a good way.

Riley and Daniel were finally getting the happily ever after they deserved, and Paige couldn't be happier. The first time Damon spotted her wiping away a tear, he rolled his eyes. The second time, he mimicked her, then blinked his eyes like he was trying to keep from crying.

She had forgotten what a tease Damon was. She'd have to find a way to get even with him later at the reception.

The afternoon and evening passed mostly in a blur. Paige cried when she gave her speech as the maid of honor, but she did manage to sneak in the story about how Damon ripped the seat of his pants jumping down from the cherry tree in the orchard. Before wrapping up her speech, she pulled a gift bag from under her chair.

"Daniel and I used to always fight over who Riley's best friend was. I figured I was because I was her only girl cousin on our mothers' side, and he argued that because they worked together on the ranch, he spent a lot more time with her." Paige's throat tightened as she thought about how lucky her friends were to have each other. "But Daniel did more than work with Riley. He carried her on his back for over a mile when she fell and split her knee open on a rock in the creek. He sang silly little songs when Riley and I got scared after

Damon told ghost stories during our sleepovers on the trampoline. Daniel spent countless hours at the rodeo arena with her, timing her and giving her tips so she could become the fastest barrel racer in the county."

Riley looked at Daniel with such love in her eyes, there was no contest anymore, and hadn't been for some time. She laid her head on her husband's shoulder, and again a little twinge of jealousy shot through Paige. Hopefully someday, she'd find a love like that.

"Daniel was also the one who drove over two hundred miles to take Riley to her senior prom. It was always Daniel who was there for Riley." She held the gift bag out to Daniel. "So today, once and for all, I concede the title of Riley's Best Friend to you, Daniel Hamilton."

Everyone watched as Daniel pulled from the bag a fancy wooden plaque that had one of Daniel and Riley's engagement pictures on it and a gold engraving that read:

This certifies that due to his unwavering support, immeasurable kindness, and enduring patience, Daniel Hamilton is officially Riley's Best Friend Forever.

BONUS EPILOGUE

Riley straightened after placing the Crock Pot on the bottom shelf of the Lazy Susan under the counter. She rubbed at the ache in her lower back with one hand while holding the underside of her swollen belly with the other as she turned in a slow circle, surveying her new kitchen.

She wasn't due for ten more days, but she'd been having some serious contractions all day. At first, she thought they were Braxton-Hicks, but now, she wasn't so sure.

Despite her family's attempts to make her sit down and let them do the unpacking, Riley had to admit she'd overdone it. She was so excited to be moving into her new home that she had to make sure everything ended up exactly where she wanted it. With the baby due so soon, she wouldn't have time to reorganize.

At least they'd gotten the kitchen and the beds, including the crib, put together. The rest would be relatively easy to do, if her back ever stopped hurting.

"Hey, beautiful." Daniel's arms slipped around her from behind, then his lips grazed her neck below her ear, sending a wave of pleasant tingles through her body. "I thought you were going to sit down and rest."

Daniel was the best. Even though it had been a long time since Riley was last triggered, he was always good to announce his presence before touching her, and his approach was always slow and gentle.

A small smile crept to her lips as she recalled their wedding night eleven months ago. He'd been so intent on taking things slow—for her sake—that she'd had to take the lead and let him know she didn't dread the prospect of being intimate with him.

"I did, but I can't sit still." She turned in his arms and slid her hands over his muscular shoulders to lace her fingers together behind his neck. "I'm too excited."

Daniel planted a lengthy kiss on her lips. "Feels surreal being in our own home, doesn't it?"

"Yes, and it's such a beautiful home." She sighed as she laid her head against his chest. "I love the idea of staying on the ranch forever."

After they got engaged, they approached Jake about buying an acre or two to build on. He'd refused to let them buy, and instead gifted them two acres of the Dry Creek parcel at the southwest end — Madam Houdini would have to find a different pasture to escape from. Daniel had already designed their dream home, so they started building shortly after they were married.

"Me too." He caressed her cheek with his knuckles. "Although, with you by my side, I'm confident I could live anywhere in the world and stay sober."

"I know you could."

He smiled. "Your faith in me makes me feel ten feet tall."

She made a scoffing sound. "I'm glad you're not that tall. I would get a neck ache every time I did this." She rocked up on her toes and pulled his head down until his lips met hers in a kiss that quickly grew passionate.

"Mmm...I appreciate everyone's help today," he murmured against her lips, "but I'm glad they're gone now." His lips shifted to nuzzle her neck again. "I'm anxious to break in our new bed." Without waiting for a response, he swept her up in his arms.

A sharp pain sliced through her back, and instead of chewing him out for trying to carry her big-as-a-house pregnant body, she cried out in agony.

"A-ah." She pressed a hand to her back.

He set her down even faster than he'd picked her up. "Are you okay? Did I hurt you?"

Riley doubled over, struggling to breathe, as the pain spread to her stomach, sharp and stabbing.

"Riley, honey, talk to me." Daniel gently stroked her back. "Is it the baby?"

She did her best to focus on her breathing like she'd learned in the Lamaze classes but wasn't much more successful than she'd been with the breathing exercises Emily had given her to help with her anxiety attacks. She'd quickly learned after Collin's second attack, that she needed to move. To do something. That's why even though she initially froze when confronted, she ended up lashing out afterward.

Daniel had found that out the hard way when she came home after the first attack. But Riley had quickly learned to divert her anger when she got upset following her second attack.

She tried to walk off the pain but found she could barely move because of the intensity. Eventually, it subsided, and she slumped back against the counter, trying to catch her breath.

"Was that a contraction?" Daniel's concerned face ducked into her line of sight. "Are you in labor?"

"I think I might be." Riley rubbed her hands on either side of her rock-hard belly.

"You think?"

"Well, how am I supposed to know? I've never been in labor before." She rubbed at her achy back. "My back has been killing me all day, but I figured I was just overdoing it."

"So, you haven't had any other pains like this?" Daniel's strong hand took over rubbing her back.

"Well, yeah I've had a bunch, but they weren't as strong as this one."

"When was the last one?"

"Right before you came into the kitchen."

Alarm filled Daniel's face as he glanced at the clock on the stove. "That was only a few minutes ago."

"I'm fine." She pushed him away and headed toward the living room. "I just need to sit down and put my feet up for a bit. The only furniture I'm breaking in over the next hour is the couch."

She'd only taken five steps when a flood of warm liquid cascaded down her legs, soaking her leggings and leaving her standing in a puddle. She gasped and looked down at the floor.

"Did your water just break?" Daniel's voice rose in pitch.

She turned wide eyes on him and nodded.

He shoved both hands into his hair, then rubbed them over his face. "But you're not due for another ten days."

That was the only reason they'd decided to go ahead and move into their new house today. Well, that and the fact that today was the anniversary of little Isaac Russell's death. Riley hoped that moving would keep Daniel distracted enough to not dwell on events in the past that always triggered his cravings.

"I know, but I think this baby is done waiting."

"Okay, we need to get you to the hospital." He patted his pocket, making sure he had keys, and took several steps toward the door then stopped. "You haven't even packed a bag yet."

"No, but I think that's something we should worry about later." The last word came out as a groan as another contraction hit. She did her best to breathe and relax through the contraction then gave Daniel the most cheerful smile she could muster. "This baby is coming whether we're ready or not."

Holding a cup full of pebbled ice, Daniel walked into Riley's hospital room to find Dr. Henderson and three nurses scurrying around the room. He hurried over to Riley's side. "What's wrong?"

He'd only been gone for five minutes.

"Your wife is finally ready to deliver." Dr. Henderson said as a nurse tied a green gown on him. He winked at Riley and grinned. "Now the real work begins."

Daniel looked at his beautiful but exhausted wife. She'd finally relaxed after getting an epidural, but she had been pushing with each contraction for the last hour in preparation to actually push the baby out.

"You've got this, honey." He scooped ice chips into her mouth then smoothed a lock of hair back from her face.

She looked at the clock. "Do you think the baby will come before midnight?"

Daniel's gaze followed hers.

Eleven twenty-five.

"Maybe, but the nurse said it usually takes a while for first time mothers to figure out how to push effectively, so it might be a while yet."

A determined glint filled Riley's eyes, and Daniel had a feeling she would reach her goal of delivering by midnight, although he didn't understand why she was so eager to get the baby here before the day ended.

"Okay, Dad, I want you to wrap your arms around Mom's shoulders and help her lean forward until she can grasp her knees." Dr. Henderson continued to alternately give Riley words of encouragement and Daniel instructions over the next twenty minutes.

Riley grew more exhausted with each push, but the determined glint remained in her eyes as she frequently checked the clock between contractions. But the closer the clock got to midnight, the more frantic she looked each time she pushed and the redder her face became.

Dr. Henderson must have seen the toll it was taking on Riley too, because he said, "Lie back and catch your breath, Mom. I don't want you to push on the next contraction."

"You're doing great, sweetheart." Daniel leaned down and pressed his lips to her forehead. "Why are you so concerned about having the baby before midnight?"

She blinked away tears. "I thought it would be good if you could look forward to this day every year, instead of dreading it."

His brows drew together in confusion, then it dawned on him what day it was. A lump filled his throat.

Celebrating the birth of their child was a far cry better than remembering the life he'd unintentionally taken four years ago. But not at the expense of his wife.

Filled with love for this woman, he pressed another kiss to her temple. "I appreciate what you're trying to do, but it's okay for me to feel remorse each year and regret my poor choices. It keeps me from repeating them." He reached into his pocket and wrapped his fingers around the two-year sobriety coin he earned last week. "I don't worry about trying to stay sober on this day anymore. It will be nice to have our son's birthday to look forward to the next day, though."

"Are you sure?" She glanced at the clock. "We still have seven minutes." Her gaze shifted to Dr. Henderson. "We're close, aren't we, Doc?"

"You're very close, but there's no need to rush this. You and the baby are both stable."

Riley locked gazes with Daniel again. The determined glint in her eyes had dimmed, but he could tell she wanted to please him.

He smoothed another lock of hair away from her face. "Let's let our son decide his birthday, shall we?"

"Okay."

After a few more contractions, Dr. Henderson grinned. "One more good push ought to get the head out."

A surge of excitement ricocheted through Daniel as he helped Riley bear down. Sometimes he felt like he was living in a dream. He still couldn't believe his best friend was finally his wife, and he'd get to spend the rest of his life with her. And now, they were going to be parents.

It took two more pushes before the head fully appeared, and Daniel couldn't help himself; he laughed at the amount of thick dark hair covering the misshapen head. One more big push brought the body, and suddenly Daniel's vision blurred as he took in his son.

The tiny, red, squirming body was absolutely perfect.

"Official time of birth: twelve o-five," Dr. Henderson said.

A few minutes later, the doctor placed the tiny, striped bundle in Riley's arms, and tears filled her eyes again. "He's so beautiful."

"Yes, he is. And so are you." Daniel pulled out his cell phone and started taking pictures.

He'd thought many times throughout his life that he'd never seen Riley look prettier, but he'd been wrong. Despite her flushed face, the tendrils of damp hair clinging to her neck, and the exhaustion in her eyes, the love that shone on her face as she looked at their son made her simply radiant.

One of the nurses stepped up beside him. "Here, Daddy, let me take some pictures of you with Mommy and baby."

Daniel handed his phone over and leaned in close to Riley. Even after the nurse was done taking photos, he continued to hold his wife and son. He pressed his lips to her temple. "Have I told you lately how amazing you are?"

"I am, aren't I?" A slow grin spread across her face.

The room remained a hub of activity for some time while the doctor cleaned Riley up, and the nurses took the baby to measure, weigh, and evaluate. When they finally finished, Daniel found himself with the tiny bundle in his arms. Heart full, he sat on the edge of Riley's bed, and together they studied their son.

"Does he look like a Wyatt or a Logan?" Daniel asked.

Those were the two names they'd narrowed it down to.

Riley gave him a timid look. "We could name him Isaac Russell Hamilton, if you want."

If Daniel thought there was a lump in his throat before, it was nothing compared to the boulder of emotion that cut off his air supply now. He'd never told Riley that little Isaac's last name was Russell.

She must have done some research, and judging by the way she lifted her chin and met his gaze, she'd given this serious thought. "It has a nice ring to it, don't you think."

"It has a very nice ring to it, and I appreciate what you're trying to do. Again. But I don't want our son to carry that weight."

"I thought it could be a nice way to honor little Isaac Russell."

"It's a beautiful tribute, but I don't want our son to ever feel like he was a replacement for someone else."

"But —"

"There will come a day when he wants to know where his name came from, and I don't want him to feel burdened by knowing it's associated with some of my biggest mistakes." Daniel stroked his son's soft cheek. "I'd rather name him after my hero."

"That makes sense." Riley nodded. "Who is your hero?"

"My dad." He tilted the bundle. "How about we name him Wyatt Zane Hamilon?"

"Sounds perfect." She laid her head against his shoulder. "You're going to be a great dad."

I hope so.

Daniel held his son a little tighter, silently promising to stay sober so he could be the best father possible. He couldn't change the past, but he could look toward the future with faith instead of fear.

He lifted his eyes to the ceiling, silently thanking God for trusting him to raise this child. Then he promised to take good care of him.

He'd teach his son how to ride a bike and a horse. Tie his shoes and rope a steer. To be a gentleman and a cowboy. And he would pray everyday his son was fortunate enough to have a best friend by his side forever.

If you enjoyed Love Rebranded, please consider leaving a review on Amazon.

Want to see Paige get her happily ever after?
Check out *Love Remodeled – Seeking Providence Book 2*

Free on Kindle Unlimited, or from Amazon.

When one door closes another one opens.

When her boyfriend's fiancée shows up for dinner on Valentine's Day instead of him, Paige Young runs—in front of a moving car. Her long road to recovery is paved with heartache, self-reflection, and a vow to never fall in love again.

Gabriel Rivera finally has his own physical therapy office, but he might blow his chance at success by falling for his first patient. Add in a terminally ill mother, a white lie—that quickly gets out of control—a meddling PT assistant, and he's soon in over his head with a fake girlfriend.

Be sure you join my newsletter, so you don't miss a new release.
www.jillburrell.com/newsletter

ABOUT THE AUTHOR

JILL HAS always been an avid reader, and romance has always been her favorite genre. If she's not writing or folding laundry her head is usually in a book.

When her father told her, "I've got a story I want you to write," she didn't think she'd ever actually do it.

But after twenty years of being a stay-at-home mom with seven children, the idea of writing and publishing a book sounded less terrifying than entering the workforce again. Boy, was she wrong!

Keep in touch with Jill Burrell
www.jillburrell.com

amazon.com/author/jillburrell

facebook.com/authorjillburrell

goodreads.com/authorjillburrell

bookbub.com/authors/jill-burrell

instagram.com/authorjillburrell

www.ingramcontent.com/pod-product-compliance
Lightning Source LLC
Chambersburg PA
CBHW070809180626
46818CB00001B/180